"*E*liza."

"Yes?"

"One last thing," Kit said. "If your curiosity persists and you find yourself tempted to experiment further in the realm of the physical, don't go to any of your other suitors. I am still your mentor." Reaching out, he stroked the edge of a knuckle over the delicate curve of her cheek. "If you wish to have more lessons in love, you need only say. I shall teach you whatever it is you care to learn."

With a last smile, he strode toward the door, leaving Eliza stock-still in the center of the room.

Also by Tracy Anne Warren

The Husband Trap
The Wife Trap

THE
WEDDING
TRAP

A Novel

TRACY ANNE
WARREN

BALLANTINE BOOKS • NEW YORK

An Ivy Books Mass Market Original

Published in the United States by Ballantine Books, an imprint of The Random House Publishing Group, a division of Random House, Inc., New York.

IVY BOOKS and colophon are trademarks of Random House, Inc.

ISBN: 0-7394-6782-4

ISBN: 978-0-7394-6782-4

Cover illustration: Jon Paul Ferrara

Printed in the United States of America

For my beloved kitties, who passed over the bridge
during the writing of this trilogy.

Marshmallow,
a beautiful boy whose light burned bright,
but far too briefly.

Sally, "the Boo,"
our sweet, funny black lovebug, who found us one
stormy Halloween night and made us her own. We
cherished your little hops and loving motorboat purrs.

Mitten, "Miss Mitten,"
my dainty, brown-striped princess. Priceless friend and
companion. Thanks for giving me twenty-two
wonderful years of meows, lap naps and love.

Chapter One

London, February 1820

This business of acquiring a husband is going to be far from pleasant, Eliza Hammond decided from her place on the saffron-and-white-striped sofa in the upstairs family drawing room of Raeburn House.

Considering this would be her fifth Season—a lowering realization indeed—she knew she would need all the assistance she could get, despite the immense fortune her late aunt had quite unexpectedly left to her only six weeks ago. At least she knew she would be able to count on the steadfast support of her dear friend, Violet Brantford Winter, Duchess of Raeburn. Perhaps with Violet's assistance, the process would not be as dreadful as she feared. Then again, thinking of the assorted ne'er-do-wells and fortune hunters already vying for her hand, perhaps it would.

"There is Mr. Newcomb," Violet stated as she reviewed the current selection of Eliza's prospective suitors. "He seems a very pleasant sort of gentleman with a genuine interest in the arts."

"Yes, he was most attentive when we happened upon each other at the gallery the other day," Eliza agreed, recalling the man's even features and straight auburn hair, a shade that had put her in mind of a glossy-coated Irish setter. "He demonstrated a definite command of the great masters. Perhaps he has an interest in historical subjects as well."

"What he has is an interest in card playing, followed a close second by a love of the dice," interrupted a deep, smooth male voice that never failed to send a pleasurable tingle down Eliza's spine, no matter how firmly she tried to suppress it.

She shifted her gaze toward Lord Christopher Winter, better known to his family and friends as Kit. Tall, broad-shouldered and ruggedly lean, he sat relaxed in a leisurely all-male sprawl upon a nearby chair. Having spent the past twenty minutes eating his way through a stack of small watercress, cucumber and chicken sandwiches, he leaned forward now to conduct a perusal of the dessert tray.

A lock of his dark, wavy brown hair fell across his handsome forehead as he selected a pair of lime tarts and a thin slice of rum cake. As he transferred the sweets to his plate, he got a smudge of whipped cream on one of his knuckles. Eliza's stomach tightened as she watched him lick it away.

She forced her gaze down to her shoes. Kit was Violet's brother-in-law and nothing more, she reminded herself. Certainly he was nothing more to *her*. True, she had once nursed a secret infatuation for him, but such silliness was long since over and done. During the nearly year and a half he had been away traveling on the Continent, she had ruthlessly purged him from her heart. And by the time he returned to England this Christmas past, she had long since grown used to giving him scarcely a thought.

Still, that didn't mean she couldn't admire him for the gorgeous male specimen he was. And Kit Winter, with his beautiful, lazy-lidded green and gold eyes, sensuous lips and infectiously charming smile, was a gorgeous man indeed. One with an infamously prodigious appetite that seemed to make no impact at all upon his trim, well-muscled physique.

He bit into one of the tarts from his plate, a tiny smile of gustatory delight on his lips as he settled back into his chair. Engrossed in the confection, he seemed utterly oblivious to the volley of disappointment he had just lobbed into the room.

Violet shot him a mighty frown. "What do you mean by that remark, Kit?"

He swallowed and glanced upward. "Hmm?" He took a drink of tea, then politely patted his mouth with his napkin. "Oh, about Newcomb, do you mean?"

"Yes, of course about Newcomb. Of whom else have Eliza and I been conversing?"

"Well, there's no need to come up cross, Vi. Just thought I ought to give you fair warning the chap is close to being dipped. Last I heard, he lost twenty thousand quid to Plimpton playing high-stakes whist, and his luck hasn't turned for the good since."

Violet and Eliza released a pair of mutual sighs.

"If that is the case, then he is out," Violet declared, turning her bespectacled blue-green gaze upon Eliza. "You certainly don't want to take an inveterate gambler to husband."

Eliza silently agreed and contented herself by sipping her tea.

"There is Sir Silas Jones," Violet continued. "He sent you that sweet nosegay of hothouse roses last week. I hear he comes from a lovely part of Kent. Owns an estate that produces a most bountiful harvest of cherries and apples each year. Has quite the way with plants, I am given to understand."

"That's not all he's good at planting," murmured Kit

as he polished off the last of the sweets on his plate and leaned forward for more.

Violet angled her attractively coiffured blond head. "I suppose by that you mean there is something wrong with him as well?"

"Depends upon your point of view. Some might say there's nothing wrong with him at all." He ate a guinea-sized crumpet topped with a generous spoonful of gooseberry jam, then silently held out his empty Meissen cup for more tea.

Without pause, Violet lifted the heavy silver teapot from a matching silver tray and poured. A delicate tendril of steam spiraled off the surface of the beverage for a moment before Kit brought the cup to his lips.

"So?" Violet encouraged when he failed to say more.

Kit set his teacup onto its saucer with a faint *clink*. "Man's a womanizer. Has six by-blows by four different women and those are only the ones he acknowledges. One might say Jones is a man who likes to plow a field."

Eliza felt her cheeks grow pink. A small guffaw escaped the duchess before Violet recovered herself.

"Kit," Violet said in reproof. "Might I remind you there are ladies present, myself included. That is no kind of talk for the drawing room."

He forced an irreverent grin from his lips. "Sorry. You are right, of course. My apologies, ladies."

"Nevertheless, I am glad to learn that Sir Silas is not a man to whom my dear friend should direct her time or attentions." Violet tapped a thoughtful nail against the scrolled sofa arm. "Of the other gentlemen who have recently extended their regards to Eliza, we know Viscount Coyle and Mr. Washburn are not to be received, the both of them known fortune hunters forever on the lookout for a likely heiress to replenish their pocketbooks."

"What of Lord Luffensby?" Eliza said. "He sent me that very pleasant book of sonnets." Wordsworth, she recalled with pleasure, the poet one of her favorites.

"Of course. I met him only once and very briefly but he struck me as a most amiable man. Very considerate and gently spoken."

A soft but unmistakable snort erupted from Kit.

Violet shot him another look, one of exasperation this time. "Pray do not tell me there is something amiss with Lord Luffensby too? Surely not. I know his cousin and she gave me to understand that he has a most comfortable income and no predilections for the usual vices."

"No, not the usual ones, that's for certain."

Violet waited for a long moment. "Oh, do go on before Eliza and I both expire of curiosity."

"I am not sure I ought to say. As you already reminded me, there are ladies present." Kit paused, glanced at Eliza. "Unmarried ladies."

"Well, dear heavens, what is it? Surely it cannot be so terrible Eliza cannot be allowed to hear. And it isn't as if she is a miss just out of the schoolroom."

Kit tapped a considering finger against his lips. "He has a nickname among certain fellows. Lord Poofensby."

Poofensby? Eliza frowned. Was Kit referring to the man's wardrobe? Luffensby did tend toward being a bit of a dandy but nothing too extreme. She looked over at Violet, whose brows were also furrowed in confusion.

"I am sorry but you'll have to be clearer," Violet said.

"Clearer?" Kit rolled his eyes, then heaved a beleaguered sigh. "You know, for a woman who reads Greek and Latin and speaks five languages, you can sometimes be remarkably ignorant."

"There is no need to be insulting. Just say it out. I am sure it cannot be so very bad."

"All right. He . . . um . . . has a liking for men."

"Well, what is so remarkable about that? A great many gentlemen enjoy the company of others of their sex. I don't see why you are making such a— Oh." Violet broke off, her eyebrows rising. "Oh! *Oooh.*"

Eliza looked between them, still not entirely understanding the message that had just been passed. Then suddenly she remembered a bit of text she had read once in one of her books on ancient history about men who cared for other men in an amorous way. She had found the notion quite astonishing at the time, yet never considered such things might still go on. Certainly not here in present-day England!

A fresh blush stole over her cheeks.

"Quite so." Kit stretched out his legs, crossed them at the ankle. "Not the sort of fellow likely to give you a family, assuming that is what you want?"

A family, Eliza thought, was exactly what she wanted. It was the single most important reason she had decided to find a husband and wed. Her shoulders dipped, her spirits disheartened by the entire conversation.

"Well, who else is there?" Violet withdrew a white silk handkerchief from her dress pocket, then removed her spectacles and began to polish the lenses. "You have received so many bouquets and trinkets, there must be someone suitable in the bunch."

"But there is not," Eliza bemoaned. "Oh, Violet, don't you see, it is simply no use. They are all of them unsuitable in one way or another. Either they are after my fortune or they have some dreadful personal difficulty they wish to conceal through a convenient marriage."

Violet slipped her eyeglasses back on, then reached out and patted the top of Eliza's hand. "Now, do not let this discourage you. The Season has not even begun yet. There is no telling all the eligible bachelors who will be arriving in the city over the next few weeks. Men who would give their eyeteeth to have you for their wife."

"Perhaps a single rotten molar but no more." Eliza shook her head. "No, the facts must be faced. The sad truth is that no suitable gentlemen wanted me before my aunt died and none of them wants me now. Some days I wish my aunt had not gotten angry with Cousin Philip and cut him out of the will. Some days poverty seems a remarkably easier choice."

"Poverty is never easy and do not spout such self-defeating nonsense. I know you would never wish to go back to that life. You lived under that old woman's miserly thumb far too many years—forgive my harsh sentiments toward the dead—not to enjoy a little comfort now. If anyone deserves her fortune, it is you."

"Maybe, but it does not seem to be doing me much good."

"What you need is a mentor," Violet said. "Someone who knows Society and could smooth your way. Teach you how to be easier in company, have more confidence so your shyness does not leave you tongue-tied and silent among others, unable to show what a lovely personality you possess."

Violet paused, tapped a thumb against the knee of her elegant lavender merino wool day dress. "As you will recall, I once had the same problem as you. So shy in public I could barely string a pair of words together. Then during those insane months when I switched places with Jeannette and married Adrian in her stead, well, I had no choice but to change my ways. Why, if it had not been for Kit—" She broke off and stared at her brother-in-law for a long, pregnant moment. Suddenly a merry laugh bubbled from her lips. "Well, of course! Why did I not think of it before?"

"Think of what?" Eliza asked.

"Of you and Kit. Why, it is perfect. Kit will help you find a worthy husband."

"I'll do what!" Kit jerked upright in his seat, his cup rattling precariously on its saucer. Only his innate sense of balance kept him from spilling hot tea all over his fashionably tight buckskin pantaloons. In no mood to risk a burn, especially in so vulnerable an area of his anatomy, he steadied the china and set it onto a nearby side table.

Eliza Hammond, he noticed, looked as shocked as he felt, her pale lips parted, her slender jaw slack with obvious astonishment.

He straightened his waistcoat with a firm double-handed tug. "I must have misheard you. Sounded like you just suggested I play matchmaker for Miss Hammond here."

"Not matchmaker, no. Eliza and I will be able to locate gentlemen aplenty, I suspect. Your role will be more in the way of mentor, just as I said. You can help vet her prospective suitors, but more importantly you can do for her what you did for me. Teach her how to be more confident in company. Give her techniques and ways of interacting in Society so she need not feel so reticent."

"Well, I hardly think I'm the proper one to help," he sputtered, anxious to put a stop to Violet's wild notions before they had a chance to propagate any further.

"But of course you are," his earnest-eyed sister-in-law stated. "You are the very best person to help. For one, you are family, so there will be no need to worry about you telling the world all the details of our little project. For another, you know absolutely everyone in the Ton. If you aren't friends with them already, you know someone else who is. Plus, you hear all the best tidbits, as you have so eloquently demonstrated this afternoon."

"I hardly know *everyone*. Been out of the country

these many months past, I'll remind you. Even now I am catching up." His lids narrowed accusingly. "And I hope you are not implying that I am a gossip."

"Nothing of the sort," Violet assured. "You are just friendly and popular, that is all. People tell you things, things neither Eliza nor I will ever be in a position to find out. Which gives us a great advantage since you will be able to weed out the fortune hunters and blackguards and leave only decent gentlemen from which Eliza may choose. That way she will be able to concentrate on deciding if she feels genuine affection for any one particular man without having to worry that he might have unscrupulous motives. No, I cannot think of a person better suited to help our dear Eliza than you."

Kit restrained the pained grimace that rose to his face. If he had known tossing out a few opinions about a couple of fellows would provoke such dire results, he would have kept his blasted mouth shut. Should have kept eating, that's what he should have done. Kept eating and kept silent.

Reminded of food and suddenly in need of sustenance, he plucked another tart off the serving tray and popped it into his mouth, the delectable flavors of raspberry and sweet cream taking the edge off his distress.

"I am not a project," Eliza said in a low, stiff voice.

"What is that, dear?" Violet questioned, turning her head toward her friend.

"I said, I am not a project, as you referred to me earlier. Neither of you need feel duty-bound to take pity upon me. I shall find some way to manage for myself." Short speech done, Eliza lowered her eyes to her lap, fingers linked together, her knuckles squeezed tight enough to turn them white around the edges.

Kit ate another tart, surprised at Eliza's small burst of outraged pride. He hadn't realized she was capable of such fortitude, quiet little brown wren that she was. In fact, she'd spoken more this afternoon than he was used to hearing her say in an entire day, not that he ever really spent enough time around her to be certain how much talking she normally did. Yet she had always struck him as one of those plain, reserved women who tended to walk into a room and fade from notice two minutes later. The quintessential wallflower. And a bluestocking, to make matters worse. Only now she was a rich bluestocking wallflower, and Violet expected him to make her over into a glorious swan.

Impossible.

Perhaps giving birth to her latest child four months before had done something to disrupt Violet's usual good sense. Maybe if he phrased his arguments just right, she would see reason and back away from this ludicrous plan.

Violet shifted toward Eliza. "Now, do not ruffle up so. You know I meant no insult, and neither of us pities you. Do we, Kit?" She gave him a stare that brooked no opposition.

"Of course not," he chimed.

"I apologize if my choice of words was poor," Violet went on. "But Eliza, even you admit that you are shy and do not feel easy in Society. And while there is no disgrace in such behavior, it does make it more difficult for others to see your true beauty. Particularly gentlemen, who—let us be frank—tend to be led by their eyes and other unmentionable portions of their anatomy."

"Their brains, do you mean?" Kit remarked, unable to restrain the quip.

A tiny smile curved across the duchess's youthful lips; her eyes twinkled. "Hmm, just so, for we all know that is what men use to think with when they are around an attractive female."

And that, Kit thought, *is precisely the problem.*

Eliza Hammond was not what any man would describe as a stunner. It wasn't that she was homely—quite the opposite, if one took the trouble to look closely enough—it was just that she did nothing to enhance what attributes she did possess.

Instead of looking thick and lustrous, her brown hair appeared ordinary, yanked back into a boring knot at the nape of her neck. Although unblemished by the sun, her white skin often seemed sallow and wan. Quite likely she possessed a pleasant figure, but who could tell since she hid her slender body inside one shapeless, hideous dress after another—though he supposed her nip-cheese aunt could be blamed in large measure for the state of Eliza's meager wardrobe, now dyed black for mourning.

She had good eyes, though, bright and luminous despite their soft, unremarkable gray color. And lovely bone structure, with a classical sweep to her jaw and a cute, finely bridged nose.

Still, turning Eliza from a frump into a fashion plate would be a truly monumental achievement. He nearly sighed aloud at the idea.

This scheme is doomed to fail.

This plan will never work, Eliza railed inside her head.

What was Violet thinking to suggest such a ridiculous thing? Imagine wanting to toss her and Kit together as mentor and pupil? She could not do it. *Would* not do it, even if he had once helped Violet overcome her diffident nature and step comfortably into her role as wife to one of the most powerful aristocrats in England. Besides, Kit obviously did not wish to help her. She could see it in his eyes. The doubt. And yes, the pity, no matter that he said otherwise.

"Please, Violet," she implored, "I am sure Lord Christopher has other, more important things to do with his time than spend it instructing me."

"I cannot imagine what that might be. Kit was just telling me the other day how bored he is with the same old round of amusements and so few people yet in Town. Is that not so, Kit?"

"I believe I confessed to feeling a slight ennui, but that does not mean I have nothing to do. Somehow, I manage to fill my days quite admirably."

"But only think how much more admirably your time would be employed assisting Eliza. With her residing here, it will be an easy thing for you to teach her."

He wiped his fingers on a linen napkin, dusting off crumbs. "If you'll remember, I'm in the process of locating bachelor's quarters and moving my things in there. If I don't find something soon, they'll be nothing decent left to rent."

"Maybe you could put that plan on hold for a while. I mean, would it really be so dreadful if you stayed here with the family for a little while longer? You mentioned that you've nearly gone through your quarterly allowance again, and I know how you detest applying to Adrian for additional funds."

"Remind me in future to stop telling you things, Vi. You remember far too much, far too well."

Violet sent him a sympathetic smile. "I also remember that you will be coming into your own money on your birthday this August when you receive your grandfather's bequest. Until then, why don't you simply remain here at Raeburn House and economize a bit? Only think how easy it will be for you and Eliza to work together. A few hours in the morning, then you can each go about your usual routine. You'll scarcely notice the difference."

She would notice the difference, Eliza thought. Until now, living in the same abode with Kit had been tolerable due in great measure to the sheer enormity of the townhouse. Her and Kit's paths rarely crossed except for the occasional meal *en famille* and the infrequent afternoon visit with Violet, such as now. But to be daily in his company? To have Kit, of all people, coaching her on ways to overcome her shyness . . . well, it seemed too intimate, far too personal.

Despite knowing that her infatuation for him had waned, she wasn't certain she would feel comfortable being so near him so often. Yet would she not be a fool to refuse his help? Assuming, of course, that he agreed to help. Assuming she even wished him to.

He sat back again in his chair, obviously wrestling with his thoughts as he rubbed a knuckle against his expressive lips. "I suppose I could stay and assist Miss Hammond."

Violet clapped her hands in delight. "Oh, I knew you would see the merit of my idea."

"But only if she wishes me to do so, that is," Kit added.

Eliza and Kit's eyes met, his clear hazel irises appearing more green than gold today, the shade enhanced by the elegantly tailored bottle green cutaway coat he wore.

Her pulse skipped at such scrutiny. What could she say? How could she refuse under the circumstances? She lowered her gaze. "At your pleasure, my lord."

"Very well, then. But if we are to proceed with this plan, I must be blunt and tell you both that it will take more than a few lessons in social comportment and style to turn the trick. Miss Hammond must put herself entirely in my hands and do as she is instructed, and that includes making an adjustment to her appearance."

Her head came up. "M-my appearance?" She was fully aware she was not the most beautiful of women. Nevertheless it hurt to hear him discuss such matters aloud.

"Hmm. If you want men who are more than fortune hunters and rogues to offer you marriage, then half measures will not do."

"Of what precisely are you thinking?" Violet questioned.

"A complete makeover from head to foot. Hair and clothes to start—"

"But I am still in mourning," Eliza protested. Defensively, she plucked at her black skirts, knowing how severe they were. Even so, they were more becoming than most of the unsightly shades her aunt had been in the habit of choosing for her. When duty had required her to dye all her old dresses black, it had come as no great loss.

"Well," he said, "you shan't be in mourning forever, and when you are not you will need a new wardrobe. You've plenty of blunt for it now, what with the inheritance you received from your aunt."

He was right about that, she mused. Although even now, weeks later, she had still not gotten used to the realization that her aunt Doris—who had never shown her anything but scorn and disapproval in her whole life—had made Eliza the sole beneficiary of a vast fortune.

All two hundred thousand pounds of it!

Eliza had not had so much as an inkling that her aunt possessed such great wealth. Why would she when the woman had forced them to live like virtual paupers? Spending the winters, no matter how harsh, bundled into layer upon layer of thick wool rather than pay to burn a few extra logs in the fireplace. Refusing to let Eliza buy new handkerchiefs or fresh gloves until the old ones were so worn through they were just a few threads shy of resembling Swiss cheese. Scoffing at the notion of purchasing a reliable team of horses, maintaining that a pair of tired, old rented hacks could do the job satisfactorily enough.

Apparently even Aunt Doris's son, Philip Pettigrew, had not realized the size of his mother's estate. At the reading of the will, he had looked as stunned as Eliza had felt, clearly reeling as much from learning the amount of his mother's fortune as by the fact that he had just been cut off from it.

Even now she remembered the sick cast to her cousin's complexion once the solicitor had finished that day. She also recalled the instant of fierce hatred that had raged in her cousin's cold black eyes before he had willed the expression away.

She shivered at the memory, pushing it aside.

Since then she had spent very little of her new wealth, and nothing on herself. She had given all of her aunt's servants a healthy, and long overdue, increase in wages. She had also instructed her aunt's man of business to pay for several much needed repairs to her aunt's London townhouse. Now *her* townhouse, since the abode had also been left to her in the will. But as a single woman, living there alone would not have been proper. And truth be told, she did not wish to live alone, not even with a hired companion.

Thank heaven for Violet and Adrian. Bless them, she thought, for so graciously inviting her into their home.

She supposed under the circumstances it was her duty to spend some of her inheritance. She gazed at Violet and knew her friend only had her well-being at heart.

And considering all of Violet's many kindnesses, how could she do anything but give way?

"A new wardrobe would not come amiss, I suppose," she agreed.

"Good." Kit nodded, flashing her a quick smile. He paused to draw his gold watch out of his vest pocket, snapping open the case to check the time. "As for the rest, why don't we talk of it tomorrow? I have plans scheduled this evening and if I don't get ready now, I shall be late."

He stood.

"Of course, go on." Violet reached out her hands, clasped Kit's to give them a friendly parting squeeze. "You won't regret agreeing to help."

"Hmm. Only time shall tell," he murmured. "Miss Hammond, until the morrow."

She nodded her head. "My lord."

She waited until he was gone from the room. Only then did she become aware of her fingers and how tightly she had them clasped together in her lap. Pain shot through her hands, blood flowing normally again as she loosened her grip. Abashed, she sighed.

Dear heavens, what have I done?

Chapter Two

"Keep up your left, my lord. That's right. Excellent."

The impact of his padded gloves connecting with his opponent's broad, muscled rib cage sang along Kit's arms like flesh hitting stone. *One, two, three,* then away. He swung around and narrowly missed taking a sharp jab to the head as he dipped and weaved. Sweat beaded on his bare chest, dampened his brow and trickled in a slow line along his temple.

The other man circled, his dark eyes searching for an opening. Kit did the same, studying the situation, knowing his reactions would have to be lightning quick, nearly instinctual, if he was to prevail. His sparing partner for the day was built like an oak, huge and solid and every bit as mighty.

No easy pickings here.

But then, Gentleman Jackson never pitted him against any of the lesser boxers who fought in his salon, knowing Kit preferred a challenge and wasn't the sort to complain if he came away with a bruise or two afterward.

Suddenly the big man moved, coming in low in an effort to make Kit drop his gloves and fall prey to the feint. But Kit was on to the tactic and held steady, ignoring the burst of pain in his side as his opponent got in a solid punch.

Before the other man had time to recover and raise his gloves, Kit struck, connecting with a solid right cross to the jaw, followed quickly by another pair of blows to the ribs. The man staggered back a few steps. Kit pursued and punched again, pummeling him with a series of clean, powerful blows.

The big man swayed, then over he went, the wooden floor reverberating beneath Kit's feet as his opponent crashed to the ground. A trainer rushed forward seconds later to help the downed man sit up, the bruiser shaking his head, clearly disoriented.

A wash of satisfaction surged through Kit at his victory. Lungs straining for air, he bent double and braced his gloved fists on his thighs as he recovered from the exertion.

A round of clapping commenced, a few gentlemen who had gathered to watch the bout expressing their approval.

"Well done, my lord," Gentleman Jackson declared, stepping forward. "Not many men can best Finke, who once defeated the great Tom Cribb himself early in his career. If you weren't a nobleman, my lord, I'd set you up in a prizefight and put my money on you to win. I fear, however, your esteemed brother, the duke, would not approve."

No, Kit mused as he accepted help from the young servant boy, who hurried forward to unlace his gloves, Adrian most decidedly would not approve of his engaging in public fisticuffs, bloodying his hands in one of the bare-knuckle boxing matches so popular these days. A gentleman might box for sport or to settle a matter of honor in lieu of dueling with sword or pistol, but he would never fight for money or fame, certainly not in front of the masses.

The gloves gone, Kit took a towel from the boy and used it to dry his damp face and rub the sweat from his chest. "Thank you for the vote of confidence, John. It means a lot coming from you. Good round today. It's left me hungry."

Jackson laughed, Kit's prodigious appetite being well known to all. "Glad to hear it, my lord. Will we see you next week at the usual time?"

Kit opened his mouth to agree, then stopped.

Deuced take it, he didn't know, he realized. Might have to tutor Miss Hammond this time next week. "I am not yet sure of my plans," he told the older man. "I'll have to let you know."

"Very good, my lord. You are welcome here anytime it's convenient."

Jackson strolled away, moving to attend to a few of the other pugilists in training. Kit turned and crossed to his sparing partner, who had regained his senses enough to be steady again on his feet. Kit shook the bigger man's hand and thanked him for the match, then turned and exited the ring.

Speaking of matches, Kit mused, *how in the blue blazes did I let myself get talked into playing matchmaker for Eliza Hammond!* Because, no matter what Violet chose to call it, that is what he had agreed to do. Granted, he wouldn't have to handpick the men for Eliza, but he had been charged with vetting them, culling the honorable wheat from the fortune-hunting chaff, as it were.

Worse, he had given his word to make her over, to turn her from a nondescript spinster into a charming Society belle—a transformation that would require nothing less than a miracle.

Good God, what was I thinking?

One minute he'd been girding himself to gently but politely refuse Violet's outrageous request and sprint for the nearest door. The next he'd been sitting there chatting with the pair of them, agreeing to outline plans for improving Eliza's coiffure and wardrobe.

Insane, that's what it was. He might be good with people but he was no mincing fop. He was an athlete. He boxed. He fenced. He rowed. He rode and drove horses. He even still partook of the occasional footrace.

He did *not* help women dress their hair and pick out clothing.

But it looked as if he was about to, beginning this afternoon. Bloody hell, if any of his fellows got wind of this, they would laugh him out the door. Laugh him out of the city, more like.

Well, at least rehabilitating Eliza Hammond would be a challenge. Mayhap the effort would help stave off some of the relentless boredom that had gripped him ever since his return from abroad. He had enjoyed the Continent, thrived on meeting new people, exploring new places. If he'd had his druthers, he would have stayed away longer. Gone on to India, the Orient, even the Americas, perhaps. But Adrian had written, telling him their mother missed him and wanted him home. Asking him when he was going to settle down, take up some sort of profession, get married and start a family.

He didn't want a wife and a family, at least not yet.

He was only five and twenty, after all, far too young for such unbreakable ties and obligations. Even Adrian— the one in the family who never shirked his duty—hadn't fallen prey to the parson's noose until his thirty-second year. But Adrian had gotten lucky. He'd found a wonderful woman he loved. A woman who loved him back just as fiercely. A wife who made every day a pleasure, and the blessing of children, who, Kit knew, made Adrian grateful for each moment he was alive and able to see them grow and prosper.

But Kit wasn't ready for marriage. And although he wouldn't mind something meaningful with which to occupy his time, he had no interest whatsoever in the usual livelihoods available for the younger son of a duke. The military and its rigid discipline would stifle the life out of him. As for the clergy . . . well, let's just say he enjoyed the varied pleasures of the flesh a bit too much to ever consider taking ecclesiastical orders. Which left little else to do other than wait for his inheritance to come through in six months' time and hope for something interesting to transpire in the meanwhile.

A hard palm suddenly slapped him on the shoulder. "Winter. What a splendid dustup. Caught the very last of it when you knocked that chap to the deck. Well done."

Kit turned, found a pair of his friends loitering near his elbow. "Lloyd, Selway, what brings you round here? Didn't know you cared for the pugilistic arts."

"Oh, I don't for myself," Lloyd volunteered. "I've too fine a sense of self-preservation to risk ruining this handsome face. But I never mind watching the rest of you foolhardy types take to beating each other stupid. Which is why Selway and I came by. We are off to a mill this afternoon in Hampstead. Thought you'd want to join us."

The offer was tempting. Damned tempting and for a long moment he considered sending a note to Violet to beg off from this afternoon's meeting with her and Eliza. But a promise was a promise and he was nothing if not a man of his word.

"Sorry, but I'll have to join you another day," Kit said. "Previous engagement."

"What sort of engagement could be more important than a mill?" Selway gave a disgusted cluck of his tongue. "Oh, unless you've received another summons from your brother?"

Kit said nothing, deciding to let them think what they liked. If they wanted to blame Adrian for Kit's refusal to join them, then it seemed a proper sacrifice for his brother to make.

"Well, at least say you can join the pair of us for breakfast," Lloyd said.

At the mention of food, Kit's stomach rumbled. "As you well know, I never turn down a proper meal. Give me a few minutes to wash and change, and I will be at your disposal."

He strode toward the changing rooms, his mind filled with thoughts of the miracle he would be expected to perform later that day. "And now for my next trick, ladies and gentlemen," he murmured under his breath, "I shall attempt to part the Red Sea."

". . . seven one hundred, eight one hundred, nine one hundred, ten. Ready or not, here I come."

With exaggerated drama, Eliza lowered her hands from her eyes and swung about, making a great show of peering around the large, sunny schoolroom painted in buoyant shades of blue.

"Now, where could those boys be hiding?" she wondered in a loud clear voice as if she were completely perplexed. "I don't see them anywhere." Setting her hands upon her hips, she turned a slow circle. "It is such a big room, how will I ever find them?"

A high-pitched childish giggle of excited delight drifted up, clearly originating from the room's far corner where a large wooden rocking horse stood complete with a real leather saddle and toy crop. Beside it sat a huge chest, filled nearly to overflowing with toys.

Pretending she hadn't heard so much as a peep, Eliza deliberately turned in the direction opposite the sound and walked slowly forward. "Could they be over here under this big chair?" She bent at the waist, looked beneath. "No, not there."

She turned and walked toward the windows that overlooked the mews at the rear of the townhouse, her footsteps ringing softly against the polished oak floorboards.

"Could they be here behind this curtain?" She paused before taking hold of a nearby drapery and yanking the cloth aside with an overacted flourish. "Fustian! Not there either."

She ambled toward the boys' hiding spot, making sure not to get too close. She caught sight of a pair of small, dark shoes protruding an inch beyond the edge of the toy chest and smiled. Her mouth curved wider when a tiny gasp of breathless anticipation broke the silence, followed by a second, separate conspiratorial giggle. When she was near enough that she could have leaned over and grabbed them, she stopped and turned her back. "Hmm, I believe I am outfoxed. Noah? Sebastian? Where are you?"

"Here I am!" Up one of them jumped, the little boy's body springing rabbit-quick out of his hidey hole.

Eliza spun in feigned surprise, a hand on her chest, her eyes wide. "Oh, you scared me," she fibbed. "And where is your brother, Noah?"

"He's not Noah. I am!" The second boy popped upright, a mirror image of the first, with short dark hair, keen brown eyes and cherub cheeks, the shape of which reminded her of their mother, Violet.

She knew which boy was which and had only been teasing them about their names, though it wasn't always so easy to tell them apart. Physically they were as alike as like could be. But their personalities usually gave them away—the elder twin, Sebastian, a bit sweeter and more pliable, the one of the pair who could generally be counted upon to give up the game—and the most information—just as he had today.

Racing from their hiding place with exuberant shouts and exclamations, they swarmed around her. Dropping down to her knees, she returned their eager hugs and joined in their laughter, loving the sensation of their small arms twined around her neck, their sturdy bodies nestled warm and resilient against her own. She closed her eyes for a brief moment and gave in to the motherly urge that made her wish, if only for an instant, that they were her own.

And this, she thought, was the reason she had decided to go along with Violet's wild plan. Why she had put aside her fears, her doubts and, yes, her pride and agreed to let Kit Winter act as her mentor when she would much rather have refused and remained the shy, quiet person she had always been.

But the plain truth was that she wanted more from her life than to spend it alone.

After her first four disastrous Seasons, she had given up all thoughts of marriage, had abandoned the notion of ever finding a husband and raising a family. She had resigned herself to the idea that she would need to take her pleasure in her friends, satisfy her desire for home and children by playing maiden "aunt" to other people's children. Forever outside watching what she wanted and would never, ever have.

Then suddenly everything changed. Suddenly she inherited great wealth and the options that came with it, and like a phoenix, hope had beaten its bright, wide wings and risen from the ashes. With her new fortune, she could have a life of independence few women ever dreamed of achieving.

Yet as a single female, her existence would be one lived in solitude. Certainly she would have friends she could visit, but she could not trade upon their kindness indefinitely. As much as she cherished living with Violet and Adrian, as much as she adored their darling children, she could not stay with them forever. They and their children were not, and could never be, her own. And when she must, out of good conscience, leave them to lead their own lives, hers would be spent in the company of a paid companion and a handful of indifferent servants.

But if she married, she could have her own children, someone to love again to replace the family she had lost so many years before when she had been only a child herself.

She remembered that day with vivid clarity, the day she had awakened from a deadly fever, her hair sweat-drenched and plastered like a cap against her skull, her body listless and weak. The local minister's wife, a woman she barely knew, had held her hand and told her with tears swimming in her eyes that both of Eliza's parents had been claimed by the angels, dead these many days past of the same fever Eliza had survived.

In those moments, she had wanted to die herself, weeping tears that only made her throat ache, her lungs labor harder for each ragged breath she drew. She had drifted into restless nightmares, wishing the illness would claim her too. But something inside her had clung to life, and at eleven years old she found herself alone.

When she recovered, her aunt had taken her in rather than see her go to an orphanage. "My Christian duty," Doris Pettigrew had pronounced with pinched nostrils and tight, humorless lips.

In the years to follow, Eliza had found no love in her aunt's house. Slowly she came to understand the deep resentment Doris bore her younger sister—Eliza's mother, Annabelle. Years before Annabelle had turned her back on her aristocratic family to run off with Eliza's father, the impoverished tutor with whom she had fallen madly in love. Doris had never forgiven Annabelle for the resulting scandal, for embarrassing the family and diminishing Doris's own chances to make a distinguished match. Her aunt had been forced to marry down socially, a circumstance for which she had never failed to remind—and blame—Annabelle's offspring, Eliza. Doris's bitterness had tainted every aspect of her adult life.

Yet astonishingly her aunt had left Eliza her fortune, giving her the means to have the one thing she desired the most—a family of her own. She was not looking for great love. She had no foolishly naive dreams that a woman like her would inspire a man to feel the sort of grand passion of which the poets wrote and romantics dreamed. But if she could find a pleasant man, a kindly sort who would give her a comfortable home and the children she craved, a man who would not abuse or harm her, then she could be quite content. And if after some while the two of them became companionable friends, she would be very glad indeed and have no room for complaint.

So if that meant letting Lord Christopher Winter instruct her, then she would allow it. She would put aside any lingering feelings she might harbor for him and learn what she must in order to win herself a husband. Anyway, spending time with Kit would give her the chance to prove to herself that she was indeed over the man once and for all. It would let her be confident in the knowledge that all she had ever felt for him was rash infatuation and nothing more.

Realizing she'd held the boys a bit too long, she gave both a quick squeeze and released them, then climbed to her feet.

"Play again," Sebastian said, clapping his hands. "Let us play again."

The sturdy footfalls of sensible shoes crossed the floorboards. "Not today, my lords," said their nurse. "I am sure you have worn poor Miss Hammond down to the ground. You must let her go on her way. Besides, it is time for you to wash up and have your midday meal."

A pair of groans resounded.

"We want Aunt Eliza to stay," Noah piped.

"Aunt Eliza, Aunt Eliza," Sebastian seconded.

"Your aunt Eliza cannot remain. She has other things to do with her day," the older woman said, a gentle undertone in her voice that softened her strict words. "Now, behave as well-bred young lords ought and bid Miss Hammond a polite farewell."

Identical mouths turned pouty, tears pooling in Sebastian's eyes.

"Now, what is this? Are those tears I see?" Violet asked as she entered the playroom.

"Mama, Mama!" Both boys raced to her, burying their faces against her thighs, clutching handfuls of her dotted apricot skirts in their small fists.

"They wish me to stay," Eliza explained, meeting Violet's curious gaze.

"Well, of course they do. The boys adore you and quite rightly so. You are their favorite aunt, more favored even than any of their natural aunts. But," Violet declared, wrapping a comforting arm around each of her sons as she bent forward to address them, "as much as she would like, your aunt Eliza cannot stay and play the day away. She has things she must do that cannot include a pair of little boys. Besides, if I do not mistake the hour, it is time for both of you to have your meal and then take a nap."

"Just as I was telling them when you arrived, your Grace," Nurse said, her hands folded at her ample waist.

"I don't want a nap," Noah said in a defiant voice.

"Me either," Sebastian seconded.

"Hmm." Violet slowly shook her head. "Well, I cannot make you sleep, I suppose, but if you do not get your rest your papa will not take you out this afternoon to ride your ponies. He says tired boys make poor riders, and he will never agree to let you take a turn on Snow and Ebony if you have not had your naps."

"I want to ride the ponies." Noah cast an entreating gaze up at his mother.

"I do too." Sebastian pressed himself closer against her hip.

"Well, I see no alternative, then, but for you to go with Nurse and do as you are told. Will you promise to be good boys, eat your meal and take a proper nap?"

"Yes, Mama," they said in unison.

"That's my sweet loves." Violet planted exuberant kisses on each of their cheeks, hugging them until giggles erupted. "Off with you now, imps."

The boys started toward their nurse. Sebastian stopped and ran to Eliza. He motioned for her to bend close. "Will you come and tell us a story later?" he whispered in a loud voice.

She smiled, melting under the spell of his innocent charm. "If I hear you have been extra good, I shall accompany your mama upstairs when she comes to tuck you in tonight."

Noah grinned from where he waited beside his nurse. "We shall be good," he piped.

Sebastian's lips curved in agreement with his brother before he gave Eliza a hug, then obediently went to his nurse. Taking a small hand in each of her own, the servant led the children away.

"Thank the stars for ponies," Violet said the moment her sons were safely out of earshot. "Heaven knows what I will be driven to bribing them with come next year. At least Georgianna is too young yet to work her wiles."

"She is a darling baby."

A look of happy pride washed over Violet's features at mention of her daughter. "She is, is she not? I am perpetually astonished at how even-tempered she is. She doesn't fuss, hardly ever cries, not even when her diaper is wet. I was just in the nursery feeding her and as soon as she finished, she drifted straight off to sleep."

Behind her spectacles, Violet's eyes sparkled. "You should see Adrian with her, cooing and making silly faces. You would think a man never had a daughter before. He is quite besotted. Did I tell you he has taken to calling her his little angel?"

And the baby did resemble an angel, Eliza thought, one with round rosy cheeks, long-lashed green eyes and a perfectly shaped head that was only now starting to grow the veriest bits of dark hair upon its surface.

"Is the christening still to be held a week from Sunday?"

"Yes. Jeannette sent ahead a note. She and Darragh

and my new niece plus most of Darragh's siblings are on their way. The whole brood of them should arrive in the next day or two, if all goes as scheduled. Their servants are madly cleaning their townhouse, making preparations for a very full house indeed."

Eliza had mixed feelings about being in the Countess of Mulholland's presence once again. Jeannette Brantford O'Brien intimidated the life out of her, managing somehow to always leave her feeling roughly the size of a small green inchworm. But Violet said she had noticed a marked mellowing in her spoiled, gregarious twin's disposition since Jeannette's marriage to her Irish lord. And since the addition of their new daughter, born only a week earlier than baby Georgianna, she had softened even more.

But could one glean such things from letters? Eliza wondered. Only a visit in the flesh would tell.

"I am so pleased we decided to wait and hold a joint christening together here in Town," Violet said. "Traditionally, family baptisms are always held at Winterlea, but since it will be both our daughters this time, I see no harm in a bit of change. Anyway, Jeannette said traveling with the baby all the way from County Clare would be exhausting enough without having to go up to Winterlea then back down here to London again. And she wants to stop in Town, since she refuses to return to Ireland without an entirely updated wardrobe."

Oh, yes, Eliza thought, Jeannette's mellowing remained to be seen since in some matters she clearly had not changed at all.

A polite knock sounded on the schoolroom door. A footman entered and bowed, then waited to be acknowledged.

"Yes, Robert, what is it?" the duchess asked.

"Your Grace, you asked to be informed when Lord Christopher arrived. He is in the yellow drawing room now, awaiting your pleasure."

Eliza's stomach dropped hard and fast as a lodestone. She didn't know if she was ready but it seemed her lessons were about to begin.

Chapter Three

"Is this the young lady you mentioned, my lord?"

A stranger dressed in a well-tailored coat and breeches of tobacco brown turned at Eliza and Violet's entrance into the drawing room. Shoulders erect, he marched straight across and stopped in front of Violet. Since he was not a tall man, his critical middle-aged gaze landed nearly at her eye level. Angling his head of wavy, shoulder-length copper hair, he conducted a bold inspection of Violet's coiffure.

"Hmm, not bad," he mused aloud, craning his head one way and then the other. "Not bad at all. Lovely color and texture but, of course, I am sure I could provide you with something far more elegant, more fashionably *au courant.* A style certain to bedazzle your friends and make you the envy of your acquaintances."

Kit cleared his throat loudly. "*Ahem,* Mr. Greenleaf. That is not the young lady we discussed but rather my sister-in-law, the Duchess of Raeburn. The young lady in need of your attention is over there, standing just inside the door."

Greenleaf's gaze shifted and fastened upon Eliza where she hovered not far from the entrance.

She watched his eyes widen, blue irises flashing first with surprise before darkening in unconcealed disappointment. His thin nostrils quivered faintly around their edges, lips rounding into a disapproving moue. "Ohh."

She stiffened, his tone and look as hurtful as a slap. After years of receiving many such similar reactions, this one ought not to have stung. Yet all she wanted to do was turn on her heel and flee the room. Only stubborn pride and a fear of further censure held her in place.

Kit stepped forward, gesturing her toward him with a hand. "Come in, Miss Hammond, come in. Allow me to make known to you and the duchess, Mr. Albert Greenleaf. Mr. Greenleaf is the best women's hairdresser in all of London."

"In all of England, my lord." Greenleaf drew back his shoulders, his angular chin pointing upward. "I am the finest hairdresser in all of England and likely the entire Continent as well. I have never seen my better."

Well, he certainly does not lack for self-esteem, Eliza mused. *Perhaps his middle name is Napoleon.*

The introductions apparently at an end as far as the little dictator was concerned, the hairdresser tapped a pair of fingers against his lips and stared at her once more the way one might study a particularly distasteful but nevertheless intriguing beetle. He walked a slow circle, tsking and humming and sighing as he went.

Nerves pinched and fluttered along her skin, buzzing like a swarm of tiny gnats. She restrained the urge to twitch and slap, holding herself steady beneath his scrutiny, her eyes cast down. Over the years she had learned to endure all sorts of unpleasant, intolerable encounters by keeping her gaze lowered firmly toward the floor.

Suddenly fingers began plucking at her hairpins, diving with rude impertinence into her tresses to brush against her scalp.

She jumped and whirled, her hands flying defensively to her head. Fingers trembling, she tried to hold up her drooping topknot. "W-what are you doing?"

"Taking down your hair. I must see it free of this dreadful bun in which you have it yanked if I am to envision any kind of improvement. Already it has been made better simply by loosening it around your face. Now, put down your hands and let me take out those pins so I may see the challenge before me."

She backed a step away. "No!"

Reddish-brown eyebrows rose, imperious as a pair of outraged monarchs. "No?" He turned to Kit, exasperation writ clearly upon his face. "My lord, if she will not cooperate then I see little point to this exercise. I am a busy man with many clients who do not balk at having a few trifling pins removed from their hair."

Kit looked between the two of them. "Well, you did rather take her by surprise. Perhaps if you ask her politely you might begin again."

The little man's nostrils quivered anew at the rebuke. Still, he turned and made her a small bow. "My apologies, Miss Hammond, if I startled you. Now, may I please be allowed to continue?"

She hesitated, desperately wanting to refuse. She looked to Kit then to Violet, seeking their help and intervention.

Compassion lapped like a gentle ocean wave in Violet's gaze. "Perhaps I could remove the pins?" Without waiting for a reply, Violet stepped forward, reached up and began to slide the remaining hairpins free of Eliza's hair.

She had not won the battle, Eliza realized, but at least she had scored a minor point, thanks to Violet.

Greenleaf sniffed. "As you wish, your Grace."

Freed of its restraints, her heavy hair swung over her

shoulders and down her back to her waist. She knew how it must appear, hanging straight and uninspiring as a mud-colored cape. Staring at her shoes this time, she struggled against the vulnerability that left her feeling naked and exposed. A woman's unbound hair was a private matter, she had always thought, an intimacy to be shared only with her lady's maid, her bosom female friends and, one day, if fate was willing, her husband. Yet here she stood with her hair revealed to all—or revealed at least to the trio currently gathered in the drawing room for the occasion.

From beneath her lashes she peeked up at Kit and found him staring, an unreadable expression on his normally open, winsome face. Hurriedly she glanced away, her heart thrumming like a plucked violin string.

Then Mr. Greenleaf stuck his hands in her hair again.

"Thick as a horse's tail," the hairdresser proclaimed, gathering her tresses inside his fists before letting the skeins gradually slide free. "Soft, but manageable with the proper applications and techniques. Hmm, yes, this might be most interesting, inspiring even, like da Vinci given a blank canvas upon which to create."

He walked around her, then reached out and scooped her hair forward, draping it so the locks cascaded over her black-clad shoulders and breasts. "Up. Chin up, please. Shoulders back, spine straight so that I may properly observe you, otherwise I shall be unable to achieve a thing."

He marched several paces across the drawing room then spun to face her.

"Up, I said." He sighed. "Please, Miss Hammond, I must have your cooperation."

Cooperation, was it? All the little tyrant seemed to want so far was obedience. Then again, wasn't that what her aunt had also always wanted? Unquestioning compliance in all matters both large and small. Perhaps that, as much as her present circumstances, was the reason for her wish to resist, and her ultimate decision not to do so. Long ago she had learned the futility of open defiance, taught beneath the painful slap of her aunt's hard palm against her cheek.

With his commands scraping along her nerves like a claw, she raised her chin.

One fist planted on his hip, another raised to his mouth, Greenleaf raked her with his eyes. Abruptly, he tossed up a hand and waggled his fingers in the air. "Yes, I have it. Don't know why I didn't think of it immediately. We shall cut!"

"Cut!" Eliza gasped, and took an instinctive step away, her hands flying to her head.

"Cut Miss Hammond's hair?" Kit stepped between her and the hairdresser, his dark brows furrowed. "I don't know, seems rather extreme, don't you think?"

"Sometimes brilliance requires extreme measures."

Violet inserted herself into the conversation. "Yes, but even I know short hair is no longer the fashion these days. Perhaps some compromise could be made."

"Compromise?" The older man gave an imperious sniff. "The Great Greenleaf does not compromise. And once I am done, short hair *will* be the fashion, mark my words."

"Yes, but if she does not want you to cut her hair, then—" Kit said.

"I thought I made myself clear from the outset, my lord," Greenleaf interrupted. "I am an artist and must be allowed free reign. If you and the others insist upon interfering, there is no point in continuing today's gathering. I shall leave and you may hire some other coiffeur. A talentless hack who will no doubt bow and scrape and do precisely as you suggest, giving you what you believe you want with far from satisfactory results. Now, I bid you adieu—"

"Go ahead and cut it," Eliza said.

Three pairs of eyes flew toward her.

"Your pardon?" Kit asked.

Eliza raised her voice to be clearly heard. "I said cut it." Mayhap Greenleaf was right, she thought. Mayhap in this situation boldness and daring were precisely what was needed most of all. She'd come this far, she decided. Why let fear convince her to toss her opportunities away? "Mr. Greenleaf seems convinced my hair will look better than it does now and if he is as good as he claims—"

"It is not a claim. I am that good," the little man declared, his slight chest puffed out like the boldest pigeon in the park.

"Then I put myself in your hands. Pray do not disappoint me."

A long moment of silence descended, then a smile as wide as the English Channel creased his mouth. "Bravo! To work, then, to work. Where shall we set up? Certainly not here in this drawing room. Your bedchamber, perhaps?"

"You may use my sitting room," Violet stated in her most authoritative duchess voice.

"Excellent." The hairdresser clapped his hands twice and stalked toward the double doors. "My staff await me below. I shall send for them and we will begin anon."

Greenleaf departed, residual energy circulating in the room as if a whirlwind had just torn through.

Violet crossed to Eliza, threaded a supportive arm around her waist. "Are you sure? You need not do this if you do not wish."

Eliza braved a look at Kit, met his green-gold gaze. "*Is* he as good as he says?"

"The best, from everything I am given to understand. But every inch as temperamental as you have just witnessed. We can find another man, if you prefer, and I shall send Greenleaf on his way."

Eliza bit back a sigh, sorely tempted to give in to her trepidation and do that very thing. But hadn't she agreed to this plan? Hadn't she pledged herself to letting Kit help her? If this Greenleaf was a master at arranging hair, then she must take the risk and let him arrange.

"I shall be fine," she assured Kit and Violet with far more courage than she felt. "Besides, if it is dreadful I can always wear a wig while my own hair grows out," she added with a wry smile.

As the next three hours passed, Eliza began to wonder if she would indeed be forced to resort to such desperate measures.

Expressly forbidden to look into a mirror, she had scant idea what the Great Greenleaf was doing to her hair. But what she couldn't see she felt, often with a sense of escalating worry and horror. Even now a tinny aftertaste remained on her tongue from the lump of misery that had collected in her belly when the little man braided her long hair then retrieved a pair of shears from a nearby table.

She'd felt the scissors clamp down like a voracious pair of jaws, heard them make a sawing noise before finally closing with a *snick*.

Seconds later, her shorn braid landed in her lap like some just-skinned pelt, dark and every inch as dead.

"A souvenir," he'd cackled with heartless glee.

She'd clutched it, stroking the soft plait as she fought back tears. But she had only a few seconds to mourn before he and his minions had set to work, vigorously scrubbing her hair with soap, rinsing it clean with fresh, warm water. After that, they had proceeded to slather her locks with one odd-smelling concoction after another, wrapping her hair in towels and rinsing in between. She didn't know what they were using but imagined she caught whiffs of blackberry, coffee and something that reminded her of dried autumn leaves and bread mold.

All the while, Greenleaf directed his staff around the room like a field marshal, ordering them hither and yon with precise, well-drilled movements. The series of decoctions at last complete, he draped a towel over her shoulders then worked her hair free of tangles using a fine-toothed ivory comb.

She assumed the ordeal was coming to an end, when he surprised her yet again by calling for the scissors— new ones this time, gleaming silver and wickedly sharp.

In a flurry of movement, he clipped and snipped, moving around her as if possessed, angling her head this way and that, pausing to stare as he drew bits of her hair through his fingertips, measuring and judging. She was starting to get drowsy by the time he stopped and roused her with a loud grunt of satisfaction. Clapping his hands, he called for the curling tongs.

She feared being singed by the heated metal rods but he worked with confident precision, her hair drying and curling all at once around her head. Handing the last nearly cold curling tong to his assistant, he reached for a pair of filigreed gold clips and placed them just behind her ears. He tugged at a pair of locks that drooped over her forehead and made one last inspection.

With a grand flourish, he swept the towel from around her shoulders. "*Et voilà!* Perfection."

One of his helpers rushed forward, a large mirror at the ready.

Eliza gazed into it and felt her mouth drop open as she stared in astonishment at her reflection.

Kit snuggled deeper into his drawing room chair and tried to sleep. And to think he could even now be enjoying a jolly fine time with his cronies in Hampstead, watching fighters fight, betting and smoking and admiring the pretty demireps who came to such events on the arms of their latest protectors.

Instead he sat, a prisoner of his promise to Violet while they awaited the results of Miss Hammond's haircut. Who would have imagined such a simple thing would take so long? He prayed the results would not be a disaster. Surely anything Greenleaf did would be an improvement, and Kit had been assured by a number of excellent sources that the imperious little man was extremely talented.

Greenleaf had better be, for what he charged. If Kit weren't a lord and above dabbling in such low professions as Trade, he might have considered taking up the craft himself for that kind of blunt.

He must have sighed—again—though he hadn't heard himself do so, since Violet suddenly peered up at him from the book she sat reading.

"Shall I go and check on her again?" she asked.

He shook his head. "They'll only toss you out as they have done thrice already. Imagine having the nerve to eject a duchess. Prideful, secretive bunch they are."

"Yes, you are right and I'm sure your mother would not stand for such treatment, but there was nothing for me to do but watch and wait anyway. I only hope poor Eliza is all right in there."

"Of course she is all right. If they were actually torturing her, I think we would have heard the screams by now."

Violet shot him a chastening look though he could see the humor playing at the corners of her mouth.

His own lips curved upward as he showed his teeth in unabashed amusement. "So, since I have been consigned to remain home for the evening, what is Chef preparing for supper?"

Violet was just beginning to tell him when Greenleaf appeared, striding grandly into the room. "My lord. Your Grace. Behold my newest creation."

A woman glided into the room behind the hairdresser and for a long, pronounced moment Kit did not know who she was. He stood and stared, then stared some more. If not for the familiar dour black dress she had been wearing earlier in the day, he suspected he would not have recognized her at all, the change was so marked.

Was this striking bit of femininity really Eliza Hammond?

He nearly blurted out the rude question but restrained himself at the last second.

Violet meanwhile leapt to her feet and rushed toward her friend. "Oh, just look at you! Your hair is precious, simply precious. Oh, I love it!"

Touching a tentative hand to her new coiffure, Eliza shared a shy but obviously excited smile. "Do you really? It is so different, I am still trying to reconcile myself to the alteration."

"It is magnificent," Violet cooed, "just as Mr. Greenleaf promised. What do you think, Kit? Do you not adore it?"

All eyes turned upon him.

"Yes," he said, a strange tightness in his throat. "It is quite fetching."

"It is more than fetching. It is divine," Violet said.

And it was divine, Kit silently agreed. The miracle they had needed. Since, quite beyond hope, a simple haircut had succeeded in turning Eliza Hammond into someone she had never been before—a strikingly attractive woman.

Where before there had been a sallow, almost grim cast to her complexion, there lay now a fresh, unexpected radiance. A gamine spark coaxed forth by the short curls that frothed and cavorted about her cheeks and forehead in a kind of wild, pagan dance. Gone was the heavy severity of her long, straight hair, as though cutting it had unleashed some great weight, freed her of an old confining burden.

And the color. The color was purely breathtaking, lush as a crisp autumn day. Her hair shone with vibrant life, glorious hints of red peeking out from beneath a mix of warm chestnut and burnt umber. How had Greenleaf achieved such a marvel? More to the point, why did the result leave Kit wanting to thread his fingers through those impish curls to see if they were as silky and seductive as they appeared?

In his mind's eye, he saw himself doing that very thing. Crossing to Eliza and running his hands through that crazy, impulsive mass of hair, caressing her skull, making her turn and smile, then laugh up at him in a gleeful way he had never before seen her laugh. Her gray eyes sparkling only for him.

Unnerved by the fantasy, he quickly drove it away.

What nonsense, he thought, giving himself a mental shake.

Obviously he must be in greater need of a woman than he imagined. But if he had such a reaction, just think how other men might respond.

Perhaps Violet was right. Perhaps this scheme of hers was not such a hopeless case, after all. Attired in the proper clothes, Eliza would look quite presentable. More than presentable, in truth. And with the promise of a hefty fortune to be had in exchange for a wedding ring, he surely could find her a suitable bridegroom.

But then he looked again, watched her shuffle in place and clasp her hands in the folds of her skirts in bashful discomfort at being once more beneath the scrutiny of others. And they were but three people, and with the possible exception of Mr. Greenleaf, her friends.

He caught himself in a sigh, realizing he had nearly forgotten the most difficult part of the task set before him.

Her shyness.

Her painful, abject, utterly withering shyness that left her all but paralyzed in moments when poise and bold-ness were essential for success. Her improved looks would help and help greatly but she needed to be able to do more than mutter a barely audible "Hello" then stare at her feet when she found herself in company.

Still, this new hairstyle was a marked improvement. With the right instruction and encouragement from him, perhaps the goal could yet be achieved.

At least that's what he hoped. Lord, how he hoped.

"Well now, miss, did I not tell you?" Greenleaf said. "A fair beauty you've become and in less than a day with my brilliant assistance. But you will need me to re-turn on a regular basis from now on. Precisely four weeks from today I will be back to do everything anew. Such splendor must be maintained."

Eliza dipped her chin in a diffident nod. "Yes, sir. Four weeks from today."

"And not a single day more. Do not think of postpon-ing our next appointment or you will find yourself suf-fering the most profound of regrets. Well, I am off, more amazing, splendorous feats to achieve."

Somehow the three of them managed to remain silent until the hairdresser was out of earshot, then they all began to laugh.

Kit was wiping a tear from the corner of one eye a minute later when Adrian walked in. Tall and formidable, his brother possessed a commanding presence that instantly filled the room.

"Do you know I just passed the most curious little fellow in the hallway," Adrian remarked. "He was muttering something to himself about being bloody brilliant, your pardon, ladies, for repeating such language."

Adrian turned and smiled at Violet, then quite absently glanced at Eliza.

He froze and stared, looking for a long instant as though he'd been smacked in the forehead by a cudgel. "Good God, Miss Hammond, whatever have you done to your hair!"

Chapter Four

"We shall have an afternoon dress in the primrose silk as well and another done in the dusty rose. Oh, and riding habits, she must have riding habits. Three at least, one made of that divine Sardinian-blue figured merino, I believe. A second in that sweet forest green poplin and the last in the amaranthus gros de Naples." Grinning like a child turned loose inside a confectioner's shop, Jeannette Brantford O'Brien clapped her gloved hands together. "Oh, how darling they shall be, do you not agree, Miss Hammond?"

Kit watched Eliza open her mouth to reply, but she didn't get so much as a squeak past her lips before Violet's twin rushed on, the countess mulling over the various trims and buttons available—the proprietress, Madame Thibodaux, all condescension and nodding agreement.

From his spot on the modiste's satin-covered, scroll-backed divan, Kit observed the proceedings, not the least bit surprised by the ongoing exchange—or lack thereof, in poor Eliza's case—since Jeannette had barely let the other girl get in a word from the moment they entered the dressmaker's shop. As for asking Eliza's opinion, Jeannette had taken over the shopping expedition like a general laying siege to a citadel, Eliza no more than a raw recruit expected to learn and obey.

As for himself, he was the superfluous male escort. Restraining a sigh, he reached for one of the pâté-topped toast points Madame Thibodaux's assistant had offered not long after their arrival.

Why did I ever agree to accompany the women this morning? he wondered as he ate the hors d'oeuvre. A man didn't belong in a feminine bastion such as this. He raised his wineglass and drank, catching a fresh glimpse of Eliza's face, her pallid cheeks smudged with raw color, and he remembered the reason. Remembered the anxious flash that had come into her eyes when she had realized Jeannette meant to accompany her to the modiste's instead of Violet.

Violet was laid low with a touch of stomach flu and regrettably confined to her bed. When Jeannette—who had arrived two days before, along with her husband, Darragh, their infant daughter, Caitlyn, and Darragh's siblings Michael, Finn, Moira and Siobhan—heard Eliza's shopping expedition was to be postponed, she had eagerly offered to help.

Who better than she, Jeannette declared, to arrange for Eliza's new wardrobe? With Jeannette's love of fashion and all things feminine, she was the perfect choice for the task. Besides, she confessed, she had been dying for literally years to get her hands on Eliza and dress her in something other than frowsy furbelows and drab shades of brown. Now, at long last, she had grinned, her chance had arrived.

Knowing Jeannette wasn't in the least exaggerating her talents in the fashionable arts, and that she really was the best person to outfit Eliza with a new wardrobe, Kit had found himself agreeing to Jeannette's offer. What he had not planned on was accompanying the ladies on their expedition. But that desperate, pleading look from Eliza had persuaded him otherwise.

Sweet Jesu, he would have felt worse than a puppy killer to ignore her silent entreaty.

So here he sat, bored and out of place. At least the toast points were tolerable, he mused, as he leaned forward to select another.

"Now, let us start on evening gowns," Jeannette pronounced. "I would say we'll need a minimum of two dozen."

"Two dozen!" Eliza gasped in a faint voice of distress.

"Of course." Jeannette nodded. "A lady never wishes to be seen in the same gown twice, so come to think of it, let us say three dozen evening gowns, just to be safe."

"But the expense—"

"You've plenty of funds. It'll do you good to spend some of them, especially if you intend to find a husband." Jeannette turned back to the modiste. "Let us begin with the oyster satin. Hmm, perhaps we should add a row of appliquéd roses along the hem? They are all the rage this Season, you know."

"Yes, my lady, roses would look lovely, and mayhap a pale rose tulle underskirt, if I might suggest."

"In what style? Have you a sketch?"

"Yes indeed. Let me find the pattern book."

As the woman hurried away, Jeannette looked again at Eliza. "My dear Miss Hammond, why don't you go to the changing room with Madame's assistant before the poor thing faints from nerves. She's been hovering so these many minutes past."

Kit saw both women gaze toward the girl, the servant waiting along the room's periphery exactly as Jeannette described.

"Your fitting must be seen to directly if the seamstresses are to have any hope of altering the pair of dresses Madame has set aside for you. Otherwise, they will not be ready by tomorrow," Jeannette continued.

"I-I can wait a few days for my new gowns," Eliza objected in a soft tone. "It is not as if I will be making any calls soon."

"You'll be attending the christening tomorrow. It won't do for you to arrive at the church in black. It is such a depressing shade."

"But I am in mourning."

"*Half mourning.* No one will think ill of you if you wear a bit of color. Ah, here is Madame returned, so run along. She and I shall do quite well on our own for a time."

For a moment, Eliza looked as if she intended to hold her ground and argue the point, but abruptly her shoulders drooped and she turned meekly away. She and the servant girl disappeared behind a curtain that led to a room in the back of the shop.

The tableau concluded, Kit propped his elbow onto the single, high arm of the divan and sipped his wine.

Less than five minutes later, Madame Thibodaux's assistant shot out from behind the curtain, an expression of deep distress marring her cute, button-nosed face. A flurry of muffled conversation ensued between the girl and her employer.

"Your pardon, my lady. My lord," the modiste said, a sharp frown etched upon her forehead. "Miss Hammond apparently requires my help. I shall return in but a moment."

Jeannette paused in her assessment of the pattern book. "Is there some problem?"

"Oh, no, no problem. Just a small delay, it would seem."

But it was more than a small delay, the modiste's obvious pleadings issuing audibly from the dressing room a scant minute later.

Jeannette set down the book. "What on earth is the matter?"

Kit raised an eyebrow and met her puzzled gaze with a curious one of his own.

Madame emerged seconds later, lips pinched as if she'd eaten an unripened persimmon. "She won't have them."

"Who won't have what?" Jeannette asked.

"Miss Hammond. She will not have the dresses we selected."

The countess gave a dainty gasp. "Of course she will have them, do not be absurd."

"I tell you, she is most adamant."

"That doesn't sound like her. Eliza Hammond is an exceptionally quiet, biddable female."

"Well, not today, my lady. She does not want the gowns and I cannot force her into them. If she does not care for my creations then perhaps she should look elsewhere."

"I am sure that is not it at all. Let me talk to her and find out what the difficulty is."

Jeannette turned and walked into the back.

But to Kit's amazement, Jeannette had no more luck persuading Eliza to try on the gowns than the other two women before her. Sea-colored eyes awash with tumult, Jeannette emerged from the dressing room, as plainly at a loss as the others.

"She's being impossible," Jeannette declared.

Kit set down his wine, came to his feet. "What did she say?"

"Nothing, that's what she said. She just sits there and says, 'No, I will not wear them,' then stares at the floor."

"Perhaps I should take a turn speaking to her," he suggested.

"Well, you can try if you wish," she said, her skepticism plain.

"In the meantime, why don't you continue selecting clothing for Eliza's wardrobe."

"Even if she won't wear what I choose?"

"Oh, she'll wear it. Unless she wishes to renege on our agreement. She's already given me her promise on the matter."

Striding across the room, he easily located the entrance to the dressing room. A discreet tap on the frame announced his presence, then without further preamble he shoved aside the gold damask curtain that acted as a door to the elegantly appointed dressing chamber.

He found Eliza seated upon a blue velvet upholstered bench, her head down, her gaze fixed upon a very dull pair of black half boots. Her chin came up, eyes widening as he strode unceremoniously inside.

"My lord, what are you doing? You can't be in here."

"Don't see why not. It's not as if there was any risk of catching you in your unmentionables. From what I hear, you won't take off so much as a stitch, let alone give either of those new frocks a try."

Color flooded her cheeks. "Lord Christopher!"

"Kit. Please, call me Kit. Never have cared for 'Lord Christopher,' always puts me in mind of some stuffy old duffer. Besides, you and I have known each other long enough to safely dispense with the formalities, don't you think?"

Eliza shifted on the bench and let her lashes sweep downward. What she thought was that he was large and male and took up far too much space inside the limited confines of the room. Anyway, why was he here? Had they sent him in to work on her as well, despite the impropriety of such an action?

"Yes, I suppose. But that does not change the fact that you should not be here. This is a ladies dressing room," she insisted, "and I'll thank you to leave."

"Not until we've talked." He moved closer and startled her by sliding onto the bench. His thigh brushed her skirts as he settled himself, the clean scents of milled soap and bay rum drifting across to tease her nostrils. She caught herself before she gave in to the urge to lean closer and sniff him like some rare, exotic spice.

"Well now," he said, resting his gorgeous hazel gaze upon her. "Tell me what is awry."

She plucked at a crease in her skirt. "Nothing."

"Must be something. I understand you've refused to try on the dresses? Why is that?"

"Because I do not wish to try them on, that is all."

"Don't you like them?" From the corner of her eye she saw him look toward the pair of gowns hanging from a built-in wooden rod. "They seem pretty enough to me, though I confess I'm only a man and don't know all the finer points of fashion. Jeannette lost me somewhere around the time she started discussing Gabrielle sleeves and palatine tippets."

"She lost me well before that," Eliza confessed, peeking up long enough to meet his grin. Finding his humor infectious, she couldn't help but smile back. "She barely listens to my opinion."

"Is that what's wrong? You'd like to be consulted?"

"Not really. It's . . ."

"Yes?"

She studied her boots again, falling silent.

Heavens, she really wished he would go. She couldn't think sensibly with him so close. He took up nearly the entirety of the bench, his wide shoulders barely an inch distant from her own.

"Come on, Eliza, tell me," he coaxed when she failed to answer his query. "I am sure whatever it is we can see it resolved. Surely it can't be as bad as all that."

It is, she silently bemoaned. *It's worse.*

"You might as well get it out." He stretched his booted feet in front of him. "Otherwise the day is going to grow very long indeed while the two of us sit here together."

Catching the tilt of his chin, she realized that he meant every word. When Kit decided on something he could dig in tight as a burrowing scallop.

She sighed and linked her fingers in her lap. "It is the color," she whispered.

"What? I didn't quite hear."

"The color," she said, forcing herself to speak louder. "I can't wear those colors."

Kit studied the dresses again. "Why not? The colors seem fine to me."

"But they're purple and gold!"

"Yes, and so they are," he said in an agreeable tone. "Don't you like purple and gold?"

"I do, but . . ."

"But?"

She hung her head, wishing she hadn't said a word. Wishing she could take it all back so she did not have to discuss her fears, especially with him. Kit would think her foolish. He might even laugh. Dear God, what if he laughed?

Suddenly she wanted to sink into the floor—or better yet, close her eyes and disappear. What a miraculous power that would be, she mused with real longing. How lovely to just wish for invisibility and find oneself fading away until nothing remained but air.

But as impossible as that might be, so too would be hiding this from Kit. She didn't even need to sneak a glance to feel his keen gaze upon her, to sense his calm patience as if it were an actual touch.

She waited for him to press her further, to keep on with the questions and the demands. Instead he said nothing, a quiet, steady presence at her side. One full minute ticked past, then a second, and yet he made no impatient moves, gave no sign he wanted to be anywhere other than where he was at that moment.

An odd resignation stole through her. "They'll stare," she finally murmured.

He leaned close, his voice deep and kind. "Who will stare?"

"Everyone." A shudder rushed through her. "If I wear those gowns, the whole of Society will stare."

And find me lacking, think me ridiculous as a plain brown sparrow trying to pass myself off as a brilliantly plumed jay, she concluded silently. Only a woman of daring could hope to wear such rich, vibrant, utterly captivating shades. What was Jeannette thinking to put her in such eye-drawing gowns? To tempt her with finery that was quite obviously unsuited to a girl like herself?

"Even if they do stare," Kit stated, "it will be with nothing but admiration."

She met his gaze and shook her head. "No, it will be in derision and scorn. They will laugh at me and wonder who I am to attempt such splendor. Everyone knows plain women should not wear bright colors."

It was Kit's turn to stare, but out of pure surprise. He studied her features, thinking at first she must be jesting. But sadly he realized she was not, recognizing the deep lines of vulnerability etched in her face. Obviously he knew of her shy nature but he had never given much thought to its cause. Did she really think people would mock her for wearing pretty colors? Did she equate standing out with being the brunt of jokes and ridicule?

"That," he declared, "is a load of nonsense. Was it your aunt who filled you full of such tarradiddle?"

Her mouth dropped open. "No, I—well, I don't know."

"Of course it must have been she. Who else could have drummed such a bunch of rubbish into your brain?" He grunted, not at Eliza but at the bitter, miserly old woman who had raised her. He slapped his hands against his thighs. "Well, whatever it is she told you about such matters, you are to forget them all. From now on you are to listen to me. I am your mentor, remember? It's my job to steer you along the right path."

"And you think these gowns are the right path?"

"If Jeannette believes so, then yes. She has excellent taste, and in this, at least, I trust her implicitly."

Eliza swallowed, her trepidation still in evidence. "B-but the colors she is choosing are too daring. They aren't at all the usual thing for an unmarried woman to wear during the Season."

"True, but then, you aren't the usual thing either. Forgive my bluntness, but we both know this isn't your first Season. Since it is not, there's no need to follow the rules and dress you in the demure pastels and dainty whites most girls wear. When you enter a room, people will look and you will want them to. You'll appear both striking and dramatic. Men will flock to your side, relieved to be in the company of a girl who has maturity and a brain filled with more than empty-headed fluff."

Her lips tightened, then quivered slightly. "How can you be so sure? Men have never liked my brain before."

"Once we are done with your lessons, they will. You'll have all the skills needed to change their minds, right at the tips of your fingers."

"But what if I cannot master the lessons? What if the gowns don't look as you imagine? You haven't even seen me in one of them yet."

"Precisely why you need to try one on."

She sighed, realizing how neatly he had maneuvered the conversation.

"I'll tell you what," he offered at her continued reluctance. "You try on one of the gowns and if you don't look positively splendid, then we'll jettison the entire plan. You and I and Jeannette will start from scratch."

She brightened a bit. "Do you mean it? You'll be honest with me even if the truth is as bad as I suspect?"

"Of course I'll be honest. You have my word as a gentleman."

She nodded, his oath apparently relieving the worst of her fears. "Very well. You may send Madame Thibodaux's assistant back in."

"Excellent." He stood and tossed her a smile before crossing to the entrance. Pulling back the golden drape, he paused. "Oh, and Eliza."

"Yes?"

"Don't ever again refer to yourself as plain. You may not be a diamond of the first water like Jeannette and Violet, but that doesn't mean you lack your own kind of beauty."

He left her with amazement shining bright as silver in her gentle gray eyes. Resuming his place once more on the curved sofa, he waited for Eliza to emerge, answering only a few of Jeannette's questions about how he had managed to convince Eliza to change her mind.

He only hoped he'd done the right thing. What if she didn't look good in the gowns? What if, for all his confident words, she wasn't able to benefit from his guidance and attract the husband she so obviously craved? As he'd told Violet, he was just a man and not a magician.

Eliza came into the room, her step hesitant as she awaited his reaction, her uncertain gaze darting toward him then away. He sucked in a sharp breath, astonished at the change something as simple as a dress could achieve. He stared and realized Eliza had been right about that—she did make him want to stare and stare some more.

Swathed in a rich shade of dark lilac, she was positively radiant. Her skin looked creamy, her eyes vibrant and her figure . . . well, her shape was even better than he'd suspected it might be. Always before she had worn gowns that were slightly too big and rather shapelessly made. But this one Jeannette had chosen fit Eliza in a way that emphasized the fact that she was indeed every inch a woman. Femininity fully formed with a pair of small but shapely breasts, curvaceous hips and a slender waist that begged to be encircled by a pair of eager male hands. As for what lay concealed beneath her skirts— well, he could only imagine and assume it must be every ounce as fine as the rest.

Realizing where his thoughts had led him, he forced his gaze toward a display of ribbons near the shop's front window.

"Oh, don't you look a picture," Jeannette declared, striding forward on a rustle of skirt. "I knew that color would suit you perfectly and it does. Look how she glows. Doesn't she just glow?"

Yes, he agreed, she did glow. In a manner he would never have thought to associate with his sister-in-law's quiet friend.

"I quite agree, my lady," the modiste concurred. "An inch off the bottom of the skirt and a tuck or two here and there and this dress will suit her well."

Despite the women's positive opinions, Eliza's uncertain expression did not disappear. "Kit? What do you think?" she ventured. "Do you . . . do you like it?"

Eliza waited, clearly unsure and as ill at ease as a first-year plebe sent before the headmaster. What a brute he was to make her suffer. He set aside his unaccountable response—the second in only three days' time starting with her new haircut—and answered her with complete and unfeigned sincerity.

"I like it very much. You and that dress are a match made in heaven." He smiled widely. "See, I told you that color would suit. You had nothing whatsoever to fear."

"Are you sure? It's not too bold?"

"Certainly not. You look amazing, Eliza, and don't ever think otherwise."

A relieved smile moved over her mouth, rising like a warm, brilliant sun.

"Now try on the gold dress," he urged. "Let us see if it's even more dazzling than the first."

"All right." On a happy turn, Eliza went back into the dressing room.

Kit breathed a small sigh of relief the instant she left, assuring himself he'd be in complete control by the time she returned. He quaffed a half glass of wine, ate a toast point and promised himself a well-deserved night on the town.

After all, what else could he possibly need?

Chapter Five

Eliza sat in a chair in a corner of the downstairs drawing room amid the crush of relatives and friends gathered inside Raeburn House to celebrate that morning's double christening.

A steady throb of conversation and laughter blended with the delicate fragrances of flesh-warmed perfume and fresh flowers. Generous arrangements of pink roses and white lilies provided an impressive natural display from the quartet of finely wrought Meissen vases that were set at intervals around the room. The aroma of food and wine drifted in from the dining room buffet, subtly overlaying the mix.

Eliza set aside her own plate, the taste of hothouse strawberries and clotted cream still sweet upon her tongue. She observed the clusters of chatting people, relieved to be on the periphery and no longer required to make any more pitiful attempts at small talk and casual conversation.

At the start of the brunch nearly an hour before, there had been a great deal of enthusiastic comment about her new lilac gown and her artfully shorn locks. In fact, several people had not recognized her immediately, including the Countess of Wightbridge, Violet and Jeannette's mother, who had stared at her through most of the christening ceremony with an expression of frustrated puzzlement on her fine-boned visage.

But despite the outward changes in Eliza's appearance, she knew herself to be the same person she had been before—a reserved, tongue-tied bluestocking who could quote passages from Euripides, but who knew almost nothing about the latest gossip or juicy on-dits. Knowing what a disaster she was at casual conversation, she had decided to spare herself and others a great deal of unnecessary suffering by withdrawing to a quiet seat in a quiet corner on the outskirts of the group.

Earlier, she had been one of the select few invited to attend the christening ceremony. A couple weeks ago Violet had asked if she would serve as Georgianna's godmother. Surprised and deeply touched, she had instantly said yes, honored to be given such an important and sacred responsibility.

Eliza hoped someday she would have a chance to ask Violet to do the same for her own child. Should she ever manage to have a child. How much easier it would be if she weren't required to find a husband first. If she could simply choose a man for the job and invite him to do the deed, as it were, without the benefit of marriage.

She smiled to herself at the scandalous notion. Half the ladies in the room would faint dead away if they had any inkling of her thoughts. And she could only speculate about the reaction of the men.

"What are you daydreaming about?" inquired a warm masculine voice whose tone skimmed like a finger down her spine.

Her gaze flashed upward to meet Kit's, scalding heat leaping into her cheeks. "N-nothing."

Mercy sakes. She had been so preoccupied she hadn't even heard him approach.

He dropped into the chair at her side, tipping his head

to peer at her. "Well, it must be something to turn you such an interesting shade." He paused for a long moment, then settled back into his seat. "But I won't plague you with teasing, I haven't the energy."

"Is it your head? Does it still hurt?"

She had noticed his frown all during the christening, the way he winced each time the vicar required him to speak his vows as godfather to little Georgianna. Darragh's siblings Michael and Moira had fulfilled the same duties as godparents for baby Caitlyn, with Violet and Jeannette each acting as a second godmother for the other's child.

Kit grunted faintly. "A bit, yes. My punishment, I suppose, for too much wine and not enough sleep last night." He cast her a sideways glance. "My pardon if I've shocked you."

"No. I had wondered if it might not be something of the sort. I confess I overheard you and Adrian talking before the coaches arrived for church this morning."

Kit's lips quirked. "Never can hide anything from big brother. It's a genuine wonder Vi managed to keep her identity a secret from him all those months when they were first wed."

Eliza still remembered her stunned amazement at learning the truth of Violet's deception. But her initial burst of hurt and anger had quickly turned to forgiveness and delight when she saw what happiness her friend had found in her marriage.

Her gaze tracked Kit's across the room to where Violet and Adrian stood, the pair of them laughing merrily at some tale Darragh was spinning with occasional gestured embellishments from Jeannette. The youthfully effervescent Dowager Duchess of Raeburn, two of Adrian's sisters and their husbands, Adrian's friend Peter Armitage and a pair of Brantford cousins rounded out the group.

"Of course, Vi doesn't keep anything from him now," Kit remarked.

She hasn't the need, Eliza thought. *When one truly loves there is no place for secrets.*

Darragh and Jeannette shared a deep, loving intimacy as well, Eliza knew. One had only to see them together to understand the strength of their union, the depth of their obvious commitment and passion for each other.

What a joy it must be to know such love.

To distract herself from wistful thoughts, Eliza turned her attention back to Kit and his malady. "I could make you a posset."

He raised an inquiring brow.

"For your head," she explained. "I know a remedy that might help."

"Thank you, you are most kind. But my valet already poured one concoction down my throat first thing this morning. Don't think I could manage another."

"This one is only warm milk and a spoonful of brandy."

"No raw egg and pepper?"

She couldn't bring herself to lie. "No pepper anyway."

He shuddered. "I think I'll pass and close my eyes for a minute instead, if you don't mind."

"No, not at all."

His eyelids came down, short dark lashes fanning in a sooty arc against his cheeks. She caught her breath at the sight, tracing the shape of his cheekbones, the refined sweep of his nose, down to his beautiful, kissable mouth.

Suddenly that mouth moved. "I thought we'd begin our lessons on Tuesday," he murmured.

She jumped slightly, relieved to find his eyes still closed. "But that is only two days away."

"Best not to waste too much time. The house should be quiet again by then, all the relations gone on their way."

She gulped. "Oh."

"If we are to proceed with this plan, we must begin. The Season will be upon us in only a few short weeks and by the time it arrives you will need to feel easy in company. No more scurrying off to hide in quiet corners."

"I do not scurry," she defended, saying nothing about the hiding part since he had her pegged quite correctly on that count.

"Never fear. I'll teach you what you need in order to get on in Society." His lids opened a slit, hazel eyes gleaming more gold than green today. "Unless you've changed your mind, that is."

Part of her dearly wished she could say yes, she had. How easy to renege on their agreement and ease the ache of fearful worry that churned inside her belly. But she was resolute. She would not let herself fail. "I have not changed my mind."

"Then Tuesday it shall be."

Two days later at precisely ten o'clock, Eliza met Kit in Violet's study. Violet had suggested they conduct their lessons there, thinking the pair would find the surroundings more relaxed and comfortable than using one of the much larger drawing rooms.

"Do not worry about me interrupting you," the duchess had told her the evening before. "I plan to spend the morning at the park with Adrian and the children, then it's off for luncheon at Jeannette's townhouse.

Mama is coming and Adrian's mother as well. Thank heavens for Marguerite. She is always a marvel at keeping Mama from lapsing into lengthy complaints about her latest ailment. Adrian's sisters will be there except for Sylvia, who has already left for the country with her brood. And Moira and Siobhan despite their not yet being out of the schoolroom." Violet paused. "You did say you did not wish to attend, Eliza? For you are more than welcome, you know."

Eliza shook her head. "Thank you but I shall be quite content to remain here." Relieved actually, if truth be told, since Lady Wightbridge would likely stare at her again then pepper her with a series of uncomfortable questions. "Besides, I have lessons."

Violet gave a conspiratorial grin. "Just so. When I return you must tell me all about your progress."

And so now, as the ormolu mantel clock chimed the hour, Eliza took a seat on Violet's pale blue silk-covered sofa. Not long after, Kit strolled in, handsomely attired in a corbeau coat and fawn trousers that emphasized the width of his shoulders and length of his strong, masculine legs. His dark hair carried a rebellious hint of wave that no amount of trimming could control, an unruly lock already fallen across his forehead in a most tempting manner.

"Good morning," he greeted in a pleasant voice.

She clasped her hands in her lap, her muscles tight, her back unnaturally stiff. "G-good morning, my lord."

"What's that now? There'll be no 'my lords,' remember? Just 'Kit' and 'Eliza' for the two of us, at least in private."

"Yes, of course." She dropped her chin, feeling the rebuke. *What is the matter with me?* she chided herself. *Why am I so nervous? It is only Kit, after all.*

He took a seat next to her, settling back upon the

cushions. "I told March to send along tea and biscuits. I thought we could use some refreshments to see things along."

She had eaten breakfast not so very long ago and wasn't in the least bit hungry. But perhaps the distraction of drinking tea would allay a few of her qualms. Kit, of course, was like a ravenous young boy—always eager for a meal, a trait she found curiously endearing.

A housemaid arrived a minute later, knocking before she entered. Setting the tray she carried onto the table in front of them, she quietly excused herself and exited the room.

Eliza sat for a moment, staring at the tea. Manners required that she pour. Her hands shook as she reached for the pot.

Kit stopped her. "Here now, put that down before you burn yourself. I'll do it."

She withdrew to let him arrange the cups and fill them, the tea hot and strong. He added milk the way she liked and passed her the cup.

"Don't spill that or we'll never get started," he cautioned. "Here, have a piece of shortbread."

When she made a murmur of refusal, he ignored it and slid a sugar-coated wedge onto her saucer.

He picked up another piece of pastry and popped it into his mouth, chewing as he lifted his own cup of tea. Helping himself to another treat, he leaned back against the cushions. "Why are you so nervous?"

Her cup rattled. Carefully she set it aside. "I-I don't know. I'm sorry."

"Don't be sorry. First rule, whatever you do, act as if you meant to do it even if you're sure you look like a fool."

"But—"

"And no buts. They show hesitation and uncertainty.

The Ton is like a pack of hounds. If they sense they've drawn blood, they'll go straight for the kill." He sipped his tea. "Tell me why you are anxious. You weren't the other day when we talked."

She pulled in a deep breath then slowly let it out. "I don't know. Anticipation, I suppose. I am simply no good at . . . well, at conversation. Sorry." She winced. "Sorry, I didn't mean to say sorry."

A small smile curved his mouth. "Drink your tea. It should be cool enough by now not to scald you should you spill it."

Kit watched her dutifully obey, taking up her cup with measured care before setting it to her lips. She drank, her throat working with an unconscious grace.

Today was going to be worse than he feared, he mused. She was touchy as a cat left out in a thunderstorm. If she didn't relax, they would never make the least bit of progress.

What to do?

"Why don't we play a game," he suggested.

She frowned. "What sort of game?"

"A playacting game. You pretend to be me and I'll be you. Ask me the sort of questions gentlemen ask ladies at parties, and I'll do the answering."

Her dove-colored eyes widened. "You'll be *me*?"

"Mmm-hmm. Or do you doubt I can?" He fluttered his lashes in an exaggeratedly coquettish manner.

A laugh burst from her lips.

"There, that's better already," he said. "Now, ask me something."

"Oh, please, I wouldn't know what to say."

"Anything."

A furrow formed between her brows. "Really, I can't." She fell silent, another "I'm sorry" lying unspoken between them.

He drank more tea and ate another piece of short-bread, letting the sweet, buttery pastry melt in his mouth. By the time he was done chewing, he had an idea. Downing the last of his tea, he sprang to his feet. "Come with me."

"What? Where?"

He grabbed her hand and tugged her to her feet. "No questions, just follow me."

"But Violet said we should conduct our lessons here."

"Violet meant well, but you'll never relax if we keep on as we are. So come along."

She trotted in his wake as he pulled her out into the hallway. "But where are we going?"

"Now she speaks," he remarked. "You'll see soon enough."

Through the mansion they went, footsteps padding soundlessly as they traveled from one luxurious Aubusson or Turkey carpet to another, her slippers and his boots ringing softly against the islands of sleek hardwood and glossy marble that lay interspersed between. Down the grand staircase he led her, the pair of them startling one of the housemaids, a feather duster drooping in her hand as they passed. Finally, they arrived at a set of inlayed double doors that Kit threw open with a flick of his wrist.

Inside the portal lay the music room.

A large pianoforte held a position of prominence between a trio of double-hung sash windows, sheer cream curtains drawn back to let a flood of winter sunshine pour like honey across the polished walnut floors. Cheerful vanilla-hued walls rose upward to a ceiling that featured delicate rococo stuccowork, while celery green appointments added refinement and a feeling of intimate warmth. Along one wall stood a gilded harp, chairs ranged in two semicircles east and west. An open area lay in the center of the room, allowing plenty of space for movement. Kit led her there, then stopped.

"Why are we here? You do not expect me to play, do you?" Eliza squeaked in an appalled voice.

Up went his eyebrows at her reaction. Did the notion of playing a musical instrument in his presence truly distress her? Come to think of it, he could not recall ever having seen Eliza perform at a social gathering as most young ladies were encouraged, and often eager, to do. Still, he knew Eliza was capable.

Only two weeks ago, he'd walked past this very room and stopped outside its closed doors to listen to the lovely Mozart sonata that was being played inside. When he complimented Violet later that day on her improved skill at the pianoforte, she had laughed and said her musical talents were as woefully mediocre as ever—the musician was none other than Eliza.

One of these times soon, he would have to speak to Eliza and convince her to stop hiding her musical abilities. She possessed a fine talent, one that truly ought to be shared with others. Most young ladies could only dream of playing as beautifully as Eliza. What a crime it would be to let her keep hiding her gift away from the world. But that, he mused, would have to be a lesson for another day.

"No," he said, "I do not expect you to play, not this morning anyway. I thought we would dance."

She gave him a blank stare.

"It is an excellent way for you to relax and learn," he explained. "With your feet occupied you won't have so much time to worry over every syllable that comes out of your mouth. Plus, it will be good practice for when you really are out on the dance floor with a partner. But blister it, I didn't think this plan through very well, did I? We've no one to play for us."

He set a hand at his waist. "Here we are in the music room and we're to have no music. You don't suppose Mrs. Litton knows the pianoforte, by any chance?"

"No, I wouldn't imagine so," Eliza said, still eyeing him quizzically.

Kit ignored her look as he considered ringing for the housekeeper to ask the woman if she could pick out a waltz on the keys. But just as fast as the thought appeared, he discarded it. Coaxing Eliza into an easy conversation was going to be difficult enough without there being an audience present to eavesdrop on every word they said.

"I suppose we ought to have gone to the ballroom despite our lack of music," he continued, "but the space is so massive I thought we'd feel lost in there with only the two of us. Besides, the mirrors might put you off your stride."

When she gave no reply, he made her an elegant bow then extended his right hand. "Miss Hammond, would you do me the honor of a dance?"

She shook her head, making no move to accept his hand. "My pardon, but I do not see how dancing will help me learn to be more at ease in my speech. I already know how to dance."

"Indeed you do, which is why I thought of it. You are an excellent dancer, Eliza. A shame more gentlemen do not realize what they are missing."

Her cheeks turned a becoming pink at his compliment.

"Have a bit of faith. I'm your mentor, remember?" he teased, shooting her a grin. "Come let us see if this will work."

Once more he offered his hand. This time she accepted.

He wore no gloves.

Eliza trembled, her pulse bounding at the sensation of his warm, naked flesh curving around her own. Her bare palm fit small and unsteady within his hold, his controlled strength evident in his touch.

Dear me. She hoped her hand didn't begin to perspire. How mortifying that would be. She wished she could pull away and rub her palm against her skirt but knew the gauche gesture would only make matters worse.

At least Kit didn't seem to notice her heightened apprehension as he set his other hand upon her waist, his grasp firm yet undemanding. With a small tug, he drew her closer, careful to leave the proper distance between their bodies. She fixed her gaze upon his firm jaw and square chin, tracing the faint dimple that creased its center.

Her pulse thumped again.

Swallowing sharply, she lowered her gaze to his cravat.

He took a step and propelled her into a waltz. Moving on blind instinct, she followed his lead.

"Dah-daa-Dum, dah-daa-Dum, dah-dah-Dum, dah-dah-Dum, dah-dah-Dum . . ."

Her eyes flashed upward as he swung her in a circle, a small giggle escaping her lips.

The improvised melody ceased, Kit's striking eyes alight with humor. "No good? I was trying to provide some music for us."

She couldn't prevent a smile. "It is fine. Just unexpected. Pray continue."

"No, I can't now, you've muddled the mood. But it's all for the best, I suppose, since I can't very well hum and talk at the same time, now can I?"

He led her easily around the floor, her feet gliding in a smooth, effortless rhythm.

"May I compliment you on your gown, Miss Hammond? It is a lovely shade of blue, if you don't mind my saying so. Is it new?"

This was it, she realized. The lesson had officially begun as Kit shifted the conversation into more formal territory, keeping his words light with just a touch of flirtatiousness.

"Yes," she said. Her monosyllabic response sounded stiff and dry as a slice of day-old toast, her neck muscles tightening as nerves returned. He waited politely for her to continue, but as usual she could think of nothing further to say.

"Acknowledge the compliment with a slight inclination of your head," he instructed in a gentle tone. "A blunt 'yes' won't lead to further discussion."

Obediently, she dipped her chin.

"Good. Now make some casual remark. Something perhaps about your preference for the color or where or with whom you made the purchase."

"I-I, all right. Thank you, my lord," she said, resuming her role. "The Countess of Mulholland suggested the shade."

"The countess has exceptional taste. The color makes your eyes sparkle."

"Does it?"

"Indeed."

"I should not be wearing it, though."

"Oh, and why is that?"

"I am still in mourning for my aunt, but the countess hates black and instructed her sister's servants to burn all my old clothes."

Kit snorted, breaking character. "You didn't tell me Jeannette had done away with your old things."

"Yes. The moment the first dresses began to arrive, she ordered my maid to toss everything out. Poor Lucy didn't have the nerve to disobey her."

"And what about you? Did you scold Jeannette for her dictatorial ways when next you saw her?"

Eliza shook her head, setting her curls bouncing around her cheeks. "Scold her? Gracious, no, I happen to like my skin exactly where it is."

Kit tossed out a laugh, white teeth flashing. "Ah, a sensible choice. I always say one should be wise in the battles one picks."

"Exactly so. The clothes were already lost by the time I learned of their sad fate. But I told Lucy if the countess comes around my room issuing orders again, Lucy has my permission to shut her out and lock the door."

He chuckled, flecks of green glittering like polished emeralds inside his lively eyes. He swung her into a gentle turn, his body moving with an unconscious grace that melted any last possibilities of concern on her part.

She expelled a breath and relaxed into the movements of the dance. Without forethought, she smiled up at him.

"So, Miss Hammond," he said, his voice rich and warm as syrup, "how do you find the weather of late?"

She blinked, not comprehending the innocuous question for a long, long moment. Then she recovered. *The weather?* But, of course, he had returned to their lesson.

"T-the weather is fine for late February," she said.

"Not too cold for your tastes, then?"

"No. Although I prefer spring. It is my very favorite time of year."

"And why is that?"

"Because everything blooms and begins anew in the spring."

"So, like most women, you enjoy the flowers," he teased.

"Of course, but it is more than just the flowers."

"Is it?"

"Oh, yes. The whole world seems to come alive in the spring," she observed, getting caught up in the sentiment. "It never fails but to give me hope, watching what has lain cold and dormant all winter burst forth once more. I often think it is nature's way of giving everything and everyone a chance to try again."

An arrested look came over his features. "A lovely thought. If only man could be half so generous in his actions, the world might yet be a better place."

Eliza nodded, pleased by the depth of his remark. "Yes, precisely."

Then Kit's moment of serious reflection vanished as he began to hum a few strains of the waltz once more. He shot her a broad smile that she couldn't help but return.

"Well now," he said after a long moment, "perhaps we should take a moment to discuss the basics."

"The basics of what?"

"Polite conversation. We've exhausted the weather, always one of the safest of topics, good for any sort of occasion and company. What else? If we were at an actual entertainment, you might make some pleasant observation about the party, remark on the number of guests or the decorations. Or you could compliment the host and hostess, assuming, of course, you can find something genuinely pleasant to say. If they are utter bores, it tends to put you in a bit of a sticky situation. Whatever you do, never lie. Silence is better than a fabrication."

But wasn't that always her difficulty? Being too silent?

"Horses, hunting and dogs are fine topics to discuss with gentlemen."

"But I do not know much about horses and hunting,

and the only dog with whom I'm familiar is Violet's Great Dane, Horatio. What a big, loveable oaf he is."

"He's a character, that is for certain. And so is Darragh's wolfhound, Vitruvius. Talk about them. Any dog lover would be most amused to hear of their antics. As for horses and hunting, you shall have to learn more. You do know how to ride, do you not?"

"Yes, but not well. Aunt Doris believed that money spent stabling a horse was a great waste. Eating machines, she used to call them, not worth the expense of feed and a groom to care for them. Hired hacks were her preference since she lived most of her life in London. Consequently, I have never spent much time around horses except for a few lessons in the country one summer."

Kit scowled. "I knew your aunt was a tightfisted old harridan but not so much that she wouldn't even maintain a single steed. Well, we shall have to find time to reintroduce you to the joys of riding."

A faint shiver rippled through her. She liked horses, but they could be unpredictable creatures, especially with a new, inexperienced rider on their back. She didn't relish the idea of being thrown. "Oh, it is all right. I do quite well as I am."

"But, at the very least, you must learn to feel comfortable again on a horse, in case you are asked to go riding. Don't worry. Adrian has a magnificent stable. I'll find you a sweet mare who will treat you like her dearest friend."

"Do horses have friends?" she blurted.

"They do indeed." He laughed and gave her a merry wink. "Besides, you have three new riding habits in your wardrobe, as I recall. We can't very well let them go unused."

To that she decided it wisest not to respond.

Moments later he brought them to a stop but did not release his hold upon her. "Shall we continue a while longer? Take another turn around the room while we engage in a new practice conversation?"

She did her best not to respond to his nearness, his body having drawn inexplicably closer since their dancing had ceased. Had he moved an inch toward her? Or had she moved toward him?

Either way, he was deliciously close.

She caught a fresh trace of the shaving soap that lingered on his clean-shaven cheeks. Enjoyed with her fingertips the soft texture of the finely wrought broadcloth that stretched across his powerful shoulders. Reveled in the sensation of her hand held so intimately within his own.

But, of course, Kit noticed none of this. And neither, she knew, should she. "Yes, let us continue," she said, determined to ignore her unwanted, wayward impulses.

He spun them around the room again, making her skirts sway. She released an inaudible sigh, aware of his body settling once more into a smooth, natural rhythm with her own.

"And how are you enjoying the delights of the city, Miss Hammond?" he began.

"London is, as always, most pleasant."

"And what sights have you seen thus far?"

"Oh, none of any note. T-there is still the last of my mourning to consider. I have not been out much this winter."

"Ah, yes. Quite correct of you."

"And then there is my mentor," she continued. "From what the Duke and Duchess of Raeburn's majordomo informs me, he keeps all my suitors at bay."

Now, from whence had that impish comment come? she marveled, amazed at herself.

Kit's lips quirked, easily catching on to the game. "A stern sort, this mentor of yours?"

"About his duties, yes. He is very conscientious."

"Doesn't sound much like the fellow I know. I have heard it said he is given to wiling away his life at trifling pursuits and idling pleasures."

"Oh, he enjoys himself, for sure, but I would not call him in any way trifling or of an idle nature."

"You ought to tell his brother that when your mentor next applies for his quarterly allowance."

A laugh burst from her mouth. "I shall strive to do so for his sake."

"Well, I have to admit I am not surprised to hear that your mentor takes his responsibilities seriously. Not with a student such as yourself. When the time arrives, he will have to beat the suitors off with a stick."

"Will he?"

"Undoubtedly."

She gazed into his eyes and felt herself begin to drown, just as a swimmer must the instant before the water closes over his head.

What am I doing? she questioned. *Am I flirting? With Kit! Moreover, is he flirting back?*

But no, she reminded herself, his responses were all pretense. Amusing, lighthearted deceits meant only to instruct and inform, none of them in any way real.

Abruptly the pleasure drained out of her like a balloon pricked by an extremely sharp pin. Throat tight, she quit dancing and pulled away, wrenching her hand from his. "I-I am sorry. Do you mind if we stop?"

Kit frowned. "What's wrong? You were doing so well."

She lowered her gaze so he could not see her expression. "I-I am tired of a sudden. Perhaps I should not have agreed to continue the dancing, after all."

"Are you sure? You are not coming down with Violet's stomach ague from a couple days past?"

"No, I—" She took another step back from him. "Just a touch of the headache. I shall be fine."

"Why don't you go up to your room and lie down, then? I'll tell your maid you are unwell and have her bring you something for your discomfort."

If only there were something she could bring, Eliza thought with irony. *If only things were so simply remedied.*

"T-thank you."

On a nod she spun and walked from the room. Alone in the hallway, she hurried faster until her walk all but turned into a run.

Chapter Six

Eliza angled her book closer to the weak light trickling in through the library window. The day was dreary and cold outside, and she hugged her patterned blue and white cashmere shawl closer around her shoulders and curled deeper into her chair, grateful for the warmth provided by the logs burning in the fireplace.

Violet sat nearby, engrossed in the sensational horror novel *Frankenstein, or, The Modern Prometheus,* a story Violet had promised to loan her as soon as she finished reading it. With his canine chin resting on his immense front paws, Horatio slumbered at her friend's feet, an occasional snuffling snore whistling from the dog's damp black nose.

Turning a page, Eliza tried to focus her attention upon the words printed there. But after no more than a paragraph, her thoughts scattered, drifting like a handful of windblown petals to dwell on her lesson with Kit. She had scarcely thought of anything else since racing from the music room the day before.

What a perfect pea goose she was, she chided herself for the hundredth time. She had gotten carried away, that's all, overcome by Kit's kind attentions and undeniable good looks. If she wasn't careful, though, she might find herself once again succumbing to his myriad charms. And that she could not afford to do.

Once, she had worn the willow for Kit, adoring him in silence, too timid to gain more than his most fleeting notice. The day he departed for the Continent, she'd thought she might shatter from the pain. For nights afterward, she had soaked her pillow in bitter tears until finally she was exhausted, with no more tears left to shed. From that moment onward, she put her stupid, useless, impossible feelings away, doing what it took to kill her love for Kit Winter.

So why, when she no longer cared for him as any more than a friend, had she run from their lesson yesterday, fleeing like some foolish green girl discomforted by a crush?

It was the dancing that had caused all the trouble, she decided. The dancing that had nostalgically reminded her of her first headlong plunge into hopeless infatuation.

Even now, she remembered the long-ago evening in all its profuse detail. The warm glow of the candlelight, the thick crowd of people, the way she had felt as she sat along the edges of the ballroom, absently listening to a cluster of gray-haired matrons gossiping nearby. Painfully alone, that's how she had felt. Painfully alone and utterly unwanted in her ugly dishwater brown taffeta dress.

She was visually tracing the shape of the ribbons on her slippers when he appeared before her. Lord Christopher Winter in all his charismatic glory. Air wheezed in painful astonishment from her lungs as he bowed.

"Miss Hammond," he said, "would you give me the pleasure of a dance?"

She couldn't speak, not so much as a word, staring at him until he simply reached down and took her gloved hand to tug her gently to her feet. Sheer instinct was the only thing that kept her upright as they took to the floor, as he took her into his arms for the dance.

Then the music began and they were whirling to the strains of a waltz. Smiling and attentive, he did his best to engage her in conversation despite her near inability to respond. With her heart beating in her throat, she managed to answer a few of his questions, though to this day she could not recall a single one. By the end of the dance, she was captivated. By the end of the evening, she was utterly in his thrall.

All that night, young gentlemen approached to lead her to the floor, one after another after another. She wasn't a fool. She realized immediately that the men were friends of Kit's, their invitations no more than favors done for him.

Perhaps she ought to have been offended, outraged that she was somehow being mocked. Instead she realized Kit's actions stemmed from charitable intentions, his kindness more than anyone else had shown her in a long time. And at midnight, he had asked her to dance with him a second time before taking her arm to escort her in to supper.

Perhaps someone had put him up to it, she still didn't know, but Kit Winter had given her one of the best nights of her life.

And she had fallen in love.

A log popped, sending a shower of red cinders blazing upward into the flue. Eliza awoke from her reverie, blinking in momentary confusion at the book that lay forgotten in her lap. A quick glance assured her that Violet had not noticed her woolgathering, her friend still completely engrossed in her own novel.

Eliza swallowed a sigh as her thoughts returned to Kit. Being around him could prove dangerous, she realized. Obviously some part of her was still susceptible to his lure, however unconsciously he cast it out. But as much as a part of her longed to run and hide as she had done yesterday, a stronger part of her was determined to see these lessons through.

She could succeed, she told herself. She *would* succeed, taking care to treat Kit as no more than a friend and teacher. If she did that, her heart would remain her own. But just to be safe she supposed she ought to give these lessons her best effort, work hard and push herself to learn everything she needed to know as rapidly as possible. The sooner she did, the sooner she could find a husband and get on with her life.

Unless she could make Kit want her.

She froze, astonished by the very notion.

Kit as her husband, her lover. How sublime. How idiotically impossible. It could never happen, and yet . . .

She was still debating the possibilities when Adrian strode into the room.

"Good afternoon, ladies," he said. "You both look cozy as a pair of cats, snuggled up with your books and your shawls. I almost hate to interrupt."

"Then pray do not," Violet said, marking her page with a finger. "The monster has just gone on a rampage."

Adrian grinned. "He'll still be rampaging by the time we get back from our ride. Or did you forget you promised to let me take you out in the new phaeton this afternoon?"

She cast him a sheepish smile as she climbed to her feet. "I confess I had forgotten, probably because of this gloomy weather. Just let me run and get my warmest cloak and muff and I'll be right back."

"Ten minutes or I am coming up after you."

Violet strolled to him and lowered her voice to a whisper. "You'd better not. Remember what happened the last time you came looking for me while I dressed."

His eyes heated, gazing at her as if he wanted to kiss

her. "Nine minutes now, minx, so you had better get moving."

Violet laughed and went on her way. Horatio lumbered to his feet to follow.

Eliza quickly looked away and pretended that she hadn't heard a word of her friends' intimate exchange.

Adrian strolled forward and took a seat in his wife's abandoned chair. Eliza glanced up at him, struck as she often was by the marked resemblance he shared with Kit. Both men were dark-haired, broad-shouldered and handsome, leaving no doubt they were related. She suspected Kit would come to look even more like his older, more powerfully built brother as the years went on.

"And what is it you are reading?" Adrian inquired.

She flipped the book over so the fine leather cover showed. "Oh, a volume of Keats's. *Endymion*. Have you read it?"

He nodded. "I have had the pleasure, although a few of the critics have been less than kind. I hear he is to issue a new volume soon, perhaps it will prove a better success. A shame about recent reports concerning his health, though. Consumption, or so I am given to understand."

"Oh, I had not heard. How very dreadful."

She and Adrian sat for a moment in contemplative silence.

"Perhaps we should speak on a more cheerful topic," Adrian said. "How go your lessons with my little brother?"

"Is that more cheerful?" she blurted.

He laughed.

"P-please d-don't misunderstand me. The lessons are going well, though we have only had one so far." Her nerves jittered at being so abruptly reminded of Kit and her recent musings about him. "But I fear that his kind efforts may yet be in vain. I am rather hopeless at making small talk and polite conversation."

Adrian smiled. "You and I are talking now. I suspect you are rather better at conversation than you imagine."

"Oh, but I know you, your Grace. It is strangers who prove my undoing."

"Then you must strive to make everyone your friend."

She gazed at him, struck by the unique wisdom of his statement.

Footsteps rang out in the hallway.

"Ah, that must be Violet returning." Adrian stood, casting a glance toward the library casement clock. "You made it with one minute to spare. Well done, my dear."

Violet crossed into the room. "You are most welcome, love. I thought I owed it to you for nearly forgetting our outing. We mustn't tarry, though. Georgianna won't sleep much above an hour, and I know she'll be hungry when she wakes."

"Then we had best depart. I don't want you or Georgianna to suffer any ill effects."

As soon as Adrian and Violet said their good-byes and left, Eliza turned once more to her book. She actually managed to put Kit from her thoughts long enough to read a few stanzas, when a discreet knock sounded on the door.

March glided on soundless shoes into the room. "My pardon, Miss Eliza, but a gentleman has arrived. Your *cousin,* he says."

She scowled. "My cousin? Mr. Pettigrew, do you mean?"

March inclined his graying head. "I have put him in the main salon."

How singular, she mused. *Philip Pettigrew here? What can he want?*

Ordinarily, with Violet and Adrian absent from the house, it would be most improper for her to entertain a gentleman caller. Even Kit was away, out visiting with some friends, she assumed, since she had canceled their lesson this morning, pleading lingering effects from yesterday's headache.

But Philip Pettigrew wasn't really a caller, she reminded herself. As her cousin, Pettigrew was family, distasteful as the connection might seem. Through the years she had done her best to be civil and pleasant when in his company, though truth be told, she had never liked her aunt's son. She still recalled how he used to collect spiders and toads when they were children, leaving them in unlikely places for her to find.

For years she had been afraid to reach into her sewing basket for fear of discovering something that crawled or hopped. And once when she was thirteen, he had slipped a cricket into her dress pocket at church. When she found the creature, her screams had shaken the walls of the stone chapel, the commotion upsetting the entire congregation and ruining Sunday service.

Even now, she cringed to remember the whipping she'd received when she arrived home, her aunt refusing to listen to a single explanation, certain Eliza had played a deliberate prank.

No, she had never liked Philip Pettigrew.

Fighting the urge to have March turn him away, she set her book aside and rose to her feet. "Thank you, I will attend to my cousin directly."

"Shall I bring refreshments?" the majordomo inquired.

"Yes, I suppose you ought." Though really she wished Pettigrew wouldn't stay long enough to drink tea or eat cakes. But maybe fiddling with the tea tray would provide her with some welcome distraction.

Smoothing her deep purple skirts, she made her way to the salon.

Pettigrew turned at her entrance, his black hair slicked straight back from his thin face to hang just a bit too long and lank around his collar. She had always thought *scrawny* the best word to describe him—scrawny and humorless, gravely serious as if a smile might do permanent damage to his face. Not that he had any looks to protect, she mused, his hooked nose and lantern jaw enough to send a shudder through any unsuspecting child.

In fact, as Eliza recalled, Pettigrew had made more than a few toddlers burst into fits of messy tears in his time, the tots terrified by his fearsome countenance and grim demeanor. Eliza was thankful Noah, Sebastian and Georgianna were tucked safely away in the upstairs nursery or he would surely have set them to wailing too.

Garbed entirely in black—his preferred color even before his mother's death—he reminded her of a crow. A carrion crow come ready to pick flesh off bones. A shiver rippled just below her skin as he approached, his large, faintly yellow teeth displayed in something that was not entirely a smile.

"Cousin Eliza, how pleasant it is to see you. It has indeed been far too long since last we met."

Had it been? She rather doubted his statement, since the last time they had seen each other was at the reading of Aunt Doris's will—cold rage radiating from every inch of his body after he learned he'd been entirely cut out of the inheritance.

What, she wondered again, did he want? She couldn't believe this was just a friendly social call, though perhaps she was being unfairly harsh in her assumptions.

Maybe his initial anger about the will had cooled over the intervening weeks. She supposed in deference to their familial connection she ought to at least hear him out before passing judgment.

Pettigrew extended a hand for her to take. She hesitated, loath to touch him. To cover her revulsion, she pretended not to see his offered palm as she brushed past on her way to the sofa. She sank down and gestured to the armchair opposite. "Won't you have a seat, cousin?"

His arm lowered to his side. To her relief, he made no comment, seating himself where she suggested.

"I am sorry the duke and duchess are not here to receive you," she said, running a finger along a seam in her skirt. "They left shortly before your arrival. A ride in the park in the duke's new phaeton."

"How unfortunate my timing was not more propitious. Though to be truthful—"

A tap came at the door. Grateful for the interruption, Eliza watched March enter the room, laden tea tray in hand. His presence surprised her since she had expected him to send in one of the housemaids as usual. Was he worried about her? Had he decided to personally perform the task in order to assure himself of her well-being within her cousin's unctuous company? Her spirits lightened at his thoughtful concern, a wide smile of appreciation on her face. "Oh, this looks lovely. Thank you so much."

"It is my pleasure to be of service, Miss Eliza." The older man set down the heavy tray, positioning it for her easy access. "Will that be all?"

"Yes, I believe so."

"Please do not hesitate to ring should you require anything else, anything at all."

She caught the look in his eyes and subtly nodded her understanding. "Thank you, March."

Once he had gone, she busied herself with the painted china cups and plates, the pretty silver spoons and forks, praying she didn't bungle the whole process and pour tea everywhere but in the cups. "Cream and sugar?"

"Neither. I prefer my tea plain."

"Oh, of course, I remember now."

How could she have forgotten? He was truly one of the most ascetic people she had ever met, less given to indulging in creature comforts than even her late aunt.

Into her own cup, Eliza added a generous spoonful of sugar and a healthy dollop of cream, enjoying the little defiance. Next, she lifted the teapot, her hand displaying only the faintest tremor as she filled both cups with careful precision. After passing her cousin his tea, she offered the selection of cakes and small sandwiches for his perusal.

Out of obvious politeness, he accepted a single cucumber and butter triangle and set it on his plate, then took a spare sip of tea. Had Kit been here, he already would have eaten at least three of the sandwiches and stacked a half dozen more onto his plate, Eliza realized, inwardly smiling at the thought. A pity he wasn't here to amuse her with his antics.

"I see you have left off mourning."

Her head came up at Pettigrew's statement. Just barely, she restrained the urge to cringe. "That's right. The mourning period is nearly done so there is no shame in wearing a few dark shades, like this purple."

For a long uncomfortable moment, he stared at her out of deep-set black eyes. "Perhaps you are right. Your change in circumstances obviously agrees with you. I have never seen you look so well."

"T-thank you."

"Though I doubt Mama would have approved of the hair."

She raised her hand, touched her fingers to the edges of her curls. "No, probably not."

He set his teacup down. "But one thing of which I am sure she would have approved is seeing the two of us reconciled."

"Oh, well, yes, of course."

"But more than that, I think she would have wished to see us joined."

"Hmm? What!" *Had he said "joined"?*

"I am glad your friends are not here. Glad we have this opportunity to be alone so I may openly tell you of my feelings."

What feelings? Philip Pettigrew didn't have feelings, at least not the sort ordinary people expressed.

"I have never before spoken of this for fear of bruising your tender sensibilities, but you have always held a special place in my estimation. A partiality, if you will."

Her mouth dropped open.

"I have heard the rumors and know you are seeking a husband, a life partner as it were. You need look no more. I know you, Eliza, know the sort of man you require. A strong protector to help guide you, help steer you through the rocky shoals of life. A man of conviction who will keep you from harm, and who will assume the sound and equitable management of your affairs so your delicate feminine nature does not cause you to foolishly squander your resources."

Suddenly he was up and out of his seat, leaping from his chair faster than a bullfrog, to land on the sofa next to her. He grabbed for her hands.

"Eliza Hammond, will you marry me?"

She squirmed away. "No!"

"No?"

"Dear God, you are my cousin." She wrenched her hands from his, or at least tried to, since he immediately reached for them again.

"How does that signify? Cousins marry all the time."

Not first cousins!

Then again, she realized that some first cousins *did* wed. It was not illegal, after all, but probably should be as far as she was concerned. Marriage to him would be almost incestuous, not to mention abhorrently disgusting.

Ugh.

She gave a visible shudder and yanked her hands from his for a second time. "T-thank you for the honor of your proposal but again I must decline."

"You are simply being emotional and have not had time to think this through."

"I don't need time. I will not marry you." She leapt to her feet. "Now, I really must ask you to go."

Something hard settled over his face. "Not yet. You have not listened to all I have to say."

"But I have listened to all I care to hear. Leave, Philip. Now."

"Yes, *Philip*," ordered a firm, wonderfully familiar voice. "The lady has told you no. Accept her refusal and leave."

Eliza's gaze darted toward the doorway, to find Kit standing there like a guardian angel. *Thank the stars.*

"Lord Christopher, I did not realize you were here. Cousin Eliza and I were just having a bit of a private discussion. Family matters, you understand."

Kit strolled into the room. "Didn't sound like family matters to me, sounded more like a marriage proposal. A proposal the lady rejected."

Impotent fury turned Pettigrew's eyes dark and cold as a moonless night. "This is not your concern."

"Oh, but it is. Perhaps you didn't realize, but Eliza is a protégé of mine. I'm instructing her in the finer points of social interaction, such as how to distinguish a gentleman from a cad. Your actions in the next half minute will determine which of those you are."

Pettigrew's hands clenched into fists at his sides as he glared at Kit. Suddenly he let out a snarl and stalked from the room.

Eliza felt her whole body sag after he had gone, only then realizing how tautly she had been holding herself, how rapidly her heart was racing.

Kit crossed to her and wrapped a comforting arm around her shoulder. "Are you all right?"

Unthinkingly, she leaned into him, resting a palm against the resolute strength of his chest. He'd been riding, she noticed, his clothes warm and fragrant with the scent of horses, clean perspiration and Kit.

She closed her eyes and pulled in a deep breath, enjoying the sensation. "I am fine. Now."

"The second I arrived, March told me Pettigrew was here with you in the salon. Did you know he planned to call?"

She shook her head. "He took me completely by surprise, as did his loathsome proposal. I had no inkling Philip had such a purpose in mind. Why would I, since he is my cousin?"

"Well, I am proud of you for tossing him out. I'm only sorry I wasn't here sooner to hustle him through the door."

"He certainly did not want to take no for an answer." She considered the matter for a moment, releasing a sigh. "Hoping to reclaim his mother's fortune, no doubt."

"That and perhaps something more."

"More? What more could there be?"

"*You,* my little wren." He gave her arm a friendly squeeze. "You've grown so uncommonly fetching of late. I am sure once he beheld you in your pretty gown and saw your adorable curls, he wanted you as well."

A jolt arrowed through her. Did Kit really find her fetching? Her? Reserved, nondescript Eliza Hammond, who had spent most of her life being looked *through* instead of being looked *at*?

"But he can't have you," Kit pronounced in a silky tone, "because you'll soon be claimed by someone else." Peering down at her, he raised a hand and drew the tip of one finger across her cheek. "Someone better."

Her heart kicked, skin tingling in the wake of his tender, featherlight touch. Lips parting, she lost herself inside his mesmerizing gaze.

What was he saying? she wondered, half-dazed. Could he, by some impossible miracle, be speaking of himself? Was *he* the someone better?

"And once the Season officially begins," Kit continued, "we'll find that man. The perfect husband for you. But we'll need to continue your lessons first. You have made definite progress, but there is much work yet to be done."

As if he had plucked her up and dropped her off a cliff, she fell, crashing hard, the rosy glow around her bursting like a handful of soap bubbles.

Slowly she came back to her senses.

What a clothhead she was. What a ninnyhammer.

Using the hand still resting against his chest, she pushed herself away, moving out from under the circle of his arm.

He seemed not to notice her withdrawal. "Is your

headache gone? We could have a lesson yet this afternoon if you feel well enough."

She fixed her gaze on the carpet as she strained to compose herself. Abruptly, she looked up. "Yes, let's have a lesson. As you say, the Season shall soon be here and I have much to learn. We had best not waste an instant."

Chapter Seven

"More wine, Winter?" Edwin Lloyd invited, holding a freshly opened bottle of Malaga.

Kit inclined his head, barely glancing up from his cards. His friend poured, replenishing Kit's glass with the fortified reddish-brown wine that was both strong and sweet. Lloyd topped off the glasses of the other men at the table, then did the same for himself before setting the now empty bottle aside.

The play continued, each of the five men taking his turn, hoping to capture the requisite trick so he would not be looed. Kit drank a single swallow of wine and waited, infinitely patient since he already held the one card guaranteed to beat everything else in the deck.

The other four groaned when he played that card at precisely the right time, tossing down what remained of their hands in defeated disgust.

With a mild grin, Kit scraped his winnings forward.

"You've the devil's own luck tonight, Winter," Selway said. "Should keep you flush for some while. Unless the angel of mercy finally flies off your shoulder and you start to lose."

"Deal another round and we'll see." Kit broke off a lump of the Cheshire cheese that lay on a small plate near his elbow.

Selway was right, Kit acknowledged, as he enjoyed

the slightly salty flavor of the food melting against his tongue. He was having a fine night at the tables. Making merry with his friends, drinking and talking and playing cards. So far he'd won nearly double the quarterly allowance Adrian provided, an allowance he would have need of for only six months longer. With his pockets filled and his independence within reach, Kit knew he ought to be ecstatic.

Instead what he felt was dissatisfaction. A kind of underlying boredom with his current way of life and the prospect of all the years that stretched out before him.

What in the hell was he going to do with all of them and with himself?

Seated opposite, Jeremy Brentholden—his old pal from university days—dealt the next round. Kit perused his cards and calculated whether or not his hand was good enough to play.

"Deuced fine mill in the offing tomorrow over near Charing Cross. Who's up for it, eh?" Vickery raised his sandy eyebrows and scanned the group.

The others nodded their agreement.

Kit shook his head. "Sorry, gentlemen, but I'll have to pass."

"Have to pass!" Lloyd clicked his tongue in obvious exasperation. "This is the second mill you've passed on in recent memory. What's amiss, Winter? Not going squeamish on us, are you? Sickened by the sight of all that blood."

Kit tossed him a look. "No, I'm not going squeamish. In fact, I'd be more than happy to spill some of *your* blood if you'd ever risk that pretty face and step into the Gentleman's ring." He slid his cards together inside his palm and tapped them against the table. "If you must know, I have a prior engagement."

"What sort of engagement?" Selway questioned. "Can't be the duke again, surely."

Kit kept his features impassive.

"If not your brother, then what?" Selway pressed. "Come to consider it, you seem to be having a lot of *engagements* of late."

"Yes, Winter, he's right," Lloyd agreed. "You have been rather cagey about your schedule over the past couple weeks. What's going on? We insist that you share."

Kit fanned out the cards in his hand again and studied them. "Insist all you like. It's a private matter and none of your business."

"Don't have something to do with that chit, does it?" Vickery said. "The one living in your brother's house?"

"What chit is that?" Brentholden asked.

"Bluestocking friend of the duchess." Vickery paused, then snapped his fingers. "What's her name? Haywood? Hampton? No, no, Hammond. That's it, Eliza Hammond."

"Hammond?" Lloyd tossed a silver coin—a crown—into the center of the table as his opening bid. "Which gel is that?"

"You know the one," Vickery said, wagging a finger. "Whey-faced chit who doesn't have a word to say for herself, permanent member of the wallflower club. She dresses dowdier than a governess and is all but on the shelf. You've seen her over the years, I'm sure. By God, you must have done, she's had so many Seasons by now they must be stacking into the double digits."

The men laughed, all except Kit.

Lloyd shook his head in continued puzzlement. "Is she redheaded?"

"No, mousy brown. Always sits along the wall with the dowagers and matrons. Stares at her shoes."

"Well, Vickery, can't say I spend much time looking at the dowagers and matrons." Lloyd shot them all a youthful grin. "I much prefer the young, pretty girls."

Kit drank a long swallow of wine, hoping the liquor would ease the irritation brewing in his belly.

"She's the one who inherited that huge fortune a couple months ago," Vickery said.

A chorus of *ohs* resounded.

"Now I know," Lloyd declared. "Had the harpy aunt."

"Exactly." Vickery tossed in his ante. "The fortune hunters are already salivating."

"For blunt like that, how can you blame them?" Selway placed his money into the pool. "There's many a man would marry for that, even if she were as ugly as the ass end of a dog."

Kit smacked a hand against the table. "*That is quite enough.* I will remind you that you are speaking of a lady. I'll not tolerate such blatant disrespect."

Selway's dark eyes bulged. "Sorry, Winter. Didn't mean to give offense."

Kit's jaw tightened. "Well, you did. Miss Hammond is neither whey-faced nor is she ugly as a dog's backside."

"Didn't say she was," Selway defended in a weak voice. "Just said *if* she were."

"Well, she isn't," Kit bit out. "She is a lovely lady and my sister-in-law's friend. I'll thank you not to speak of her again unless it is to proffer a compliment."

The other man bobbed his head. "Of course, Winter. Sorry, old chap. Won't happen again."

Kit lifted his glass, tossed back the last of his wine.

Vickery looked across the table. "So, it's true, then, is it? What I've heard?"

"And what have you heard?" Kit asked, one hand curling tight against his thigh.

"That you're coaching her. Miss Hammond, that is."

"Coaching her in what?" Brentholden questioned, breaking his silence.

Kit meet Vickery's gaze. "And where did you hear that?"

Vickery tapped a finger against the side of his nose. "Little birdie in the servants' wing. You know how the staff grapevine goes."

Obviously one of the Raeburn House servants liked to gossip, Kit thought. He would have to have a word with Violet and March and see if anything could be done, though he supposed such things were inevitable.

He shrugged. "As I said earlier, what I do with my time is none of your concern. Now, are we going to play cards or not?"

"Oh, we'll play *after* you divulge a measure of the truth." Vickery rocked forward on his chair. "I hear you are her matchmaker."

Lloyd snorted, plainly amused by the notion.

"I am *not* her matchmaker." Kit scanned the expectant looks on his friends' faces and knew he wouldn't be getting out of this without providing some sort of explanation.

He bit back a curse. Damn Vickery for his meddling ways. The man was a steady fellow, the kind you could count on to watch your back in a fight. But he was also a first-rate quidnunc, a veritable magnet for innuendo and rumor, lapping it up with the relish of a dog with his snout buried in a dish of black pudding.

"The lady is shy, there is no denying the fact," Kit said, rubbing a thumb along the stem of his glass. "She wishes to feel more at ease in company. I am merely providing her with some guidance, acting as a mentor, if you will."

Lloyd smirked. "Mentor, are you? Never thought to see you in such a role. No disrespect intended, but you've got your work cut out for you with that one."

"A regular Pygmalion, our Kit," Vickery teased. "Be interesting to see if he can transform Miss Hammond into the fair Galatea, chisel a new version from the stone, as it were. I, for one, await the outcome with baited breath. So when will you be publicly revealing your creation?"

"She isn't my creation." Kit scowled, not liking the direction of the conversation.

"If you say so."

"I do. And I would prefer not to continue this discussion." Kit stared at Vickery for a long moment. "Why don't you put yourself to some good use and fetch us another bottle of wine?"

Vickery laughed then rose to do as he was told.

The game resumed soon after, Kit losing a couple hands before quickly recouping his losses, plus a bit more.

At the end of the evening, his pockets flush, Kit climbed into Brentholden's carriage for the journey home. Selway and Vickery accompanied them, jumping down at their separate destinations to wave weary good nights.

Now, at almost two in the morning, Mayfair's residential streets stood in virtual emptiness, the sound of horses' hooves and carriage wheels intruding rhythmically upon the night quiet, the mellow glow of the streetlamps helping to illuminate the way ahead.

Kit leaned his head against the carriage's plump, upholstered squabs and closed his eyes.

"You like her, don't you?"

His eyes came open at Brentholden's softly asked question. "Like who?"

"Your little bluestocking. Miss Hammond."

"She's not *my* little anything. She is merely a family friend whom I am trying to help out."

"Family friend or not, I've never seen you so fierce about defending a lady's honor."

"I've never before had cause to defend a lady's honor, but it needed to be done. Didn't care for the things Selway and Vickery were saying nor the way they were saying them. Miss Hammond is a sweet girl and doesn't deserve to be mocked, not even behind her back."

"Just as I said, you like her."

He rolled the statement through his mind. "Maybe I do like her, but not in the way you are implying. I have no designs upon her if that's what you are wondering. She's more like a sister, a little sister who just needs a guiding hand. She wants a husband, a decent man, not some blasted fortune hunter who will make her life a misery."

Brentholden sniggered softly. "So you *are* her matchmaker."

"Nothing of the sort. I'm her mentor, there to smooth her way in Society. The matchmaking I leave strictly up to Miss Hammond and my sister-in-law."

"So you won't mind if your plan succeeds and men start flocking around her in droves?"

A quick fist knotted inside Kit's stomach before he forced it to dissolve. "Lord, no. Why should I mind?"

"Hmmph."

"What is that supposed to mean? *Hmmph*?"

"Nothing. Just thinking that this year's Season should prove to be quite an interesting one, quite an interesting one indeed."

Kit made no further comment as the carriage continued on its way toward Raeburn House.

* * *

Three days later, Eliza hooked her knee over the side-saddle's pommel before securing the foot of her opposite leg in the stirrup. She shifted, fighting to maintain her balance while surreptitiously attempting to arrange the voluminous skirts of her Sardinian blue riding habit in as ladylike a way as possible.

Once she stopped squirming, Kit handed her the reins. From her perch, she peered down at him where he stood next to her mount.

"How does that feel?" he asked.

"High," she confessed with complete honesty.

He chuckled. "Cassiopeia isn't all that large a horse, barely fifteen hands. If you want a tall horse, you should see the hunters, big brutes a couple of them are. But you have nothing to worry about with old Cassie here." He stroked a palm along the bay's neck, then gave it a gentle pat. "She's as gentle as they come. A real darling, aren't you, sweetheart?" he cooed to the horse.

Cassiopeia's ears flicked and she bobbed her head slightly as though agreeing.

A couple of stable lads paused in their early-morning chores to watch the goings-on. Eliza pretended not to see them, relieved when a fierce look from the head groom sent them back to work.

Kit clipped a lunge line to the horse's bridle. "I'm going to lead you around the yard a couple times just until you feel comfortable."

She sat, ramrod stiff, as she waited for him to proceed.

Kit touched her elbow. "Relax, you'll be fine. You did say you know how to ride?"

"Yes, but it's been many years. What if I've forgotten?"

"You never forget a thing like that. Once we go around a few times, it will all come back."

And Kit was right—the feel of the saddle, the movement of the animal beneath her, the clip-clop of hooves against the mews's cobblestoned yard, the slight weight of the reins lying in her hands all soon combined to put her at ease. By the time Kit brought Cassiopeia to a halt, Eliza felt almost comfortable.

He unclipped the lead. "You try it now. Take her around a couple times, just a gentle walk like before. Reins loose and keep your knee soft against her shoulder. Cassie's a good girl, she doesn't need much direction."

With barely a touch, the horse began to make the circuit once more. Eliza went around three times before she stopped, a smile on her lips. "That was fun."

"I am glad to hear it. Well done, Eliza. So well done, in fact, I suggest we go to the park. It's early yet, no one but the birds up and about at this time of day."

Her hands tightened involuntarily, sending Cassiopeia back a step. She brought the horse to a halt with a gentle loosening of the reins. "I don't know, Kit. Are you sure?"

"Of course I'm sure. Let me get my mount."

Twenty minutes later they rode into nearby Hyde Park, Kit's solid black gelding, Mars, walking at an easy stride beside Eliza's mare. Just as Kit had predicted, the park stood nearly empty, the hour far too early for other members of the Ton to venture out. A street hawker, toting his small barrel of ink and basket of quills, hurried by, his head down as he cut through the park to his destination.

Birds hopped and fluttered in the bare tree branches, singing out their avian delight in the sunny new day. A crisp breeze bumped lightly across Eliza's cheeks, making her grateful for the comforting warmth of her riding habit and gloves. Still, she didn't mind the brisk weather, too invigorated by her surroundings to have any real concern.

Kit led them toward the Serpentine, where bands of ducks and geese congregated, a pair of white swans floating in majestic splendor upon the glassy surface of the lake.

"This is lovely." She turned her face up to a ray of yellow sun. "I am glad I let you convince me to rise so early for our riding lesson, though I am still surprised that *you* wanted to do so."

He tossed her a look of mock offense. "I am not the inveterate slug-a-bed you may think me. You would be surprised to know how often I am up in time to see the sunrise."

"See it, you mean, whilst coming home after a night on the town," she teased.

"Here now, miss, you had better watch that tongue. I can tell if I'm not careful it may yet turn sharp."

Her smile became a grin, one that he returned with alacrity.

"Morning truly is the only time one can actually ride in the park," he said, steering their conversation back to its original topic. "Even now, with the Season not yet begun, the grounds are so crowded in the afternoon there is scarce room to do more than travel at a sedate walk. Besides, I didn't imagine you would enjoy having to stop and chat every few feet as you would be required to do were we to arrive here later in the day."

She shuddered faintly at the idea. "Definitely not, and my thanks for your thoughtfulness. Though I can tell you obviously planned all along for us to come here to the park this morning."

"So long as you didn't fall off Cassiopeia back home

in the stable yard, yes, I figured I'd see if I couldn't coax you farther afield. What do you say we attempt a trot?"

She met his eager, encouraging gaze, a spot of nervous tension lodging like a handful of warm pebbles beneath her breastbone. On a sharp exhale, she shoved the feeling aside and nodded her assent. After a series of quick and efficient instructions, Kit urged her and her obedient little mare into a trot that he soon pronounced "not half bad for a novice."

Eliza was just beginning to find her confidence in the clipped gait when Kit dared her to increase her speed even more.

"Come on, Eliza," he encouraged, grinning over at her from atop his impressive black steed. Kit controlled Mars with effortless ease but the horse's pent-up excitement was almost palpable, the animal clearly longing to stretch out his powerful legs and enjoy a good run. Cassiopeia's ears perked up as well as she sensed the possibilities. The instant Kit gave Mars his head, Eliza knew her mare would chase after the gelding.

The little spot of anxiety re-formed inside her chest. "What if I fall off?" she asked, striving not the let her voice quaver.

"You won't fall off. You've got a good seat. Just settle your weight and let your horse do the rest."

If she told him no, she knew Kit would abide by her decision, and not even chide her for her temerity. But as tempting as a refusal might be, another part of her urged that she not take the coward's way out. Isn't that what she had spent most of her life doing? Knuckling under to her fears? Withdrawing into her own tight little cocoon so that nothing and no one could harm her again?

On that thought, she lifted her chin. "All right, let's canter."

A wide smile split Kit's mouth as he let out a very un-gentlemanlike whoop. With a light flick of his reins, Mars sprang forward, hooves racing over the park's grassy fields. Eliza's small bay mare followed, sending Eliza's heart leaping into her throat as Cassiopeia charged forward, speeding to keep pace with her stable-mate.

Eliza forced herself not to look down as the ground flashed by far too fast for comfort. And they were only going at an easy canter. Think how fast a gallop must be, she mused, awestruck at the realization. Still, she maintained her balance and trusted her mount to do most of the work, just as Kit had advised.

The yards flew by, and as they did her fears began to dissolve, drifting away like acorn pinwheels in the brisk wind that whipped against her cheeks and tugged at her hair.

She laughed and turned her head to meet Kit's gaze.

"Fun?" he called.

"Oh, yes."

"Up for a gallop?" he dared.

Another laugh billowed from her throat. "No, no, this is quite fast enough for me."

He relented and held them to a canter. Side by side, they rode along the horse paths, startling birds from their roosts, making the occasional squirrel stop and stare as it hung suspended by its tiny clawed feet from the side of a tree before dashing away.

Kit let his horse run the faintest bit faster, as if testing Eliza's meddle. She increased her pace, keeping up admirably.

Suddenly her hat came free of its mooring and flew off into the bushes. Kit reined in. She did the same, though Cassiopeia had already slowed to a walk, taking her lead from the other horse.

A steady hand on the reins kept the bay mare from following as Kit turned Mars around to trot after Eliza's lost millinery. He returned quickly, beating a smudge of dirt off the end of a bobbing ostrich feather.

"Your errant chapeau, Miss Hammond." He extended her hat with a flourish.

"My thanks, milord," she said as she accepted. Touching a hand to her hair, she realized why her hat had come lose. "I seem to have lost my hat pin."

"Then we shall have to content ourselves with a walk back so that your hat doesn't fly off again."

The pair of them turned their mounts to retrace their path across the park, settling into a very gentle pace.

"A crime you haven't been riding," Kit said. "You have a genuine aptitude for it. By this fall, I bet we could have you ready to join in the Hunt."

"Oh, no, not the Hunt. I could never manage the jumps. Besides, I always pity the poor fox. I would be rooting for it to escape the entire time."

"Would you indeed? You'd set the Hunt master on his ear, for sure." Kit's smile faded as he leaned forward. "Truth be told, I feel bad for the poor creatures too. People call them vermin but they're only trying to survive. To the fox, eating people's eggs and chickens is just their version of dinner. No worse than a man would do, only the fox can't pay in coin for his meal after he's done."

A warmth curled inside her that had nothing at all to do with her recent exertion. She couldn't begin to name all the people she knew who were incapable of showing so much as a glimmer of sympathy for anything that did not walk on two legs.

"Still," Kit murmured in reflection, "I can see the farmer's dilemma when those eggs and chickens are the only things keeping him and his family from starvation. If there were less poverty in this country, perhaps there would be more compassion for creatures like the fox."

"If only our politicians could be half so perceptive."

He barked out a cynical laugh. "That would be a miracle indeed. A sorry lot so many of them are, too busy looking out for their own interests to be bothered seeing to the interests of those they purport to represent."

"Then perhaps you should change that."

He shot her a look of amused surprise. "And how would you suggest I do that?"

"You could run for Parliament. You would make a fine member of the Commons."

"Me? In the Commons?" A full, rolling laugh boomed out of his chest. "You are a wit, my little wren, and I didn't even know it."

Her eyebrows wrinkled. "I was entirely serious."

Kit chuckled again, meeting Eliza's steadfast gaze as he visibly fought to wipe the humor from his features. "Yes, I can see now that you are. Well, my thanks for the vote of confidence but I think I'll leave such weighty matters as politics to those who enjoy meddling in the affairs of others."

"But why should you?" she questioned with great eagerness. "You have a good head on your shoulders, despite the carefree facade you choose to show the world."

He sobered. "And why do you imagine my carefree nature is a facade?"

Her fingers tightened on the reins. "I don't know. I just . . . well, I have sensed that you do not always seem perfectly contented with your circumstances. Forgive me if I mistake the matter."

He was silent for a long minute. "No, you do not mistake the matter. Not that I am unhappy, mind you," he hastened to add. "I like my life and take a great deal of

delight in the varied amusements in which I engage myself. I lead a blessed existence, filled with privilege and
pleasure and yet, as you say, I sometimes . . ."

"Yes? Sometimes . . . ?"

Kit stared at her. At the clear, guileless gray of her
eyes, and wondered why he was telling her these things.
He never talked of such matters—not to his friends or
his family, not even, in large measure, to himself. "Sometimes I grow a bit bored," he offered without intending
to do so.

"You want more from your life."

"Yes, I suppose. Though what more is there? As a
younger son I have limited options." He caught her expression, saw her mouth move and knew instinctively
what she was going to say. "And no, I don't want to run
for Parliament. Truly, politics and I would not be a good
fit."

She shifted slightly in her saddle, then caught one corner of her lower lip between her teeth in contemplation.
"What about the foreign service? I have heard you talk
of your travels and can tell they brought you great pleasure."

"Yes, but I don't see how a penchant to go wandering
could be of any use to the foreign service."

"Of course it could. You have an inquiring mind,
open to new people and new places. You have a natural
affinity for getting along well with just about everyone
you meet. I am sure you could put those skills to valuable use. Why, you might even become an ambassador
one day."

Kit smirked. "Oh, now I'm an ambassador, am I? You
are a dreamer. Can you imagine His Royal Highness en-
trusting *me* with the responsibility of negotiating important treaties and lucrative trade agreements?"

He laughed, waiting for her to join in.

Her features remained serious. "Yes, I can. In fact, if you truly set your mind and your heart to a goal, I suspect you could do almost anything you desire."

As they rode past the gated entrance to the park, he used the moment to compose his thoughts. She surprised him, seeing depths, abilities and ambitions in him that others did not. Not that his friends thought him useless, just a little uninspired, perhaps. No better or worse than many of his peers.

He grimaced. Maybe Eliza was right and he *should* consider pursuing loftier goals than debating whether to eat kidneys or kippers for breakfast and pondering which color coat would be the best choice for attending a race meeting.

Blister it, he sounded vain. Vain and foolish. Is that how Eliza saw him? When all was said and done, did she find him lacking, not academically or politically inclined enough for her erudite tastes?

His jaw tightened in uncharacteristic annoyance as they made their way toward the Raeburn House mews. For all that he was mentoring her, teaching her how to succeed in Society, did she in truth find him absurd? A ridiculous wastrel too full of his own aimless, selfish pursuits to be of any genuine consequence?

So he didn't like reading Latin. What of it? Did that make him less of a man? And was it really so terrible that he preferred spending a day at Tattersalls rather than sitting at home reading a book?

Not that he begrudged Eliza her love of books and ancient languages—her scholarly tendencies had never troubled him the way they would many men.

Yet what of her? Did she begrudge him *his* choices? Would she think better of him if he was less a creature of his own whims and passions? And more importantly, why did her opinion suddenly matter so much?

Side by side, they rode into the stable yard, the horses' hooves ringing out against the cobbles, the scents of straw and manure and sweet hay mingling like an earthy perfume in the air. A stable boy emerged from one of the outbuildings as Kit swung down from his mount. As the boy led his horse away to be cooled and watered and fed, Kit went to Eliza to assist her from the mare.

She gazed down at him out of solemn eyes. "Kit, is anything amiss? You turned awfully quiet of a sudden. Did I . . . did I say something wrong?"

He reached up and slipped his hands around her waist to lift her down. She was light as a feather, her weight barely enough to register in his grasp. He let her slide a couple inches then held her, her feet dangling in the air, their eyes level with each other's.

And in the next moment, as he gazed into the forthright sincerity of her eyes, he knew one thing for certain—he was a fool. Steadfast and unaffected, Eliza was the same gently quiet girl she had always been, open and honest and much too innocent for her own good. Whatever she had said to him today had been said with good intent. He could see that, he didn't need to ask for proof.

So she thought he could be an ambassador? The absurdity of the idea made him smile.

"I have only been doing a little thinking. A very little," he joked, slowly setting her on the ground. "Nothing is amiss, nothing at all."

A relieved smile enlivened her face, and for a moment he thought he had never seen anything quite so pretty or quite so appealing in his life. He found himself wanting to draw her closer.

A groom came forward to take Cassiopeia's reins.

Abruptly Kit withdrew his hands from Eliza's waist and stepped back. "What do you say we change into fresh clothes, then have some breakfast? I, for one, am famished."

She chuckled. "Of course you are. And after our ride, so, my lord, am I."

Chapter Eight

"Which gown would you like me to press for tonight's festivities, miss?"

Eliza set down the book she was reading and looked across her bedchamber toward Lucy. Standing before the room's large walnut armoire—its double doors thrown wide—her abigail held up two evening gowns, each garment as lovely as the other.

Eliza considered both dresses with a frown. "I don't know. What do you think, Lucy?"

"Hmm? If it was up to me, I'd wear the rose one. Then again, this jade green is awfully smart, sure to catch the eye. On the other hand, the rose is very pretty and will put lots of color into your cheeks. It's a frightfully hard choice, isn't it?"

Eliza sent the other young woman an amused yet exasperated smile. "Lucy, you're even more hopeless than I, and that is no compliment to either one of us."

Studying both gowns again, Eliza dithered between the two.

Just pick one, for heaven's sake, she thought. What possible difference could it make? Especially since most of the company coming to Raeburn House tonight would be family. Most, but not all, and that was what had her worried.

At this evening's gathering in celebration of Violet and

Jeannette's birthday, Eliza would perforce be expected to speak, to carry on—or at least attempt to carry on—an articulate conversation with the other guests before and after dinner, and with those on either side of her during the meal.

But in spite of her recent lessons, was she ready? What if her mind went blank and she forgot everything Kit had been teaching her? What if she made a dreadful muddle of her sentences and reverted to her old bad habits of hesitant stammering and long, mortifying bouts of silence? If she failed tonight, she would not only embarrass herself, she would embarrass Kit and that would by far be the greatest shame of all.

Over the past three weeks, Kit had spent literally hours each day with her, striving to teach her how to master the nuances of small talk and general conversation, while also continuing his instruction on how to ride.

Most mornings now the two of them began their day on horseback, setting out early for the park to exercise Cassiopeia and Mars and to work on improving Eliza's equestrian skills. She discovered, after their first outing, that Kit was a great deal more exacting an instructor than she would ever have expected. She received scant sympathy from him as he put her through her paces, constantly reminding her to straighten her spine and not slump in the saddle, to keep her hands light and balanced on the reins in order not to bruise her horse's delicate mouth.

Once the riding lesson was complete, they would return home to share breakfast before devoting the remainder of the morning to her social lessons—an exercise she could never seem to begin without discovering a stultifying lump wedged inside her throat.

In the beginning, she thought their efforts were useless, the games of verbal pretend he insisted they try causing her to fall mute as often as they encouraged her to speak. Yet Kit remained cheerfully persistent, refusing to let her give up or grow dispirited, counseling her to have more confidence in herself, suggesting techniques and strategies so her tongue would no longer be her enemy but her ally and friend.

During the second week, he asked Violet and Jeannette to join them for a few of their sessions so Eliza could practice speaking to ladies and not just gentlemen. Chatting with Violet hadn't been too taxing, but as for Jeannette— Eliza still quaked to remember. Yet for all her no-nonsense stares and glib-tongued remarks, Jeannette had been surprisingly kind, never once laughing at Eliza's mistakes, advising her in a patient tone to simply begin again whenever she faltered. During their last lesson, Eliza had actually relaxed enough to forget they were rehearsing and enjoyed several minutes of the conversation.

Tonight's small party would be her first real test. A chance for her to "dip her toes into the water," as Kit put it. If only she could figure out which gown to wear.

"The green one," she told her maid. "No, the rose. No, definitely the green. Yes, the green, and put the other one away before I change my mind yet again."

Lucy smiled and dipped into a quick curtsey. "Yes, miss. I'll be ironing in the servants' quarters if you need me for anything. Oh, and it's nearly one. You asked me to remind you so you wouldn't be late for nuncheon with the duchess and her sister."

"Oh, that's right. Thank you, Lucy, or I would indeed have let the time get away."

Eliza marked the page in her book, then rose and crossed to the washstand while her maid hung the rejected gown in the wardrobe. Pouring tepid water into a flowered china basin, Eliza washed her hands and dried them on a soft towel, then turned to consult Lucy about her hair.

"It looks lovely, miss," Lucy declared. "That Mr. Greenleaf certainly gave you a fine trim and color when he came yesterday. The man's a tyrant, if you ask me, but he's a talented tyrant so I suppose we have to abide by his uppity ways."

"He does seem to enjoy clapping his hands and ordering everyone around," Eliza agreed.

Her abigail hurried off moments later with Eliza's green evening gown draped neatly over her arm. Eliza followed, walking in the opposite direction toward the family dining room.

Jeannette paused in her conversation with her twin as Eliza entered the room, the countess's gaze roving appraisingly over Eliza's bronze-striped muslin day dress and slippers, a matching ribbon threaded through her hair.

Jeannette's sea-colored eyes brightened with approval. "Oh, don't you look dear in that gown. I knew you would the instant I saw the material at the linen-drapers. And the vandyked sleeves, I simply adore them, don't you? They are the very latest thing, you know, *très de rigueur.*"

"I am extremely pleased with my new wardrobe."

"As you ought to be, and you are most welcome. Shopping is always a true delight for me, as Darragh can strenuously attest. He was complaining only this morning about the amount of the shoemaker's bill. When I asked him if he would prefer to see me go around barefoot, he said it wouldn't bother him a bit. First thing tomorrow I plan to go out and buy another six pairs just to teach him a lesson. A lady has a need for shoes that no male will ever understand. Besides, the wretched beast bought three new pairs of boots for himself and he has the gall to complain about me. Truly, I don't know why I adore him so, but I do."

Subject exhausted, Jeannette shared a wide smile with Eliza and Violet. "Shall we eat? Impolite of me to say, but I am utterly famished."

"Good, then you won't disappoint François," Violet declared, gesturing for them all to take their seats at the table. "In honor of our birthday, he has made your favorite tournelles of beef and mushrooms in puffed pastry and my favorite dessert, *gâteau au chocolat*."

"Speaking of birthday presents," Jeannette said to her twin, a curiously wicked gleam in her eyes, "I have something interesting for you, sister dear. But I shall save it for later, after we eat." She angled a look at Eliza. "Now, tell me, which of your beautiful gowns shall you be wearing at this evening's party?"

The meal passed in convivial harmony, the three of them doing admirable justice to François's delectable fare. After polishing off the last bites of rich, tender chocolate cake, Violet ordered tea to be delivered to the family drawing room.

The beverage served and sipped, Jeannette went to collect her reticule before returning once again to take her seat on the sofa. With a secretive little smile playing around her lips, she pulled open her silk bag and withdrew a small rectangular object wrapped in pretty flowered paper and tied with a bright pink ribbon.

"I have another present for later," Jeannette explained, "but I thought I ought to give this one to you now while it was just us girls."

Eliza watched as Violet reached out to accept the gift. "Well, thank you, I have a pair of presents for you too. Mayhap I should go—"

Jeannette waved a dismissive hand. "No, no, I'll enjoy them more this evening. Do go on and open it."

Bowing her head to the task, Violet slipped the ribbon free then pushed aside the paper to reveal a slim, well-worn volume bound in plain green leather. "Oh! A book. How lovely. Is it poetry?"

Jeannette smirked, leaning forward slightly with unconcealed enthusiasm. "Of a sort."

Violet opened the cover to reveal the first page. "*Albanino's Postures.* What a curious title," she mused aloud.

She flipped through a few more pages before she abruptly stopped, blue-green eyes bulging in their sockets.

"Oh!" Violet exclaimed, snapping the volume closed with a loud *whap,* cheeks flaming red as a field of scarlet poppies.

Enjoying her twin's astonished reaction, Jeannette let out a merry chortle.

"Where on earth did you get such a thing?" Violet said, lowering her voice to a sotto voce hiss.

Eliza darted a look between the two women, wondering what the book contained. Obviously whatever it was, the subject matter was scandalous enough to have shocked Violet to her toes.

"I found the decadent little gem in a trunk of Darragh's belongings back home in Ireland," Jeannette said. "Several months ago, I was having the castle attics cleaned when I happened upon it quite by accident. When I showed the book to Darragh, he told me a friend of his had given it to him as a gift during one of his trips to Italy. Seems he'd packed it away after his return and completely forgotten about it." She touched her hands to her knees. "Well, always eager for a bit of adventure, I persuaded him to test out a few of the more interesting illustrations. There's one about halfway through that is well worth the effort despite how improbable it looks." Arching her delicate eyebrows, she concluded her little speech with a giggle.

Violet's mouth dropped open. "You are beyond anything, do you know that?" She paused, casting a plainly apologetic glance toward Eliza. "And we really ought not to be discussing such things."

"Why not? Oh, you mean you're worried about Eliza's delicate sensibilities? Well, if she is serious about getting married, then a little education on the subject might not go awry."

"I am *not* showing her this book!"

"I never suggested you do, but I hardly think being privy to our conversation is going to ruin her." Jeannette focused her gaze on Eliza. "What do you think, Eliza? Do you want to scurry out of the room like a demure little maiden or stay and listen?"

Her imagination run amok, Eliza sat mute and unmoving, waiting for the next act of this very interesting drama to unfold. Just what, she was dying to know, was inside that book?

"See," Jeannette declared, "she doesn't want to leave."

"Here, take it back." Violet shoved the book toward her sister. "I know you meant well, but I couldn't possibly keep it."

"Oh, but it's yours. I have the original still at home. This is a copy I asked a rather discreet bookseller here in London to ferret out for me. I thought it would make a delightful gift that you *and* Adrian could both enjoy."

Violet flushed again. "Adrian and I do not need books. We do quite well in that area all on our own."

Jeannette grinned, refusing to accept the volume Violet was trying to push at her. "I am sure you do very well, but a little variety never hurt anyone. Just thought you'd have some fun."

"We have fun. *Plenty* of fun, so thank you but no thank you." She tossed the book into Jeannette's lap. "Give it to your friend Christabel. Now, there's someone who looks like she could use a bit of assistance in the bedroom."

Jeannette clutched the small book in her hands and burst into renewed laughter. "Oh, Violet, I must say you've developed an edge. It's what must come of having spent all those months pretending to be me. But here, I insist you have the book. Try at least one of the sixteen. If you don't like it, I promise I'll take the volume back and say nothing of it again."

Violet shook her head and sprang to her feet. "Adrian and I are very happy as we are, and our private life is . . . well, private. Now, you had best be getting back to your own townhouse so you can get ready for tonight's dinner. I shall see you then."

Jeannette stood and opened her mouth as if to argue, then released a sigh. "Very well, but let me know if you change your mind—about the book, I mean."

"I shan't but thank you again for the . . . the thought." Violet crossed the room and went out into the hallway.

Eliza stood and started to follow her friend from the room. At the doorway, she turned in time to see Jeannette hurry across to a small ladies escritoire on the far side of the room, a desk Violet used on the occasional evening. Sliding open the top drawer, Jeannette popped the book inside, then turned with a conspiratorial grin.

"*Shh,*" Jeannette said, setting a finger across her lips. "Let her find it. I know she'll be glad." Crossing, she took Eliza's arm. "Best hurry before she wonders what is keeping us."

Eliza cast one last curious glance back at the escritoire, then accompanied Jeannette from the room.

Convivial laughter and smiles filled the music room as the assembled guests watched Jeannette and Violet open their birthday gifts. Side by side on the damask-covered sofa, they made a perfect tableau, Eliza thought, their lovely blond heads bent to their work as each unwrapped present after present.

By far the more impatient of the pair, Jeannette ripped into her gifts with unencumbered relish, tossing paper and ribbon aside to land where it willed. Violet took a milder approach, devoting more time to the process, yet collecting a small mountain of wrappings at her feet just the same.

From her place on the sofa opposite, Eliza sipped a slender glass of after-dinner ratafia and enjoyed the twins' patent expressions of delight. Jeannette squealed like a schoolgirl when she opened Darragh's gift, leaping to her feet and into her husband's arms for an enthusiastic hug and kiss before turning around so he could fasten around her throat the glittering ruby necklace he had given her. Violet, for her part, was every inch as thrilled with the gift she received from Adrian, a very rare and delicate volume of ancient history that nearly brought tears to Violet's eyes when she opened it.

The unique book was certainly a far cry from the one Jeannette had presented to Violet only hours past. Eliza considered the racy bit of literature that was even now residing in the upstairs escritoire, wondering if it was truly as shocking as Violet's reaction suggested. So what would Violet do when she found the book? Send it straight back to Jeanette? Or decide to keep it, after all, and maybe even give it a try?

Eliza felt her cheeks warm and hoped anyone looking at her would assume her blush had been caused by the spirits she drank.

As soon as all the presents were opened, the servants slipping discreetly in and out to carry away the discarded wrappings, Darragh got to his feet.

"Shall we have some music, then?" he declared. "What do you say, Moira. Will you give us a tune?" He glanced at his sister, who returned his grin with a quiet smile of her own. "She plays a grand melody on the harp. Be a good lass and pleasure us with your skills."

"Yes, Moira, do," encouraged her brothers Finn and Michael.

At barely sixteen, Moira was not yet *out*. During their nuncheon, Jeannette had told Eliza and Violet how excited Moira was to be included in tonight's celebration, since girls her age were not usually invited to adult parties. But considering this was a private gathering with only family and a few select friends in attendance, Jeannette and Darragh had agreed it would be acceptable.

On the other hand, his youngest sister, thirteen-year-old Siobhan, had been mightily put out when she discovered she would have to remain at home. But no amount of tears and pleading on her part had convinced them to change their minds, despite the pangs of guilt the girl had roused in them both.

Pretty and personable, auburn-haired Moira gave her brothers another becoming smile, then got to her feet and crossed the room.

The girl has more nerve than I do, Eliza thought, glad she wouldn't be called upon to perform. Despite the enjoyment she derived from playing piano, her efforts were strictly for her own amusement. Years ago, she had once tried to play for a group of her aunt's friends and had ended up shaming herself and her aunt when she froze at the keys, unable to hit more than a few stumbling notes. As she recalled, the notes she had managed to play had sounded worse than an organ-grinder's monkey. She'd left the room in tears. From that day forward, she had vowed never to make such a public mockery of herself again.

As Moira settled gracefully onto the harp stool, Eliza sensed Kit walk up to stand behind her, leaving only the sofa back between them.

He touched a hand to her arm. "Would you care for another glass of wine?" he asked.

She shook her head. "No, I believe I have had more than I ought, as it is."

He bent down so his mouth was close to her ear. "You are doing very well tonight, by the way. I wanted to commend you."

A delicious quiver trickled down her spine; his voice was as darkly intoxicating as the fragrance of his brandy-scented breath.

She turned her head to meet his gaze, ethereal notes of harp music floating like shimmering diamonds upon the air. "I have been trying to remember all my lessons."

"I can tell. Bravo." He gave her shoulder a light, almost barely noticeable squeeze, then straightened, his touch withdrawn as abruptly as it had been bestowed. Still, he didn't walk away, towering solid and strong, his presence a distraction and yet a comfort at the same time.

All through dinner she had wished him at her side instead of a half a dozen seats away, but even she had to concede the evening would not have offered much of a test with Kit at her elbow.

Instead she had found herself seated between the Dowager Duchess of Raeburn on one side and Michael

O'Brien on the other. She'd surprised herself by managing to hold reasonably entertaining conversations with both, finding Violet's flamboyantly French mother-in-law reassuring and kind, while Michael O'Brien made her laugh more than once with lively tales of his life as a country veterinarian, told in his lilting Irish-accented voice.

The half hour after dinner had proven more difficult, the ladies leaving the gentlemen to their brandy by retiring to the drawing room to talk and sip tea and cordials. Eliza had nearly choked on her tea when Jeannette's old friend Christabel Morgan—now Lady Cloverly—sat down in a chair directly across from her.

Eliza marveled to think they were both of an age—only three and twenty years. Compared with Christabel and the veneer of practiced sophistication she wore like a second skin, Eliza felt green as new-mown grass.

Christabel stared out of dark eyes that Eliza had always found coolly beautiful. "I hear tell you are on the lookout for a husband again this year," Christabel drawled.

Eliza forced herself not to squirm and raised her chin a notch instead. "That is right, my lady."

The other woman raked her gaze up and down. "Well, at least you are making an honest attempt at it this time. That gown is very becoming."

It took her a moment to respond, since Christabel had never before breathed so much as a kind word in her direction. "Lady Mulholland chose it for me."

"Jeannette has always had exceptional taste. Heed it, and you may actually get an offer. Assuming you give up those books of yours. Gentlemen don't care for too educated a female."

Eliza bit her tongue and swallowed her rebuttal. She might not often have much to say, but on this particular subject she could be quite vocal. How easy to point out the fact that Violet was a lady who could be termed a "too educated female" and yet it had not hurt her reputation. Then again, Violet was the Duchess of Raeburn, a title that had earned her forgiveness on many fronts. Yet remembering Kit's advice to never, ever be argumentative in company no matter the provocation, Eliza consigned herself to a noncommittal nod.

Shortly afterward the gentlemen had joined the ladies, everyone repairing to the music room to continue the birthday festivities.

Now harp strings resonated on a few final sugar-spun notes, the melody as lovely as the youthful musician who had made only a pair of barely noticeable mistakes throughout her endearing performance. Applause rang out at the end of the song, Moira's fair complexion pinking up in pleased reaction.

As the girl stood to return to her seat, Kit leaned down and spoke in a low voice. "Eliza, why do you not go next? It would be a wonderful opportunity for you to share your talent with everyone."

Her stomach flip-flopped in abrupt horror. "N-no, I could not," she whispered, shaking her head in fierce resistance against the idea.

"Why not?" he pressed softly. "You are among friends here. Go on, you need the practice and it would be an excellent chance for you to perform in front of others."

"Oh, do you also play the harp, Eliza?" Darragh asked, having overheard the last of the nearby exchange.

"The p-piano, m-my lord. B-but not well, I am afraid."

"Nonsense," Kit retorted in a carrying tone. "I have heard her and she plays like an angel. A veritable virtuoso in our midst."

Inwardly, Eliza cringed and closed her eyes. How

could Kit do this to her? How could he trap her into such a situation, push her into doing something he must surely have known she would never voluntarily have agreed to do?

And that's when she realized he was doing it deliberately. That he had lain in wait like some predatory jungle cat for exactly the right moment to pounce, betting she would give in to his urgings rather than humiliate them both in so public a forum.

Her lips tightened with anger. Raw, resentful anger, an emotion she had never before felt toward Kit.

It would serve him right, she thought, if she kept her seat and shook her head in stubborn refusal. But to do so would ruin all her hard work, make jest of her lessons and shatter her future plans. After all, as Kit said, if she could not perform here in front of these people, who were in large measure her friends, then how would she ever be able to cope in front of strangers during the Season?

Knowing Kit had her neatly ensnared, she climbed to her feet. She just prayed her legs didn't give out between the sofa and the piano bench. "Very well, I shall play," she said in as brave a voice as she could muster. "But don't say I did not warn you all beforehand."

A few people laughed at her quip as Kit accompanied her across the room. Refusing to look at him, she sank down upon the padded seat.

With his back to the group, Kit bent near. "You're angry."

She flipped through a few sheets of music, trying not to let her hands tremble, so nervous she could barely read the printed titles, let alone concentrate on the notes.

"I knew you would be cross with me," Kit said for her

ears alone, "but I didn't know any other way to get you to play."

"Get me to make a fool of myself, you mean," she accused under her breath.

His compelling green-gold gaze caught and held her own. "You won't look a fool. You play far too beautifully for that. Remember what I've been telling you all these weeks, believe in yourself and have faith you will not fail."

"Easy for you to say. You don't have to perform."

"I'll stay with you if you like. I can turn the pages."

"Of what? I cannot even choose a song," she hissed in panic.

"Relax and play what you were playing the afternoon I heard you. It was Mozart, I believe."

Mozart, one of her favorites. Yes, she supposed she might be able to pick out the melody and not make too bad a hash of the more difficult passages. But where was the sheet music?

Kit had already found the precisely inked score, setting it on the stand and opening it to the first page of notes. "You'll be fine, and I'll be with you."

Kit stepped slightly aside to reveal Eliza to her waiting audience. She took a deep breath and set her fingers, icy cold with nerves, onto the keys.

Trembling, she forced herself to begin. She played ten quick notes before she hit the wrong keys in a resounding, cringe-inducing mistake. As abruptly as she had begun, she stopped, tears stinging the insides of her eyelids. Wanting to die on the spot, she hung her head in shame.

"Eliza, look at me," Kit commanded. "Look at me."

Slowly, she forced up her head and gazed in misery into his eyes.

"Begin again."

She shook her head.

"You can do this. Forget about them and just play. Play as if there were no one else here. Pretend there are only the two of us in the room. Play for me, Eliza. Can you do that? Can you play just for me?"

And suddenly, as she stared into his warm, steady, beautiful eyes, she felt her nerves dissolve, untangling like strands of silk caught in a pale breeze. She took a breath, in and out, and steadied her fingers once again over the keys.

She began to play again.

The notes flowed out of her this time as if the composer himself sat before the instrument. Rapid then slow, then rapid again, changing tempo and rhythm in smooth precision as the melody directed. Lyrical and haunting, the music built toward a gradual crescendo that was as sweet and passionate as a heated summer night. She lost herself to it, to those evocative strains that filled her spirit with a quiet, almost invincible jubilation.

Kit stood beside her, turning the pages to music she no longer needed to consult. And in those moments, he truly did become the only other person in the room. On she played, adrift upon their small island of two. Then the piece concluded, her fingers racing over the keys in a last powerful flourish.

Silence engulfed the room as the final note faded away. Stunned by the experience, she listened to her heart hammer in her breast, fearing for an instant that no one but her had liked it.

In the next second, all she could hear was applause. Warm, genuine, real applause. She blinked in amazement as the outpouring washed over her, before glancing upward to meet Kit's triumphant gaze as he too brought his palms together in hard claps of obvious pride.

"Bravo, Miss Hammond," Adrian called.

"Yes, well done," several of the others exclaimed. "Superb."

She smiled, uncertain how to behave in the face of such glowing approbation—approval the likes of which she had not experienced in her entire life.

Kit captured her hand and drew her to her feet, brushing a kiss over her knuckles. "Magnificent, Eliza. You outdid even my grandest expectations."

She tingled beneath his touch, feeling as if her feet were no longer touching the floor. Then she laughed, surprising everyone in the room yet again.

Chapter Nine

Two days later, Eliza was still floating in the aftermath of her success. Even now she couldn't quite believe how well she had performed, how her nerves had eased and she had been able to play as she had never played before in her life.

Even Jeannette and Christabel had been impressed with her musical ability, insisting she must exhibit her skills this Season whenever the opportunity might arise.

Eliza just hoped her newfound confidence didn't fade. Without Kit at her side, she did not know if she would be able to find the courage to perform in front of a crowd, in front of strangers. But as he had shown her last night, perhaps she owed it to herself—and him—to try. Despite his underhanded maneuvering, and her subsequent distress, he had taught her a valuable lesson, one she knew she would never again forget.

Only a few days now remained before Easter and the official start to the Season. Invitations had already begun to arrive at the townhouse, many of them with her name on them, much to her great surprise. As for her former bevy of fortune-hunting suitors, Kit had sent each and every one of them on his way. If more should appear, he promised he would send them packing as well.

For a young lordling with a reputation for carefree irresponsibility, Kit had become a fearsome protector. If only he didn't see himself as her surrogate brother, she mused. If only he could somehow feel more.

Putting aside such foolhardy thoughts, Eliza made her way into the family drawing room.

Up until a few minutes ago, she had been with Violet and the children in the nursery, enjoying another round of hide-and-go-seek with the boys before pausing to rock baby Georgianna in her arms for a few delightful minutes. Then nap time arrived for the twins, as had a meal at Violet's breast for little Georgianna.

With her lessons complete for the day, and Kit out of the house, busy with his usual round of activities and his legion of friends, Eliza had decided to busy herself by answering correspondence from her barrister, Mr. Pimm.

Along with inheriting her aunt's money, she had also inherited a plethora of business concerns—investments, annuities and the management of a few rental properties. In general, Mr. Pimm handled the day-to-day details, but he needed her authorization to proceed on several matters.

In search of pen and paper, she crossed to the rosewood escritoire and pulled open the drawer. She froze, her gaze riveted to the little green book lying inside.

The naughty little green book that Jeannette had placed there for Violet to discover. Obviously Violet had not yet found her twin's prurient birthday offering, unaware the book even remained in the house.

Trying to ignore it, Eliza withdrew a few sheets of foolscap and a quill pen, then set the items on top of the desk. She moved to close the drawer but paused, casting a quick glance over her shoulder to make sure she was still alone.

Alone and free to peek.

What could it hurt? No one would ever know but her.

Fingers hovering, she hesitated for a last few seconds before succumbing to the delectable temptation. Flipping open the book, she let the pages settle where they would, landing on a section of verse somewhere near the center. The text was written in old Italian that likely dated from the fifteenth or sixteenth century. She read a couple lines of the flowing, heavy black script.

Mercy, she mused, *does that mean what I think it means?* She read it again and frowned, unsure if she understood the stanza, after all. Perhaps her Italian was getting rusty. She turned a page and felt herself grow saucer-eyed. Though well executed and drawn in a lush Renaissance-style pen and ink, the illustration was indeed explicit—depicting a naked man and an equally naked woman passionately entwined on a bed. The man lay atop the woman between her spread legs, her ankles hooked, of all things, over his shoulders! His wide palms clutched the woman's large, overflowing breasts, his bent knees and taut, naked buttocks and the back of his powerful thighs prominently revealed.

Eliza tipped her head to one side and studied the scene from a different angle. *Stars and garters, isn't that uncomfortable?* Apparently not, based on the expression of intense rapture on the woman's face.

The thin wool of Eliza's afternoon gown grew suddenly hot and faintly itchy against her skin; another, unknown kind of heat—one that disturbed her on many levels—pooling low between her legs.

She turned a page, found another illustration.

This one was even more amazing and more alarming, the woman lying on her side with one leg raised, the man kneeling in between her splayed limbs, his genitals fully exposed as he prepared to . . .

She tried to swallow, finding her mouth strangely dry. She knew men were anatomically quite different from women—she had seen Greek and Roman sculpture, after all—but those artists had never sculpted men like this one.

This one was *large*. Huge, actually. His male member big and long as a ripe summer squash.

Jiminy, she wondered, how did a man walk around with something like that between his legs? For that matter, how did he fit the thing into his breeches? Wouldn't someone notice with it sticking out that way?

That's when she deduced the part must grow, and grow a lot! Soft and small when tucked inside a man's breeches. Long and hard when . . . Eliza's cheeks ignited as if they were on fire, her whole body burning with a combination of heat and shock.

Suddenly she heard a voice in the hallway and a low murmured reply. Violet, speaking to one of the servants. *Oh, goodness, what if Violet comes in here and catches me?*

Pulse skittering as fast as a rabbit racing from a hound, Eliza closed the book, returned it to its hiding place and slammed shut the escritoire drawer.

At least she *tried* to shut the drawer, the deuced thing catching at the midway point. She tugged and shoved and pushed, doing everything she could to get the drawer to slide closed. The entire piece of furniture quaked when the drawer finally shot home with a loud *bang*, the inkwell rattling, its top jumping free to roll across the desk.

The heavy brass cap landed with a *thud* on the carpet. She bent and scooped it into her hand, managing to yank out the delicate French rosewood desk chair and plop down onto its seat only seconds before Violet strolled into the room.

"There you are," Violet greeted. "Robert said he

thought he had seen you come in here. Are you working on your correspondence?"

Correspondence? What correspondence? Eliza thought wildly, realizing how thoroughly the naughty little green book had wiped her memory clean, eradicating all thoughts of the letter she had come into the drawing room to compose.

In as casual a manner as she could evoke, she shifted around on her seat. "Hmm, yes, though I h-haven't gotten much done yet."

She hoped Violet didn't come near enough to notice that she hadn't gotten *anything* done yet.

"Georgianna ate her fill then dozed straight off," Violet continued as she moved farther into the room. "And the boys actually settled down without a fuss. I guess all that play with their favorite aunt must have worn them out." She sent Eliza a warm smile. "So I thought I would join you in here while you work on your letter. Go ahead and don't mind me. I brought a book, so I shall be perfectly content over here in my chair near the window."

At Violet's mention of books, one of the bawdy images from *Albanino's Postures* quick-flashed into her mind. Fresh blood sluiced into her cheeks, replenishing the heat and color in her skin.

Violet's pale brows crinkled. "Are you all right? You look flushed."

"I'm fine. Just a tad warm. The . . . seasons are changing and this dress . . . I ought to have worn one of my lighter gowns."

"Maybe you are coming down with something. Here, let me see."

Eliza sprang to her feet, but before she could elude her friend, Violet was already setting outstretched fingers upon Eliza's skin to check for fever. "Your cheeks are warm but your forehead feels cool enough. Even so, perhaps I ought to have Agnes make you an herbal tea. With the start of the Season so near, it would be dreadful if you came down ill."

"I am not coming down ill and I don't need an herbal tea. But my thanks, all the same."

"Well, if you are sure—"

"I am well, truly. You needn't be such a mother."

Violet shot her a startled look, then laughed self-deprecatingly. "If I am behaving like a mother, it is only because I *am* a mother. You'll see how it feels when it happens to you."

"*If* it happens to me," Eliza said on a wistful note.

"Of course it will happen to you." Violet slipped an arm around her shoulders and gave a quick, comforting squeeze. "I realize your past Seasons have been disappointing—goodness, my past Seasons were disappointing—but this one will be different. You are doing splendidly at your lessons and your progress with Kit is everything I had hoped and more. Even Lady Cloverly . . ." Violet paused, pursing her lips and rolling her eyes in mockery of the woman, "remarked upon your talent at the pianoforte."

Eliza burst out laughing at Violet's imitation of Christabel Morgan's haughty ways.

"If you can win a nod of approval from her, you can win over anyone."

Eliza exchanged a warm, conspiratorial grin with Violet, remembering exactly why it was they were such good friends. For a brief second she considered telling Violet about the book in the drawer. It stood to reason she didn't have to admit she had looked inside, only that she had found it. But the moment she opened her mouth, Violet would know. Better, she decided, to say nothing. Some things were quite simply best left unsaid, even among friends.

"There's that flush again," Violet remarked. "Are you quite certain you are well? Agnes won't mind making her special tea. You know how she loves to fuss."

Eliza wanted to refuse, but maybe a cup of tea might not be such a bad idea, after all. She was still a bit overset. "Yes, all right."

With a satisfied nod, Violet crossed to call for her maid.

It was only then that Eliza noticed the ink stopper still clutched inside her palm, faintly sticky with perspiration. Giving it a surreptitious polish on her sleeve, she placed it back atop the inkwell.

"It is early yet, not quite three, so we shouldn't encounter too many people," Kit said two afternoons later as he and Eliza walked their horses along Hyde Park's Rotten Row. "The throngs don't descend for another hour and a half at least, so you should have no cause to feel overwhelmed."

"Speak for yourself," she murmured under her breath.

"I heard that," he said, a laugh in his voice. "You will do fine, Eliza. Just remember to stop when you see someone with whom you ought to speak, say a few polite phrases, make an inquiry or two, then ride on. No need to devote more than five minutes to any one individual or group."

Good, she mused, since at the moment she did not know if she could recall more than five minutes' worth of conversational topics despite all Kit's lessons.

She would much rather have come riding this morning as usual, but last night Kit had announced his plan for them to take an afternoon ride in order to "test out" her new skills. If they arrived early, he explained, she would have far fewer people to face. That way she could get a taste of the park experience without enduring the Fashionable Hour at its zenith.

Still, there were plenty of people already gathered—carriages and riders and couples, many strolling together arm in arm as they traversed the grounds.

Not that this was her first outing to Hyde Park during the Fashionable Hour. In years past, she had come on occasion with her aunt. But their few outings had been in her aunt's hired carriage. Silent and respectful, she had sat uncomplaining while Aunt Doris paused to talk with her own friends, middle-aged women and men of an older generation who exchanged nods and a brief greeting with Eliza before turning away to talk to her aunt until it was time to move on.

So today's excursion would indeed be a kind of first. Her first without her aunt and the carriage and her first since her weeks of study with Kit. Now she had only to prove herself.

If she could.

Her muscles tightened at the thought, her mount, Andromeda, shifting restlessly beneath her, sensing Eliza's unease. She wished she were riding her usual horse, Cassiopeia, but the sweet little mare had come down with colic a couple days ago. The head groom had dosed her round the clock until the crisis passed. Although she was now on the mend, she needed to remain in her stall for a few more days.

So Kit had chosen another horse for Eliza to ride, a smooth-gaited chestnut mare with a temperate nature. A younger horse, Andromeda tended to be slightly more playful, but with Eliza's improved riding skills she wasn't having any difficulty controlling her, especially since she and Kit were constrained to move at a pace no faster than an easy walk.

"Here comes Lady Shipple, Lady Eelsworth and Lord Turtlesford, and no sniggering at any of their names," Kit murmured low. "Although truth be told, Turtlesford has always reminded me a little of a garden tortoise. It's those protruding eyes of his."

"You are outrageous!" Eliza exclaimed on a laugh, as she and Kit drew their horses to a stop.

"Ah, Turtlesford. Ladies. How do you do this afternoon?" Kit declared, flashing a broad smile. "You are, of course, acquainted with Miss Hammond."

From inside an open-air carriage, the group turned their collective sights upon Eliza. Three pairs of eyes narrowed in momentary puzzlement as if trying to place her among their peers then abruptly widened in astonished recognition.

"Miss Hammond, well, of course, what a pleasure," Lady Shipple said, recovering first. "I did not realize you were in Town."

Until a few seconds ago, you probably didn't remember I existed, Eliza thought.

"Yes," Eliza said. "I have been residing with the Duke and Duchess of Raeburn this winter and spring."

"Ah, yes, since your aunt passed on to her reward." Lady Eelsworth inclined her dark head, a few touches of gray showing along the edges of her temples. "Very sad, always difficult to lose a relation, but such is the nature of things." She paused, sweeping an arched look over Eliza. "I must say you are looking remarkably well, better than I have ever seen you. Your aunt's death obviously agrees."

The woman smiled slyly.

For a long moment, Eliza simply stared. *What a rude witch.* The old Eliza would have stayed silent and lowered her eyes, wishing the whole incident away. But the new Eliza decided a reply was most decidedly in order.

Eliza met the other woman's gaze. "It is not her death that agrees but rather her money, is that not what you mean to say?"

This time it was Lady Eelsworth who stared. "Well, I—"

"It was very good of my aunt to leave me her fortune," Eliza continued. "And you are correct, my lady, her money has made my life far more comfortable. It bought me this riding habit. What do you think of the color and cut?"

Lady Eelsworth had the grace to flush. "I think it a most becoming gown."

"Most becoming indeed," Lord Turtlesford stated with cheerful enthusiasm. "I'd say it was money well spent."

Eliza turned her head and smiled. "Thank you, my lord."

"Why, I hardly recognized you at first, you've turned so dashing. If this is the result, then I say spend and spend some more."

Eliza laughed. "And so I shall, my lord. So I shall."

The five of them chatted for another minute or two before saying their farewells. She and Kit each urged their horses forward.

"I was about to step in to protect you from that nasty cat but I see I had no need." Kit tossed her a grin. "I've rarely witnessed a nicer set-down. You'll be giving me lessons soon."

She shook her head. "Oh, I don't think so. I'm still trembling from the encounter. I can't believe I said that to her."

"Neither can she. Word will soon get round that you have come out of your shell and are no longer to be meddled with or ignored. I predict a far different Season for you, my little wren, than any you have known before." He looked ahead of them on the path. "Ah, here comes a new group. Be kind and promise not to hurt them too badly."

But there were no verbal mishaps or confrontations with that group or the next one or the one after that. To her profound amazement, Eliza handled herself with gracious aplomb at each encounter, incrementally gaining confidence and poise in both her responses and her behavior. It seemed that all of her hours of drilling with Kit, all his tips and tricks and techniques had become so firmly lodged in her brain that they rolled off her tongue the way drops of rain fell from the sky during a storm.

She was quivering with astonished delight by the time Kit decided they should turn toward home.

"Lady Dolby was very kind," she said as they walked their horses toward the entrance gates. "She said she would send around cards for her party next week."

"Hmm, so I heard. You shall likely receive a great many invitations soon, far too many to accept."

"I shall leave it up to you and Violet to decide which entertainments to attend. I—"

A loud shout came from behind them. Turning her head, she saw curricle bearing down, racing far too fast for the park lanes as people hurried to get out of its way. Andromeda shied and danced to the side, letting out a whinny of fear.

Eliza held steady and fought to direct the mare out of harm's way. She caught a glimpse of the driver, seeing his vivid yellow-and-green-striped coat and the shock of coal black hair on his youthful head, his face appearing scarcely older than that of a child. Then she didn't have time to see more, as he drew abreast of her, flicking his long coach whip with an audible *crack*.

But the whip missed its mark, its vicious tip connecting with Andromeda's hindquarters. The mare released a cry of pain and reared, slashing her front hooves through the air and tossing her head so fractiously that she jerked the reins out of Eliza's hands.

Somehow Eliza kept her seat, but without the reins she could do nothing to control the mare. Terrified, the horse came down onto all fours and shot forward into a gallop. Relying on instinct, Eliza leaned low and dug her fingers into the mare's thick mane, hanging on for dear life as she prayed she didn't crash to the ground. In her ears came the thunder of her beating heart, a sound so loud she could hear nothing else. Across the greens the horse raced, veering wildly around trees and groups of startled people. The lost reins dangled like writhing serpents, frightening Andromeda even more, keeping her running when she might otherwise have stopped.

The scent of fear and horse sweat was sharp in Eliza's nose as she clung with all her might, her own perspiration dampening her hands, turning them perilously slick. But she dared not shift so much as an inch, or she risked toppling off.

Suddenly a male arm came into her line of vision, reaching out to take hold of the bridle. From the corner of her eye she could see a polished Hessian boot in its stirrup and the flashing of his mount's hooves pounding into the turf next to her horse.

Kit, she thought in relief, *Kit has come to save me.*

With a soothing, deep-throated command, he slowed the horses, urging Andromeda to break stride and slow. Moments later, the horses came to a walk then finally a complete and blessed stop.

Eliza began to tremble, full-body shakes she could not seem to control. She heard Kit dismount, sensed him hurry around to her side. And then she was in his arms as he set her carefully upon her feet.

Only, the man who held her wasn't Kit.

Her eyes widened as she gazed upward, way upward, into the face of male perfection—the blond, blue-eyed stranger quite possibly the most handsome man she had ever seen, as if Adonis himself had been brought to life.

She gasped, then gasped again—dizzy—as he showered her with the radiance of his smile.

Chapter Ten

Kit heard the shout and looked behind him to see the carriage barreling recklessly along the lane toward him and Eliza, people and animals and vehicles jostling in a frantic scramble to get out of the way.

Damned jingle-brained fool, Kit cursed, catching a glimpse of the driver's boyish face. *Must be doing it on a dare,* he concluded in an instant, recognizing the unmistakable signs of a foolish young man egged on by his idiot friends—none of them considering the consequences or the fact that someone was bound to get hurt.

Then he forgot all about such thoughts as Eliza's mare spooked and did a fretful sideways dance across to the opposite side of the path. The carriage streaked between them, wheels rumbling, his view of Eliza obscured. The crack of a whip split the air, followed by Andromeda's scream as the animal reared. Kit watched in horror, time momentarily slowing, as the mare thrashed her head and yanked the reins from Eliza's grip. Then the horse was off, racing at a full gallop as Eliza clung to her mount's back.

A fist of terror punched into his stomach. Seconds later, he set Mars into motion, pushing the horse for speed. But try as his loyal steed might, the gelding's way was blocked by the chaos left in the wake of the boy's crazed stunt. Women were crying, men shouting, riders and drivers fighting to calm their own frightened animals.

Finally he broke free and set off after Eliza. *Please God, don't let her fall,* he thought. *Don't let her be injured, or worse.*

He caught sight of her and pushed Mars harder to catch up. Across the grounds he charged, intent upon reaching her and bringing her to safety. But it seemed another man had the same idea, a horse and rider appearing ahead, his mount's hooves churning up chunks of grass and mud as he pounded after Eliza's wayward mare. At full charge, the man drew abreast of them. In a display of impressive equestrian skill, he shifted sideways and grasped Andromeda's bridle, bringing the frightened horse to a stop.

Even from a distance, Kit could see how badly Eliza was shaking, her tremors a clear indication of her own fearful reaction to the wild ride.

The man dismounted and sprinted to Eliza's side, lifting her out of the saddle and onto solid ground. He kept his arms secure around her as she swayed and blinked upward as if in a daze.

Only then did Kit recognize the other man—Lord Lancelot Brevard—tall, blond and heroic as the fabled knight whose name he bore. It had been a frequent jest among the fellows at Oxford that Brevard ought to have been born the son of a baronet instead of a viscount, despite the lesser status, so he could have been known as Sir Lancelot in name as well as deed.

In Kit's first term at Oxford, Brevard had been in his last, already a legend among his peers and professors. An affirmed leader, Brevard took first in everything he did whether it be academic or athletic, his record a mile-long litany of awards and honors and accolades. He led a charmed life of perfection, or as near perfection as any human man could achieve. Brevard was one of those rare people who it seemed could do no wrong, and who did no wrong, as honorable as he was talented, as compassionate as he was competitive.

Brevard had personally proven the fact that spring term when Kit—eager to test his own worth and valor—challenged the older man to a swim race. A strong swimmer and confident of his abilities, Kit had arrived full of arrogant bravado and swagger, boasting he would prevail. In the end, his unfamiliarity with the river's cold, swift current and his opponent's unflagging stamina had been his undoing. He'd put in a formidable effort and nearly won, but "nearly" hadn't been good enough.

Instead of listening to his body's warnings as he ought, Kit had challenged Brevard to another race, which Brevard clearly had not wanted. But with honor at stake, they agreed. Strength flagging, Kit had pushed on long past his endurance and nearly drowned as a result of his stubborn, idiotic pride. It was Brevard who had saved his life. Brevard who afterward had refused to mock him as others in his position would surely have done, instead taking Kit under his wing and turning his young, would-be rival into a friend.

And that was the diabolical magic of Lancelot Brevard. No matter how much a fellow might wish to despise him, it simply could not be done. Man or woman, dog or cat, bird or beetle—everyone and everything liked Brevard.

And now, wouldn't you know, the bloody great hero has raced to the rescue and saved Eliza. Of course, Kit was glad she had come to no harm. Even so, a part of him didn't understand why Brevard couldn't have come on the scene just a minute or two later and let Kit do the rescuing. After all, Eliza was in *his* charge—*his* student and *his* responsibility.

Kit drew his gelding to a halt, vaulted to the ground. "Eliza, are you all right?" He hurried toward her.

She didn't turn her head, continuing to stare up at Brevard with a peculiar expression upon her face, her gray eyes slightly glazed.

Is she in shock?

After her experience, Kit wouldn't be surprised. He touched her arm. "Eliza, it's me, Kit. Are you all right? Are you injured? Say something, please."

Her lashes fluttered. "Kit?" Only then did she glance at him. "Kit. Oh, you are here."

"Yes, I'm here. Everything will be fine. You've taken quite a turn but you're safe now." He flicked a glance at the other man. "Hello, Brevard. Quite a save. My thanks as well as the lady's."

"Winter, well met. I expected we would tap elbows here in Town but not under such unusual circumstances. You are acquainted with the lady, I take it?"

"Eliza is a friend of the duchess and is staying with us at Raeburn House for the Season. She and I were enjoying the afternoon promenade when some young chucklehead decided to race his carriage up Rotten Row. Did you catch sight of the fuss?"

Brevard shook his head. "I was too far off but I heard it, screams and shouts enough to wake the dead. And then this lady suddenly appeared, her horse obviously out of control—so, of course, I had to help."

Oh, of course, Kit thought.

Brevard returned his gaze to Eliza, a smile playing at his lips. "Be so good as to introduce us, would you, Winter?"

Kit caught the gleam in Brevard's eyes. Was that interest he saw, male interest for an attractive female? For Eliza? Kit's chest tightened, and for the merest instant he wanted to refuse the request.

Then he brushed the impulse aside, puzzled by his unusual reaction. "Brevard, allow me make you known to Miss Eliza Hammond. Eliza, Viscount Lancelot Brevard."

"A pleasure, my lord," Eliza murmured, "and thank you. Once I lost hold of Andromeda's reins I didn't know how I would ever convince her to stop. If not for you, well, I would surely have come to harm."

No, you wouldn't, Kit mused in irritation. *If not for him, I would have saved you. It just would have taken me a minute longer.*

Brevard waved aside her exhortations of gratitude. "Pray do not distress yourself, Miss Hammond. No thanks are necessary. I am only relieved I saw you when I did and was able to lend my assistance. And may I say I thought you exceptionally brave—"

"Oh, I was not," Eliza denied.

"But you were. Many ladies would have tumbled off straightaway and done themselves a great injury. You had the presence of mind to keep your seat and your wits about you in spite of the danger. You are to be commended for your resourcefulness, a refreshing and admirable trait to be found in any woman."

Attractive color dusted Eliza's cheeks, replacing her fear-induced pallor. "You are most kind, my lord, but truly I was terrified the whole time and am not at all deserving of praise."

Brevard shook his head. "You are far too modest and far too lovely. And though I perhaps ought not say this, I confess I cannot be completely sorry your horse decided to bolt."

Eliza's brows scrunched. "Whyever not?"

"Because then I would not have had the delight of meeting you."

Eliza giggled.

Actually *giggled,* like some ingenue fresh out of the schoolroom.

Kit restrained the urge to snort and instead reached out and took her arm. "You must be exhausted after your ordeal. We really ought to get you home now so you can rest."

Eliza turned toward him as if she only then remembered his presence. "Yes, I suppose, though oddly enough I am feeling rather better now." She stuck out her free hand. "See, no more shaking."

"Brave. Just as I said." Brevard showered her with a wide smile, then he winked.

Eliza giggled again.

"Andromeda seems calm now, so it should be safe for you to ride her again," Kit declared, gently steering Eliza toward the mare. The horse, along with the other two geldings, had her head lowered, leisurely grazing on park grass.

Eliza hesitated, her step reluctant. "Kit, I don't know if I . . . feel safe riding again so soon."

"No point in delaying. It's best if you get back on now so you don't lose your rider's confidence. Otherwise you may never have the nerve to climb back in the saddle again at all."

Eliza dug one hand into the heavy skirt of her riding habit. "I'll feel perfectly safe on Cassiopeia once she is recovered. I just don't want to ride anymore today."

"I can have my man send round for a carriage," Brevard offered. "It won't take above five minutes."

For Eliza's own good, Kit knew she needed to conquer her fear and conquer it now. So why did he suddenly feel like the worst sort of bully? "Thank you, Brevard, but Eliza will be fine. It is but a short ride home."

Reaching for Andromeda's reins, he brought them around and coiled them against the horse's neck. He moved to take up a position at the mare's side, then bent down and linked his palms together so he could boost Eliza into the saddle.

She visibly trembled, a long moment passing before she set a hand upon his shoulder and slipped one foot into his waiting palms. He had her up and in the saddle in an instant, moving to arrange the reins firmly inside her grasp.

"There, how do you feel? All right?"

For the first time he could ever recall, she refused to look him in the eye. "Fine," she said, her voice barely audible.

A bony finger of guilt jabbed Kit in the chest. "I'll be right with you and we'll go at a slow, easy walk."

She did not look reassured, particularly when a faint shiver rippled just beneath Andromeda's glossy coat.

"Why don't I accompany the two of you home?" Brevard suggested in a bolstering tone. "I'll ride on your left, Miss Hammond. Winter can ride on your right, and you'll be tucked snug as a bug in the middle."

Eliza gave Brevard a tiny smile. "That sounds lovely, my lord, but I would not want to inconvenience you in any way."

"Oh, it's no inconvenience at all. What do you say, Winter?"

The word *no* came straight to his lips, though for the life of him he couldn't understand why he was feeling so peevish and perverse. Brevard's plan seemed a sound one, a method well suited to offering Eliza reassurance so she could ride home without fear of further calamity. Yet even knowing that, he still wished to refuse Brevard. He wondered why.

Must be this damnable afternoon, he supposed. That bloody boy who'd started all this to-do had a great deal for which to answer.

"Yes, all right," Kit agreed, striding across to Mars to jump smoothly into the saddle. Brevard quickly did the same, sitting his horse with a natural grace, almost centaurlike, as if he and his animal had merged into a single being. Kit assumed a flanking position at Eliza's side, Brevard opposite. Walking three abreast, they urged their respective mounts into motion.

By the time they arrived at Raeburn House, Eliza was relaxed and smiling, laughing at one of Brevard's stories. Kit laughed too, the tale far too amusing to resist despite his initial efforts to hold on to his irritation. Brevard had a knack at telling tales just as he seemed to have a knack with everything else in his life.

"Well, Miss Hammond, it would seem we have arrived without mishap," Brevard declared.

Before Kit had time to dismount, Brevard was off his horse, busily assisting Eliza from hers.

Eliza smiled up at the other man. "Thank you again, my lord. I cannot tell you how grateful I am for your help today."

"It was my pleasure. Believe me, Miss Hammond. And perhaps we shall meet again soon at one entertainment or another? I can regale you with another story, tell you of my time in India."

Surprised pleasure turned Eliza's eyes a deeper shade of gray. "India? How very interesting. Is it as exotic as they say?"

Ordinarily Kit would have wanted to hear more about India too, but not today. "Good to see you again, Brevard," he interrupted, coming around to stand next to Eliza. "I am sure we will see each other at one of the clubs. We must make plans to have a drink, play a hand or two of cards."

Brevard shifted his blue gaze to meet Kit's. "Yes, let's.

In fact, Crowe and I were just discussing getting up a group for a race meeting. Care to join us?"

"Yes, of course. Send round the particulars, won't you?"

On a nod, Brevard turned back to Eliza. "Miss Hammond, after your ordeal in the park, you must surely be wanting to rest, so I will bid you adieu. For now." He executed an elegant bow, then swung up onto his horse. "Winter." Touching the brim of his hat, he rode away.

A pair of grooms came forward to lead the horses away.

Without a word, Eliza turned and walked up the townhouse steps, March already in attendance to hold the front door wide. She gave the majordomo a murmured greeting as she passed into the house.

Kit came in after her. "Eliza, is anything wrong?"

"I am fine."

She didn't seem fine. She seemed annoyed, even angry. Maybe she was still upset that he had made her ride home on Andromeda. "Sorry if I pushed you back there in the park, but I thought it necessary. For your confidence, you understand?"

"Yes, I understand." Her expression did not brighten.

"And I'm sorry Andromeda spooked so badly. She took you on a wild ride, and you had every right to be frightened. I am only relieved you weren't hurt." He frowned. "You weren't, were you?"

"No."

"Then what is amiss?"

"Nothing, I am merely tired. I believe I'll go to my room now." Holding up her long skirt, she crossed the foyer and started up the main staircase.

Kit hesitated for a moment, then came after her, taking the stairs two at a time to catch up. "Eliza."

She kept walking, her skirts swaying in a sibilant whisper, boots silent against the hall carpeting.

"Eliza, wait." He reached for her elbow, drew her to a halt. "What is it? You seem distressed."

Slowly she turned and met his gaze. "You were rude."

His jaw loosened in surprise. "Was I? When?"

"When I was speaking to Lord Brevard. You . . . you interrupted, and I had the impression that . . ." Her gaze dropped to the floor.

"That what?" He bent his head and tried to get her to look at him again. "Go on. Tell me," he encouraged.

"That you really rathered I had not continued speaking to him. Was I saying or doing something wrong? Did I make some error?"

He gave an emphatic shake of his head. "No, you made no errors, no errors at all today. Actually, you were quite splendid, both during our promenade and later as well."

Her dark brows furrowed, her soft eyes confused. "Then what is the difficulty? Unless you were trying to warn me off him? Is there something about Lord Brevard that I should know? He isn't a fortune hunter, is he?"

"Nothing of the sort. Quite the opposite, in fact. Brevard is the very best of fellows—educated, well traveled, well spoken and rich. Even richer now, I understand, since his time in India. No, there is nothing wrong with Brevard. He is a model gentleman, honorable to the core."

"Is it me, then? My connections, perhaps—"

"Don't be ridiculous. There is nothing wrong with your connections," he said, outraged on her behalf. "Who ever put that maggot in your head?"

"My aunt, she . . ." Eliza paused, tugged at the fingers

of one dun leather riding glove and pulled it off. "She always said my father was nothing but a lowly, insignificant tutor who had dragged down the family name. That my mother was a disgrace for running off with him. I have never cared before because they were my parents and I loved them, but perhaps it is not only my shyness that has kept the suitors away all these years."

"And do you think I feel this way? That I believe your connections lacking?"

"No, but others may." She pulled the second glove free, gripped the pair in one hand. "I just wondered if you were cautioning me. Again, for my own good." She looked up at him.

"I have nothing about which to caution you, not in that regard. You are worthy of any man in Society, never think otherwise. As for your shyness, it is resolving nicely with the help of our lessons. Only a couple more, you know, and we shall be finished."

A peculiar sense of loss crept through Kit at the realization. He ought to be thrilled to have his days made once more his own, free to sleep in or racket around with his friends or do anything else he wished to do. So why wasn't he filled with happy anticipation? He *would be,* he assured himself, once the day actually arrived.

"Next Tuesday is your first ball," he said, shaking off his unfathomable emotions.

"I know," she agreed. "I hope I am ready."

"You will be. Actually, you are ready now, though a little more brushing up cannot hurt." He gave her a smile. "Is all well again? Am I forgiven for being rude? A lapse for which you have my most profound apology."

"Yes, of course. You know I cannot stay angry for long, and certainly never with you." She returned his smile.

"Well, that is a relief." He waggled his brows. "I don't like turning you cross."

She laughed, her entire face lighting up, dove-colored eyes sparkling and alive with amusement. His chest tightened at the sight, his gaze drawn down to her lips, so pale pink and pretty. They looked soft as velvet and sweet as a dish of summer strawberries. Ripe enough to pick. Delectable enough to taste. He leaned closer and caught the faintest hint of honeysuckle on her skin.

"Oh, good, you two are back."

Kit snapped straight and spun on his heel to watch Violet stroll down the corridor toward them, Horatio loping obediently in her wake.

Reaching them, she stopped, looked first at him, then at Eliza. "I hope I am not interrupting."

"No, not at all," Kit said. "Eliza and I were only discussing our outing."

"Oh, good, since it is what I came to hear. How did it go?" Violet demanded, slipping a hand around Eliza's elbow. "Any difficulties?"

"Ladies, if you'll excuse me . . ."

Violet gave him a smile and an absent nod, then turned Eliza to lead her back down the hallway in the direction from which Violet had just come. The big Great Dane trailed behind. "Did you meet anyone particularly interesting?" he heard Violet ask.

"One person. Viscount Lancelot Brevard. He rescued me just like a knight of old . . ."

Walking in the opposite direction, he headed for his rooms.

Andromeda reared and yanked the reins from Eliza's hands, the horse's cry of terror shrill in her ears. Thrashing hooves struck the ground with a jarring thud, *equine* muscles rippling as the mare surged forward, leaping into an all-out gallop that pushed for every ounce of speed at the animal's command.

Eliza clung with sick terror, her heart drumming so hard her rib cage ached. She dug her fingers deep into the horse's thick, resilient mane and fought for purchase, fought not to be hurled to the ground that raced by so quickly she could see it only as an indistinct blur of greens and browns.

She closed her eyes and prayed.

A hard, male arm suddenly curved around her waist. In a deft move, he lifted her free of the saddle and set her sideways before him on his own charging steed. She clung again, this time to the man, wrapping her arms around his strong back, laying her head against the firm warmth of his chest.

Safe. So safe.

He slowed his mount, bringing the horse to an easy walk before stopping altogether.

She tipped back her head, caught a glint of fine golden hair and a face that was almost too handsome to be real. His teeth gleamed white and straight as he smiled down upon her. She stared into his eyes, blue and pure as a Scandinavian lake.

He blinked, and when his lids lifted his eyes had changed, green now, dark and vital as summer leaves after a soaking afternoon rain. Around each pupil lay an encircling ring of gold, a few flecks of the same scattered outward to float inside his irises like pinches of gold dust.

He grinned in that boyish way she knew so well, making her pulse points flutter wildly. She smiled back, gentle and slow, and watched his eyes change yet again, growing lambent and intent in a way she had never *known before as his gaze lowered to caress her parted lips.*

She drew in his scent, thrilling to the sensation of it swimming in giddy delight inside her head. Allowing it to linger, she breathed in again and again until the fragrance seemed to seep into her pores and bones and become almost her own. Lifting a hand, she threaded her fingers into the thick silk of his dark hair, reveling in its texture.

He bent closer, then closer still, pulling her nearer inside his embrace. With barely a breath separating them, she whispered his name.

Kit.

And then his lips touched her own.

Her body tingled from head to toe, awash in the most intense sensation. Sweet bliss lighted her up from within and left her floating on a cloud of decadent pleasure. Stretching her arms upward, she locked them around his neck and pressed tighter. But it wasn't tight enough, close enough. She wanted more. She wanted everything.

Nor was it enough for him.

He reached down and caught hold of her leg, shifting her to face him in the saddle. She gasped as he draped her spread legs over his powerful thighs, tugging her so she fit against him, pelvis to pelvis.

Then they were kissing again, wild and wanton and hungry.

At length, he drew away. "Oh, don't look so shocked. I know all about that naughty little book you were reading."

Her eyes flashed open, a whimper of dismay escaping her lips as she awakened. Faint dawn light skimmed along the edges of her bedchamber's window curtains. The shapes of the room's furnishings were only just starting to become visible, still shrouded in pools of night shadow. Shifting against the fine linen sheets, she pressed a hand between her breasts and listened to the sound of her own ragged breathing.

Stars above, she thought, *what a dream.* Even now she could feel the sensation of Kit's lips on hers, the strength of his long, firm body pressed snuggly against her own, his delicious masculine scent invigorating her senses.

And every bit of it was false. A fancy spun like some intricate tapestry that was all dazzle and shape without a bit of real substance. Her body had thought it real, though, she realized, becoming aware of the faint, damp ache that lingered between her thighs. Warmth crept across her skin as she remembered how she had straddled Kit in her dream. How she had clasped her thighs around his hips with a brazen abandon worthy of one of the women depicted inside *Albanino's Postures.*

At least they hadn't been naked.

Her nipples tightened at the idea, the ache twinging anew between her legs. She rolled over, mildly ashamed of responses she scarcely understood. Ashamed as well of how her mind had jumbled together the events of the day—Andromeda's wild ride, her feelings of terror and panic, Lord Brevard coming to her rescue.

Dashing, gentlemanly Lord Brevard. She had liked him, liked him very much. His attentive demeanor and kind voice. She had liked as well the way he made her laugh and smile. He was a man any woman could desire.

But it hadn't been Lord Brevard she had dream-kissed, no matter how undeniably handsome he might be.

It was Kit.

She thought of his eyes in the dream, then thought of his gaze when he had been talking to her yesterday in the hallway. He had been Kit. Normal, regular Kit who never looked at her with anything other than patient friendliness and a sort of brotherly affection. But then, there at the last, something had changed, his gaze altering for a split second as it roved across her mouth. In that instant, it appeared to her that he had leaned closer, ever so slightly. For a moment, it looked almost as if he had been thinking about kissing her.

Or had she only imagined it, the event no more substantial than her dream?

What would it be like to kiss Kit for real? she mused.

For that matter, what would it be like to be kissed at all?

In her entire three-and-twenty years, no man had ever so much as attempted to take advantage of her innocence. Young, unmarried ladies were not supposed to kiss or touch young gentlemen prior to marriage, but, of course, she knew such intimacies occurred. And though no one would ever speak of such a thing aloud, many would be surprised to find a woman of her advanced years wholly untried, without even the experience of a single kiss.

So when this Season began, would anything change? Might a man finally wish to kiss her? And would she want him to? What if she didn't like his touch and reacted badly? What if he thought her a complete pea goose for her naiveté?

Perhaps for her final lesson with Kit she ought to ask him to teach her to kiss, she thought on a humorous note.

Seconds later her lips parted in astonishment as the idea settled deeper into her mind. No, it was ludicrous even to contemplate such a thing. Kit's eyes would jolt from his head, and the both of them would be mortified with embarrassment after his refusal.

But what if he did not refuse?

She thought again of his gazing at her lips yesterday afternoon. *Had* he been considering leaning down for a kiss? Or was it only her own wishful longings playing tricks?

There could be only one way to find out.

But did she have the nerve? Or would fear hold her back? And if she didn't act, would she forever after regret not finding out if Kit's real kisses were as sweet as the ones in her dreams?

Chapter Eleven

From her place on the satin-covered peach settee in the duchess's dressing room, Eliza watched her friend's maid set a final pin into Violet's elegant coiffure.

"I am sorry you aren't coming with us today, but I suppose it isn't as if you haven't already seen Astley's Amphitheatre and Bullock's Egyptian Hall," Violet remarked. "Jeannette says Moira and Siobhan have talked of little else since she suggested the outing. Even Finn is excited, though he tries to act as if the idea is all a great humbug and he is being forced to come along. You know how young men are at that age, worried about maintaining their reputation at the expense of all else."

"I don't think men change in that regard no matter their age," Eliza observed.

Violet laughed, shifting around on her seat to face Eliza now that Agnes had finished dressing her hair. "How very true. Adrian and Darragh have been making grumbling noises as well, but I don't think they are all that loath to be accompanying us. Still, I shall miss you not taking part."

"Oh, I don't mind. With my first ball only two days away, I ought to take this last opportunity to practice with Kit." Eliza's throat tightened at the thought of what she hoped to be practicing.

"Well, I think you have done splendidly," Violet congratulated, reaching over to pat her hand. "But I suppose one more lesson cannot hurt."

An hour later, Eliza sat on the sofa in Violet's study, her mouth as dry as one of the tomb artifacts she knew Violet and the others must by now be viewing at Bullock's Museum.

Opposite her at the other end of the sofa, Kit relaxed in leisurely masculine ease. He bit into one of the cookies on his plate, then washed down the treat with a long swallow of hot tea. Manners ingrained, he wiped his mouth on a cloth napkin before moving on to the next confection on his plate, his enjoyment apparent.

Kit always liked to have some sort of refreshments available during their lessons. Sustenance to tide them over, he claimed, since a man could go only so long without a meal.

Not the least bit hungry, Eliza set her own cup and plate aside, the one small cake she had taken out of politeness going untouched.

"Are you not hungry?" Kit inquired with a nod toward her abandoned sweet.

She shook her head. "I had a more than adequate breakfast."

"Breakfast never stays with me and nuncheon is hours away yet."

He ate one more pastry, then swallowed the last of his tea, setting his cup onto its saucer with a faint tap. "Ready to begin, then?" He wiped his mouth and his graceful, long-fingered hands, then folded his napkin and set it next to his empty cup. "Drawing room conversation or ballroom? You have mastered both quite nicely, but a final polish cannot go amiss. So which shall it be today?"

She stared down at the pale blue sofa cushion between

them. Stomach quivering, she ran the tip of one finger-nail across the expensive fabric. Her mind raced.

Should she do it? *Could* she do it? Because once the words were out, there would be no going back.

She trembled and swallowed hard then plunged ahead, knowing if she did not proceed she would turn coward and dash her chances forever. "I thought . . . that is . . . I wondered, since it is our last lesson, if we might perhaps do something a little different."

"Different? Such as?" Not one to stand on formality, Kit leaned forward and reached for the teapot. Sliding his cup into place, he began to pour.

"I thought . . . well, I have been thinking that . . . did you know I have never been kissed?"

His eyes jerked upward to meet her gaze. "*What?*"

"No man has ever kissed me and I want you to do it."

Hot tea splashed across his fingers. "Bullocks!" He released the teapot, letting it drop onto the silver tray with a cringe-inducing *thud*. "Sorry. What did you say?"

"Oh, mercy, are you all right?" She stiffened in alarm at his injury. "Are you badly burned? Oh, I shouldn't have spoken . . . I didn't mean for you to be hurt."

"Never mind that now. Repeat what you just said, not about being burned but the other."

She pulled in a breath, her voice lowering to a near whisper. "I said I want you to . . . kiss me."

He stuck his scalded knuckle into his mouth and stared.

"It's not so much that I want *you* to kiss me," she pressed on, ignoring the fact that her cheeks must be stained as red as pomegranates. "It's only that I want to be kissed . . . in case it happens this Season . . . so I don't make a fool of myself."

Little liar, she thought. Of course it was him she wanted to kiss, but something in her warned she ought not let him know that particular fact.

He pulled the finger out of his mouth. "And which gentlemen do you imagine may be in urgent want of kissing you?"

"Oh, well, no one in particular."

"*Brevard?*" His jaw visibly tightened.

She shrugged, marveling at her unexpected bravado. "I do not know, but since you seem to think I shall finally *take* this Season, I only wish to be prepared. And you are my mentor."

His mahogany eyebrows winged upward.

"I thought you could teach me . . . a little . . . so I would not be afraid, should it happen, that is. But only if you want to. I'll understand if you don't." At that, her speech dwindled into nothingness, her mock courage draining away as abruptly as it had arrived. She lowered her gaze to her lap, her fingers squeezed tightly together.

A long, pronounced silence fell before he spoke. "So let me make certain I understand this. You want me to teach you how to kiss?"

Her head came up. "Yes. A simple kiss will do."

"And I am to do this so you won't be alarmed should another man want to kiss you in future? A man who may very well become your husband. Do you not think he ought to be the one teaching you how to kiss?"

She frowned. "Well, perhaps, but . . ."

"But what?"

"But if I never kiss any other man, how will I know if he is the right one for me? Violet says I ought not settle for the first man who asks, unless I am certain he will suit me best. Of course, this Season may go no better than the others, and the whole matter shall remain utterly moot."

"I do not think you need to worry. I shall be very much surprised if you do not receive at least one or two respectable offers this year."

"Because of my money, you mean?"

His gaze softened. "No, because of *you*. Isn't that what all our lessons have been about?"

She nodded, warmed by his words.

But when he said nothing further, her chest tightened. *He is going to refuse,* she thought. *Obviously he feels nothing for me.* So much for all her ridiculous musings about the way he had looked at her in the hallway the other day.

Suddenly she wished she could shrink into herself, curl up and die.

"All right."

At first she wasn't sure she had heard him, his voice so low and rough. Had he said "all right"?

Kit shifted closer on the sofa. "Are you sure you want this?"

Her heart skipped up into her throat. "Yes."

"And I assume you wish to begin now?"

She nodded. "Everyone is away, and this *is* our final lesson. It might be awkward later."

His mouth curved up in a wry smile. "It might be awkward now, but let us begin, if such is your desire."

Hmm, her desire. Now that she had committed to this plan, she realized what a dangerous game she was playing, as if she had decided to thrust her palm directly over a roaring fire. All that remained to be seen was how badly she was going to end up getting burned.

He stood and crossed the room, closing the door with a quiet *click* of the latch. It showed her scattered state of mind, the fact that she had utterly forgotten about the door—half open for any passing servant to glance inside and see what they were about to do.

Kit returned and sank down beside her on the sofa, one trouser-covered thigh brushing her hip, a long arm stretched along the top of the settee at her back. In that moment, she became more vitally aware of his size and masculinity than she ever had before.

Leaning nearer, he placed a pair of fingers beneath her jaw and tipped up her chin. "Relax," he murmured. "It won't hurt, you know."

She gave a shaky laugh and a nod, but she could say nothing further, her hands curled into fists of anxious anticipation in her lap. She closed her eyes and waited.

At first, she barely felt it when he touched his mouth to hers—light and smooth and tender, like the dusting of a feather against her skin. The contact increased ever so slightly, the shape and texture of his lips becoming better defined as they rested in undemanding warmth against her own. She caught a whiff of the earthy bay rum he liked to wear, became aware of the gentle susurration of his breath as it moved slowly in and out through his nose.

Then as inauspiciously as the kiss had begun, he pulled away and eased back.

Her eyes fluttered open to find him watching her, his face only inches away. She swallowed, aware of a vague sense of disappointment. Somehow she had expected more, something dramatic—like the earth tipping abruptly on its axis, perhaps.

She blurted out her dismay. "Is that it?"

A smile brightened the green in his eyes. "You said simple. I didn't want to frighten you."

"Oh." She digested that for a moment. "I am not afraid."

"Hmm. Then shall we try again? Something more involved?"

"Is there more?"

"Oh, yes, volumes. That last scarcely qualified as a kiss at all. Now, really try to relax this time. Oh, and part your lips."

"Do what?"

"Your lips, let them open a little so they aren't tight as a stitched-up seam."

Was he implying she was stitched up too? Well, come to think of it, perhaps she was. A bit.

When she hesitated, he reached up and skimmed a thumb across her lower lip. Her mouth parted of its own volition, her body obviously understanding better than her mind.

"Good," he said. "Now tip your head."

"Tip?"

"Mmm-hmm. Like this." He edged closer and cocked his head slightly to one side.

She studied him for a second then repeated his move exactly, tipping her head at precisely the same angle and direction as his own.

Amusement curved his lips. "No, the other way, like a mirror image."

"Oh." She didn't completely understand the objective of his instruction until she tipped her head the opposite way. Then it all became suddenly clear, the realization that when they kissed, their noses wouldn't bump, that their lips would fit together as naturally as interlocking pieces of the same puzzle.

He slid a broad palm around the back of her neck, his thumb angling her head ever so slightly upward. And then his mouth came down upon hers and showed her just how unremarkable their first kiss had been.

Her pulse leapt, beating like tiny drums in her wrists and throat after only a few seconds inside his embrace.

Hotter and slightly moist, his lips became a revelation, a world of ripe discovery as they roved and plucked, firm and demanding, yet infinitely sweet. Captivated, she was utterly at his mercy as he coaxed and played, using a mixture of slow, sweet, heady persuasion she had no desire to resist.

Her fingers uncurled to lie relaxed in her lap as a mellow buzz began to cloud her brain. Her head feeling suddenly too heavy for her neck, she was relieved that Kit held her steady in his grasp. Dizzy and dreamy, the room spun around her in a way that reminded her of the time years before when she had drunk too much wine and ended up having to be helped upstairs to fall delirious into her bed.

Modulating the pressure and the angle of his kiss, he teased and cajoled, subtly urging her to respond. "Kiss me back," he said, pausing long enough to murmur the command against her lips.

Her brows furrowed. "How?"

"Follow my lead. Do what I do and you'll understand."

At first she didn't, confused as she attempted to obey his instructions. Remembering his words about parting her lips, she opened her mouth a fraction wider in hopes it would satisfy him. She jolted a second later when he soughed a warm exhalation directly into her mouth.

Her toes curled inside her slippers, and her entire body flashed hot. She closed her eyes and pressed her lips harder against his, driven by an instinct she hadn't known she possessed.

His lips curved against hers as he smiled, wordlessly encouraging her to proceed.

In easy, gentle circles, he rubbed his thumb against the base of her skull. A whimper escaped her, followed by a delicate trembling that threatened to combust her already enflamed senses. She whimpered again and deepened their kiss, slanting her lips across his, greedy and hungering, wanting more and knowing instinctively that she would never, ever get enough of his captivating embrace.

This time Kit was the one to groan, the one to press his mouth harder and more passionately against hers.

She jolted when the hot, wet tip of his tongue edged out, skimming across the delicate, inner flesh of her mouth. Her lips throbbed at the contact, her pulse skipping as fast and hard as a stone across the glassy surface of a pond.

She broke away on a gasp. "Oh, my!"

His gaze roved over her heated features, his breath coming in shallow drafts. "Too much? Shall we stop?"

She trembled then shook her head. "No."

"Perhaps we've gone far enough."

"No."

For an instant, he looked as if he was about to change his mind regardless, and put a hasty end to their lesson. Then she licked her lips.

The gesture was innocent but his response was not as his gaze darted downward to settle upon her damp mouth. Before she had time to consider his reaction, he groaned and captured her lips again.

Bold and brash, he plunged both of them deep. Eyelids fluttering, she gasped again at the renewed touch of his tongue on her mouth. Catching her lower lip between his teeth, he nibbled for a long moment before giving a gentle tug that coaxed her mouth wide.

Then his tongue stroked inside, astonishing her anew. Her senses spun as he teased and tantalized, exploring the contours of her mouth with an intimacy that left her blissfully shaken. Over teeth and tongue he roved, across the tender flesh of one inner cheek before moving on to trace the other.

She trembled as he pulled slightly away. "All right?" he asked.

"Mmm-hmm," she murmured, half-dazed. "You taste like shortbread."

He smiled and gave her a pair of quick, openmouthed kisses. "And you taste like honey."

"I haven't eaten any honey."

"Then I guess you're just naturally sweet."

Before she had time to think about the remark, he kissed her again, tangling his tongue with hers in a powerful mating. In and out went his tongue. And in and out again, withdrawing after each foray until she realized he wanted her to come after him, to thrust her tongue into his mouth.

She quivered at the notion, her belly clenching in a low ache. Inside he came again, plundering and pleasuring until she scarcely had breath left in her lungs. When he withdrew again, she gathered the courage to follow, chasing his tongue, skimming past his teeth and forging deeper.

Time spun away after that as she lost herself to the sensations, lost herself to everything but Kit and the exquisite ecstasy of his kisses.

Restlessly she shifted her legs, thighs brushing against his thighs. She forgot where her mouth ended and his began as they tangled lips and tongues in an explosive coupling that threatened to blow the top off her head. She had wanted the earth to shift on its axis, and Lord above, it was shifting.

She cried out, reaching up to caress his jaw and smoothly shaven cheeks. Traveling farther, she plunged her fingers into his thick hair and pulled him closer.

He moaned and toppled her backward into the sea of plump sofa cushions at her back, following her down. Sliding his hand between their bodies, he cupped her breast, massaging her pliant female flesh. Her nipple tightened under his questing thumb.

A door slammed somewhere inside the house.

Kit stiffened against her and drew away, putting an abrupt end to their kiss.

She blinked in confused lassitude. "Kit?"

"Lesson's over," he said, his voice harsh and throaty as he sat up.

Lesson? She had forgotten all about their kisses being a lesson.

"Sit up," he ordered. "And tidy your hair."

"Oh." Deciding not to take offense at his brusque tone, she struggled upward out of the nest of pillows, then brushed her fingers through her curls. "Better?"

He cast her a hard look, then reached out and tugged a couple locks into place. "You'll do. Thank God your hair is short. Otherwise . . ." He left the rest unsaid.

She reached toward him, but he jumped off the couch and began to pace. "That last . . . well, that went a bit further than I originally planned. My apologies, Eliza."

Apologies? Was he already regretting what had passed between them, before their bodies even had a chance to cool?

"Kissing is like that sometimes," he explained.

"Is it?" A sick sensation of dread twisted in her stomach.

"Yes. It's easy to get carried away, to lose oneself in the moment."

"I see."

"Do you? I hope so, because there is no need for any awkwardness to exist between us in future. What we did amounted to no more than an exercise in human physicality. You wanted to know how to kiss and I showed you. Apart from that, it doesn't mean a thing."

Does it not? she mused, sorrow crystallizing like ice shards in her blood. Maybe it meant nothing to him, but it had certainly meant something to her.

Kit folded his arms over his chest. "You were curious and now you needn't be any longer. Though for your sake I suggest you not put your advanced knowledge to use anytime soon."

Her jaw stiffened. "So you don't think I ought to improve my technique this Season by letting interesting men lure me off behind the shrubbery?"

A fierce scowl ruffled his eyebrows. "Certainly not!"

"I don't see why not. You do."

"Do what?"

"Lead girls behind the shrubbery. I have seen you do so numerous times over the years, so I suppose that is where you come by your obvious experience in the seductive arts. Today's lesson, I realize, was not the first you have ever given."

His scowl grew more fearsome, if that was possible. "What I do, or do not do, with girls behind garden shrubs is none of your concern."

She felt his rebuff like a slap. "No more than what I choose to do with gentlemen is any concern of yours."

She glanced down, afraid of the anguish he might see in her eyes. "Well, thank you for a most enlightening instruction. There is a book I bought at Hatchard's the other day that I have been longing to begin, so if we are through . . ."

His face grew shuttered. "Yes, we are through."

She rose to her feet, smoothed her dress into place, then made for the door.

"Eliza?"

She stopped, her hand on the knob, her heart kicking into a faster rhythm. "Yes?"

"Just be careful, whatever you do. Don't let yourself get hurt."

"Pray do not fear," she said in a breezy tone. "I am never anything less than careful."

As for not getting hurt, his warning came far, far too late for that.

Chapter Twelve

Kit tossed back the last of the champagne inside his flute glass and watched Eliza whirl by in the arms of her latest dance partner.

When they'd arrived at the Lymondhams' rout nearly two hours ago, she had been apprehensive.

What if I forget how to make small talk? she had whispered to him in strangled tones as he assisted her from the ducal coach.

What if all the tips and techniques, everything you have taught me over the past weeks, flies straight out of my head? she demanded of him as he had escorted her up the main staircase, Adrian and Violet in the lead.

What if—a long, horrified pause—*no one asks me to dance and I begin this Season the way I began all the others—as a neglected wallflower?*

But she need not have worried.

For one thing, she looked lovely—vibrant in a gown of rich rose satin that put color in her cheeks and brightened her eyes to a silvery shade that appeared anything but plain. Her dark curls bounced around her face in a pert come-hither, drawing more than one interested male glance.

The four of them had barely left the receiving line and their brief conversations with their hosts when a gentleman approached to solicit Eliza's hand for the first dance.

For a long moment, she had looked like a doe caught in a hunter's sight. Flicking a nervous glance toward Kit, she had sought his support and his silent approval of the man—a perfectly respectable baronet's son—which he gave with a barely perceptible nod. Only then did she find her voice and accept the offer with gracious alacrity.

The dance went well, though Kit played witness to a great deal of murmured speculation and any number of surprised stares in Eliza's direction as he strolled casually around the ballroom. Many could barely reconcile her changed appearance, while others could whisper of nothing but the extent of Eliza's increased fortune. Kit did his best to dismiss such comments, knowing people would talk regardless of anything he said or did.

At the conclusion of the set, the baronet's son returned Eliza to Violet's side and departed with a polite bow. Kit was wondering if he ought to seek out a fresh partner for her in case one didn't turn up, when his friend, Lord Vickery, appeared at Eliza's side and made her a bow.

Kit hurried forward to intercept the pair, reading the mischievous twinkle in the other man's familiar gaze, having seen it more than a time or two across the card table. But it was too late, Vickery and Eliza were already strolling onto the dance floor.

A toast of the Ton and a wag with a cutting edge to his tongue, Vickery would shred Eliza for sure. Yet, less than a full minute into the dance, Vickery tossed his head back in great good humor, and not, Kit was relieved to see, at Eliza's expense. Kit watched as Eliza slowly captivated his friend, Vickery returning with Eliza's hand clasped over his arm as if the man did not wish to part with her.

She was being whisked away by yet another gentleman when Vickery stopped and slapped Kit on the shoulder. "I owe you a case of my best French champagne, old fellow."

"Oh, what for?"

"For Miss Hammond, of course. I didn't think it could be done, but you truly are a miracle worker. Not only has she turned pretty in ways I would never have imagined, but she is a delight. Told me some story about the duchess's big dog that was as amusing as anything I have ever heard. The real Eliza Hammond has obviously been hiding, and you, clever boy, have found the key to set her free."

Is that what I have done? Kit mused. *Set Eliza free? Or has she done that for herself?*

If she had changed since their lessons began, it was only because she had brought those qualities out of herself. Perhaps he had helped buoy her deflated confidence, beaten down by years of neglect, but it was her own depth of spirit that had helped her lead the way, allowing the woman inside to flourish and blossom like a radiant flower finally given sunshine and warmth.

He watched her swing by in yet another man's arms, her face alive with merriment.

Deuced take it, he thought, when *had* Eliza turned so pretty? For that matter, when had she become so desirable?

Two days had passed since their interlude in the study and still he could not get their kisses out of his mind. Nor could he seem to rid himself of the taste and scent of her that lingered in his senses like a never-ending embrace. Her kisses may have been untutored at the start, but she had caught on to the game quickly enough. Caught on and joined in with an aptitude that made mockery of her quiet exterior.

Even now he could remember how warm and soft her lips had felt beneath his. How sleek and delicious the texture of her mouth and tongue. How his blood had beaten hot and strong, swimming in his head until he'd nearly lost all sense of propriety.

Though, to be perfectly honest, there had been nothing at all proper in what they had been doing. He should have refused her suggestion from the start. What madness had possessed him, agreeing to teach her how to kiss?

Kit reached for another glass of champagne, drank a long draught that bubbled over his tongue and eased the uncommon dryness from his throat.

Well, his and Eliza's moment of mutual insanity was over, he thought, never to be repeated again. She was his friend—Violet's friend, for God's sake—more like a little sister really than a woman. Though he'd certainly never felt the urge to play a game of tonsil tennis with Violet, nor could his behavior toward Eliza be construed as anything remotely in the nature of a brotherly act.

But their lessons were finished now, leaving both of them free to continue on with their separate lives. Of course, he would keep a watchful eye open throughout the Season, always on the lookout for unscrupulous suitors—fortune hunters, rakes and rogues—to make sure Eliza came to no harm. But otherwise he felt confident she now possessed the necessary skills to pursue her own successful husband hunt.

So why did the knowledge lie like a greasy lump inside his belly?

She was doing beautifully tonight, surpassing even his most hopeful expectations as she held her own among the Ton's haughty elite.

He should be thrilled for her. He *was* thrilled for her.

At least he would be, he assured himself, once he had a chance to relax and enjoy the party. With that thought in mind, he put down his glass and set off in search of an amiable dance partner. The prettier, the better, he decided.

He was in a much improved humor two rounds of dancing later. He returned the beauteous Miss Quigby to her doting mama—secretly relieved to escape the debutante's proclivity for giggling—then turned on his heel to scan the crowd for Eliza.

He frowned when he found her seated in a chair along the periphery of the room, not far from a cluster of matrons. Perhaps the evening wasn't going as well as he had imagined, after all.

He crossed the room, nodding but not pausing to talk to the mix of friends who eagerly waved him in their direction as he passed.

"Eliza, what are you doing over here?" he questioned without preamble as he slid into the chair next to her.

Her chin came up, an easy smile on her lips. "Oh, Kit, I thought you were dancing. I saw you out on the floor not long ago with a very lively-looking brunette."

"Miss Quigby, yes," he said, instantly dismissing the other girl. "Why aren't you dancing?"

"Oh, I have been. Too much, actually, which is why I decided to take a brief respite from the festivities." She stuck out her feet and wiggled the toes of her satin slippers. "My feet are not used to all this exercise, I have discovered."

Tension eased from his shoulders. "So you are not feeling neglected?"

"Not at all. The evening has been splendid so far. People have been much more receptive to the new me than I had anticipated. And a few old acquaintances have actually had the grace to look embarrassed at not immediately recognizing me, as well as for their less than kind treatment of me in the past. Terrible to admit, but I have rather been enjoying their discomfiture."

Kit grinned. "Well, seems to me you are entitled to your pleasure, however you may come by it. Now, what do you say we take a turn around the floor, if your feet are sufficiently rested? We haven't danced yet tonight, you and I. And since this next set is the supper dance, we can share a meal. I know just the table—"

"Sorry, Winter," a smooth, familiar voice interrupted, "but the lady has already promised the supper dance to me."

Kit glanced up. "Brevard, I didn't realize you were here this evening."

"Arrived a bit late. My little sister is taken ill with a dreadful cold, so I wanted to make sure she was well settled before I left the house. I nearly decided not to come, but Franny wouldn't hear a word of it. Shooed me on my way, blowing her poor little red nose all the while." Brevard's chin dipped in sympathy.

"Is that not thoughtful of Lord Brevard, to care so much for his sister?" Eliza said, sending the viscount a warm smile.

If he cares so bloody much, then he ought to have stayed home, Kit thought to himself.

Kit stood, one of his gloved hands curled into a loose fist at his hip. He forced a smile. "So how is young Franny? She was scarcely more than a baby when last we met."

"She's all grown up now or so she thinks. Eighteen and ready to make her come-out. She would have been here tonight if not for her illness. She was quite distraught to be missing all the fun. I have been assigned the task of providing a full rendering of events over tomorrow's breakfast."

"I am sure you will do an admirable job, my lord," Eliza said. "Only do not forget to take note of the ladies' gowns. Likely your sister will want to know what colors and styles were most in vogue tonight."

Eliza had learned her lessons well, Kit thought, since even a month ago she would not have thought to consider fashions at all. Of course, a month ago she wouldn't have been conversing so easily either. A moment of pride washed through him; he felt profoundly pleased by her accomplishment.

Then Kit forgot all about such matters as Brevard turned his blue gaze upon Eliza, adding a blinding flash of his straight white teeth. "Thank you for a most excellent suggestion, Miss Hammond," Brevard said. "I shall have no difficulty remembering how to describe your lovely raiment, or the even more lovely lady who is wearing it."

Kit restrained the urge to glower.

Eliza dipped her head at the compliment. "You are too kind, my lord. Pray be so good as to give my regards to your sister and wish her a speedy recovery."

"I shall. She will be most cheered, and sorry not to have made your acquaintance."

"We will meet when she is feeling better. I look forward to the day."

"As will she. But now, if my ears do not deceive me, I believe the next set is forming."

Brevard was right, Kit saw, as he noticed the small quartet of musicians resume their seats across the room and play a few practice notes on their instruments in preparation for the next song.

Brevard extended his arm to Eliza.

She rose and laid her hand on top of his sleeve.

"Winter." Brevard nodded at Kit.

Eliza sent Kit a well-contented smile. "Lord Christopher." Then she let the viscount lead her away.

Lord Christopher?

What in the blazes was that? She hadn't called him by that stuffy name in weeks. But in company he supposed the formality was best.

They could no longer address each other as Kit and Eliza, not in public anyway. A lot of things would be different between them now. He should be glad, he told himself. His mentoring duties were done.

So why had the enjoyment suddenly gone out of the evening?

Not wanting to consider the why, he strode out of the ballroom and made his way to the card parlor, no longer at all in the mood to dance.

"Well, you must be floating on a cloud."

From her place on the coach seat next to Violet, Eliza peered through the night-darkened interior at her friend, Adrian and Kit taking up the seat opposite.

"Now that you say it, I believe that I am," Eliza agreed in an amazed sort of wonder.

"As well you should be." Violet reached over and patted Eliza's hand. "You were brilliant tonight, *the* talk of the evening, and I mean that in the very best sort of way. Everyone was commenting on how attractive you look and how you have put off your shyness and come out of your shell. And you danced nearly every dance, the gentlemen could not stay away."

"It was a lovely evening."

More than that, it was the best party Eliza had ever attended, with the possible exception of that memorable night long ago when Kit had danced with her, then afterward compelled his friends to do the same. But she had needed no assistance tonight from Kit, at least not in that regard, a more than gratifying number of gentlemen soliciting her hand, apparently of their own volition.

She had arrived at tonight's entertainment not knowing what to expect, quaking in fear that she might muddle up everything and inaugurate yet another dismal failure of a Season. But more quickly than she could have imagined, she found herself singled out by one attentive gentleman after another. The experience had been quite novel, the impact of which was even now still sinking in.

"And you danced twice with Lord Maplewood," Violet continued. "He is a few years your senior and a widower but a pleasant man all the same."

"Yes, he was very nice. We spent most of the time discussing plays. He is an avid theatergoer with a keen knowledge of Shakespeare. I quite enjoyed myself."

"And I saw you with Mr. Carstairs and Lord Vickery and, of course, Viscount Brevard, who claimed you for the supper dance. Quite a few young ladies had their noses out of joint over that. Jeannette says Brevard is the catch of the Season, a very elusive catch, I am given to understand. At the risk of sounding like my mama, I hear he is worth twenty thousand a year, so there is no need to fear his interest in you has anything to do with your wealth."

Eliza traced a gloved finger over her pelisse. "I suspect he was only being gallant and has no particular regard for me."

"Well, we shall see. But particular or not, I must admit one cannot complain of his company, he is so very dashing and handsome."

"And what are you doing noticing dashing, handsome men, madam?" Adrian questioned out of the darkness opposite. "Might I remind you, you are a married woman."

"Hmm, but not a blind one. And despite my scholarly

proclivities, I have long admired the turn of a handsome male face. Why do you think I fell in love with you?"

Adrian snorted in obvious good humor and settled deeper into his seat.

"Kit, you have been rather quiet," Violet prodded. "What do you think of Eliza's grand evening?"

He cleared his throat. "Me? Oh, I agree, the evening was an obvious triumph. Eliza did a splendid job and surpassed all of my expectations. As her mentor, or former mentor now that her lessons are finished, I must say she has been an apt and most attentive pupil, well deserving of praise. You were marvelous tonight, Eliza."

"Due to your tutelage."

He waved off her compliment. "No, no, it was all you. And because of your success, I am sure you shall have no trouble finding a most excellent husband. The house will likely smell like a florist's shop come morning, crammed with a veritable garden of bouquets from all your many admirers. Before you know it, you'll have a ring on your finger and we'll all be cheering and waving you off on your honeymoon trip. What a glorious day that will be, don't you think? Your wedding day, the event Violet's entire scheme was designed to achieve."

"Yes, of course," Eliza said softly, glad for the coach's concealing shadows so none of them could see her expression.

Marriage and a husband was exactly what she wanted, she reminded herself, just as Kit said. But did he have to sound so ebulliently excited about it? Did he wish to see her settled and out of his life so very badly?

The pleasant little glow she'd been hugging to herself since leaving the party evaporated like a mist caught beneath the rays of a merciless sun. She folded her hands and listened to the clack of the coach wheels on the street, the cry of a night watchman calling out the time.

"Here we are," Kit announced in a pleased tone when they arrived at Raeburn House a couple minutes later. Kit leapt down first, then Adrian, who turned to assist Eliza and Violet from the coach.

"Did you ask François to set something out for us, Vi?" Kit asked as the four of them crossed into the house. "Or shall I have to go down to the kitchen and rattle around to see what I can scrounge out of the larder?"

"You know you are forbidden to go anywhere near the kitchen." Violet drew off her gloves and handed her evening mantle to a footman. "François nearly gave his notice the last time you decided to *rattle around* in his domain, and good French chefs are far too valuable to risk offending. I know fully a dozen households, including one of the royal dukes, who would snap him up in an instant. But in deference to you and your endless appetite, I left instructions for a light repast to be served in the drawing room."

"You are the best, Violet." Kit winked at her. "So who else could do with a snack?"

"I wouldn't mind a brandy," Adrian said, heading for the stairs.

"Nothing for me." Violet lifted her skirts and followed in her husband's wake. "I need to go check on Georgianna since she is likely the one who really is in need of a meal."

Eliza walked up the stairs after Kit, both of them pausing when they reached the landing. Almost as an afterthought, he turned to her. "Eliza? Will you join us?"

A lump formed in her throat and she shook her head. "It has been a long, exciting night. I think I had best seek my rest."

"Good night, then." For a moment he hesitated as if

he was about to say something more. Instead he closed his mouth and kept it closed. Bouncing on his heels, his impatience to be gone was more than apparent.

"Yes, good night," she said.

Her footsteps heavy and listless, she made her way to her bedchamber.

Chapter Thirteen

Raucous laughter flowed out of the downstairs salon.

"What is all that racket?" Kit asked March as he came through the Raeburn House front door. He passed his hat and gloves to the majordomo as another shout of hilarity split the air.

"Afternoon callers for Miss Eliza, my lord. Mostly gentlemen callers."

Kit digested the news. *"Hmmph."*

"His Grace had much the same reaction and departed for his club about half an hour past. Mentioned something about wanting to be able to hear himself think."

Kit smiled faintly. "So how long have they all been here?"

"There has been a steady stream of visitors in and out of the house since just past nuncheon." March paused. "If you don't mind my saying, it must be most gratifying, my lord, to see Miss Eliza prospering so well this Season. The staff and I couldn't help but be aware of your lessons and how hard Miss Eliza worked. We are all so pleased for her, and for your lordship as well. You must be delighted."

Kit forced away a frown. "Yes, of course, very delighted."

Seconds later, a tall man in a dark blue coat strode out of the salon, his footsteps sounding on the marble floor.

Kit's eyebrows rose upward. "Vickery? What are you doing here?"

The man looked up, a faint expression of chagrin on his face. "Winter. Have you just returned from the Raycroft sale?"

"Yes, just." Kit crossed his arms. "I had rather thought to find you there as well. An impressive selection of prime horseflesh on the auction block, a shame you missed it."

"True, but I've a full stable already, and I had . . . um, other plans for the day."

So he could see. How long had this been going on? Vickery paying court to Eliza Hammond? To think the man had once sat across from him and verbally sliced Eliza to shreds. Would she turn Vickery away if she knew?

"Well, good to see you," Vickery said. "I suppose we might bump into each other again tomorrow since I am promised to take Miss Hammond driving in my high-perch phaeton."

Now the man was taking her driving. How serious was this?

Kit repressed the urge to scowl. "See to it you don't drive so fast she falls out when you round a sharp corner."

Vickery stared at him for a long moment, then smiled, assuming Kit spoke in jest. "*Ha-ha,* don't worry, she'll be safe as a baby in a cradle."

"Cradles have been known to tip too."

"This one won't. She will be fine. I'll make sure."

"I trust you will."

Vickery flashed him an uncertain half smile then gratefully accepted his hat from March. He jammed it on his head and went on his way with a nod.

Before March could close the door behind him, another gentleman arrived.

"Hello, March," Viscount Lancelot Brevard greeted with obvious familiarity. "How are you this fine afternoon?"

"Very well, my lord. And yourself?"

"Splendid."

"Miss Hammond is in the salon, my lord," March volunteered, clearly aware of the purpose of the viscount's visit.

Brevard thanked the servant, then turned his blond head. His eyes flashed. "Winter. Didn't see you standing there."

Kit thrust his hands into his trouser pockets. "Didn't realize I was lurking."

Brevard chuckled. "Are you about to go in?" More laughter issued from the salon. "Sounds as though everyone is having a lively time."

"So it would appear. But no, I am on my way to my rooms." He flicked a finger across the lapel of his coat. "Plans tonight."

"Ah, then we won't see you at the opera, I suppose."

"We?"

"Yes, Miss Hammond has agreed to accompany my sister and me there this evening. I have come to apprise her of all the last-minute details."

"Don't much care for the opera as a general rule."

"Well, yes, it can be an acquired taste." Brevard rested a set of knuckles against one hip. "Sorry to have missed you the other day at Gentleman Jackson's. You have quite the reputation there. Hear you pummeled yet another of Jackson's best."

Kit inclined his head. "I keep my hand in the game."

"We must have a match one of these mornings," Brevard invited with a cheerful grin.

"Indeed. Sounds like fun."

"Well, best go make my bow to the ladies. Good day to you, Winter."

"Good day."

Brevard strolled into the salon, Eliza's gently melodic greeting ringing out above the fray.

So she was going to the opera tonight with Brevard? He hadn't even realized. Actually, he no longer knew a great deal about her daily schedule, not as he once had done. In the three weeks since the Lymondhams' ball and her reentrance into Society, their lives had gradually drifted apart.

For one thing, their lessons were done—no more mornings of instruction and practice conversations. Neither did they ride together in the mornings, Eliza taking Cassiopeia out in the afternoon now to promenade in the park. Caught up in the social whirl of constant balls and parties, she had taken up the Town habit of sleeping late and frequently taking breakfast in her room. Often, he caught glimpses of her at various entertainments, but she was always surrounded by her small but dedicated coterie of admirers, so he left her to them and did not interfere.

Of course, he still kept watch over her. When a rake with a less than stellar reputation at both the gaming table and with the ladies began to insinuate himself into Eliza's circle, Kit had quietly taken the man aside and let him know his overtures were not welcome.

In fact, Kit's fierce protectiveness of Eliza had not gone unnoticed, a few of his cronies ribbing him about his new little "sister" until they realized he was not amused and decided it might be safer to keep their quips to themselves.

Kit stared at the door to the salon. For a long moment, he considered following Brevard inside. Instead he turned on his heel and strode across to the staircase, racing upward two steps at a time. He had no interest, absolutely none, in watching Eliza flirt and flutter with her beaux. For a woman who used to be so timid she would barely dare to meet a fellow's gaze, she had certainly taken to her new role of charming ingenue with alacrity, he sniffed. Some days he barely recognized her, wondering where the sweet, shy girl he'd once known had gone.

But hadn't that been the whole point of their lessons—to make the old Eliza disappear in favor of the newer, bolder version? He ought to be delighted with her, as well as for her.

Instead he felt . . . hell, he didn't know what he felt anymore. All he knew for certain was that he missed her.

He stopped, hand gripped tightly around the banister.

Missed her? Missed quiet, reticent, academically minded Eliza Hammond, for whom he'd once held so little regard that years earlier Violet had practically pushed him out onto the dance floor in order to get him to stand up with her?

But as he'd only just seconds ago reminded himself, Eliza was no longer particularly quiet nor reticent, and he had long since gotten over any reluctance to lead her into a dance. Nor did he mind her company. In point of fact, he'd come to enjoy it, rather a lot, he realized.

Her soft smiles and intelligent observations. Her laughter and the deliberate way she would let a sentence hang before delivering the choicest part. Her gentle manners and occasional uncertainty, looking to him for guidance with those dove-hued eyes before rousing her own kind of bravery from within. When she spoke, it was with interesting purpose. When she fell silent . . . well, he no longer found her silences awkward, but restful, like a peaceful breeze on a warm, sunny day.

And her kisses. His loins tightened at the memory of her kisses. He shook his head and continued up the stairs. He had no time for such thoughts. No time for missing her either. Eliza Hammond was destined for a life that did not include him, except perhaps as an occasional friend.

The idea brought a frown to his face. No, he mused, he definitely did not want her for a friend. What then did he want her for?

An amour?

He scowled at how much he liked the outrageous thought. He could imagine it. How thrilling it would be to lead her off for further lessons, ones that went beyond a few heated kisses. But such a course was fraught with peril and temptation, forbidden temptation the likes of which a man such as him would do well to steer clear. Best, he decided, to do absolutely nothing. Besides, he wouldn't miss her for long. By next week these aberrant feelings would have faded like an unwanted suntan.

A volley of laughter carried faintly out of the downstairs salon.

He growled under his breath and stalked to his room. With uncharacteristic temper, he slammed the door hard behind him.

"Thank you for a lovely dance, my lord."

Eliza opened her fan and waved it slowly in front of her face as Lord Maplewood escorted her off the dance floor. Slight as it was, the air came as a refreshing relief against her overwarm cheeks, the ballroom far too close and crowded tonight.

Apparently noticing her discomfort, Maplewood dipped his salt-and-pepper head her way. "Would you care for a glass of punch, Miss Hammond?"

She raised her gaze to his. "Oh, I shouldn't wish to put you to any trouble."

"It is no trouble. No trouble at all." He gave a gentle smile, then removed her hand from his arm with infinite care. "Wait here and I shall be back in a thrice."

She stifled a sigh as she watched him disappear into the throng of milling partygoers, wishing that instead of punch, she might have asked to have the Raeburn carriage brought round so she could return home. But there were another few hours remaining before she could hope to make her excuses. After all, she was here to have fun, dance, converse and make merry until the wee hours of the morning.

Not that she was miserable or having a dreadful time—quite the contrary. Her usual group of admirers had been keeping her well entertained, whirling her around the floor, then regaling her during the intervals with funny stories and bits of poetry designed to make her laugh and smile. But that was before she had seen Kit stroll by, a willowy redhead in a diaphanous, low-cut emerald green gown parading on his arm.

The Dowager Marchioness of Pynchon, if she wasn't mistaken, a young, beautiful widow who wasn't more than a year older than Kit. Eliza's stomach had given a sick squeeze, as she was unable to help but notice Kit and the widow flirt and cavort.

Was she his mistress? Did Kit caress her? Stroke his hands over her while he devoured her mouth with clever kisses that turned her knees as weak and wobbly as a storm-tossed rowboat? Did they make love, entwine their naked bodies together in one of the postures Eliza had glimpsed between the pages of the naughty little green book? Well, whatever Kit and his widow did or did not do, it made no matter to her.

In the days following their never-to-be-forgotten kissing lesson—at least never to be forgotten by her—a small, idiotic part of Eliza had hoped Kit would change his mind about their interlude and seek her out. Show her in words—or better yet in deed—that he had been as moved by their passionate encounter as she. But he had made no such overtures, his behavior toward her as friendly—and indifferent—as ever. Apparently he was relieved to be done with his duty now that she was successfully relaunched into Society. Glad that he was no longer forced to seek out her company.

But to her great surprise, she did find herself in demand, with other eligible gentlemen seeking her out in a way that continued to amaze her even now, a full month into the Season. All that remained was to see which of her suitors, if any of them, offered for her hand in marriage. And more to the point, to which one she would say yes.

She glanced again at Kit and the widow, relieved when Lord Maplewood returned with her glass of punch. She thanked him, then sipped the almond-flavored concoction, fanning her cheeks while she listened to him tell her about his five-year-old daughter, whom he quite clearly adored.

At the end of the interval, Lord Brevard appeared at her elbow. "Good evening, Miss Hammond. You look lovely as a rose tonight, if I may be so bold." He made her an elegant bow then showered her with a dazzling smile that would have made a dead woman's heart tremble in her breast.

Eliza discovered she was no exception.

Ever polite, he nodded to Maplewood. "My lord. How are you enjoying the ball?"

After exchanging a few more pleasantries, Lord Maplewood bowed to them and withdrew to seek out his next partner.

Brevard extended his arm. "Shall we take to the floor? The next is a quadrille, I believe."

"My lord, would you mind terribly if we did not dance but went for a stroll instead? The room is so close and warm tonight."

"It is, is it not?" he agreed, sharing a conspiratorial grin. "A squeeze, as they say. Why do we not go out into the garden? I believe our hostess is known for her flowers, though it may yet be too early in the season to find any roses in bloom."

"Blooming roses or not, a walk through the garden sounds quite refreshing."

Setting her hand onto his sleeve of tailored black superfine, she strolled with him toward the doors that led down into the gardens beyond. A few night creatures hummed and croaked, playing a tune quite different from the lively one now coming from the ballroom.

A light breeze stirred her skirts, easing some of the unpleasant warmth from her skin. Eliza breathed deeply, glad to be out of the crowd, if only for a few minutes.

"Better?" Brevard inquired, their shoes crunching lightly against the pebbled pathway.

"Very much so. I suppose I must seem a terrible goose for wishing to escape the festivities."

"Not at all. Some balls are best taken in small doses."

They walked in silence for a few moments.

"I wanted to thank you again for escorting me to the opera last week," Eliza said. "I so enjoyed it, the wonderful costumes and the glorious singers. It was a truly delightful evening."

He angled his head, showered her with another smile. "For me as well."

"And your sister is such a pleasant girl. I saw her earlier this evening just after I arrived. We had a most excellent conversation about art."

"Oh, Franny loves art. If you let her, she'll talk your ear off on the subject. Mr. Turner is one of her favorites, so unless you wish to hear everything there is to know about the man and his painting, I warn you to say nothing."

He grinned and Eliza chuckled.

"In fact," the viscount continued, "Franny has just wrung a promise out of me to take her to the opening of the summer exhibition at the Royal Academy. Would you like to accompany us? You would make a perfect addition to our party."

She paused for moment, struck once more by his asking her to join him and his family on an outing. For most men, such an invitation might be construed as romantic interest. But he couldn't be seriously courting her, she thought, not a man like Viscount Brevard. He could have any woman of his choosing. He couldn't want her. She was sure he was only being kind.

"Yes," she said, "that sounds like a most entertaining afternoon. I should be glad to accept."

"Good." He paused and set his gloved hand atop hers where it rested on his sleeve. "Now, has the air grown too chilly for you, or shall we stroll a bit more?"

"The air seems fine to me. Let us stroll."

They walked deeper into the garden, the music playing dimly, the shadows heavy where the vegetation grew thick and leafy. Eliza caught a hint of lilac in the air, enjoying the sugary sweetness of its perfume.

Brevard drew her to a halt. "Have I told you how beautiful you look tonight?"

"I appreciate the compliment, my lord, but you need not flatter me. I know I am not beautiful."

"You do yourself a grave injustice, Miss Hammond, but then, you obviously cannot see yourself as I do."

"I suppose not. Nevertheless, you are very kind, my lord."

"No such thing. Friends do not lie, and I like to think

we know each other well enough now to consider ourselves friends?"

She shared a genial smile. "Indeed, yes."

"Then, *friend,* might I be permitted to call you by
your given name? Eliza?"

She considered his request. "I can see no harm. Yes, of
course you may."

"And you must call me Lance."

His voice floated deep and debonair on the night
breeze. She thought of another person, another "friend"
blessed with an equally compelling voice and wondered
at her strong reaction to both men.

She had told Kit she wanted comparison, although at
the time her protestations had been nothing more than
a ruse designed to invite his embrace. Yet here she was
standing in a shadowed garden with a devastatingly
handsome man. Given that, perhaps she ought to experiment, make good on her as yet unfulfilled declaration to
spread her wings and test her new boundaries.

A faint shiver ran through her at the idea.

"You *are* cold," he accused gently. "Here, let me take
you back inside."

She turned to face him. "In a minute. First, I would
ask you a question."

He waited, listening.

She drew on every ounce of her nerve before gazing
upward into his brilliant blue eyes. "Lance, would you
kiss me?"

She could read his surprise, one of his golden brows
winging skyward. Then he smiled. "If you would like it,
Eliza."

"I would like to see *if* I like it."

He gave a slow, leonine smile. "Then let us give it a
try."

She drew in a preparatory breath, slowly releasing it as Lance drew her into his arms.

How would his kiss feel? she wondered. Surely different from Kit's, but would it be better or worse?

He bent his head, joining their mouths an instant later. She closed her eyes and allowed herself to relax into the sensation. *Nice,* she thought, definitely pleasant, his lips warm and inviting as they moved against hers in confident certainty. Sensing her willingness, he deepened the embrace, demanding more.

She kissed him back, parting her lips as she gave herself fully over to his touch. Suddenly she wanted passion and heat, wanted him to make her mind melt with desire, wanted him to burn clean the memory of everything she had ever felt for Kit Winter.

She poured herself into the embrace in a kind of fragile desperation. Her heart sped faster, her skin growing warmer in spite of the cool air. But her mind remained completely, and all too indisputably, her own. Lance's kiss was skilled and gratifying, and she was sure most women would by now be rendered half senseless by the power of his expert touch. His kisses were lovely, except for one thing.

He was not Kit.

She drew away, bending her head so he could not read the sadness that must surely show in her eyes. "You must think me dreadfully forward."

"No, I think you are delightful," he said, winded as if he could not quite catch his breath.

Had their kiss done that to him?

She realized then that she ought not to have kissed him, since plainly he had liked it so much more than she. She forced herself to look up at him and smile.

* * *

From behind a conveniently placed evergreen hedge, Kit watched Brevard kiss Eliza. He held back the shout of outrage that sprang to his lips, his hands curled so tight his knuckles ached from the strain.

He'd come outside to indulge in a few quiet moments to himself, to enjoy a refreshing breath of night air. He had also wanted to put some much-needed distance between himself and Marvella Belquirt, the widowed Marchioness of Pynchon.

He should never have begun a flirtation with her, nor kissed her three nights ago in the library at the Nightons' ball. She had a reputation for taking lovers, young virile lovers who were the antithesis of everything her nearly eighty-year-old, now thankfully deceased, husband had been.

Tangled in her embrace on the library sofa, he knew she would have let him enjoy a great deal more than a few kisses and a quick grope. How easy it would have been to toss up her skirts and sheath himself inside her feminine heat, to ease all his recent frustrations and confusions over another woman, for whom he knew he ought not have any feelings at all.

But just the whisper of Eliza's name inside his mind had been enough to deflate his lust and put a halt to the passionate tryst.

So when Marvella had started flirting with him tonight, he should have put an immediate halt to her amorous overtures. But just as he had opened his mouth to send the widow away, Eliza had swung by on Brevard's arm, laughing in obvious delight at whatever the other man was saying.

And now Eliza was in Brevard's arms and they were kissing!

Testing out her newfound skills just as she had promised. Was Brevard the first or had she let others of her coterie lead her outside to partake of a small sample of her sweet lips? Had she let Maplewood kiss her? Or Vickery?

In his heart he knew she had not, would not. For all her bold talk that day in Violet's study, he knew Eliza was no tart, no tease, but a lady through to her bones. If she was kissing Brevard, it was because she must have feelings for the man.

His supposition seemed to prove true when Brevard and Eliza drew apart. As Brevard held her, she bent her head and rested it against his shirtfront as though she was trying to steady herself. Was she so affected, then, so overcome by the passion of their kiss that she needed a moment to recover?

Then she looked up at Brevard and smiled, brilliant and dazzling as if his touch had lighted up her entire world.

Kit glanced away, unable to witness another moment.

He wanted to leave but couldn't, for fear they would hear him and realize they had been observed. So he waited until they returned to the ballroom.

Only then did he emerge to make his way slowly inside.

Kit patted sweat from his face, then flipped the towel back to the waiting servant boy, who caught it with a deft hand. He accepted a glass of cooled lemon water and drank it down in a few deep-throated gulps.

Kit glanced over at his sparing partner. The big man was leaning against one wall of the boxing salon, quite literally attempting to catch his breath. He and Jackson's man had enjoyed a good, long practice this morning, warming up by going through the various kinds of footwork before transitioning on to handwork—jabs and punches and feints and counterpunches.

In what anyone would have confirmed was a surly mood had they been foolish enough to mention it, Kit had gone hard and straight into the practice. Refusing to pause between rounds, he had pressed even harder, moving from one skill to the next as if he were a man possessed.

And perhaps he was at that, Kit had mused, hoping he could use a pair of boxing gloves and a healthy opponent to beat out the demons that lurked inside him. But all he had succeeded in doing was making his body sweat and tiring out his opponent. At length, he had realized what he was doing, realized that the other man needed to stop but couldn't, not until ordered to do so by Kit or the Gentleman himself.

So Kit had stopped.

"Good round, Jones," Kit told the other man. "Go on and get cleaned up."

"Thank you, my lord." Jones gave a weary nod then made his way from the practice room.

Kit dropped down onto a smooth wooden bench and put his elbows to his knees. Despite the morning's exertions, he was barely winded, pent-up energy still buzzing like an arc of electricity through his muscles and inside his veins. He supposed he could ask Jackson to provide him with a new sparing partner to work off the rest of his excess reserves, but the salon was busy and he didn't want to make a bother of himself.

Huffing out a breath, he decided he might as well give up for the day. Perhaps he would take Mars out to one of the less crowded parks, Green Park or even Richmond Park if he was in the mood to roam farther afield, and let the horse have his head. A good gallop might be exactly what he needed to clear his mind.

He had just climbed to his feet when Brevard strode into the room. Brevard's attire, an open-necked white linen shirt and loose-fitting tan breeches, was not much different from the clothing Kit was wearing, though Kit had long since stripped off the shirt. He despised the sensation of sweat-dampened material clinging to his flesh.

Noticing him, Brevard crossed the room. "Winter, good morrow." He offered a hand.

Kit accepted and returned the handshake, quick and extra firm.

"Already went a few rounds this morning, I see," Brevard remarked, eyeing the few drops of perspiration Kit knew still clung to his skin.

Kit nodded. "Just practice, though, didn't actually get into the ring."

"I've yet to warm up, but I am looking forward to a good session."

A good session. Isn't that exactly what he'd been sitting here craving? Someone new he could pummel? A worthy opponent upon whom he could direct the force of all his excess energy? Not even the Gentleman himself would be a better adversary—especially since Kit didn't have an urge to pound the Gentleman into the floor of the boxing ring.

An image of Brevard kissing Eliza flashed through his mind. *Old friend or not,* Kit thought, *I am going to enjoy this.*

"Why don't we have that match," Kit suggested, "when you're ready, of course. You did promise me a bout, as I recall."

Brevard cast him a look of surprise. "Do you mean today?"

"Yes, today. Both of us are here. Why wait?"

"Don't know if I'd feel right challenging you today. Doesn't seem sporting somehow."

"Oh, how so?" Kit crossed his arms over his chest.

"Well, you've been here for some time already, working and practicing, while I have only just arrived. Seems that would give me an unfair advantage, coming at it fresh as I am."

"Not at all. I was on the verge of asking Jackson for a new sparing partner anyway. I wore my first one out and had to send him off to recover his breath."

Brevard considered for a long moment. "If you are sure—"

"Of course I am sure. I'm ready whenever you are."

Kit did a few limbering stretches to keep his muscles warm while Brevard went through his own routine on the other side of the room. Anticipation hummed through Kit. He was barely able to keep himself still as he allowed one of the servant boys to lace him back into his gloves. Gloves on, he smacked one hard, padded fist into the other, enjoying the sense of power as the impact reverberated up his arms.

Oh, yes, I am going to enjoy this.

Then Brevard strode across, stepped up and into the ring. Kit followed, swinging inside the boxing area with easy familiarity. This was his territory, and he knew exactly how to put it to use.

Various practice matches ceased around the room, gentlemen and commoners alike gathering to watch the bout. Towel boys hunkered low, slipping through the crowd to the front like lithe little monkeys, so they would be able to see the action. Even the retired champion himself, Gentleman Jackson, strolled over to witness the competition.

Inside the ring, Kit and Brevard touched gloves in a sportsmanlike salute, then the fight was on.

Kit danced backward, gloves instantly raised and ready. He circled slowly, studying his opponent, judging and measuring as he tried to anticipate what Brevard's opening move might be.

That move came an instant later in the form of a jab toward his ribs. Kit was prepared, tucking his arms tight to his chest to deflect the blow. He countered with a jab of his own, a sharp uppercut that connected with Brevard's jaw. He heard the smack as leather met skin, Brevard's head snapping sharply to one side.

The viscount shook his head, the blow plainly harder than he had been expecting. "I heard you had a solid punch, Winter. Now I know what they mean."

"What? That little tap?" Kit jogged a few steps in place, shook out his arms. "Ready to go again?"

Brevard pinned him with a faintly wary look. "This is a friendly match we're having, right?"

"What else would it be? Are we not both gentlemen?"

The viscount's gaze cleared. "Quite right. Let us proceed."

They moved around each other, gloves poised for action. Kit let Brevard come at him in his own time and at his own pace. When he did, Kit met his jabs, glancing blows he countered without strain. He waited, repelling two more series of jabs and counterjabs, giving the other man enough space to lure him where he wanted him.

Then suddenly the moment was right. One, two, and straight into Brevard's ribs. The viscount winced, instinctively tucking in his elbows after it was already too late. The blows must have hurt, Kit knew, but they hadn't been hard enough to break anything.

Smiling, Kit dropped back a few steps. "You need to keep up your right, my friend. You were wide open."

Brevard's eyes narrowed as he sent Kit another penetrating look. "I'll remember that." He paused. "You know, Winter, I have no wish to hurt you."

"How very decent." Kit displayed his teeth. "Guess that will make the match all that much easier for me to win."

They fell silent and circled again, trading punches and jabs at random. Brevard connected a couple times, light, glancing blows that felt more like bee stings than real hits. Then the viscount caught his rhythm and came in, landing a pair of solid punches to Kit's stomach that drove the air out of his lungs. Kit pulled back to recover, thrusting up his hands to shield his midriff before another blow could fall.

Time was called, each man given a small period to rest and take fluids. Kit toweled his face dry and eased the dryness from his mouth with a couple swallows of lemon water. His breath and strength restored, he stepped again to the center of the ring, ready for another round.

He didn't wait more than a few seconds before he came at Brevard again, striking hard and fast in a series of rapid, hammering punches. Brevard reacted, attempting to protect himself and get in a punch of his own. But it was Kit who landed the successful blow, a knock that landed on the other man's cheek and nose.

A trickle of blood leaked out of Brevard's nostril. He wiped it onto his shirtsleeve.

"Sorry. Guess I got too rough," Kit said, his tone clearly unrepentant.

"This whole bout seems rough. Is there something the matter?" the viscount demanded in a low tone meant only for Kit's ears. "If I didn't know better, I would think you really are out for blood. Which coincidentally enough, you just drew."

Kit shrugged. "Don't know what you mean. Come on, Brevard. Let's fight."

The viscount shook his head. "Not until you tell me what it is we're *really* fighting about. This is more than just a practice match."

"What gave you the idea I was practicing?"

Kit came at him again, the viscount getting his gloves up a fraction of an instant before Kit would have knocked him another hard one-two in the ribs. Kit pressed on, using alternating rhythms—three punches then two then three again—thrown in unexpected groupings and at varying speeds to keep the other man off balance and squarely on the defensive.

Kit's lungs were laboring for air, his skin running slick with sweat by the time another round was called. Brevard, he saw, was no better off, skin flushed, chest heaving to catch his breath. Arm and leg muscles quivering, Kit could feel a mild weariness creeping up on him, but nothing serious, nothing he couldn't overcome, still invigorated by the competition.

Rest period over, he and Brevard converged once more in the center of the ring, calls and shouts coming from the crowd to urge the pair of them on, wagers having obviously been made.

Kit threw a combination of punches, then the viscount returned the same, neither of them doing any particular damage. When Kit drew close enough to strike, the viscount reached out and yanked him into a rib-crushing hug.

"Out with it," Brevard said into Kit's ear as they wrestled. "What's behind this ire of yours?"

"A lady," Kit spat.

"What lady?"

With a growl, Kit threw off Brevard's hold, then laid in with another couple swings.

"*Ouf.*" The viscount bent forward and curled his arms around his bruised belly.

Not wanting to risk being overheard, Kit came in close. "The lady you lured out to the garden last night."

"Oh." Brevard's blue eyes widened a second before Kit socked him with another double pummel to the gut. The viscount stumbled back but caught himself before he fell.

Shaking off the blow, Brevard came forward. "She's a friend, almost a sister to you, I know, but you've nothing about which to worry."

Kit renewed his attack.

"My intentions are strictly honorable," the viscount said, fending off Kit's punches without making much effort to counter.

"They didn't look honorable to me." Kit landed another punch.

"Well, they are. She needs time yet, but I am seriously contemplating asking her to be my wife."

"*What?*" Kit's mouth fell open, his arms sagging downward.

In some vague part of his brain, Kit saw the punch Brevard had already started to throw coming toward him, but he could do nothing to get his gloves up in time. Wide open, he took the blow straight to his face.

His head swam, pain exploding in his cheek, little spitting sparks of light floating before his eyes. He blinked and swayed, then he was falling for what seemed a very, very long time. Wooden planks shuddered under him when he finally hit the ground. He groaned, his body turning into one instantaneous ache.

"Winter, are you all right?"

He squinted upward, Brevard's concerned face spinning above him.

Deuced odd, he thought. *Why is Brevard spinning?*

Another male hand appeared in his fractured line of

sight, giving him a light smack across the undamaged side of his face.

"*Hey,* what in the bloody blue blazes?" Kit complained, trying to roll away from the abuse. It was Gentleman Jackson, Kit realized in spite of his groggy confusion.

Jackson glanced up to address the crowd. "He's fine."

A wave of murmured grumblings and exclamations floated on the air.

"*Had two quid on him.*"

"*Blast it all, first time Winter's ever gone down.*"

Brevard, his gloves now off, extended a hand to help Kit to his feet. Only then did Kit remember what the viscount had confessed just before he had knocked Kit flat.

Brevard is considering marrying Eliza?

Kit blanched and suddenly felt like retching. He shook off the feeling—a result of the blow to the head, he told himself. He swayed and gazed bleary-eyed at the viscount.

"Well, Brevard," he muttered. "Looks like you won this round."

Chapter Fourteen

For once Eliza did not have any fixed afternoon engagements. Tonight she would be attending the Fitzmarions' musicale, where assembled guests would listen to the soaring soprano voice of opera's currently reigning queen. Until then Eliza was free to do as she chose, and what she chose to do was read a book.

After sharing a late-morning visit with Violet and the children, she detoured to her bedchamber to retrieve the novel she was reading from the nightstand. About to step inside, she turned at the muffled sound of footfalls, to find Kit making his way up the hall.

"Good day," she said.

His step slowed, and he raised a hand in greeting. "Eliza."

He winced, at least she thought he winced, failing to directly meet her gaze. In fact, he seemed to be holding his head at a rather strange angle, as if there was something he did not wish her to see. When he drew close enough to pass, she got a better look at him.

"*Kit!*" she gasped. "Oh, good Lord, what has happened to you?"

Despite his obvious reluctance, he stopped and exhaled a deep gust of breath. Wincing anew, he straightened and met her gaze. "It's nothing," he mumbled.

Reaching out, she caught his chin in her hand and angled his face so she could inspect the wound. Purple as a blackberry pie and clearly painful, a livid bruise rode his right cheekbone, a small, blood-encrusted cut curled at its outer tip.

"It certainly *is* something!" she declared in anxious tones. "What on earth has befallen you?"

"Just sport, nothing serious. I dropped my guard when I ought to have kept it up."

"Fisticuffs, do you mean?"

She knew Kit enjoyed athletic pursuits, frequenting Angelo's Fencing Academy and the boxing establishment next door, the one owned by the famous Mr. Jackson.

"Exactly so," he confirmed.

Her eyebrows crinkled. "Well, it must not have been a fair fight, if this is the result."

"It was fair. Don't worry yourself over it."

"How can I not, when you are so obviously injured? You need medical attention. I'll send for the physician."

He shook his head, grimacing at the movement. "You'll do nothing of the kind. I appreciate your concern, but I won't have some quack poking and prodding me. He'll only make things worse."

She wanted to argue further, but she knew Kit well enough to realize her entreaties would prove useless. "If you won't see the doctor, then at least let me do what I can. A fomentation should help to relieve the bruise before the worst of it sets. I have a book of herbal remedies here in my room. Come in and sit down while I find the recipe."

Too concerned to worry over the proprieties of inviting Kit into her bedchamber, she caught his wide palm inside hers and drew him into her room.

"You needn't fuss," he said. "I've suffered much worse than this over the years."

She responded with a delicate snort. "If you have, then I am glad I did not have occasion to see the results. Now, sit." She pointed him toward an armchair not far from her bed.

With an obedient shrug, Kit crossed and sank onto the seat.

Hard as he might pretend his wound didn't trouble him, his face throbbed like the very devil. Restraining the urge to groan, he watched Eliza as she bustled across the serenely feminine room, which was painted in soothing shades of eggshell and blue, her destination a bookshelf that stood in one corner.

Count on Eliza Hammond, he mused, to have what amounted to a small, private library at her disposal. He smiled and instantly regretted the movement.

Silently, he observed her as she pulled out one book after another, muttering under her breath as she flipped through the pages, searching for the promised herbal potion. After a pair of minutes, she turned. "I've found a couple decoctions I believe will help but not the one I really wanted. I don't know why, but I cannot find the right book." She tapped a fingernail against a shelf and sighed.

"Maybe you left the volume out," he suggested.

Her brows furrowed in consternation. "I do have a few titles scattered around, as you can see."

And so she did, he realized, noticing a foot-high tower of books stacked on a chair near the window, and another set of volumes arranged between the legs of her nightstand.

"Mayhap it's one of these." He motioned toward the titles on the floor.

She shook her head. "Those are mostly for pleasure reading. It wouldn't be one of those."

"What about in here? Sometimes I stash notes and

such in my night-table drawers, thinking I'll remember precisely where I've put them, only to have to cudgel my brain later in search. Maybe you're like me and have only forgotten." He slid open the drawer.

Inside he found a slender volume bound in scuffed green leather. "Here's something," he said, lifting out the book. "Is this the one?"

A horrified gasp rent the air. "*No!* Put that back."

He cast a quizzical glance her way, surprised by the alarmed expression on her face, her eyes as big and round as shooting marbles. "What is the matter?"

"Nothing." She raced forward, hands outstretched. "That's not the right book."

"You're sure?" He thumbed open the title page. "*Albanino's Postures.* Could be a medical work."

"It's not, it's . . . please give it to me." Her words quavered, sounding oddly desperate.

"Why? What is it?"

Instinctively deciding to play keep-away, he lifted the volume up and out of her reach, then flipped to the center of the book. Seconds later, his mouth dropped open, his eyes widening as he stared in utter stupefaction at the illustration before him.

"Bloody Christ!"

He stared for another long minute before turning the page, only to discover another picture so lasciviously remarkable that he had to spin the book around to take in the tableau from a different angle.

"Where did you get this?" he demanded, shooting Eliza an incredulous glance.

Lobster red all the way to her hairline, Eliza parted her lips to speak, but no sound emerged. Squeezing her eyes closed, she swallowed and shook her head.

He turned another pair of pages, pausing to read one of the poems. His lips twitched. "I guess one could say

this is an educational text, just not the sort I was expecting to find in your possession."

Her eyes popped open.

"So, how does a gently bred girl like you come to have
bawdy books in her nightstand?"

"Book. There's only the one," she croaked.

"And where did you get *the one*?" He closed the
book, then waggled it in her direction.

Her cheeks flashed hotter. "I . . . um . . ."

"Yes?" he drawled encouragingly.

"I'd rather not say."

"I suspect you wouldn't, but being as I'm the curious
type, I won't be able to rest until I have a full confession
from you. So confess."

*Just where had Eliza come across the prurient collec-
tion?* he mused. Had some friend given the book to her?
And if so, what sorts of friends did she have these days?
This was the kind of book men generally passed around—
he'd seen its like in his days at Oxford—handed secretly
from one lustfully inquisitive fellow to the next. Surely
one of her suitors hadn't loaned the volume to her?

At the thought, his brows bunched into a fearsome
knot.

Eliza heaved an audible sigh. "Very well, but you
can't tell her I have it."

Her. Relief surged through him. At least the mystery
person was female. "Tell whom?"

She hesitated for another long moment. "Violet."

Surprise jolted him like a thunderbolt. "*What!* You
mean this book belongs to Violet?"

"Well, it does now, though it originally came from
Jeannette. She gave it to Violet as a gift."

"Good God."

"Jeannette thought Violet and Adrian might enjoy—"
Eliza broke off, her face flushing again, crimson as a

vine-ripened tomato. "Well, never mind what she thought. Violet refused the book, so Jeannette put it in a drawer in the drawing room and . . . well . . . um . . ."

"You took it?"

At her nod, he burst out laughing, groaning moments later at the jab of pain that slashed through his abused cheek.

Her look of embarrassment turned instantly to concern. "Oh, you're hurting, aren't you? You need that poultice and here we are jabbering away about incidentals."

He raised the thin, green volume. "I would hardly call this book *incidental*."

"Nevertheless, you need something on your poor battered face," she said, obviously eager to change the subject. "Your cheek looks even more swollen now than it was when I first saw you. L-let me go down to the kitchen to put something together."

"I told you before, I'll do fine on my own."

"N-no, sit. Wait. Please." She raced across to the bookshelf and gathered up one of the books on herbs. Looking in a great hurry to be gone, she moved toward the door. As she passed him, her gaze flickered uneasily toward the slender volume he still held in his hands.

"You won't tell her, will you?"

He shook his head. "No. It'll be our secret."

"Then would you please put that back in the drawer?" she asked.

"What I should do is confiscate it, but I suppose that would be a bit like closing the stable door after the horse has galloped off." Giving her one last amused look, he set the book inside the night-table drawer, then slid it closed.

The tension in her shoulders eased slightly. "I'll be right back."

"Take your time," he called, but she was already gone, scurrying out the door as if a pack of tiny dogs was nipping at her heels. Shaking his head in continued amazement at his unprecedented discovery, he sank into the chair once more, and crossed his booted feet at the ankle.

Cheeks as hot as if they had been doused with lamp oil and set ablaze, Eliza hurried down the hallway, the herb book clutched tightly to her bosom. She knew if she let herself stop and consider what had just occurred, she would collapse into a puddle of misery.

Oh, the shame! The mortification! How was she ever going to face Kit again? How would she ever look him in the eye without thinking about that scandalous book? Without remembering his expression when he'd found it and opened it to see all the ribald depictions.

Yet she had to admit that once Kit had had a moment to overcome his initial shock, he had not been condemning, not the way she might have expected. Even Violet would have had a difficult time accepting the situation, and she certainly wouldn't have laughed the way Kit had done, at least not so quickly.

But gracious, what must he think of her? That she was a horrible, lascivious person, that's what. Oh, why had she given in to her darker impulses and taken the book? She'd only succumbed to the temptation yesterday when she'd found the volume still inside the drawing room escritoire and been unable to resist. Why, she'd hardly had a chance to look at it again. Stupid to have put it in her night table where anyone might see, she berated herself. But then, she hadn't expected anyone to look inside her nightstand.

Her maid was very good about respecting Eliza's personal papers and belongings. Actually, the girl had little use for books, shaking her head whenever she thought herself unobserved, mumbling about how many there were, and how they littered every spare corner of the room. So if her maid had happened upon the little green book, she wouldn't have thought a thing of it, wouldn't have even had the urge to peek inside.

Kit, on the other hand, was a fount of inquisitiveness, ever eager to peek.

Feeling a little ill, but determined to follow through on her promise to tend Kit's injury, Eliza forced her feet onward toward the kitchen. Perhaps the labor of mixing and heating the herbal fomentation would prove distracting enough to take her mind off her humiliation.

Back in Eliza's bedroom, Kit couldn't help but consider the encounter just passed.

Who would ever have imagined, he mused, that formerly shy, reserved Eliza Hammond had those sorts of hidden cravings churning within her? Who would have considered she would be anything but aghast to view such an explicitly sexual book? But apparently she'd been curious enough to take the volume, and hide it here in her bedroom so she could peruse the concupiscent illustrations at her leisure.

His loins stirred, remembering the kissing lesson they had shared, recalling the delicious fervor of her untutored touches and caresses. Yes, she was passionate. Or would be anyway with the proper instruction.

What a pleasure, he considered, to give her more love lessons. But no, he shouldn't let himself think that way. Hadn't he already warned himself against getting involved in such treacherous tangles? Yet if she was curious to explore that side of her nature, might she not turn to another man?

A memory flashed of her kissing Brevard. His fist tightened, lip curling up in a sneer at the image. Damn, he thought. Was she hoping Brevard might tutor her in the amorous arts? And might the viscount be willing to oblige her, even if his intentions were as honorable as he claimed? If she gave Brevard a little encouragement, why would he resist? She wasn't a girl in her first blush of youth. At twenty-three, Eliza was far more tempting fare, even if she was still an unwed, inexperienced maiden.

He was mulling these thoughts over in his brain when he heard her footfalls in the hallway.

She walked into the room, a plain, blue china bowl in her hands, a towel draped over one arm. He noticed that she was careful not to meet his gaze as she approached, nor as she set the contents of his treatment onto the nightstand.

"Lean your head back, please," she murmured.

Without a sound, he complied, settling his head comfortably against the high padded back of the wing chair.

Efficient as a nurse, she draped the towel beneath his chin and over his shoulder to catch any potential drips, then lifted the poultice from the bowl. "This may feel quite warm for a few minutes, but the heat should ease the ache and relieve a measure of the stiffness. I'm having a fresh slice of beefsteak sent to your room for later to help draw out the worst of the bruising. I want you to keep the meat on your face for half an hour minimum."

"I'd rather have it cooked and served with a hearty glass of port," he quipped.

"It will do your wounds no good in your stomach. Now, close your eyes."

He did, then drew in a sharp breath seconds later as she placed the linen-wrapped pouch against his injured face. A rush of heat flooded over his skin, prickling slightly, the pungent mix of herbs strong in his nostrils.

"What's in this?" he asked.

"Some ground mustard seed and crushed nettles,

among other things. Violet keeps a well-stocked herb cabinet for just such occasions."

Grunting, he relaxed as the initial discomfort subsided, a pleasant warmth spreading over his skin and seeping deeper into the muscle.

"Better?" she said, her voice as gentle as birdsong.

"Hmm, yes."

"I brought some gauze toweling to help secure the poultice in place. If you'll keep holding it against your face, I'll be back in a moment."

She shifted slightly, the side of her leg brushing against his thigh. Reaching upward as she directed, he covered her hand where it lay atop the poultice, effectively sandwiching her palm in between. But instead of letting her slip free, he held on, curling his fingers around her wrist.

Kit opened his eyes and caught her in his gaze. "You're still feeling awkward about the book and you have no cause."

Flinching, she glanced away. "I am fine."

"You are embarrassed," he stated, "and you needn't be. Curiosity is part of the human condition, as are feelings of lust and desire, all perfectly normal and natural, even for ladies."

Her gaze flashed to him, then away again. "Let us forget about it."

"We can try, but it's easier to just be honest and open. You and I are comfortable together these days, are we not?"

"Yes, but—"

"No buts and no dissembling."

"I should get the gauze."

"In a minute. First I want to know something. Did you like kissing Brevard in the garden the other night?"

Eliza jumped as if he'd poked her with a toasting fork. "*What!*"

"I saw the pair of you. How was it?"

She tried to pull her hand free of his grasp, but her efforts only made him tighten his hold. "*How it was* is none of your concern," she replied.

"Better than my kisses? Or worse? I assume you were conducting an experiment, just as you told me you might."

"Kit," she admonished.

"Eliza." He gave her a small half smile.

"It was . . . I was . . . yes, I let him kiss me. And yes, I wanted to know what it was like. There is no crime in that."

"I didn't say there was. So? How was it?"

She paused for a long minute, plainly deciding whether or not to refuse to speak. "It was nice."

"Nice? That doesn't sound terribly thrilling."

"It was *very* nice. Lovely, actually."

"Lovely, hmm?"

Kit didn't know if he liked the sound of *lovely,* aware the word could mean anything from banal to sublime.

Maintaining his hold on her wrist, he drew his thumb across the inside of her palm in a long, slow sweep. His spirits rallied in response to her answering quiver, and again when her lips parted on a small, involuntary inhalation of breath. His gaze traced the shape and texture of her mouth, noticing the color, pink and silky and lush, like summer roses in full bloom.

Without pausing to consider his actions, he set a hand on her hip and toyed with the gently rounded flesh he discovered there. "And was my kiss *lovely* too?"

Her eyes darkened, turning silver. "It was . . ."

"Yes?"

"Different."

"Different?"

"Than his. I can't describe in what ways."

"Then mayhap you require another kiss to refresh your memory. That way you'll be able to judge more effectively."

Sliding his hand downward, he cupped the lithesome fullness of her bottom, giving the pliable feminine flesh a gentle squeeze. Seconds after, he tugged her forward and drew her head downward so he could capture her lips.

Even with the poultice pressed to his cheek, he was skillful enough to manage the task, plundering her mouth with a gentle thoroughness that quickly drew a humming whimper from her throat. Gathering her nearer, he gave himself over to the rush, her scent a heady perfume clouding his brain, her touch an enchantment that made him forget all about the ache in his face, and concentrate instead on the one now lodged between his legs. Knowing he was playing with fire, one that could blaze from a spark to a conflagration in mere instants, he permitted himself one last ravishing kiss, then set her gently from him.

Eliza swayed and reached out a hand to steady herself. "Gracious."

"I completely agree." Easing the poultice from his face, he set it aside.

"You should keep that on," she urged.

"I believe I'll manage now without it. You have my thanks, since I do feel better, though perhaps that is more an aftereffect of the kiss than the compress," he added with a smile.

Her already flushed face pinked even more. When he made to rise, she stepped back.

Kit climbed to his feet. "I should be going. I fear I've

tarried in your room far longer than I ought, especially considering what just occurred."

She nodded, the slight glaze of desire still shimmering in her eyes. "Oh, don't forget. Put the raw beefsteak on your wound. It should help draw out the bruise and aid in faster healing."

"Once again, my gratitude for your concern, little wren. Your wishes shall be my own." He took a step toward the door, then paused. "Eliza."

"Yes?"

"One last thing. If your curiosity persists and you find yourself tempted to experiment further in the realm of the physical, don't go to Brevard, or any of your other suitors. You and I may not be meeting for daily lessons anymore, but I am still your mentor." Reaching out, he stroked the edge of a knuckle over the delicate curve of her cheek. "If you wish to have more lessons in love, you need only say. I shall teach you whatever it is you care to learn."

Her lips parted, her gray eyes widening in obvious amazement.

With a last smile, he turned on his heel and strode toward the door, leaving Eliza unmoving and stock-still in the center of her room.

Chapter Fifteen

The beautiful voice of the opera singer soared through the room, lithe and majestic as an exotic butterfly floating on a silken breeze.

Yet Eliza scarcely heard the perfect notes, her thoughts tuning out the aria, just as they had tuned out all the elegantly attired ladies and gentlemen seated around her inside the Fitzmarions' ballroom.

All she could think about was Kit.

Kit's words. Kit's kiss. Kit's undeniably provocative invitation. Even now, hours later, her heart still fluttered in wonder and astonishment. Had he meant it? Did he really wish to experiment—with her? To give her—what had he called it?—more lessons in love?

From the enthusiasm of his kisses there in her bedchamber, she rather thought he did mean it. She could scarcely credit that dashing, debonair Lord Christopher Winter might actually desire her.

After so many unnoticed years and unrequited dreams, she couldn't quite wrap her mind around the notion, telling herself she must be imagining what he'd said, cautioning herself to stop being a ridiculous ninnyhammer, and put the whole thing out of her head. But improbable as circumstances might seem, she knew she hadn't conjured the interlude, the blue and purple bruises that mottled Kit's cheek and jaw proof enough of that.

So then, what was she to do?

Say nothing and go on as before?

Or say yes, and take him up on his tantalizing offer?

Her body tingled at the thought, simmering both with nerves and with something else, something darker, the kind of urges that had led her to this pass in the first place. Yet what a delightful pass it was if it meant sharing further intimate pleasures with Kit.

How far might he take those pleasures? How far would she let him? How far did she dare? And if it was true that he wanted her, desiring her with the same interest and depth of passion he displayed with his other ladyloves, what then could she expect?

Would their interludes amount to nothing more than a mild flirtation? A few innocent kisses and caresses shared in some dark, quiet corner, rushed and playful, meant only as a dalliance? An instructive tease, as it were?

Or might his new interest in her lead to more, lead deeper? Was it possible, with the right incentive, that he might come to care for her? He liked her already—she felt confident of that—but could he love her? If she tried hard enough, could she make him want her, need her so much that tumbling into love would be the easiest, most logical next step?

And what of marriage? Family? She still wanted those things intensely. Should she race after Kit in the hopes of catching him, or resume her original quest to make a solid, achievable matrimonial alliance?

Fear of failure made the blood cool in her veins. But even as she shrank away from the idea of taking this risk, she knew she could not let it go. Just as she had decided to put aside her fears and her shyness this Season, she knew she must pursue this chance no matter the potential cost.

And honestly, how could she say no to the chance to have more love lessons from Kit? Only a fool or an ice princess would refuse.

Despite her preoccupation, she weathered the remainder of the evening with an aplomb that apparently satisfied everyone's expectations, and drew no attention to her distracted musings. Once again at home, she drew off her cloak and handed it to the waiting footman with a murmur of gratitude.

Hearing all of them in the hall, Kit emerged from the salon where he had been entertaining himself with what he said was a deuced dull game of solitaire.

"With this face," he remarked, "I thought I ought to stay in for the evening rather than risk scaring all the ladies."

Violet cooed and clucked over him, while Adrian asked a pair of salient questions to confirm that Kit hadn't landed himself in the boughs over some dispute. Reassured by his brother's innocent explanations, the four of them repaired to the family drawing room for a light late supper. Violet excused herself soon after to go look in on the children. Adrian followed a brief while later.

Eliza remained, slowly sipping her tea. She gazed across at Kit, feeling abruptly nervous in a way she had not felt around him in a very long time.

Now that the moment was upon her, she didn't know what to say. "How are you feeling?" she blurted in a soft voice that sounded tremulous even to her own ears.

He gave her a quiet look, then carefully touched a pair of fingers to his battered cheek. "Not as badly as I would have done, I think, had I not had your cures."

"You used the raw beefsteak, then?"

"Exactly as promised. I told you I would." He smiled gently.

Her heart kicked hard in her chest, quickening at the

devastating flash of his sensuous lips and straight, white teeth.

He drank a swallow of brandy.

"Kit?"

"Hmm?"

"I have been thinking . . . about what you said." She ran her fingers along the material of her skirt, pleating the fabric between her knuckles in spite of the fact that the dress had no pleats.

"About what?" His eyes twinkled like gemstones of green and gold.

Was he teasing her or was he really not sure?

She trembled, her voice scarcely above a whisper. "You know. What you said earlier about . . . experimenting . . . if I wanted to."

His eyes flashed again. "Ah, yes, *that* thing. And?"

Her fingers pleated faster. "And well . . . I . . ." She stared at her shoes, unable to meet his gaze. "I think . . . that is . . . I . . ."

"Eliza. Look at me."

Compelled by his command, she obeyed.

"Don't be shy," he said. "You have no need to be, not with me. Not ever with me. Now, say what it is you wish to say."

She exhaled, the tight muscles of her shoulders and neck relaxing. Kit was right, with him she had no cause to feel shy, especially considering the intimate nature of the step she was about to take.

Forcing up her eyes, she met his gaze. "I have thought about what you said, and yes, I want to."

His eyelids drooped slightly, a lambent light deepening the color of his irises. "Are you sure?"

She nodded. "Yes. When can we begin?" Suddenly she was breathless.

His lips curved in a wry smile. "I wish I could say

right now, but that would be far from wise. Why don't you retire for the evening while I consider the best way to proceed."

"Oh," she said, mildly deflated. "All right." After a moment, she rose to her feet.

He did so as well, as politeness dictated a gentleman do. Only it clearly wasn't politeness that made him step near, nor what urged him to cup her cheek inside his palm and bend down to kiss her. Eliza quivered in delight as he tenderly crushed his lips to hers, stealing her breath and her willpower in the same instant. Suspended in his embrace, she was his to compel, his to command. Her eyelids fluttered closed as she let him have his way.

Slowly, reluctantly, he eased back. "A little taste to tide you over," he murmured, feathering her cheek with a last, lingering caress of his fingertips. "Sleep well, little wren."

Eliza shivered, knowing that tonight she wouldn't be sleeping at all.

What in the saint's name am I doing? Kit wondered after she had gone.

When exactly had he decided to seduce Eliza Hammond? He wasn't sure he had ever actually made the decision, not in a rational, logical sort of way. He had simply made the impulsive suggestion of giving her love lessons and she had accepted. Now that she had, he couldn't say he was the tiniest bit sorry.

Desire yawned inside him, his senses still heightened from their brief kiss. If a simple kiss could render such a response, just think where a truly passionate encounter might lead.

He shouldn't want her, he knew. Propriety and prudence warned that he ought to rescind his offer and tell her there would be no lessons. But when had he ever been prudent? Hadn't he always believed that risk was the very spice of life? The thing that put vigor in the blood and brought satisfaction to the soul?

And considering the provocative little book he'd found in her possession, he knew she was ripe for a bit of risk herself. Who better than he to provide a measure of relatively innocent dalliance? Unlike her current array of suitors, he genuinely cared about Eliza. He would be careful to keep things light and playful, cautious to take their encounters no further than they ought. They would both enjoy themselves for a time, then part as friends.

What he was planning to do with her, he told himself, was not so much different than the flirtations he'd engaged in with lots of other girls over the years. A few stolen kisses and touches had never harmed anyone, and they wouldn't harm him or Eliza.

Really, when he considered the matter, he was protecting her. If she asked another man to help her "experiment," the fellow might take advantage, might misinterpret her guileless nature and use her in ways she would not understand until it was far too late.

And what of Brevard, who claimed an interest in marriage?

Kit raised his glass of brandy to his lips and tossed back the remains in a single, sharp-tasting gulp. He set down the glass with an audible *click,* his hand tight at his side.

He wasn't going to think about Brevard, he decided, carefully stretching the muscles in his neck to relieve the sudden tension that had collected there. If—and that was a big if—the viscount decided to give up his bachelorhood and offer for Eliza, the matter would be dealt with then. A notoriously elusive catch, Brevard might well decide to withdraw his interest—he'd been known to before—and move on to new territory. For now, Kit would concentrate on himself and Eliza, he wouldn't worry about Brevard or any of the rest.

Carpe diem, he thought, ruefully acknowledging the fact that the short phrase was one of the few bits of Latin to have stuck with him since he'd completed his formal education. But he'd always found the expression apt.

And so seize the day—and Eliza Hammond—he would.

"Splendid rout, eh?"

Eliza smiled at her dance partner, a nice young man whose brown hair was already starting to thin at the crown despite his lack of years. "Yes," she agreed, "it is quite festive. Our hostess has outdone herself with all the fresh flowers and the live fish pond in the center of the buffet table. It is quite the talk of the evening."

"I know. I am fascinated by the engineering. A marvel what can be created these days."

Eliza smiled again and let him talk, enjoying the fact that he didn't seem to expect her to participate a great deal in the conversation. Once their dance concluded, he escorted her from the floor. Her small but loyal group of suitors gathered around at her return.

She was laughing at an amusing tale about a bird who had built a nest inside a hat display at a Bond Street haberdashers when Kit appeared at her elbow.

"Might I have a word?" he murmured near her ear.

She cast a glance upward at him. "Of course, give me a moment." After listening to the conclusion of the story, she excused herself amid jovial groans of complaint from the other gentlemen. Laying a gloved palm on Kit's black-clad forearm, she let him lead her away. Together, they began to stroll the ballroom's perimeter.

"You have had so many social engagements these past three days," he said, "I've scarcely caught more than a glimpse of you in passing, even at the townhouse. Rather than resort to sending you a note, I decided to take the direct approach and steal you away from your admirers."

"I am sorry. I know I have been far too busy of late."

"Not to worry. You've taken so well this Season you are greatly in demand, just as we had hoped you would be." He paused and drew her away from an approaching couple, providing himself and Eliza with at least the illusion of privacy. "I wanted to talk to you about our discussion of the other evening. I assume you are still interested in pursuing the matter?"

Air suddenly squeezed from her lungs, leaving her abruptly grateful for the support of his arm. "Yes. I am still interested."

He sent her an intimate smile. "We could always duck out into the garden now, but things can become deuced awkward sometimes when trying to return undetected."

Could they? she mused. But then, she supposed he would know all about such matters, considering the practice he'd had in the past. Biting the corner of her lip, she shook off the whisper of jealousy that sighed through her, reminding herself that finally she was the girl he would be leading astray.

"I was thinking," he continued in a low voice, "of something a bit more leisurely for our lesson, something at home."

"You mean at night in one of our rooms?" she whispered.

"No, our rooms are far too risky and far too much of a temptation. A lazy afternoon would serve our purposes much better. Mayhap you could find a reason to remain behind one day while everyone else goes out. Be laid low by an unexpected headache, perhaps."

Gracious, she had never considered such a notion. How deceitful. How deliciously wicked. Her pulse beat like tiny hearts in her wrists.

"Yes, I suppose I could. But my maid will surely wish to dose me with lavender compresses and hot herb tea."

"So let her dose you, then claim a quick recovery."

"And after? Where shall we meet?"

His gaze locked with her own, his eyes deep and penetrating. "Where do you often go when you have a few spare moments in your day?"

"The library."

"Precisely."

"But won't someone see us if they come in?"

"Not if we two are snugged up tight in the loft. The servants only go up there to dust and they won't come into the room if they know you're already in there."

She gulped, anticipation warring with anxiety, making nerves do a high-stepping jig inside her stomach. For a long minute she and Kit continued to promenade, looking, she hoped, as if the two of them were discussing ordinary topics instead of boldly arranging a romantic assignation.

Vaguely short of breath, she stroked her fingers against the fine black material of his coat sleeve. "All of us are invited to a luncheon party in Richmond on Friday. I shall do as you suggest and plead an illness."

"What if Violet offers to remain home with you?"

Yes, what then? Her friend would be distressed to hear she was not at the peak of health. But no matter how Eliza hated dissembling, she would tell a lie if it was the only recourse. The promise of an afternoon spent in

Kit's arms was too wonderful to pass up, so no matter the price, she would find a way to pay.

"I shall convince her not to stay," she told him. "Violet has been looking forward to the outing since the invitation arrived. She and Adrian can take the children along, you see. Given that, I do not think she will be too hard to persuade."

"Then Friday it is." He covered her palm with his hand and gave a light squeeze. "Now, if I am not mistaken the next set is about to begin and your dance partner is heading this way."

She glanced across the ballroom and saw that he was correct, Lord Maplewood was striding toward them in a direct line.

"A shame I have to let him claim you," Kit murmured just moments before the other man arrived. "She is all yours, my lord," Kit greeted, relinquishing her hand. "For now anyway."

Feigning illness a couple afternoons later didn't prove terribly difficult for Eliza, since by the time Friday arrived she was a true bundle of nerves.

Inside her bedchamber, she pleaded the excuse of a headache, her fingers trembling faintly in her lap.

Violet's eyes immediately filled with concern. "Oh, you poor dear. You do look peaked. Is the pain very terrible?"

Eliza winced, guilt plunging deep and sharp as a blade. Touching a pair of fingers to her forehead, she glanced down. "Hmm, I confess I am not feeling my usual self."

That was the truth anyway. Ever since she and Kit had arranged their assignation, she hadn't felt *usual* at all.

"We should cancel," Violet said. "I'll stay home."

"No, please, I'd feel horrid if you didn't go to Richmond Park today." Horrid and disappointed, she thought with a fresh twinge of remorse. "I'll lie down for a while and be good as new by the time you return."

Would she and Kit be lying down during their "lesson"? She shivered at the bold images the idea conjured in her mind.

Violet wrinkled her pale blond brows. "I'm not sure, you look flushed all of a sudden. I shall worry the whole time I am away."

Drat my annoying propensity to blush, Eliza scolded herself.

Struggling to control her reactions as well as her wayward imagination, she rushed to reassure her friend. "You have no cause to fret. It's nothing more serious than a headache, and your being here will make no difference to my recovery. Please, go on or I shall come with you, after all, if only to make sure I haven't ruined your day."

"You could never do that." Violet patted Eliza's hand. "Very well, then, I'll go. But I insist you let Agnes brew you some tea, and make a compress for your head."

"Of course."

With a last worried look, Violet allowed herself to be persuaded to leave.

Flopping back onto her pillow, Eliza blew out a sigh of relief. Seconds later, the butterflies in her stomach began fluttering their wings again, anticipation rising at the knowledge that soon she and Kit would be together.

Alone.

A brief, racketing clamor echoed through the house as Violet, Adrian, the children and their nurse made their way out the door and into their coach. After their departure, a peaceful calm descended. Tucked snuggly under a cotton throw, pillows stacked comfortably beneath her head, Eliza let Violet's maid and her own abigail bustle around her, offering tisanes and compresses and soothing words of comfort.

Miserable with guilt, she nearly worked herself into having a real headache. But once she had been thoroughly tended to, and left to rest quietly on her own, her "symptoms" quickly disappeared. Forcing herself to wait, she remained in her room. When she heard the door open half an hour later, she kept her eyes shut and pretended to be asleep, knowing it was only her maid peeking in to check on her.

Once the girl had gone, Eliza tossed the coverlet aside and leapt to her feet, edgy anticipation tingling through her system in a balmy rush. Creeping out of her room, she closed the door with a soundless click and started down the hallway.

If she was lucky, no one would realize she was gone. And if they did discover her absence, she would simply tell them the truth—that she was feeling better and had gone to the library.

The familiar scents of leather and beeswax greeted her when she entered the room, but today they offered none of their usual comfort, her senses too overwrought for such plebian consolation. Glancing upward, she spied the second-story reading loft with its carved walnut balcony and balustrades, and its elegant trio of arched mullion windows. Sunlight spilled down in a glittering curtain of gold, blocking her ability to see whether or not Kit awaited her above. Crossing to the spiral staircase set along the rear wall, she began the climb upward.

Once there, she walked along the balcony, her thin, fawn leather slippers quiet against the polished wooden floor, her gown of leaf-green spotted muslin whispering a sibilant song around her legs.

For a moment she thought herself alone. Suddenly she

heard a faint tap and caught a glimpse of movement as Kit stepped into full view.

Smiling a roguish welcome, he extended a hand. She placed hers inside, quivering when he brushed a leisurely kiss across her knuckles. "Well then, are you ready to begin, my little wren?"

Chapter Sixteen

Knowing Eliza as he now did, Kit had expected her to be a bit nervous. And when the anticipated time of her arrival came and went and she had not appeared, he'd wondered if perhaps she had changed her mind about meeting him and decided to remain inside the chaste confines of her bedroom.

He hadn't realized just how disappointed he would have been at her absence until she stood before him, her wholesome beauty stealing the very air from his lungs, firing a lusty hunger that raged in his bones and blood.

How, he wondered incredulously, had he ever found her ordinary?

Holding out a hand, he smiled, exultant when she laid her own within his grasp. After exchanging a few words of greeting, he led her forward to the small sitting area he had prepared for them. Wanting her relaxed and comfortable, he had spread out a blanket picnic-style on the carpeted floor. Atop that, he had heaped masses of plump throw pillows, gathered from the nearby sofas and chairs.

"My goodness," she said on seeing the unique arrangement. "Are you expecting us to sit on the floor?"

His lips tilted up on one side. "That was the general idea. I wanted you to feel at your ease."

"Oh, well, it appears comfortable enough. I've just never sat on the floor before."

"Not even as a child?"

She furrowed her brow. "Perhaps as a very little girl before my parents died. I know I certainly never sat on anything but the furniture in my aunt's house."

"Then it is time you expanded your boundaries. That is what today is about, is it not? Learning and experimentation."

Her lashes swept downward, her tone low and unusually throaty. "Yes, it is."

He raised her hand and pressed another warm kiss upon its top. "Remember, no shyness allowed. Relax. It's not as if I'm going to bite you. Well, no more than a nip here and there."

Her eyes widened as she checked to see if he was teasing. Then she surprised them both by laughing. "I trust it won't hurt."

"You'll feel nothing but delight, I promise."

Helping her onto the blanket, he sat down beside her, making sure she had a pair of pillows at her back. Once her comfort was assured, he reached behind himself and drew forth a bottle of wine and a corkscrew. Next came a pair of wineglasses and a plate with a selection of fresh fruits and sweetmeats.

She laughed again. "Count on you, Kit, to never forget the food."

He gave her a solemn look. "Food is one of life's most sensuous pleasures. A fine meal tempts all of the senses. Touch, smell, sight, taste . . ."—he paused and popped the cork on the wine—"even sound. Added to the act of lovemaking, food can create a truly transcendent experience."

Tipping the bottle, he poured a liberal splash of sweet, white Sauterne into each glass before passing one to her.

Savoring her reaction, he watched as she bent to breathe in the delicate, flowery bouquet of the wine, stilling her before she had a chance to drink.

"Allow me," he said.

Imprisoning her gaze, he dipped the tip of one finger into his glass, then brought it out again, a single drop clinging to his skin. Before she had any idea what he intended, he reached out and dampened her lower lip, painting across her soft skin with a deft touch.

Eliza shivered visibly, her mouth glistening and tremulous. Leaning forward, he hovered for an instant with their mouths barely a breath away, then glided the edge of his tongue across her lower lip to capture the flavor of the droplet, and a hint of her own taste as well.

"Delicious," he murmured, leaning back. "Now it's your turn."

She blinked, her eyes darkening to silver. Her hand trembled on her glass, making him fear for a moment that she might spill the wine. Then she steadied herself and slowly dipped a finger into her glass.

Desire swelled within him as he waited in a sudden fever of anticipation for her touch. He didn't exhale until she made contact, her caress one of innocent, unstudied seduction. The drop of wine flowed in a cool, wet slide against his warm, dry flesh. Without thinking, he caught the tip of her finger between his lips and drew it into his mouth up to the knuckle, sucking upon her as if she were as sugary sweet as a peppermint stick.

Kit nearly groaned, feeling each pull all the way to his vitals.

Eliza appeared to feel it as well, a concussive glaze of desire spreading through her eyes. After a long minute and one final tug, he let her finger slip from his mouth.

She stared at him, obviously amazed that so simple an

act could have the power to evoke such a profoundly physical reaction. "They didn't do that in the book."

He raised a brow and smiled. "That type of book tends to focus on the basic rather than the sublime, and though such literature has its uses, there's a great deal more to the art of *l'amour* than the fundamental act itself."

Needing to moisten his throat, Kit drank a mouthful of wine. Eliza followed suit, sipping more slowly, her gaze locked upon his as she swallowed. Darting out her tongue, she licked her lips.

Hunger pounded through him, urging him to kiss her and kiss her hard. Instead he reached toward the small plate waiting not far from his elbow.

"Close your eyes," he murmured.

"My eyes? Why?"

"Because I am going to feed you. Lean back and once your eyes are firmly shut, you are to eat and tell me what you taste."

Eliza gazed at him again, then sank deeper into the feather pillows at her back. Obediently, she lowered her eyelids and waited.

This lesson, she mused, was nothing like she had expected. From the moment she sat down on the blanket next to Kit, he had kept her surprised and off balance, held her teetering on a blade-sharp edge of craving and desire the likes of which she had never imagined.

And he hadn't even kissed her yet!

Heat scalded through her, immediately chased by a shivery cold, her breathing unsteady while she awaited his next move. Moments later, something slippery and cool brushed across her bottom lip.

"What is this?" His words held a faintly teasing quality, his tone deep, dark and delectable, like a cup of the most incredibly rich cocoa ever brewed. She struggled to focus on the task at hand rather than on his nearness.

She considered the texture, tried to catch a hint of fragrance, but the soft whatever-it-was against her mouth remained a mystery. "I don't know."

"Come now, this is an easy one. Something you've eaten often."

He rubbed again, grazing her upper lip this time, then her lower. Despite the touch, she was perplexed. Why hadn't she paid better attention to the fruit and treats on the plate? Because she'd been too busy thinking about all the soul-stirring things Kit was going to do to her. And so far, he had not disappointed her.

"Here, taste it and you'll know."

Parting her lips, she let him feed her. Round and slick, the treat was light and unexpectedly firm. Biting down, a sweet, tangy squirt of juice filled her mouth.

"A grape," she declared after she swallowed. "It is a grape."

"Hmm, and so it is. Here, let me have a sip."

Bending across, his mouth claimed hers, playing in a lazy exploration that teased and cajoled. She sought to return his kiss, meeting his tongue as he dipped inside to gather the flavor of the fruit in a most thorough and pleasing way.

"Tasty," he said, easing away. "Something else now, I think. Eyes closed," he warned.

She quivered and waited. She didn't have long before he pressed another selection against her lips. Unlike the grape, this delicacy wasn't cool, nor was it slippery, an almost flowery fragrance teasing her nostrils.

Fruit of some kind, she concluded.

"Take a bite," he urged.

She did, sinking her teeth into what seemed like living velvet. Peach pulp and juice flooded her mouth in a sugary wash, enchanting her senses. Chewing and swallow-ing, she tried to catch every drop but a single one es-caped, sliding over her cheek. Reaching up, she moved to wipe away the errant drop.

But Kit caught and held her hand. "No, no, this one is mine."

Her eyes popped open as his lips glided over her skin, dropping kisses and giving tiny licks to erase the line of sticky juice. He laved her cheek until not so much as a trace remained. Her feet arched inside her slippers, body humming from scalp to toe.

"One last," he pronounced.

She stopped him. "Wouldn't you like something first? Let me feed you. Anything you want."

His eyes flashed emerald and gold. "You shouldn't make such suggestive remarks, my little wren. Another man might take you at your word."

"Any sort of *food* you want, then," she amended.

He considered for a moment. "Very well. You can pleasure me with a slice of fresh fig." Reaching out, he plucked one off the plate, then used a small knife to cut the fruit into quarters. Setting the blade aside, he handed her the section.

"You know what they say about figs, don't you?" he remarked, angling his body forward, his arms braced on either side of her waist.

She shook her head, extending the offering so he could partake. "No. What do they say?"

"That figs are erotic, their centers resembling the core of a woman's most secret place. I'm surprised that naughty little book of yours didn't make mention."

Her eyes widened as he bit deep, his lips grazing the tips of her fingers as he caught the fruit and drew it into his mouth. Chewing, he gave her a thoroughly wicked grin, one that shot straight to the spot he'd mentioned.

She shifted, her legs abruptly restless.

"I'm sorry, Eliza," he said, once he'd consumed the fig. "I oughtn't tease you so. It only makes you confused and me deuced uncomfortable."

He leaned over, stretching to choose yet another offering from the plate. As he did, she got a glimpse of precisely *how* uncomfortable he was, his dark blue trousers no longer fitting with their usual easy drape and flat lines.

A starburst of heat flashed through her like a log popping on a roaring fire. She forced herself to calm, despite the near impossibility of the act, watching him when he turned back to see if he might be dismayed. But Kit appeared his usual self, obviously unconcerned and showing no signs of awkwardness or discomfiture.

So, she concluded, if Kit wasn't discomposed by his body's unfettered response, then neither would she let herself be. She remembered the way the men had looked in the illustrations she'd viewed, realizing that such reactions must apparently be normal. And if she had any lingering doubt about the honesty of Kit's desire for her, she didn't any longer.

Propped on his bent elbow, he settled full-length next to her. "This," he stated, holding up a small, round ball of creamy white, "is a confection not to be missed. They are known as *Capezzoli di Venere*."

Instantly, she translated the phrase, the tips of her ears turning warm and, no doubt, pink. "You're teasing me, aren't you? They are not really called . . ." she couldn't bring herself to say the words in English, "what you just said?"

He tossed back his head and laughed. "They most certainly are. Do you really believe I could make up a candy called Nipples of Venus?"

One of her eyebrows arched upward. "Actually, I do."

He chuckled again. "Thank you for complimenting my imaginative powers, but I fear I cannot take credit. I discovered this particular confection on the Continent in a most amiable Viennese sweet shop. The owner was delighted to make up an entire box for my exclusive delectation. I assure you I enjoyed each and every one." He held the sweet toward her lips. "Here, try a nibble."

A nibble of a nipple, she mused with scandalized humor. There seemed something intrinsically wrong with that to her way of thinking. "What are they made of precisely?"

"Well, in plain and simple English they are brandied chestnuts dipped in a sugar cream coating. You like chestnuts, don't you?"

"Hmm, I do. But it isn't winter. Where did you come by chestnuts this time of year?"

He gave her a slow smile that displayed the dimple in his chin to devastating effect. "I have my ways. Now, I insist you take a taste and tell me if you don't agree this is one of the most sinfully divine experiences you've ever had."

All her experiences with him this afternoon were sinfully divine as far as she was concerned. Yet wasn't that the point? she reminded herself. To indulge her emotions and inclinations, to yield to passion and persuasion in ways she never had, enjoying everything each had to offer? To savor and be savored, and in doing so prove to Kit that she was the perfect woman for him.

Mustering her courage, she raised her head and bit into the sweetmeat, the rich, buttery chestnut flavor filling her mouth. As luscious as promised, the *Capezzoli di Venere* melted with pure decadence against her tongue, making her smile. She took a second small bite, and when she did Kit joined her, biting down from the other side so that their lips met around the confection. They finished the treat that way, laughing and sharing, their mouths awash in sugar and sensation.

But once they were done, all laughter ceased, playful candy-coated kisses turning into long, deep, drugging forays that made her mind whirl like a strand of dandelion fluff caught in a blustery summer gale.

Giving herself over to the passion singing through her blood, she followed Kit's lead, letting him take her on a journey of carnal exploration, exactly as he had promised he would. Held tight inside the safety of his arms, she kissed him with all the meager skill at her command, taking his lessons and putting them to what she trusted was good use.

Kit certainly had no complaints, murmuring encouragements even as he paused occasionally to make a suggestion or show her a new trick designed to maximize her pleasure and his own.

Then, as though his kisses weren't satisfaction enough, he began to touch her.

Light caresses at first. The brush of a fingertip across her cheek. The slide of his hand along the length of her throat. The devastating pressure of his teeth as they clamped, ever so lightly, around the fleshy end of her earlobe. She nearly swooned, right then and there, when he added a final, tiny nip, a sound that was part sigh, part whimper escaping from her lips.

He smiled and moved to nuzzle the underside of her jaw. Laving her collarbone, he dappled kisses across the narrow area of exposed skin that lay above her bodice. She groaned, her heart kicking hard when he stopped his kisses to lay a hand over her breast.

For a long moment, he did nothing, letting her adjust to the weight and shape of his palm cupping her. On a deep breath, her chest rose, unconsciously pushing her muslin-covered breast more fully into his grip. He added a second hand and held her, then slowly rubbed his thumbs over her aching flesh.

As if governed by a will of their own, her nipples sprang to attention, peaking fast and hard beneath the deft, clever stroke of his fingers. She gasped for air, her mouth growing dry. His every caress set her afire, making her yearn in ways she hadn't known she could.

A ravenous hunger flashed like glittering emeralds in his eyes seconds before he lowered his head and crushed her lips to his. Savaging her mouth, demanding she match him kiss for kiss, he fondled her more fully, each squeeze and stroke and brush of his dexterous hands shooting straight to her core as if the two were somehow connected. The ache between her legs intensified, leaving her quivering and incautious, focused only on him and the wicked, wonderful things he was doing to her body.

She was barely aware when his nimble fingers went to work, loosening the buttons and ties of her bodice and stays. Material sagging, he smoothed the cloth downward and revealed her naked breasts.

Their gazes collided for an explosive moment as she lay exposed before him.

"Now, these," he murmured, "are real nipples of Venus, worthy of the goddess of love herself."

He flicked a thumb over one taut, pink peak, wringing a moan from her lips. He touched the other breast, lightly rubbing around the aureole in a circular glide before tweaking that nipple in a way that made her writhe.

"God, you're beautiful, Eliza. And so passionate, so perfect. Where have you been hiding all these years?"

Right here, she thought, half-dazed. *Always right here, waiting for you, for this.*

He played upon her, how long she didn't know, too caught up in the sensations, in the rhapsody of his touch, to do more than feel. When she thought she could bear no more, her nerves so sensitized she wondered if she might shatter, he did something that stunned her afresh.

He took her nipple into his mouth and rolled his tongue around her flesh before giving a drawing pull.

"Hmm, I was right," he said. "The *Capezzoli di Venere* taste delicious, but you, my little wren, are as scrumptious as they come. I could literally eat you up."

And then she could barely think, her brain turning to the consistency of porridge as he kissed and laved and suckled. Sinking her fingers into his hair, she stroked his head and his cheeks while he pleasured her.

She let him do as he wished, caught in the grip of a fever she had no will to resist. His hand dipped beneath her skirts, traveling in an unhurried slide from stocking-clad calf to bare hip. Fondling her curves, he stroked her below, even as he kissed and caressed her above. Around her knee, over her thigh, across her hip bone, he wandered, lightly skimming in lazy, gliding circles. Curving his palm around the fullness of her upper leg, he fanned a thumb across the tender flesh of her inner thigh, back and forth, each stroke inciting an increasingly fierce ache. She shuddered, her eyes rolling back in her head, when he blew a stream of breath across one kiss-dampened breast. His fingers glided, creeping higher against her thigh. Just when she wondered in some vague recess of her brain where his touch might journey next, he stopped.

Muttering what sounded like a curse, his fingers curled together, squeezing into a steely fist. Burying his face between her breasts, he lay silent and still, a shudder running through his muscles like a man in the midst of a terrible battle. The inner struggle raged for several tense moments until, with obvious reluctance, he withdrew his hand from beneath her skirts.

Pausing to drop a lingering kiss upon each of her naked breasts, he huffed out a ragged groan, then levered himself away.

Without the sheltering warmth of his embrace, Eliza lay confused and bereft, dismayed by his hasty withdrawal. "Kit?"

Out of the corner of her eye, she caught sight of him, seated with one knee raised, a hand spread across his face like he was in the grip of some dreadful agony. Considering the hunger still burning in own her body, perhaps he was.

"Kit, come back," she beckoned.

Yes, she thought, *please, please, come back.*

Splaying a pair of the fingers on his face, he peeked out at her from between the spread digits. "Can't, my dear. We have to stop."

But why? she wondered, when everything he did felt so exquisite, his every touch and kiss like tiny glimpses of heaven. "But I don't want to," she complained, petulant for perhaps the first time in her life.

The corner of his mouth turned up in a wry smile. "I don't want to either, but we must. We dare go no further, not today." He paused, drew a deep breath, then blew it out in a sigh. "Anyway, there will be other chances, with more lessons ahead. No need to rush the process along too quickly."

Lessons? Somewhere along the way, she'd forgotten all about the lessons, their lovemaking going far beyond her imaginings, her senses focused solely on Kit and the sheer glory of being in his arms.

But now, as the misty haze of passion began to clear from her mind, she supposed he was right. Calling a halt before their passions truly escalated beyond any semblance of control was the prudent course to take. Honestly, she didn't know how he had mustered the fortitude to stop. Having never before been caught in the clutches of unfettered desire, she hadn't realized how difficult it would be to tear herself away. If he hadn't ended things when he had . . . well, she supposed her innocence would now be lost. Of course, she wouldn't really have minded, since Kit was the man to whom she would have gifted her maidenhead, the man she wanted to be her first, her last, her only.

But a gently bred lady didn't give her virginity away except inside the bonds of matrimony. Would Kit ever wish to wed her? Or was she a simpleton to pin her hopes on such an outcome, believing one day he might come to love her and ask her to be his wife?

Yet all these years of waiting primly for him to notice her hadn't worked, so perhaps passion was the way to win his heart. At least he wanted her now, saw her as a desirable woman instead of his sister-in-law's ordinary little friend. And she was making progress, this afternoon her proof. If someone had told her a month ago that she and Kit would do all the wonderful, passionate things they had done today, she would not have believed them.

And so she would let this whatever-it-was between them play out, hoping in the end his need for her would lead to love. She tingled inside at the idea of more lessons, her body still aquiver from the one he'd given her today. Truly, she had no notion what might come next, and she could hardly wait to find out.

Outside, a cloud passed, blocking the rays of warm

sunlight shining in through the upper-story windows. She shivered, becoming acutely aware that her breasts were still bared. With a trembling hand, she tugged at her bodice and stays, pressing both garments flat against her chest as she struggled to sit up.

"Here," he said, "let me help you."

She glanced downward, unaccountably shy. "I am fine."

Tucking a finger beneath her jaw, he raised her chin and forced her to meet his gaze. "What did I say about no shyness when we are together? There is to be no shame either. Please do us both the favor of remembering that."

Beneath his patient, accepting gaze, her discomfiture faded. "Yes, Kit."

"Now, if you'll release that death grip you have on your bodice, I can help lace you up again. I ought to act as your maid anyway, since I'm the one responsible for putting your clothes into such disarray."

She chuckled softly. "Do you know how to act as a lady's maid?"

"I've had a bit of practice in my time, enough to do the job properly," he said, moving around behind her. With a skillful hand, he reached for her laces. "Seems a damned shame to conceal those beautiful breasts of yours, though, since they truly are magnificent. Then again, it will only give me something to look forward to, wondering when I shall next feast my eyes upon them."

"Kit!"

Laughing and clearly unrepentant, he skimmed a kiss over one bare shoulder, then proceeded to cinch her in. With her dress once more in place, he stood, then reached down a hand to lift her to her feet. Plucking at her coiffeur, he set her hair to rights, then brushed a hand over her skirts to free them of wrinkles.

"Good as new," he pronounced.

To return the favor, she gave his waistcoat a tug, then reached up to straighten his neck cloth.

Finished, she brushed a stray lock of hair off his forehead. "When shall we meet again?"

"Hmm, I am eager too, but we shall have to see. I suppose it would look odd if you started coming down with lots of unexpected ailments."

She nodded. "Yes, it would be suspect. Violet would insist I see Dr. Montgomery, sure something is dreadfully wrong."

Sliding his arms around her, he pulled her close. "Perhaps I will surprise you, then. That way you'll never know when a kiss might be waiting just around the corner."

Her mouth grew suddenly moist in anticipation.

Bending his head, he kissed her, long and lingering.

"My thanks for a most exquisite afternoon," he said after their embrace ended. "I shall cherish it always."

Her heart leapt. "As will I."

"Hurry on to your room before you are missed, if you haven't been missed already. Oh, and here—" He broke off, crossing to a nearby shelf. Reaching up at random, he pulled out a book. "Take this."

She glanced at the title. "A treatise on theoretical calculus?"

He tipped his head in surprise, then shrugged. "You like improving your mind, don't you?"

"Yes, but even I don't like math."

He chuckled and kissed her hand. "That makes two of us. You'd better be on your way."

Clutching the book to her chest, she did as he bade.

Kit enjoyed the sway of her hips as she walked to the spiral staircase and down, disappearing from view. On the floor below, she reappeared, pausing to glance up and back to see if he was watching.

He was, unable to keep himself from approaching the railing. Raising a hand, he offered her another smile to send her on her way. She smiled back, showing him a flash of her pretty teeth before she turned and hurried away, lithesome as a young girl.

An odd pressure squeezed in his chest.

How was it, he wondered, that she grew more lovely with each passing day? And her skin, she glowed as if illuminated from within. Had their lovemaking given her that radiance? Added the vibrant shine to her eyes?

He knew he'd brought her pleasure, her every kiss and sigh one of open, artless delight. She'd certainly returned the favor, her innocent, unguarded touches scalding him to the core. Even now, unsatisfied desire held him in its merciless grip, demanding to be slaked. Halting their coupling had been a near thing, every fiber of his being insisting that he take her, sheath himself deep into her willing flesh. But by a force of will he hadn't known he possessed, he had ended their interlude.

So much for keeping things light, he mused with an ironic twist to his lips. Turning around, he strode toward the scene of their mutual seduction. Scooping up an armful of pillows, he moved to replace them in their original locations.

Just as he'd halted their lovemaking today, he ought to call a halt to this whole affair. Already she tempted him more than he'd dreamed possible. More, if he was honest, than any other woman he'd known.

But infatuation could be a powerful motivator, dare he say a compulsion, and even as he considered the idea of telling Eliza there would be no more lessons, he knew there would be. The thought of doing without her kisses, forgoing her caresses was simply unbearable.

And so he would continue their loveplay despite all the dangers inherent in the plan.

Perhaps he was making more of the risks than need be. He'd controlled himself today. He could control himself again, could take both of them to the edge of the precipice, but no further.

He hoped so anyway.

Chapter Seventeen

"Is your headache improved?" Violet asked the next morning over breakfast.

Eliza set down her china teacup with its delicate banding of blue and gold stripes. She blotted her lips with her napkin. "Oh, yes, I am completely recovered."

"Good. I am relieved to know you needed nothing more than a quiet afternoon here at home to feel yourself again."

Eliza smiled then bit into a slice of toast spread with butter and marmalade. She wouldn't exactly say her afternoon had been quiet or that she felt precisely like herself, but there was no need to tell Violet that.

With an appetite she found surprising considering the flutters still trembling inside her belly from yesterday's tryst, she ate a forkful of eggs. She swallowed them, together with the juicy confession that hovered on the end of her tongue. She was dying to tell Violet about her and Kit, but knew such secrets were best kept to herself.

Instead she listened while her friend regaled her with stories about the outing to Richmond Park. The children, it seems, had especially enjoyed the excursion, the twins running and tumbling in the fields, stopping at a pond with their father to exclaim over the frogs they desperately wanted to catch and bring home.

Eliza interjected an occasional question, but let Violet

do the majority of the talking. Despite her interest in "everything she'd missed at the park," her thoughts drifted time and again to Kit and their assignation in the Raeburn House library.

She shivered again just to remember.

Kit had said he would surprise her. How long, she wondered, would she be forced to wait?

Not long, she was thrilled to discover when Kit happened upon her in the hallway that afternoon and pulled her into an alcove for a quick but heated embrace.

From that moment forward, she never knew when he might steal her away for a few clandestine kisses, a few savory caresses. She began to live on a knife's edge—one side a slice of heaven, the other a sort of hell.

And always he took care, making sure that neither of them were seen together in anything but chaste circumstances, either at home or in public.

Otherwise, her days became alarmingly routine. Morning and afternoon calls, followed by parties, routs, balls and soirees. There were breakfasts and luncheons to attend, teas and musicales and an occasional evening at the theater or the opera.

Her suitors called upon her most afternoons, congregating in the salon before one of them, by prior arrangement, would have the privilege of escorting her for a carriage ride or a promenade in the park.

She spent one day with Viscount Brevard and his sister, who invited her, Violet and Jeannette to go shopping on Bond Street. Among the vendors visited, they stopped in Hatchard's bookstore, where Eliza found a wonderful first edition of Burns's poetry. Later, they concluded their excursion with a trip to eat ices at Gunter's.

She did her best to enjoy herself—since this truly was the best Season she had ever known—but underneath every action, every thought, was Kit. He even stole into her dreams, leaving her aching and empty when she awakened to find herself alone, the object of her desire sleeping only just down the corridor.

But she counseled herself to have patience. She had waited for him this long, she could wait a while more.

Three weeks to the day after her first love lesson with Kit, she came down the stairs after breakfast and received the news that she had a gentleman caller.

"Lord Maplewood is here?" she repeated to March, knowing it was most irregular for the baron to call at such an early hour of the day. "Has the duchess been informed?"

The majordomo inclined his regal head. "Her Grace is aware of his arrival and asked that you go ahead into the salon. She shall join you both in a few minutes."

Well, Eliza mused, if Violet thought she should entertain Lord Maplewood on his own for a few minutes, then it must be all right.

With a murmur of thanks for March, she crossed and entered the salon. To her surprise, the majordomo closed the doors behind her. She stared for a moment, a suspicious little frown between her brows, before turning to offer a cheery hello to her visitor.

Impeccably attired in a conservative, Wellington brown coat and trousers, his thick salt-and-pepper hair neatly brushed back from his temples, Maplewood came forward and cut her an elegant bow.

"My dear Miss Hammond, how good of you to receive me so early in the day."

"But, of course, my lord. I am always glad of your company." Sinking onto the sofa, she straightened her skirts, then gestured to a nearby chair. "Would you care to take a seat?"

He shook his head, twirling a small gold and amber

signet ring around on his pinky. "My thanks, but I would prefer to remain standing, if you do not mind."

"Not at all."

Was he nervous? Eliza wondered. How unusual, since Lord Maplewood was one of the most stalwart, level-headed men she had ever known. She waited quietly, deciding it best to let him speak first.

Around went the signet ring one more time before he looked up and met her gaze. "Miss Hammond . . . first let me tell you how deeply I have enjoyed the time we have spent together these past weeks. Of all the ladies I have met this Season, you are by far the kindest and most amiable. And lovely, of course," he hastened to add.

Faintly bemused, Eliza inclined her head.

"I am not a man much given to flowery speeches, so I will speak plainly instead. As a widower, I am in need of a wife, and more importantly, a mother for my young daughter. You have expressed your affection for children, and I believe you would make an exemplary parent. I know Clarissa will love you." He broke off and gave a self-deprecating laugh. "I love you too, though perhaps I ought to have mentioned that first."

The air whooshed out of Eliza's lungs. Before she had a chance to recover or respond, Maplewood reached down and gathered her hands into his own.

"Miss Hammond," he said, a warm look of hopeful entreaty in his eyes, "pray relieve my present anxiety and say you will marry me."

Her head whirled.

She had not been expecting a proposal, though why she had not she couldn't say, since Lord Maplewood had been one of her most dedicated suitors from the very first. He wanted to marry her. She was flattered, of course, but how should she answer him?

As little as a month ago, she would most certainly have said yes. Maplewood was everything she claimed to want in a husband. Considerate and kind, intelligent and educated, pleasant to look upon—well, really more than pleasant, since he drew rapturous sighs from the ladies whenever he happened near.

He was a good man, who would never berate or abuse her, who would do his utmost to provide her with every comfort and happiness she could want and who had no need of her wealth since he possessed an immense fortune of his own. Added to that was his daughter, a sweet girl by all accounts, who often earned a sad shake of the head from those who had known her late mother.

"Such a darling child," they would say. "Such a dear woman, Lady Maplewood. A pure tragedy that she had to die so young."

If Eliza married Maplewood, she would be the child's mother, instantly fulfilling another of her most cherished dreams.

If only there were not a difficulty.

If only she did not love Kit.

And, in that instant, she had her answer.

"My lord," she began, "you do me a great honor with your proposal. You are a wonderful man whose friendship I sincerely cherish." Gently, she tugged her hands from his grasp. "But I am afraid I cannot accept."

He blinked and straightened, disappointment clear on his features. After a moment, he seemed to recover his equilibrium. "May I at least have the satisfaction of knowing why?"

She glanced down at her hands. "I do not believe we would suit."

A single dark eyebrow rose. "I beg to differ. I believe we would suit very well. We have similar interests and compatible personalities." He paused and rubbed a hand over his jaw. "If this is because of Clarissa, because you are worried about taking on so much responsibility so quickly—"

"No, my lord," she entreated, cutting him off. "This has nothing to do with your daughter. She sounds like a lovely child, obedient and sweet and most deserving of your obvious love for her. She is one reason why I would be tempted to accept you, but . . ."

"Ah, but . . ." He paced a couple steps across the floor. "Is it me? Do you find the idea of me as a husband unappealing?"

"No, not at all."

"Then it is my ham-fisted proposal, perhaps? The fact that I did not stress from the start how great an affection I hold for you. If you would let me, perhaps I could persuade you."

She shook her head and gave him a gentle smile. "You could try, but my answer would remain the same."

He studied her for a long moment. "Then there is someone else. Ah, I can see from your expression that I am right. I assume this affection is serious, and you have expectation of an offer forthcoming from this man?"

Lowering her gaze, she traced the edge of an embroidered flower on her skirt. She didn't know why, but she decided to be honest. Lord Maplewood deserved that much.

"I hope he will make me an offer," she said, meeting his gaze. "Although I do not at present have the right to say I have a firm expectation of one from him. He and I . . . we are . . . still courting."

Maplewood scowled. "Well, he is a fool if he does not come up to snuff and make you his wife. I suppose you love him? He is not a penniless scoundrel, is he? Someone who may be taking advantage of your kind nature?"

"Oh, no, my lord. He is a most honorable man, and you have no cause to suspect such a base motive of him. And yes, I do love him."

Shoulders lowering in defeat, he glanced away.

She stood. "My lord, I am so very sorry. I never intended to cause you sadness or distress. And I meant it when I said you are a wonderful man. I know you will find a woman one day who is worthy of your admiration and affection."

Emotion softened his strong features. "I believe I already found such a woman, but her heart, it seems, is otherwise engaged." Reaching for her hand, he raised it to his lips and brushed a kiss across the top. "I wish you every happiness. Adieu, Miss Hammond."

On a nod, he exited the room.

Not long after, she heard the front door open and close, then the sound of his team of horses moving away down the street.

With his departure, she flopped onto the sofa.

Violet arrived less than a minute later, rushing in with a look of barely suppressed excitement enlivening her features. "Well, what did Lord Maplewood say? And why has he left already? I thought surely he would stay long enough for the two of you to share your news. You do have news, do you not? I mean, I wasn't mistaken that he came to propose?"

"No, you were not mistaken."

Violet clasped her hands to her breasts. "And?"

Eliza repressed a sigh. "And I refused him."

Violet's hands fell to her sides. "But why? I thought you liked Lord Maplewood. You always seem to have such a fine time in his company, and the two of you share so many interests, including a love of literature. He struck me as a splendid match for you."

"He thought so too. And I do like him. He is a very amiable man. But . . ."

"But?" Violet encouraged gently.

Eliza gazed into her friend's ocean-tinted eyes. "But I do not love him."

"Oh."

"Is it so wrong of me to want to love the man I marry?" She jumped to her feet. "Am I so desperate I must accept any gentleman who is not a villain or a gargoyle?"

"No, of course not, and I never meant to imply as much." Violet came forward and wrapped an arm around Eliza's shoulders. "You have every right to expect love, even to demand it in the man with whom you will spend the rest of your life. I had not realized but I have been quite inconsiderate. I cannot conceive of being married to anyone but Adrian, nor know how I would go on without the joy and reassurance of the bond he and I share. It was wrong of me to imagine you could be contented with any less. Forgive me."

"There is nothing to forgive." She returned Violet's hug. "At the start of this matrimonial hunt, I said I wanted a man who is pleasant and kind, and not a fortune hunter. Lord Maplewood by far fits those requirements, truly he exceeds them and would make a most excellent husband. But I find that I want more, I want to love and be loved in return."

"And so you should." Violet squeezed Eliza's shoulder before lowering her arm to her side. "Is there any particular gentleman among your suitors for whom you do have a special affection?"

Eliza hesitated. Should she tell Violet? Reveal the depth of her love for Kit and her quest to win him and his elusive heart? As always, the urge to share with her friend rose within her.

"Not exactly," she said, "but—"

"What is this I hear?" Kit interrupted, striding into the salon. "Do I understand correctly that Maplewood paid an unexpected call upon Eliza this morning?"

Violet swung toward him. "I see the house grapevine is working with its usual blistering speed and efficiency. But yes, you are quite right. Lord Maplewood was here."

His gaze flew to Eliza. "What did he want?"

Was that anxiety she read on his face, or was it only her own wishful thinking? Eliza wondered. She drew a breath and unconsciously straightened her shoulders. "He asked me to marry him."

"Did he?" A scowl creased Kit's dark brows in a way that made her glad.

"I did not accept," she added in a soft voice.

For a long moment he stared, a glimmer of an emotion she could not interpret flickering inside his eyes. Then he gave a nod. "I should think not. No cause to take the first fellow who comes up to scratch, don't you agree, Vi? Maplewood's too serious for Eliza. He'd have the pair of them inurned in the countryside, prosing over boring estate business and reading to each other in the evenings before bedtime. Makes me yawn just thinking about it."

Violet laughed. "Kit, you are horrible! Lord Maplewood is a delightful man, very considerate and good."

"Didn't say he wasn't good, just that he needs to loosen up a bit."

"Like you, I would imagine," his sister-in-law teased.

"Nothing wrong with having a bit of fun every now and again." With a shameless smile, he turned his twinkling gaze on Eliza and gave her a bold wink. "Is there, Miss Hammond?"

The force of his personality struck her like a fireworks display, leaving her simultaneously bewitched and bedazzled. Pulse points hammering inside her wrists, she fought not to show her reaction, aware that Violet was watching them both.

Eliza dipped her chin. "No, my lord, nothing wrong at all."

The next evening, applause erupted inside the theater, startling Eliza from her private daydreams. Below on the stage, the actors took a quick bow before withdrawing behind the curtains to make ready for the second half of the play.

Viscount Brevard turned from his seat next to her. "How do you like it, then?"

She stared for a long second of incomprehension, finally realizing he must mean the play. Luckily this was not the first time she had seen *Othello*.

"Very affecting," she said, "though I never understand how Othello allows himself to fall prey to such an obvious deceiver as Iago. He would do well, after the interval, to put more faith in his bride, but alas I know he will not, yet again."

Brevard gave a sad shake of his head. "No, I fear a tragic end yet awaits poor Desdemona. The fair lady is doomed to die."

The viscount, his sister and one of Franny's young friends, Miss Twitchell, had joined Eliza and the rest of the duke's party at the theater tonight. Seated in the ducal box, Eliza had an excellent view of the entertainment.

She also had an excellent view of Kit, who had arrived solo, then sought out a group of his cronies in a box across the way. Despite her best attempts, the action on the stage had not held her attention, not enough to keep her eyes from straying time and again toward Kit. He'd been watching her as well, she was sure of it, though it was difficult to tell for certain in the dim theater lighting.

Now the interval had arrived.

Would Kit seek her out? Her senses throbbed at the notion before she told herself to put away her fancies. Kit might continue to "instruct" her in private, but he was always careful to project an air of the benevolent, platonic friend whenever they were together in company. Sometimes she wished he would forget his practiced facade and let his passion for her show. Of course, what she truly wished was that he would join the ranks of her suitors, then order all of them to be gone, declaring to the world that she belonged to him.

But until that time she would continue to play the game, continue to let gentlemen like Viscount Brevard shower her with their attention. With that determination in mind, Eliza met Brevard's gaze and shared a warm smile.

He smiled back, eyes as blue as a June sky.

His sister, blond and pretty as a spring daffodil, appeared beside them. "Lance, may Jane and I have permission to go across to Lady Margate's box? Her daughters are in attendance, and we should very much like to talk with them."

The viscount looked between his sister and Miss Twitchell, both girls waiting with expressions of eager hopefulness on their faces. "Very well—" he began.

The girls interrupted with claps and whoops.

"So long as Miss Hammond consents to accompany me," Brevard continued. "We shall walk behind the pair of you, so I can be assured you have arrived at the Margates' box without incident. Most people here in the upper levels are quite well mannered, but one never knows when a ruffian may slip up the stairs to accost unescorted young ladies." He turned to Eliza. "So what do you say, Miss Hammond? Would you care for a stroll?"

Eliza nodded. "Yes, of course. Miss Brevard and Miss Twitchell would be quite cast down if I did not. And taking a turn around the theater sounds vastly refreshing."

The viscount stood, then extended his arm for Eliza to take. She paused to let Violet and Adrian know their destination, then the four of them were on their way.

The girls, Franny and Jane, preceded them out into the corridor, walking arm in arm as they chatted to each other. Eliza and Brevard strolled behind, careful to give the pair enough room not to feel crowded.

They soon arrived at the Margates' box, Lady Margate and her daughters cheered to receive them. A trio of handsome young gentlemen were also in the box. Another reason, Eliza surmised, that Franny and Jane had been so eager for the visit.

After a couple minutes of polite conversation, Lady Margate bid Eliza and the viscount farewell, promising to bring the girls back to the duke's box before the play resumed. Assured of his sister's and her friend's safety, Eliza and Brevard resumed their stroll.

"Shall we continue on in the direction we have been walking before making our return?" Brevard inquired.

"Yes, let's. There are several minutes left in the interval, and after so much sitting a stroll sounds just the thing."

But their perambulations were slow due to the multitude of elegantly dressed ladies and gentlemen thronging the corridor. Conversation was also not as easy to conduct as one might imagine, the haze of noise so thick it drifted on the air like a cloud of smoke. Tiny, oil-burning wall sconces lighted the way, giving off a muted, almost golden light. She and the viscount stopped often, pausing to exchange pleasantries with one acquaintance after another.

They had made their turn at the end of the corridor, and were about halfway back to Violet and Adrian's box when a tall, wiry man slithered through the crowd. With hair and eyes as black and flat as a bottomless chasm, he crept forward, his gaze scraping over her like the brush of an icy claw.

Philip Pettigrew.

She had not seen him since that unnerving encounter at Raeburn House the day he had practically demanded she marry him. Perhaps after that, he had gone away from Town. Obviously wherever he had slunk off to, he had now returned, dressed as usual like an undertaker in unrelenting black.

She considered turning away and pretending she had not noticed him. But there was nowhere to retreat and if she publicly cut him, the incident would cause a stir among the gossipmongers. Steeling herself, she kept a firm hold on Brevard's muscled arm and forced a pleasant expression onto her face.

"Cousin Eliza," Pettigrew declared, drawing to a halt before them. "What a pleasure to find you here this evening. I did not realize you were in attendance until I happened to spy you among the crowd only a moment ago."

Now, why, she wondered, did she think he was lying? Shaking off the unsettling feeling, she nodded her head in greeting. "Cousin."

An awkward instant of silence fell, Pettigrew quite plainly waiting for an introduction.

"Lord Brevard," she said, "pray let me make you

known to my cousin, Mr. Philip Pettigrew." She paused, not meeting Pettigrew's gaze. "Cousin Philip, Viscount Lancelot Brevard. I assume you gentlemen do not have a prior acquaintance."

"No, I have not had the occasion. Pettigrew." The viscount thrust out a palm.

The men shook hands.

"I didn't realize Miss Hammond had family in Town," Brevard remarked.

"Cousin Eliza does not possess many relations," Pettigrew said, "her own dear parents having long since gone to their maker. Her aunt and myself were really Eliza's only close relatives. But now that Mama is gone, God bless her sainted soul, there is only myself. A shame we do not see more of each other, is it not, Cousin?"

Eliza stared at him, fighting a frown. If she said "No," as he surely must know she longed to do, she would sound churlish. And if she agreed, he might take advantage of the opening to ingratiate himself upon her again.

Taking the middle path, she made a noncommittal noise. "Good to happen upon you, Cousin, but I believe his lordship and I should be returning to our seats now."

"Oh, there is still plenty of time remaining in the interval, enough to chat for another minute or two."

She cringed inside, wanting to walk away regardless of Pettigrew's assertion, but manners long ingrained held her in place.

"You must be enjoying the Season this year, Cousin," Pettigrew said. "Your name is on everyone's lips, remarking on the swath you've been cutting among the Ton." He paused, showing his discolored teeth. "Quite a change from your prior Seasons. How many were there?"

A gleam in her cousin's eyes showed her he knew exactly how many there had been.

She stiffened and refused to rise to his obvious bait. "I really could not say."

"Well, however many it is," Pettigrew continued, blinking in a slow, direct way that put her in mind of a reptile, " 'tis commendable of you to maintain your optimism. Most women of your years would have donned a spinster's cap and set themselves firmly on the shelf ages ago. All your success this Season must be gratifying. Although I confess surprise that I have not yet heard news of an engagement."

Brevard's arm tensed beneath her hand, but before he could respond, a familiar voice entered the fray.

"I am sure the lady will reveal her choice of husband when she is ready to do so, and not a minute before," Kit said, his tone carrying a hard, implacable edge she had never heard him use. "You can read the engagement announcement in the paper when the time comes, Pettigrew."

The disdain in Kit's words carried like the smack of a glove across the other man's gaunt cheek. For a second, a malevolent light flickered in Pettigrew's obsidian gaze, then vanished as quickly as it had arrived.

"Lord Christopher," her cousin said with false warmth, "a pleasure as always."

"If you say." Kit made no effort to greet the other man as good manners dictated.

"Obviously you feel I have overstepped, but I meant nothing untoward. As Cousin Eliza's closest relation, I am merely concerned for her future welfare and happiness."

"Oh, I am sure you are," Kit said, his words dripping with sarcasm. "And still lamenting the loss of your mother's money as well, no doubt." He leaned forward, tall and intimidating despite the fact that he and Pettigrew were of a similar height. "Whatever wild permutations are rumbling around inside that head of yours, you can put them away. Eliza and her wealth are out of your reach. She refused you once, and she won't be entertaining your unwelcome advances again."

"You wound me, my lord. I merely stopped to converse and reacquaint myself with my cousin. Surely I have a right to speak with my own family?"

"You've spoken to her. Now be gone."

An unnatural flush colored Pettigrew's usually pallid complexion, his upper lip trembling. "I should call you out for your insulting behavior and the accusations you have made about myself and my intentions."

Kit crossed his arms over his chest, clearly amused. "Want to fight, do you? I shall be happy to oblige. Brevard here can act as my second."

The viscount gave a firm, tacit nod of agreement.

"So, what shall it be?" Kit dared. "Pistols or swords? Either choice makes little difference since I am proficient at both. Or if you're worried about dying, we could meet in the ring at Gentleman Jackson's. I am sure I could provide you entrée, since I know you do not hold a subscription."

At the mention of violence, alarm squeezed inside Eliza's chest. "Oh, Kit, please, stop. Do not do this."

Without glancing her way, he reached out and patted the hand she had laid on his arm. Otherwise, he kept his attention centered on her cousin.

"Well, Pettigrew? I am waiting."

To Eliza's dismay, she saw that Kit was not the only one waiting. A small cluster of ladies and gentlemen had congregated and were pretending, not very successfully, to be minding their own business, when in actuality they were riveted to every word.

Visibly bristling, Pettigrew puffed out his scrawny chest and thrust forward his bony chin, his Adam's apple bobbing up and down like a buoy. Just when everyone was beginning to wonder if he might actually be foolish enough to agree to meet Kit, he growled low, spun on one heel and elbowed his way through the crowd.

"Appears his threats are as empty as his pocketbook," Kit quipped in a voice loud enough to carry.

Their audience tittered and made a couple of choice remarks. Since the interval was about to end, they had the grace to quickly disburse and return to their seats.

Once the corridor stood deserted, Kit turned to Eliza. "Are you all right?"

She had not thought herself affected, but now that the entire encounter was over, she began to tremble.

Seeing her condition, Kit gazed at Brevard. "As you can see, Miss Hammond is overset. If you would be so good as to inform my brother and his wife of our departure, I shall escort Miss Hammond home."

"There is no need for you to leave. I shall be fine," she told Kit.

He shook his head. "You won't be fine with half the audience watching you for the remainder of the evening. You know how quickly word spreads. Let me take you back to Raeburn House. Adrian and Violet can handle any uproar that follows. Since weathering their own scandal a couple years ago, they've grown quite skilled at quashing unwanted talk."

"Winter is right, Miss Hammond," Brevard urged. "You would only cause yourself unneeded grief if you remained. And most likely by the time you awaken tomorrow, there'll be some new fodder for everyone to start chewing on, and they will forget all about yours."

She worried her lower lip with her teeth, then nodded. "Very well. But please tell the duchess not to be alarmed and to stay for the rest of the play. I do not wish to be the ruin of her evening."

"You won't be," Kit assured her before turning to the other man. "Thank you, Brevard, and good evening."

She tossed a weak smile to the viscount. "Yes, thank you, my lord. Pray give my regards to your sister and Miss Twitchell."

With a nod and a farewell, Brevard bowed, then strode away.

Kit offered her his arm. "Come, my little wren, let us away."

She set her hand on his sleeve and together they departed.

Chapter Eighteen

Outside the theater, Kit took the coach seat opposite Eliza and waited while the servants closed the door and made ready to set the vehicle in motion.

All evening long, Kit had kept his distance from Eliza. At first, he'd fleetingly considered attending the theater with the rest of the family, but had known the wiser choice would be to sit with his friends across the gallery, instead of inside the box with Eliza. Being so near her, he knew he might give in to the temptation to steal a quick touch or two, a craving that lately was beginning to border on obsession.

So he'd contented himself by watching her instead, gratified to catch occasional glimpses of her watching him back from across the darkened venue.

But during the interval, when he'd come upon Pettigrew publicly accosting her, his intention to remain discreetly in the background had vanished, his only thought to come to her aid and erase the expression of distress from her face.

Now as they sat together alone in the coach, he was doubly glad he had.

The coach lurched slightly as the driver flicked the reins, giving a command to send the team forward. As soon as the horses were moving, so was Kit, levering himself up and across to sit beside Eliza.

Curling an arm over her shoulders, he pulled her close. "Feeling better?" he asked.

She nodded. "I am now."

"Then what are these shivers?" he admonished gently, rubbing soothing fingers across the strip of bare skin that lay between the edge of her short, silk sleeve and the top of her elbow-length glove.

From underneath her lashes, she cast him a glance. "I am a little cold, I guess."

"Here, then, let me warm you up."

Without further warning, he lifted her off the seat and onto his lap, setting her snuggly against him, his arms wrapped tight. "Ah, now, this *is* better."

She wiggled for a moment in obvious surprise, her bottom brushing against him in a way that drove a rush of longing straight to his loins. As if she knew exactly what sort of difficulty she'd put him in, she stopped squirming, but her efforts came too late.

He couldn't complain, though, enjoying the sensation of holding her so near. On a quiet sigh, she leaned her head against his shoulder.

Stroking her arm, he gave her a light kiss. "Relax, sweet. You're safe."

"I know. Just as I know I was never in any real danger, it's only that he's so very dreadful."

"That he is. A wart on the world's backside. But Pettigrew is gone now, and I don't want you worrying about your cousin bothering you anymore. I'll keep you safe."

Snuggling closer, she slid an arm around his waist. "I never did thank you for stepping in the way you did. I think Lord Brevard was about to try, but—"

"But he doesn't know what a snake your cousin is, or what a coward. I guess everyone in the Ton will know now."

Eliza raised her head to meet his gaze. "Philip was furious, Kit. You oughtn't to have goaded him the way you did."

"I wouldn't have been in any real peril, I assure you, even if he had mustered the nerve to fight me."

"Oh, I know that. I was only concerned that if you killed him, you would end up having to flee the country, particularly considering the number of witnesses there were to the event."

Kit stared at her for an instant before tossing his head back on a hearty laugh. He was still chuckling moments later. "That's what is so enchanting about you, Eliza, you're always so delightfully honest. It's a refreshing quality that few people possess. Promise never to lose it, my little wren, no matter how old you may one day grow."

A dreamy smile blossomed across her lips, her cheeks glowing with a pleasure visible even in the tenebrous interior of the coach. "I promise," she murmured, her voice solemn and husky.

The humor inside him faded as quickly as it had come, desire stirring once again to life. Tightening his hold, he reached up and stroked the warm, satiny skin of her cheek, before roving downward in a gradual glide, tracing the slender column of her throat as he went. At the base, he curled gentle fingers against the underside of her jaw, then tipped back her head to position it for his kiss.

He dusted his lips across one cheek. "You said something about wanting to thank me." He bent to pay homage to the other cheek. "I believe I know just the way. Why don't you show me what I've taught you and exactly how much you've learned."

With that invitation, he waited, earning his reward seconds later when she buried her fingers in his hair and dragged his lips down to hers. As Eliza plundered his mouth with impressive thoroughness, Kit realized she had indeed learned a great deal under his tutelage, her touch sending his senses reeling, turning his brain to mush.

Like she always did, Eliza experienced a blaze of emotion, a sizzle in her blood that by rights should have sent up sparks. Toes curling inside her satin evening slippers, she poured every ounce of passion and skill into her embrace.

His tongue tangled with hers in a wild dance, dynamic and intense, showing her that her efforts were proving effective. Groaning, he slid his hand lower to cup her breast, rubbing the taut peak of her nipple through the delicate silk of her gown.

Shifting on his lap, she encouraged him to take more, and to her profound delight, he did. Tugging down a sleeve and one side of her bodice, he freed a single breast, giving it a tantalizing squeeze before raising her up enough to fasten his mouth upon her willing body.

The pull of his lips and teeth and tongue against her sensitive flesh sent her skyward. Needing desperately to touch him, she reached under his coat and waistcoat to pluck frantically at his thin lawn shirt. Unable to find bare skin, she contented herself by stroking him through the cloth, relishing his heat and the firm shape of his hard, male muscles.

Growling, he suckled upon her more deeply, even as he reached down a hand to drag her skirts high. Up moved his fingers, gliding as they had that day in the library, along the length of her calf, over knee and thigh. He caressed her leg and hip for a full span of minutes, but instead of withdrawing this time, he continued on.

Stroking her inner thighs, he made her shudder, her eyes closed in hot, dreamlike bliss. Seconds later, her eyelids popped wide as he inserted a finger inside her in a way she had never imagined she might ever be touched.

"*Oh, dear God,*" she whimpered, crying out as he began to finesse her there, deep between her legs. Claiming her mouth again, he caught the tiny moans and sighs and panting groans that issued from her throat, the sounds completely out of her ability to control.

An ache built where he caressed her, escalating higher with each subsequent inner stroke. Just when she thought it couldn't possibly feel better, he added another finger and thrust inside her, deep and slow, taking his time so she could adjust to the added width.

She arched and gave a shout, the noise muffled inside his mouth. No longer capable of forming a coherent thought, she lay utterly helpless in his arms as he stroked her to the breaking point. Grasping at the cloth of his shirt, she hung on as if in peril for her very life.

A cry rang from her lips when the crisis came, her whole body shaking as a burst of blinding pleasure spiked through her, fierce and profound as a lightning bolt, singeing her blood and bones and sinew.

Panting for breath, she clung to him as the tremors of delight gradually began to subside. Only then did she become aware of Kit's own physical state, the length of him pressed like a hard rod against her bottom. Acting on pure instinct, she curled slightly to one side then reached a hand between their bodies.

His flesh leapt at her touch, even through the satin of his evening breeches. He bit his lip to restrain a groan, squeezing his eyes closed in an expression that was a mix of ecstasy and agony, as she traced the shape of his rigid arousal.

He lowered his hand and covered hers, patiently but firmly showing her the exact manner in which he wished to be touched. Gladly obeying his direction, she caressed him, amazed at the differences in their bodies, and the similarity of their response.

Obviously wanting more, he reached up to unfasten the buttons of his falls.

Just then, the coach came to a halt.

For a second, the vehicle's sudden cessation of movement made no sense to either of them. She and Kit stared at each other, frozen as they both tried to comprehend.

She heard sounds—the whickering of the horses, the jangling of their bridles as they waited in eagerness to unload their passengers and make the last short trip around the house to the mews and the comfort of their stalls. She heard too the muted, easy conversation of the coachman and footman, as the second man sprang down to open the coach door.

Quicker than she'd ever seen him move, Kit tugged her bodice into place, flung her skirts down over her legs, then lifted her bodily and placed her onto the seat at his side. Sliding as far away as the coach seat would allow, he raked a hand through his disheveled hair and plucked at the front of his breeches as if hoping to somehow ease the stiffened flesh beneath.

He curved an arm across his lap and leaned farther back into the darkened corner.

The door opened, light from the nearby streetlamps and Raeburn House's own lanterns spilling inside in a pool that tonight seemed unnecessarily bright. The footman waited for them to descend.

"We'll just be a minute, Robert," Kit told the servant in clipped tones. "Miss Hammond and I were having a . . . conversation."

"Of course, my lord."

"And shut the door, would you?"

Robert sent them a curious glance. "Yes, my lord."

Moments later, the door closed.

Kit heaved a sigh and leaned his head against the velvet squab. "Good God, if we'd been even a second slower . . ." He left the rest of the statement unsaid.

Half-dazed, her body continuing to tingle and throb in any number of unmentionable places, Eliza could only agree.

"What must they think?" she whispered, shooting a sideways glance out at the servants waiting for them to emerge. Even March stood at the entrance, the front door open in readiness for their ascent.

"They may think we've having a quarrel," Kit said. "At least let's hope that's what they think. On the other hand, if I make an attempt to climb down from this coach in my current state, none of them will have to guess at anything."

Her gaze shot to the substantial bulge between his legs, a bulge that seemed to grow larger beneath the force of her stare.

Kit raised a brow. "I would advise you stop doing that unless you wish to stay here and finish what we started."

Her eyes flew upward, heat scalding her cheeks.

"I would also suggest you go ahead inside," he continued in a gentler tone. "Will you be all right if I don't escort you to the door?"

She nodded. "Yes, but what about you?"

"I'll travel on to my club. That should take the wind out of my sails, so to speak."

"Oh," she murmured, downcast that he would not be going inside with her, even though she knew he was making the prudent choice. Her hand trembled faintly as she readjusted her bodice and smoothed out her skirts.

After a deep inhale, she shifted toward him on the seat. "How do I look?"

A gleam blazed in his beautiful green-gold eyes.

Catching her hand in his own, he pressed a kiss onto her palm. "Stunning. But then, you always do, my dear."

Radiant warmth clamored inside her heart.

Leaning forward, Kit rapped on the door, then lowered himself back onto the seat. Shifting slightly, he once again draped a strategically placed arm across his lap and crossed his legs.

Robert opened the door.

"Assist Miss Hammond inside, if you would, Robert. Then inform Josephs I will be driving on to Brooks Club."

The footman bowed. "With pleasure, Lord Christopher. Miss?" he said, extending a hand to help her navigate the small metal coach steps.

March gave her a cheerful greeting as she mounted the stone staircase to the main entrance. Once she was safely across the threshold, the coach door slammed, then the vehicle rolled away down the street.

Hours later, Kit let himself into the darkened townhouse with a small key he kept for just such occasions. His footfalls rang out softly on the marble floor, the residence silent, even the servants abed at three o'clock in the morning.

He had not wanted to go to his club earlier that evening.

Not when every cell inside his body had been screaming for him to follow Eliza into the house, hustle her inside one of their bedrooms and spend the rest of the night ravishing her.

And damned if he might not have done that very thing—in spite of the servants, in spite of Adrian and Violet—if it hadn't been for the look of naive puzzlement and shock in Eliza's eyes when the pair of them had been on the verge of being discovered inside the coach.

The forceful reminder of her innocence had awakened his brain, along with his sense of right and wrong. So he'd set her aside, then worked to cool his lust on the ride across Town.

Despite his need for rest, he crossed into the downstairs study where he knew Adrian kept a decanter of brandy. Maybe a draught of spirits and a few minutes' contemplation in front of the fire would ease the restlessness still brewing inside him, enough for him to fall asleep anyway.

Lighting a single candle to dispel the heavy shadows, he went to a cabinet along the far wall. Locating a glass and the promised crystal decanter of brandy, he poured himself a drink.

He'd just replaced the stopper and was downing his first swallow when a filmy glimpse of white flashed into his line of sight.

Surprise made him choke. Sputtering, he spun and locked gazes with Eliza. He coughed twice before he managed to catch a proper breath. "*Plague take it*, I wasn't expecting anyone. Whatever are you doing up so late?"

A tiny line creased her brow. "I could not sleep and came down for some warm milk. I'm sorry if I scared you."

He waved off her apology, then decided to brave another sip. The alcohol slid down his throat with a satisfying warmth before he set the snifter aside.

Only then did he notice the tumbler in Eliza's hand—a glass of warm milk, no doubt. In imitation of his actions, she took a drink, then moved to place the glass carefully onto the same table as his brandy.

As she drew closer, the honeyed scent of her skin teased his nostrils, his earlier desire roaring vividly to life. Dark and tousled, her curls framed her face in seductive disarray, her nightgown and robe of fine, white lawn draping her slender curves in a way that hid far too little from his view. If he'd had a little more candlelight, he could probably have seen through the gown. And her feet were bare.

Hot blood rushed to his groin. Cursing inwardly, he scowled.

"How was your club?" she asked.

He stared for a moment at the non sequitur. "Brooks was fine. I won a hundred pounds playing faro."

"Oh, that's good. You'll have to buy yourself something nice, something you've been wanting."

What he wanted was her.

At his side, his hands curled into fists.

She glided a single step closer, her dove-gray eyes dark and mysterious in the low light. For a long moment, neither of them spoke, their gazes speaking for them.

Every muscle in his body grew rigid as he fought the need to drag her into his arms.

"Go to bed, Eliza," he growled in a harsh voice. Perhaps if he sounded nasty enough, he could convince her to leave. Surely even she must realize this was no time to be playing games.

But she held her ground. "I told you, I can't sleep. I think I need more than warm milk. Don't you think . . ." she said on a near whisper, "that I need more?"

Body trembling, he held himself in check.

His restraint lasted all of ten seconds before he broke and hauled her against him. Their lips met and fused, locking together in a blistering explosion of passionate need. Kissing her greedily, he claimed her mouth in long, deep, hungry draughts that permitted no denial, and demanded nothing less than her complete capitulation. On a breathy murmur, she gave him everything he asked for and more, turning the tables so that soon he found himself as tightly ensnared in the web they were weaving as she.

Catching her buttocks under his arm, he lifted her up and fit his hips to hers. She moaned, clasping her arms around his neck to stroke his shoulders and neck, back and waist, touching him in all the places her arms and hands could reach.

Head spinning, Kit gave one last thought to setting her down and pushing her from him, as good sense warned he must do. But even as the idea formed, it slipped away, disappearing like a piece of driftwood snatched by the tide and swallowed whole.

Running his hands over her, he traced her shape, learning the blithe lines and vivacious curves of her body as if for the first time, his access enhanced now that there were no petticoats and stays to impede his exploration. Soft and warm and pliant, her femininity held a kind of divine perfection. He let himself drown, reveling in her scent and touch and taste, the sensation of her in his arms as close to heaven as a man could come.

And yet, as near as she was, she wasn't near enough. He needed more, needed to sheath himself inside her and sate the hunger that pounded within him, strong as a beast rattling in a cage to be free.

Throwing the bonds of caution aside, he gently lowered Eliza to the thick soft woolen carpet, then followed her down, laying over her as he let his lips and touch roam at will. Kissing her wildly, he lost himself, aware only of his, and Eliza's own, aching desire.

Abandoned to a drugging haze of sensuality, Eliza gloried in every hot, delicious thing Kit was doing to her mouth and body. Tingling from scalp to foot, she let him guide her where he would, doing what small things she knew to do to intensify his pleasure.

Sighing, she caught her lower lip between her teeth, and quivered in delight as he unfastened the small placket of buttons that ran along the front of her night-gown. She watched as he pushed back the cloth, pleased by the look in his eyes as he gazed once more upon her naked breasts. He cupped them in his hands, and then began to lavish her with caresses and kisses and the occasional perfectly placed nip that shot fire through her veins.

By rights, she ought to have experienced some sense of reticence, some feeling of shyness or shame. Instead she knew only excitement and joy, safe in the arms of the man she loved, confident beneath the power of his every caress.

Fingers trembling, she reached up to return the favor, a fever of curiosity rising inside her to see his own flesh laid bare. With only partial success, she managed to unfasten a couple buttons before he took over the task, hastily shucking off his coat and opening his waistcoat before yanking his shirttails out of his breeches.

Tunneling her arms under his shirt, she sought out his skin, marveling at the byplay of textures she discovered. Warm, velvety skin layered over hard muscle and bone. Crisp, springy hair that clung to her fingers when she threaded them into the soft curls that grew close to his chest.

Shivering at her touch, he buried his face between her breasts and sent the ache shooting hot and high. Her longing spiked even more when he shoved her night-gown to her waist and began to touch her as he had earlier in the coach.

She whimpered and moaned as he drove her to a feverish pitch, her body growing slick in ways she hadn't realized it could, her inner flesh clinging to his fingers with a sweet suction that made her half crazy.

Curling her fingernails into her palms, the pleasure suddenly caught her, making her buck and cry out. Shuddering, she rode the crest, swamped by a cascade of sensations and emotions. She was still gathering her breath, drawing her thoughts back from the brink of oblivion, when she felt him reach between their bodies and free himself from his breeches.

Sliding a hand under one of her knees, he parted her legs, using his knee to grant him even greater access.

Leaning across her, he plunging his fingers into her hair and savaged her mouth, his kiss raw and elemental. Without breaking contact, he lowered his hands to clasp her hips and position her to accept his penetration.

He began pressing inside her, slowly at first, then with increased pressure. Tensing against the initial feeling of invasion as he thrust, she worried suddenly whether or not she would be able to take him. He was large, she knew, given what she had felt of him earlier that evening in the coach. Fear coursed through her. Was he going to fit? But Kit must believe he would, she mused, or else he wouldn't be attempting to push himself inside her.

Forcing herself to trust him, she closed her eyes and bit her lip against the discomfort, and the mild sense of panic.

Breathing heavily, he paused, obviously sensing her need for time, and for an opportunity to adapt to his size and the sensation of their joined flesh. Murmuring tender words, he urged her to raise her legs and hook them around his narrow hips. Compliant, she obeyed, her feminine flesh opening wider to take more of him inside.

Taking advantage, he plunged again and gained another few inches, then paused to let her adjust. Reaching up, she slid her hands across his naked back beneath his shirt, finding his skin slightly damp with perspiration. Needing to hold on, she curled her fingernails in to anchor herself. He grunted in surprise, then kissed her, letting her know he didn't mind the mild pain.

Pulling back, he thrust once more, hard and firm and to the hilt, seating himself fully.

A sharp burst of pain spread deep within her. She cried out against the hurt, but to her surprise found the ache fading almost as swiftly as it had arrived.

"All right?" he grunted, his eyes dark green flame, sparkling fiercely in the ruddy glow of the fireplace light.

Overwhelmed, she could only nod.

Cupping her face in his large palms, he brushed his lips over hers. "It won't hurt again. I promise."

She gazed up into his beloved face, reading the signs of both his strain as well as his restraint. Until that moment, she hadn't realized Kit had been holding back, keeping firm control of his actions and his needs.

Trembling above her as if he could take no more, he caught her mouth in a frenzied kiss and began thrusting. In and out he plunged, taking her in long, deep, powerful strokes, his movements establishing a primal rhythm that rocked her to her center.

She lay still, quite prepared to endure whatever might come next, but as he drove into her, hunger sprang to life once more. Her spine arched of its own volition, her body heating, proving it knew what it wanted, even if she didn't fully understand. Sweet yearning engulfed her, flooding her senses so that she was rendered incapable of catching a proper breath, her sanity taking flight as he swept her toward the pinnacle.

Pumping her hips in naive instinct, she tried to match his pace, hands sliding and grasping, nails scratching as she fought toward her pleasure. She yielded her body utterly and completely to him, knowing he would keep her secure.

When a wail ripped from her throat, she barely recognized the sound as belonging to herself, the intensity of her release both frightening and fulfilling. Gliding aloft the way birds must as they soar above the clouds, she sobbed out her pleasure, shuddering violently before drifting gradually downward.

Aftershocks pinged and popped inside her, her mind and body drowsy with rapture and repletion.

But Kit had not yet taken his satisfaction, stroking inside her a few last, powerful times, before stiffening and calling out her name. Smiling, she held him as he quaked, then cradled him as he collapsed upon her and tucked his cheek against her own.

Lying together, she knew he loved her. How else could a man do what they had done and not feel more than simple lust? Her heart burst wide at the thought as she sifted her fingers through the damp silk of his hair.

I love you, Kit.

The words trembled on her lips, about to spill forth when suddenly she noticed a change in him, a slight cooling of his skin, a new tension that tightened the muscles in his neck and shoulders.

Exhaling, he eased himself from her body and rolled onto his back beside her.

"Dear Lord," he groaned, lifting a hand to cover his eyes, "what have we done?"

A shiver raised gooseflesh on her skin, her buoyant glow of happiness fading like a doused candle. She frowned. Was that regret she heard in his voice? Did he wish they had not made love after all? Surely she must be wrong.

Quiet fell over the room, the gentle hiss and spit of a last log burning in the fireplace, accompanied by the soft ticking of the rosewood casement clock that stood in a distant corner.

Raising his hips to tuck his shirttails into his breeches, Kit fastened his falls, then sat up.

And that's when she realized she was not mistaken.

Suddenly, brutally, she became aware of her rumpled state, sprawled on the study floor like some doxy, with her nightgown bunched around her waist, her breasts naked and exposed. A draft of air washed over her, making her nipples pucker, but from cold this time, not desire.

Reaching down, she struggled to cover herself, plucking at her nightgown and robe, and the open top of her gown.

"Here," Kit murmured, "let me."

With an irritation wholly unlike her, she considered slapping his hands away. Instead she allowed him to help her into a sitting position, only then noticing the rude smear of blood on her thighs, a few crimson drops staining the white cloth beneath.

She stared.

Her lost virginity, she mused. Given in love. Defiled by remorse.

Obviously unaware of her thoughts, Kit drew her skirts down over her legs, concealing the evidence of their recent coupling. When he moved his hands toward her bodice, she hunched her shoulders and turned away. "I'll do it."

He paused, then dropped his arms to his sides. "As you wish."

Ignoring the stiff, clumsy movement of her fingers, she forced herself to fasten every last button, all the way to her chin, then did the same with her robe.

Standing, he extended a hand and assisted her to her feet.

Instead of releasing her, he pulled her against his chest

and bent to brush a kiss over her forehead, tender and almost sexless, as though he were comforting a child.

"Forgive me," he said, his expression grave, his voice gruff and serious, more serious than she had ever heard him. "I completely lost my head tonight. But the responsibility is all mine and you are not to worry. I am fully prepared to do as honor requires."

Honor? What was he saying?

"It's very late, or very early depending upon your point of view. Either way, you should go to bed now and sleep." He skimmed a palm over her hair, then set her from him. "Tomorrow will be soon enough to discuss our plans."

A line formed between her brows. "What are you talking about? I am afraid I do not understand."

"No, you are far too innocent, even now." He sighed and dragged his fingers through his hair. "We must wed, Eliza. Duty leaves us no choice in the matter."

Wed? He wished to marry her?

But no, she realized, he did not wish it. He spoke of duty and honor and, yes, obligation, saying they had no choice.

A deep ache formed inside her chest.

"I'll apply for a special license, and we can do the deed as early as this weekend, assuming the archbishop gives us his consent. Under the circumstances, I am sure he will have no objection."

Deed! Is that what marriage to her would be? A task that must be performed no matter how disagreeable? A kind of penance from which he could not escape? He made the idea of their union sound about as pleasant as a trip to the tooth-drawers.

A splinter of pain stabbed beneath her breast. She wondered if it might be the breaking of her heart.

"No," she said in a low, steady tone.

The word stopped him in his tracks. "No? What do you mean?"

"I will not marry you."

For a moment, she couldn't believe what she had just heard herself say. Had she really turned down an offer of marriage from Kit? Miserable an offer as it most certainly was.

Isn't that what she had always wanted? What she had craved for so many, long years now? The chance to be Kit's wife, to live with him and share his life and bear his children. And yes, sleep in his bed. Despite the dreadful circumstances, she ought to have been jumping at the opportunity, willing to accept him on any terms, no matter how grim.

But she couldn't do it, not now, knowing he desired her but nothing more.

Knowing he did not love her.

And when the desire faded in time, as it surely would for him, what would be left for her but bitterness and sorrow?

No, she vowed, she would not bind them inside an uneven marriage. One he obviously did not want. One that she knew with certainty would tear her soul apart a single, small piece at a time.

She would have been better off accepting Lord Maplewood. At least with him she could feel an equal and not a burden forced upon him because of a single, imprudent act of passion.

No matter how much she loved Kit, she deserved better. And so, she thought, did he.

Kit shot her a fierce look. "You have to marry me."

She shook her head. "I do not. Now, it is late, as you said, and I am tired. It has been a long . . . eventful day."

"Eventful? Is that how you describe losing your virginity?"

His question brought heat into her cool cheeks.

He clasped his hands around her upper arms, pitching his voice to a gentle timbre. "I took your innocence, Eliza. I compromised you and now I must make amends."

Her resolve hardened, whatever ambiguity she might have been feeling about her decision dropping away.

"I thank you for your sacrifice, but there is no need. You are not the only one who participated in tonight's activities. I wanted you as much as you wanted me, perhaps more. With all these lessons we have been having, my curiosity has been running rampant. I must admit you more than satisfied my wildest fancies. You're better than any book, even a naughty one."

She drew in a breath to carry on her lighthearted act. "So you see there is no need for gallantry. I shall be quite fine, just as I am."

"But Eliza—"

She hushed him with a finger across his lips. "Please, don't persist. You do not wish to marry me, and I"—she swallowed—"do not wish to marry you. Let us leave it at that."

His green-gold eyes looked troubled. "But what if you are with child? You could be, you know."

Her eyes widened. No, she thought, she had not realized that such a thing could happen after only one time. But as she considered the possibility, she knew in her heart she had not conceived. A part of her cried at the knowledge.

She shook her head. "I feel sure I am not."

"But you could be, and if—"

"If anything should happen, I will let you know."

He sighed, whether from frustration or relief she could not tell.

Suddenly, needing one more touch, she rested her palms against his cheeks and pulled his head down for a final kiss. A last, wonderful, blindingly sweet kiss that rocked her to her toes.

"Thank you for a thrilling evening," she whispered. "I know I shall never forget it for as long as I live."

Then, already weeping inside, she turned and let him go.

Chapter Nineteen

A long while later, Kit made his way to his bedchamber, a newly refilled glass of brandy in his hand. Quaffing a healthy swallow, he proceeded along the hallway of the family quarters, his shoes silent against the finely patterned carpets.

As he neared Eliza's room, his step slowed. He stopped outside her door.

Was she already asleep? he wondered. Dreaming? And if so, of what? Of him? Of their lovemaking? Or something else? Her mind utterly calm and at peace?

He clenched a fist at his hip and drank another mouthful of spirits, desire firing his blood every bit as strongly as the drink. Despite their recent lovemaking, he was honest enough with himself to admit he wanted Eliza again. Even in her virgin state, she had been a magnificent lover, warm and ardent and inviting.

A few kisses from her satiny sweet lips, a couple caresses from her delicate hands, and he'd been lost to all reason and good sense. So far gone had he been, in fact, that he'd taken her there on the study floor like a barbarian. What must she think of him? Although, as he recalled, she had made no protest, welcoming, even encouraging his advances.

He had no excuses, though, castigating himself for his

weakness, his all-too-human frailty. He was the one with experience and control, the "teacher," who ought to have found a way to stop, no matter how impossible his need, or her own.

Afterward, his body brimming with sexual satisfaction, the magnitude of their act had rushed upon him. With stark clarity, he realized that he had done what no gentleman would dare to do outside the marriage bed. He had taken Eliza's virginity, stolen the virtue that by rights should have belonged only to the man she would one day wed.

In the next moment, he'd known that man must be him.

But when he offered her marriage, she had refused. Shock still radiated through him to remember her words.

What was it she had said? *You do not wish to marry me, and I do not wish to marry you. Let us leave it at that.*

But how could he leave it? How could he, in all good conscience, do as she said and simply forget? Behave as though the night just past had no real significance? As if their lovemaking had been nothing but a mad, impetuous, passionate mistake?

Yet hadn't it been precisely that? A night of loveplay gone much, much too far?

He supposed he ought to feel relieved. After all, she had released him from his obligation, given him back his freedom with no strings attached. Many men would be glad, secretly congratulating themselves on their lucky escape.

So why didn't he feel lucky? Quite the opposite, truth be known. His reaction made no sense, not even to himself.

It wasn't as if he really wanted to marry her. Not that marriage to Eliza would be so very bad. In fact, a union between them could have its definite advantages. He liked Eliza, liked her a lot, and they were clearly compatible, both in bed and out. She would be an excellent companion and a good friend. His entire family adored her, and undoubtedly she would make a wonderful mother for any children they might conceive together.

It's just that he wasn't ready to marry right now. He had far too much living to do before he settled down. And yet . . .

Before he knew what he meant to do, he reached out and took the cool metal knob to her bedroom door in his grasp.

He stopped, fighting his compulsions and his confusion as he debated whether or not to give the handle a turn.

If he went inside her room, what would he say to her? Wake her to demand she marry him, no matter her wishes? Insist she be his bride?

And once inside her bedroom, might he not be tempted to take her again? Climb between the sheets and tangle them both in a spell of seduction and sex so heated neither could refuse?

Deciding he had already acted in haste enough for one night, he released the doorknob. Maybe the best thing would be to give her a little time, a few days to reconsider her actions. Some time as well to consider his own.

On a sigh, he downed the rest of his brandy and shuffled down the hallway to finally find his bed.

Eliza roused abruptly.

She'd heard a noise, or at least she thought she had, as

if someone had been standing outside her door. Lying in the dark, she listened again, hearing nothing but quiet. Perhaps the sound had been made by one of the servants. Though that answer seemed unlikely since the hour was still too early for any of the staff to be moving around the house.

Swinging her legs out of bed, she crept to the door. Easing it open, she gazed out.

The hallway stood in shadow, dark and utterly devoid of life.

Closing the door, she padded back to her lonely bed.

Only a dream, she mused.

Who had she thought it was? Kit come to tell her he loved her and they must be wed, after all?

A hollow laugh erupted from her throat, quickly turning into a sob.

Burying her face in her pillow, she wept.

"More tea, miss?"

Eliza gazed up from her ruminations, realizing she had been woolgathering again. "Yes, thank you," she told the young footman, waiting while he filled her china cup with the steaming, delicately flavored brew.

She turned her attention back to Adrian and Violet's breakfast table conversation, relieved neither of them seemed to have noticed her brief lapse. Lifting a buttered triangle of toast to her mouth, she ate a bite, then set the slice aside, wanting no more.

Violet's gaze shifted her way. "Is that all you are going to eat? You've barely touched your meal."

"Sorry. I don't know why, but I'm just not hungry this morning."

"You haven't been hungry the last few mornings. Is anything amiss?"

Eliza forced a reassuring smile. "Of course not. I am perfectly well." She lowered her voice and leaned toward Violet. "Just that time of the month," she whispered.

"Oh," Violet said, obviously sorry to have pried in so public a forum.

Adrian, ever the gentleman, turned a page of his newspaper and pretended he hadn't heard a thing.

Violet sent her a bolstering smile, then gently moved the conversation on to safer topics. Eliza sipped her tea and let her friends talk, doing her best to ignore the dull cramping settled low in her belly.

Right on schedule, her flow had arrived this morning. She'd burst into tears when she'd realized, a stupid reaction since a baby now would have proven a disaster, forcing Kit to offer his hand again and her to accept this time. She ought to have been relieved since she did not want a marriage based on necessity and obligation, no matter how much she loved Kit.

And yet irrational as it might seem, the news had hit her like a small death. What she and Kit had together was through. Even their passionate, clandestine encounters were over. She could excuse her earlier actions as a kind of naive insanity, fueled by love and youthful ardor. But to ever find herself in his arms again would make her something far different, and far, far worse.

Of course, now that he had lain with her, whatever sexual appeal she had held for him might very well be gone. She had heard whispers that men could be like that sometimes. And Kit had never struck her as a constant lover, having watched him over the years flit from girl to girl like a bee gathering pollen.

Over the three short days since their night together in the study, she had barely seen him. Both of them were admittedly busy with social engagements, but not so much so that their paths would not have crossed at all. She wondered if he might be avoiding her.

The only thing she knew for certain was that he did not love her.

Cruel as it might seem, it was the truth.

So she must accept the fact, put away her foolish, idiotic dreams and move on.

Misery engulfed her.

She never should have done it, she chided herself. Never should have risked her heart on such an unlikely chance at love. What had she been thinking, to place herself in such jeopardy again, when she'd barely managed to recover from the first time he'd stolen her heart?

Gazing across the breakfast table at her friends, a harsh stab of envy rose inside her. *Look at them,* she thought. *So happy. So perfectly suited to each other. Their union rooted in friendship and respect, and above all else, a deep, abiding love that will last them all the rest of their days.*

Why couldn't she have that? Why couldn't Kit love her? If not with his whole heart, then at least a little. Just enough to let her pretend his proposal had been motivated by affection instead of duty.

Seconds later, Kit strode into the room. Her pulse jittered as he paused just inside the doorway. Immediately he fixed his gaze upon her, his lips curving upward, warm and tender. The power of his beautiful smile impaled her to the core, as if he'd tossed a lance straight through her heart.

She did not smile back.

Lowering her eyes, she lifted her teacup to her mouth and forced herself to swallow a sip that very nearly made her choke.

What did he think he was doing? Smiling at her like that?

"Good morning," he greeted in a sunny tone.

Adrian and Violet offered up pleasant replies.

Eliza mumbled a response, then pushed a cold toast half, with its smear of congealed butter and jam, around in a circle on her plate.

She heard him cross to the sideboard, take a plate and begin helping himself to the tempting array of offerings carried up from the kitchen.

Meanwhile, the young footman came forward and set a fresh china cup and saucer in the place directly to her left.

She wanted to protest. Why couldn't a seat be arranged on the opposite side of the table, beside Adrian? She did not want Kit sitting so near.

The servant moved away but quickly returned, pouring steaming coffee into the cup, the staff aware that Kit generally preferred a more robust beverage than tea in the morning.

Kit crossed and set down his plate, heaped with food. "Shall I bring anyone anything while I am up?" he offered.

His brother and sister-in-law both declined with appreciative refusals.

Kit inclined his head toward her. "Eliza? What about you? There are some very delectable-looking red raspberries. I know you've a partiality for them. Why don't I bring you a dish?"

She made herself lift her chin. "My thanks, but no."

"Are you sure? I tasted one and they're very sweet. Let me get you a few."

Her brows drew together.

Why was he being so conciliatory? she wondered. Was he trying to smooth the way between them again? Did he imagine they could be friends? That they could put their intimate relationship aside and forget they had ever lain naked in each other's arms?

Well, she could not forget. Nor could she be his friend. Not anymore.

Suddenly, desperately, she had to get away.

Tossing down her napkin, she jumped to her feet. "If you will excuse me, I need to go to my room. I am driving out with Mr. Vickery today and need to change my attire."

Violet sent her a look of concern. "Oh, of course, do run on. It is quite all right."

Without glancing again at Kit, Eliza hurried from the room.

As she departed, she heard Kit demand to know what was wrong. She didn't wait to hear Violet's reply.

Kit cooled his heels for nearly two hours before Eliza finally emerged from her room and came down the stairs.

She looked as lovely as a crisp autumn morning in a marigold-colored carriage dress, a small, delicate bonnet with a whimsical little feather perched coyly atop her brunette curls.

For a moment, he had to remind himself to breathe, had to caution himself not to sweep her close inside his arms and give her the sort of thorough kissing a woman of her undeniable appeal deserved. Instead he folded his arms across his chest and finished watching her descend.

Her gait slowed for a moment when she saw him, but she recovered nicely, barely pausing as she navigated the last few steps.

He waited until she stood next to him at the base of the staircase. "Eliza, might I have a word?"

She glanced across the immense entryway toward the

front door. "Lord Vickery is due to arrive any moment, so I don't believe—"

Annoyance set lines across Kit's forehead. "Vickery can wait."

Without asking further permission, he placed a hand on her elbow and turned her toward the study. He could have chosen the salon, Kit knew, instead of revisiting the scene of their recent wayward night together, but decided the smaller room would allow them easier privacy.

She balked for an instant when she noticed where he was taking her, but quickly gave up any attempt at resistance and followed along.

Once inside the room, he closed the door behind them.

As soon as he did, she slipped free of his hold.

He decided to make no comment about the distance she placed between them, gathering himself to ask the question uppermost in his mind.

Eliza lifted a brow. "What is it you wish to say to me?"

The pendulum of the room's tall, corner clock swung in a placid rhythm, its pace at complete odds with the emotions warring inside him.

"That I was worried, for one," he began. "Considering how you rushed out of the breakfast room this morning, I wondered what was amiss. Violet tells me you are unwell, but she was very vague on the particulars." He met her gaze. "I know it's only been a few days, but do you know already? Are you carrying my child?"

Before she could speak, he hurried on. "Because if you are, we must marry quickly. That way no one will even suspect you conceived prior to our marriage. A week one way or the other will make no difference at all. I shall apply for a special license this very afternoon."

The feather on her hat bobbed gently as she shook her head. "You have no need to procure a license, special or otherwise, since your assumptions are incorrect."

"What?"

She averted her gaze and traced a fingertip over a golden ribbon decorating her sheer silk spencer. "My monthly arrived this morning, and that is why I am not feeling my best. You may rest easy in the certainty that I am most definitely not with child."

"Oh."

He stood unmoving, momentarily nonplussed by her statement. In the hours since Eliza had left the breakfast room in such haste, he'd convinced himself she was pregnant and that they must marry, after all. He'd had everything planned, down to taking her to a summer cottage in Middlesex, where they would spend their honeymoon, and share endless nights of passion before returning to set up their new household.

But she said there was no child.

Tension leeched out of his shoulders, muscles he hadn't even known were knotted suddenly easing. Yet to his dismay, the overriding emotion he felt was not one of relief, but of disappointment.

He scoffed at the idea, telling himself not to be a fool. Surely he hadn't actually wanted her to be with child? And it was ludicrous to imagine he had been genuinely excited by the prospect of making her his bride.

"That's good, then, is it not?" he stated with forced cheer.

"Yes," she said in a low voice. "Quite the best possible outcome."

Tugging at her gloves, she refastened a tiny, pearl button at one wrist. "Lord Vickery must have arrived by now. I should not keep him waiting any longer."

"No, I suppose you should not." He reached out and wrapped a palm around her arm. "Are you sure, Eliza?"

Her gaze flew upward to meet his. "About what?"

"About us? About your decision that we not wed. I realize there is no baby, but still . . ."

A faint light softened her dove-colored eyes. "Yes?"

"I don't feel easy knowing I have compromised you. I was supposed to be your mentor, your protector. Instead I let desire get the best of me. I robbed you of your innocence."

The light winked out inside her eyes. "It was my innocence to give, and I gave it freely. You need not suffer any guilt."

"Yes, but—"

She blew out a breath that sounded almost angry. "Pray do not act the martyr, Kit. It is a role that does not suit you well. Now, I have a carriage ride to take."

Pointedly, she gazed down at the hand that held her arm.

Relaxing his grip, he let her move away and step toward the door.

Following behind, he trailed her into the hallway, watching as she welcomed his friend with a warm smile and a very pretty greeting.

A skillful trick, he realized. One of the many he had taught her.

Vickery glanced up and saw him, and nodded his head. Kit strode forward out of obligatory politeness, and stood in the entryway while they exchanged a few pleasantries.

Eliza looked as if she hadn't a care in the world, as if the two of them hadn't just been closeted inside the study discussing topics that would have scandalized most genteel young women.

Is that what he had brought her to? The prime lesson she had learned at his hand? How to dissemble? How to lie and pretend with the rest of Society's shallow brethren?

He didn't like it, didn't like it at all.

Nor did he enjoy the sight of her a minute later as she offered him a sunny farewell, then turned and strolled from the house on Vickery's arm.

Chapter Twenty

The next two weeks flew by as if borne aloft on wings.

Determined not to give in to her own inner agony, a secret despair that hovered just beneath the surface, Eliza threw herself into the social fray with unheralded enthusiasm. Accepting as many engagements as possible, she kept busy from morning to night. Sparing herself no extra moments, she would find herself so exhausted by the time she laid her head upon her pillow that her body and mind had no choice but to let her sleep.

Violet commented on her relentless pace, but Eliza assured her she was simply having fun. Even Jeannette noticed Eliza's uncharacteristic élan, remarking how zealously she seemed to be embracing the last few weeks of the Season, Jeannette's words tinged with apparent admiration for Eliza's seemingly boundless energy.

As for Kit, Eliza did her utmost to avoid him without being obvious. Surrounding herself with her small but faithful band of suitors, she let them act as a kind of shield. Careful to keep at least one of them always by her side, she managed to spend relatively little time in Kit's company.

If he objected, he did not say, although she found his gaze upon her more frequently than she wished, a brooding expression glittering in his jewel-toned eyes.

At home, she took breakfast in her room before

bustling downstairs to plunge into the myriad events comprising her day, careful to leave no opportunity for a chance meeting or private coze with Kit. Despite her earlier determination, she didn't trust herself to be alone with him, fearing how easy it would be to fall prey to his magnetic charms yet again.

This afternoon, however, she could not elude him completely, numerous members of the Winter family, Kit included, having gathered just outside of London for an outing at the estate of one of Adrian's cousins.

From her perch inside a small rowboat, being expertly steered by Viscount Brevard, she had a clear view of the thirty-odd guests arranged in leisurely groupings on the grassy shore. Some were seated upon blankets beneath the shade of mature, leafy trees, while others strolled the verdant grounds and gardens.

Counted among their number were several children, including the twins, Sebastian and Noah, and baby Georgianna, who, at eight months of age, had developed a lively crawling style that kept Violet and the children's nursemaid scrambling to keep up. Jeannette and Darragh had brought little Caitlyn as well. A playmate for Georgianna, she charmed everyone with her infectious, infant laughter. Darragh's siblings were having a merry time visiting with other young people near their own age, including Franny Brevard and her friend Jane Twitchell.

Three of Adrian's sisters and their families were also in attendance, including Sylvia and her husband, both of whom had recently come up to Town to spend a few weeks. Unwilling to leave their brood, they had brought their children as well, all six of them—five boys and Emma, the much-cherished only daughter.

Screams and squeals resounded in the air as the children raced and played, the adults letting them do mostly as they pleased with only an occasional reprimand to quiet them down.

Off to one side moved a small contingent of servants, busily working to set up the elegant alfresco buffet where the whole party would dine in a short while.

Eliza caught sight of Kit as he strolled up to one of the tables and snatched a handful of what appeared, from a distance, to be fresh berries or nuts. He ate his pilfered bounty, laughing and teasing one of the serving girls as she halfheartedly tried to shoo him away.

With an uncomfortable tightness squeezing her throat, Eliza forced her gaze aside and focused again on Viscount Brevard. He was telling her about his estate in the Cotswolds, his voice infused with an unmistakable pride for his ancestral home. From the description of the place, he had every right to feel boastful, the house and grounds appearing a veritable haven, with several thousand acres of prime land and two natural, deep-water lakes.

Currently being rowed across a far less vast, yet nonetheless lovely artificial lake, Eliza dipped her fingers into the water, enjoying the sensation of cool wetness flowing against her skin as the little boat glided forward. She angled her parasol to catch a moment of warm June sunshine on her face before returning the silk covering to its proper position so her skin did not burn.

"Are you comfortable?"

She glanced toward Brevard where he sat at the opposite end of the boat, plying the oars in a smooth, easy motion.

"Very comfortable," she answered in complete truthfulness. A light breeze stirred, luffing against her cheeks, teasing her short curls. "I am glad you convinced me to come out. I have rarely been boating and never in such fine style."

"Then I must remember to take you out onto the water more often. In fact, it would be my very great pleasure if you and the duke and duchess would join me at my estate sometime during the coming weeks. Fall, in fact, is a perfect time to visit a pleasant stone pavilion I have that sits along the shore of my northernmost lake. Franny and I have been known to take a meal there on occasion, enjoying views of the waterfowl and other wildlife that are brave enough to venture close. I know you take delight in nature. I believe you would enjoy the experience."

Visit his home? she thought. Gentlemen asked ladies to visit their estate only when they were considering a more serious attachment. Was Viscount Brevard thinking about asking her to be his wife?

She had her answer to that question a moment later when the viscount lifted the oars from the water and set them dripping in their side hooks.

Allowing the boat to drift, he leaned toward her. "Miss Hammond, Eliza, I realize this is not the most conventional of locations in which to speak my heart, but it is one of the few that affords us utter solitude."

She held her breath for an instant, unsure whether or not she wanted him to proceed.

Meeting her gaze, his eyes appeared a vivid blue, far bluer than the lake water surrounding them. "Surely you must not be unaware of my regard for you," he continued. "From the moment of our first, albeit unconventional, meeting, where I spied you on that runaway horse, I have been captured by your beauty and grace and, yes, your amazing bravery. Since that time, I have come to discover how sweet and wise you are, how generous and kind, all qualities a man desires in the woman with whom he would choose to share his life."

Reaching out, he folded one of her hands inside his own. "Eliza, I love you. Please say you will be my wife."

Staring at the hand to which he'd laid claim, she wrestled for an answer. What to say when joyous acceptance did not rise immediately to her lips? And yet how could she refuse him?

She had already turned down Lord Maplewood, an admittedly good man with whom she could have made a fine life. To refuse Brevard as well would be sheer insanity.

Heavens above, he was the undisputed catch of the Season. If she accepted him, shock would ripple through the Ton. Astonishment was rippling through her right now, since she had never seriously believed he would offer for her.

And yet, inconceivably, he had. So what to do?

In a thousand years, she knew she could not hope to find a better man. Why, he was practically perfect. Handsome and charming. Intelligent and well educated. Rich and titled. Without question, he would give her everything she desired. A beautiful home. Lovely children. Companionship and protection. He even said he loved her. If only she could feel the same.

Thoughts of Kit flooded into her mind. Lips firming, she pushed them away, along with consideration of his own marriage proposal. Given under duress as it had been, his offer hardly counted. And yet . . .

And yet what? she demanded to herself. She had refused him, twice. He was hardly likely to ask again. And even if he did, she still could not say yes, not when doing so would place her in a position of emotional subordination, leaving her to beg for cherished crumbs of his attention and affection.

But would agreeing to wed Brevard be fair to him? And what of her? She had not given up her wish to have babies. She did not want to live her life unmarried, comfortable in her wealth but distressingly, wretchedly alone.

No closer to an answer, she decided she would offer him the truth, and let him direct her path.

Gently drawing away her hand, she curled it in her lap, then gazed upon his gorgeous, chiseled features. "Lance, before I give you my decision, there is something that I believe you have a right to know."

He smiled in inquiry, one blond brow arching upward. "Oh? What is that?"

"I am not the young lady you may imagine me."

"Of course you are. You are utterly wonderful."

"I do not know if you will continue to think that after I tell you what I have to say. I am by no means infallible or without weaknesses. Lance, there was . . . well, it is over now . . . but there was someone else. A man."

"What man?"

"His name is not important. What is of relevance is the fact that if I marry you, I will not come to you with my . . . purity intact. I am no longer . . ." She broke off, her cheeks growing hot beneath the shade of her bonnet. "Well, I'm not."

For a long moment, he was silent. "I see. Did you love this man?"

"Yes."

"And it is finished, you say? There is no hope for a reconciliation?"

She shook her head. "No."

Another silence descended.

At length, he spoke. "Well, I suppose you are of an age where I should not be wholly surprised. After all, you are not a young girl just out of the schoolroom. Still . . ."

"I understand, and you need say no more, but I could not consent to a marriage between us knowing you be-

lieved something about me that is not true. You are far
too honorable a man for that."

He reached again for her hand. "You are very coura-
geous to tell me; many ladies would not."

"You must think me dreadful."

"No, I think you are a woman who lives by the gov-
ernance of her own heart. So what does your heart say
about me? Could you love me, Eliza?"

Just as she had not lied before, she could not lie to him
now. "I can try. I make no promises, but I should like to
try, Lance, if you will have me."

From his vantage point on a slight rise near the buffet
table, Kit observed Eliza and Brevard. The pair were
rowing out on the lake, but from what he could see,
their boat wasn't moving. In fact, Eliza and the viscount
appeared to be in deep conversation.

On what subject?

His jaw tightened, the sweet flavor of the black raspberries he'd eaten turning bitter in his mouth.

For the past two weeks, he'd stood by, silent while
Eliza took the Town by storm, sallying forth on the arm
of one man after another in a way that was unprecedented, particularly for her.

From all appearances, she was having the time of her
life.

And she was doing it—quite determinedly, it would
appear—without him.

Since their night together in the study, they had barely
spent more than a handful of minutes in each other's
company. At first, he'd thought perhaps she was feeling
shy and awkward in his presence after the intimacies
they had shared.

But soon he realized her reticence stemmed from

something else entirely. As always, she was sweet and friendly to him, smiling and behaving very much as she had always done. Except that something essential was missing now. An underlying warmth that no longer shone in her eyes. A special radiance to her smile that she used to reserve exclusively for him, but no more.

Out of necessity, their love lessons had come to an abrupt halt. Obviously without benefit of marriage their dalliance could not continue unchecked. Yet all the logic and good intentions in the world had not kept him from desiring her, could not prevent him from craving her with a kind of single-minded obsession that bordered on madness.

During the day, he caught himself spinning fantasies, mental wanderings that left him semi-aroused, sometimes in the most untenable of locations and company. At night, she came to him in dreams. Hot, earthy, boldly sexual dreams that left him aching and unsatisfied, sheets twisted around his limbs, his loins throbbing when he came awake.

But what of her? From everything he'd observed, Eliza appeared to have put their night behind her with a sort of cold finality. Could she really turn her passions on and off so precipitously? She said she had wanted him that night, said she had taken great pleasure in their joining. Innocent as she had been, he knew from her earnest, open responses that she had not been lying.

And yet now that their passion was consummated, did she want nothing further? Had their lessons really meant no more to her than a chance to dip her fingers into the dark waters of the forbidden? To experiment in the secret world of libidinous delights, as she had once told him she wished to do?

Such behavior didn't seem like Eliza.

Then again, her behavior of late didn't seem like her either.

He didn't understand what she wanted. For that matter, he barely knew what he wanted, except for one thing.

He wanted Eliza, needed her back in his arms, in his life. Desiring her with a hunger that burned as hot as flame even now. Whatever this spark was between them, he couldn't let it die. But to have what he wanted meant marriage.

And therein lay a stumbling block.

He'd already proposed—twice—and she had said she did not want to wed him. But he realized now that his words had been those of duty and honor, couched in rather unemotional terms. Perhaps if she understood how much he wanted her, how desperately he craved her touch, she would consent. Many marriages had been built from far less than what the two of them shared. They were friends. If the passion between them should ever fade, their friendship would remain. If he had his druthers, he would wait to marry. And yet the more he considered the idea, the more he liked it.

Yes, he thought, watching as Brevard finally began to row himself and Eliza to shore, Kit would propose to her again.

Only this time she would accept.

Eliza pushed aside her uneaten slice of cake.

Although the bountiful fare at the outdoor luncheon was delicious, she'd found herself mostly picking at her food, using her fork to slide various offerings around on her plate in pretense of actually eating.

Had she made the right choice? she pondered again, as she had done repeatedly over the course of the meal.

Was her decision the best one for her future life, her future happiness?

Her indecision was only compounded by her awareness of Kit. On some level, she was always aware of him whenever they were in proximity of each other. Yet today her senses were on the alert, catching his sharp, lazy-lidded gaze focused upon her more than once.

She caught it again now, that gaze, as he lifted his wineglass to his lips and drank. She quivered, feeling the visual touch as acutely as if he had reached out and traced his fingertips slowly along the length of her spine.

Stifling a sigh, she turned her face away so she could not see him anymore.

She would not, could not, think of him that way again, she warned herself. Such intimacies were over and done with between them. They had to be, now that she had made her decision.

Then suddenly that decision became all the more real, all the more fixed, as Viscount Brevard climbed to his feet. With a raised hand and a few effortlessly pitched words, the attention of the assembled guests turned his way. Radiating a comfortable, outgoing charm, he thanked their host and hostess for a lovely outing and a most memorable day. After a few more well-chosen words, he turned a smile upon Eliza.

"My dear friends," he said, "this day is special to me for another reason, one I hope you will all help me in celebrating. It is with great joy that I wish to make an announcement. This very afternoon, here in this idyllic setting, I asked Miss Eliza Hammond to be my wife. To my most profound relief, she agreed. Eliza?" Reaching down, Brevard pulled her to her feet, gasps and exclamations erupting into the air.

Down the table, a *thunk* sounded as Kit's glass toppled over, red wine flowing across the white linen like an obscene gush of blood.

Eliza's gaze collided with Kit's. His jaw hung slack, an expression of profound shock marring his handsome features. But it was his eyes that stopped the breath in her lungs, his look one of puzzlement and, if she didn't mistake, pain.

Then she had no further time to consider what she had—or had not—seen, as well-wishers swarmed around her in a sea of congratulations.

Violet caught her in a tight hug, releasing a cry of happiness and surprise, before alternately bombarding her with questions, and scolding her for not saying so much as a word about the viscount's proposal.

A long while later, the flurry of excitement died down enough for her to look for Kit.

Moments after, she realized he was gone.

Come with us to Newmarket.

Kit's friends had been urging him to join them at the race meeting for the past two weeks. Originally he'd been reluctant to agree, what with circumstances so unresolved with Eliza.

Now he couldn't wait to get away.

"See to it these are carried down," Kit's valet, Cherry, instructed a footman, pointing to a large brown leather portmanteau and another small traveling case that sat near the door. The footman collected his burden and made his way out into the hallway.

"If you need nothing further, my lord, I shall await you below."

Kit glanced at the other man. "Go on, Cherry. I'll be along directly."

The servant nodded, gathered up a last couple of items of his own and exited the room.

Kit checked the amount of money in his possession, then tucked his coin purse into his suit coat pocket. He added a small penknife and a silver brandy flask before crossing to pick up a copy of the latest racing news he planned to peruse on the journey north. Deciding he had everything he needed for his trip, he strode out into the corridor.

Not expecting to encounter anyone this time of morning, he rounded the first corner at a brisk clip and nearly collided with Eliza.

She let out a faint cry, obviously as startled as he, and took a stumbling step backward. Instinctively, he caught her, steadying her with a firm pair of hands on her upper arms. Becoming suddenly aware that he was holding her, and enjoying the sensation, he let her go, setting her away from him as if she carried the plague.

"Kit. I didn't see you." Her voice sounded breathless, no doubt from her surprise.

"Nor I you."

They stared at each other for a long moment, an awkward silence between them.

"Well, I had best be going." Kit leaned down to retrieve the copy of the racing news he had dropped onto the floor.

"Oh. Do you have an engagement?" she asked.

He nodded brusquely. "Traveling up to Newmarket for a race meeting."

"Ah."

Another uncomfortable pause settled between them.

He tried not to look directly at her but couldn't help himself, tracing hungry eyes over her face. Drawing a quick breath, he immediately regretted the action, his body tightening as her familiar fragrance wound inside his head, sweet and intoxicating as apple blossoms in the spring.

Almost violently, he squeezed the pamphlet in his hand, fighting a battle of conflicting urges—half of him wanting to shake her for agreeing to marry another man, the other half wanting to yank her into his arms and kiss her senseless, kiss her until she begged for no one and nothing but him.

He did neither, holding himself in check.

"I never offered my best wishes on your upcoming nuptials," he said, unsmiling.

Her eyelashes fanned across her cheekbones. "No, you did not."

And I'm not going to either, by God, he growled to himself.

Flattening a palm against the wall next to her head, he leaned close, effectively caging her with his much larger body. When he spoke, his voice registered barely above a whisper, sounding rough as gravel even to his own ears. "So? Does he know?"

"Know what?"

"About us? And more to the point, the fact that he won't be getting a virgin bride."

She drew in a harsh breath, her gaze wide and deeply gray. Her shoulders stiffened. "Actually, he does know."

His brows arched. "Now I am shocked. How amazingly understanding of Brevard. He's never struck me as the liberal sort. So he doesn't mind sharing you with me, does he?"

"He isn't sharing me at all. And he doesn't know it's you, not specifically. I told him there was a man. I also told him the relationship between us is over."

A jagged pain lanced through his chest, a pain that made him want to strike back. "Over, is it? I wouldn't be entirely certain of that. You may find after a few nights in his bed that you'd much rather be back in mine. If you ask nicely, I may decide to let you."

Before either of them knew what she meant to do, her hand flashed up, making solid contact with his cheek. The blow stung, but not as badly as the wound to his dignity, the damage to what remained of their old, comfortable friendship, tatters now of its former self.

Nerves raw, he moved away, cursing himself for the punishing need that still roared inside his veins. Even now, he wanted her with a hunger he could barely control, and was helpless to deny.

"I'm late and my carriage awaits me below." He executed a curt bow. "Good day, Eliza."

Forcing himself not to look at her again, he strode away.

Chapter Twenty-one

The last days of June arrived, each one warm and long and crammed full of activity. Word of Eliza's engagement to Viscount Brevard spread quickly, like fire through an old-growth forest, an instant topic on everyone's lips.

As a result, Eliza had even less time to herself than before, deluged by a constant barrage of visits, inquiries and invitations from all manner of well-wishers and curiosity-seekers. Part of her took comfort in the frenzy since it helped keep her troubled thoughts and emotions at bay. Kept her from questioning her decision to marry Brevard. And more importantly, from dwelling on Kit, especially their last encounter with each other.

Even now she couldn't quite believe she'd slapped him. Until the moment her palm actually connected with his cheek, she hadn't realized she was capable of such an action. But Kit seemed to draw the full range of emotions from her, from sweet tenderness to raging temper.

How could he have said such things to her? Never before had she heard him be so scathing to anyone. For a second, it was as though he wanted to hurt her, as if she had injured him and he craved a measure of revenge at her expense.

But why?

Wounded pride, she supposed, his self-esteem pricked by her agreeing to marry another man so soon after his own proposal. She considered the glimpse of shock and pain she thought she'd seen in his eyes the day of the picnic, just after her engagement had been announced. Had the look been one of real distress? Surely if he did feel something more for her, he would have declared himself instead of saying such horrible things to her. Instead of making her cry.

After their confrontation, she'd fled to her room and sobbed for an hour straight. The bout of tears left her nose stuffed, her eyes swollen and her head aching so fiercely she'd had no need to prevaricate to her maid, or to Violet, about feeling unwell.

Later that evening, she had composed herself enough to attend the opera with Lance, telling herself over and over again that he would make her happy if only she would give him the chance.

And in the days to follow, he had certainly tried. No woman could ask for a more attentive bridegroom. At every turn, he went out of his way to please her, seeing to her every comfort, surprising her with one gift after another.

He'd begun first by presenting her with a magnificent diamond engagement ring, the stone so large and glittering, it drew envious comments from every woman who viewed it. And last night he'd given her a beautiful pearl and diamond bracelet to match. Ear bobs, he'd hinted, just might be next.

She gazed down upon the gemstones now and sighed.

At least the Season was nearly at an end. Soon Jeannette, Darragh and their family would return to Ireland, while she, Violet, Adrian and their children traveled to Winterlea. They would remain there for a month, then journey north to visit Lance and his sister in the Cotswolds, so she could become acquainted with her future home.

The thought made her tremble. Quite frankly, she didn't know if she was cut out to be a viscountess. Lance assured her she would do splendidly, leaving her to hope his prediction proved true.

She took comfort in knowing he didn't expect her to be a great hostess. Already he had assured her they could remain in the country much of the year, if that is what she preferred, saying that he loved the quiet, rural life.

She was lucky to be marrying him, she told herself. Lance was a marvelous man and he loved her. If only she felt the same intense devotion for him. Guilt jabbed her with a nasty finger, then poked a second time when memories of Kit flooded into her mind.

Closing her eyes, she fought to banish him from her traitorous thoughts.

"Is everything all right?" Violet asked from her place next to Eliza on a bench in the Raeburn House garden. "That's twice now that you've sighed."

"Is it?" Eliza murmured in consternation, watching the duke and his rambunctious sons playing on a nearby patch of green lawn. Adrian was giving the boys piggyback rides, much to their giggling delight.

"Indeed it is," Violet continued.

"I am fine."

A small silence followed.

"I wasn't sure," Violet said. "You have seemed . . . well, not always your usual, happy self lately."

"Have I not? Do not worry, I am only a touch weary of the heavy press of social rounds and obligations."

"Well, you have been running yourself ragged these past few weeks. Why don't you stay in a little more. Adrian and I shan't mind turning down a few invitations and having the occasional night at home, I assure you."

"I appreciate the suggestion, but I don't want to disappoint Lance."

"Do you think he would be disappointed? We could invite him here to take dinner with the family. I do not believe he would object."

Eliza gave a genuine smile. "No, likely not. Yes, all right, but only for an evening or two."

Violet turned her eyes forward to watch her husband and children play. "And is everything well between you and Lance? You are glad of the engagement, are you not?"

"Of course. Lance is everything a woman could want."

"And you love him, yes? I know that is what you wanted, to love and be loved in return. If you are not certain—"

"Of course I am certain. I am very much in love."

Violet reached across and squeezed her hand. Eliza smiled and said nothing further to correct her friend's mistaken assumption.

She hadn't lied, Eliza thought. She *was* in love. Just not with the man Violet imagined her to mean.

Kit slumped in his chair before the fire.

A few feet distant, his friends sat circled around a table in one of the inn's two private parlors, playing cards and drinking, the last of their dinner long since cleared away.

Groans of defeat rose from three of the men, while a fourth crowed in victory as he scraped his winnings toward himself.

Vickery grinned over at Kit. "Come play, Winter. We're just about to begin a new game, and I could use fresh pickings."

Kit raised his glass of port in a silent salute, then waved the other man off. "I am content to remain here with my wine. Lost too much already at the races today."

Actually he hadn't lost much at all, a pound or two in total, but he was in no mood tonight to indulge in cards. Lately he was in no mood for much of anything, and hadn't been since he'd left London. He didn't know how his friends tolerated him, he'd been in such a foul, black humor. When he'd arrived in Newmarket, he had hoped that convivial company, entertaining sport and a change of scenery would provide sufficient diversion to rid him of his impossible craving for Eliza.

But it had not. If anything, his absence from her had only made his longing increase, made the terrible melancholy inside him grow deeper and darker. During the day, he tried to ignore his discontent, but at night such attempts became impossible as he tossed against the sheets in a torment of restless frustration, unable to escape thoughts of her even in his dreams.

What was she doing tonight? he brooded. Out on the town no doubt with her fiancé. He tossed back his wine and set down the glass with a sharp snap that came close to breaking the stem.

Engaged.

He still couldn't believe it, his mind even now shying away from the reality of that nightmarish day a little more than a week ago when he'd been slapped with the news.

Why in the blazes had she done it? How could she have promised to marry Brevard when she had refused Kit only a couple weeks before?

Well, if she preferred the viscount, so be it, he derided. The pair of them would probably bore each other to death with their incessant politeness and perfection, while he remained free to do as he chose without encumbrance or responsibility.

And since he was able to do as he wished, what he ought to do was go down to the inn's taproom and find a willing bed partner. There was one wench in particular who'd been giving him the eye ever since he'd arrived, smiling and flirting with him every time she sauntered near. Pretty and young, she had enough padding on her to give a man a hard, healthy ride, and a huge bosom that would surely overspill even his large, inquisitive palms.

But even as he considered the notion of taking the girl to his bed to slake his hunger, his body remained unmoved.

Instead he found himself craving another pair of breasts, smaller but utterly exquisite, with nipples the color of rose petals and skin that smelled every inch as sweet. Delicate, slender arms, legs and hands that could stroke and twine and intoxicate. And gently flaring hips that pressed against his own as if they had been formed by a divine hand, fitting in perfect accord as if their two separate bodies were meant to join as one.

Body thrumming, he forced himself to retreat from such dangerous musings. Wallowing in his present gloom would do him no earthly good. He would simply have to find a way to get over his desire for Eliza. The days and weeks would pass, and with them his near desperation for her would wane until eventually the yearning disappeared altogether. Physical passion was always like that, and so it would be again.

At least that's what he was going to tell himself.

If only he didn't have to go back to London tomorrow. But the races were finished, his friends ready to return. He supposed he could go in search of other entertainment—Selway and Lloyd were always prime for new adventures—but racketing off to another town would smack of cowardice, no more than a febrile excuse designed to put off the inevitable.

He would have to see Eliza again sometime, so he might as well get it over with as soon as may be. And perhaps if he was lucky, he would return to find her hold upon him diminished, the magnetism of her allure weakening already.

Still, he was no masochist. When the household left soon for Winterlea, he would not be traveling with them. Perhaps he would spend a few months at his country house instead, invite Brentholden and the others to go shooting with him come fall. By the time Christmas arrived and he was forced to put in an appearance at the family estate, he would be done with this insane infatuation for Eliza.

Closing his eyes, he prayed he would be over her.

Loud exclamations issued from the card table, his friends growing increasingly noisy in their exuberant play. Deciding he'd had enough company for the night, Kit climbed wearily to his feet.

"Ho there, Winter. Where are you off to?" Selway questioned, the other three men at the table turning inquiring gazes on Kit.

"If you must know, I'm off to bed."

"At this hour? It's barely midnight. Surely you can't mean to hie off to your sleep like some plaguey old man?"

"We have a long day's travel tomorrow and I'm in no mood to be miserable through it."

"You can rest in the coach," Lloyd muttered. "Best thing to do in a coach, if you ask me."

He could think of other activities, Kit mused, then

wished he hadn't as heated memories of Eliza washed through him. An ugly scowl descended across his brow. "Nonetheless, bed is where I am bound."

"Sad waste, if you ask me," Selway persisted. "Surely we can coax you into playing one hand of cards."

Brentholden cast Kit a long, quizzical look before turning back to the others. "Leave him be. Now, are we going to finish this hand or not? Vickery, I believe it was your bet."

As his friends returned to their game, Kit let himself out into the inn's narrow hallway. Once inside his bed-chamber, he stripped off his coat, neck cloth and boots, then flopped back upon the inn's adequately comfort-able bed.

He should have invited the serving girl to join him, he decided. A shame she wasn't the woman he craved. Forcing his eyelids to shut, he tried to sleep, knowing that even if he managed the trick, his dreams would all be of Eliza.

Two days later, a note arrived on Eliza's breakfast tray.

"The footman said the message came for you early this morning, miss," her maid remarked as she set the tray onto a small table near the window.

Covering a yawn with a hand, Eliza climbed out of bed and crossed to take up the note, her maid moving busily around the room, pulling back the draperies to let in the morning light.

Eliza opened the missive.

Meet me in the park at ten o'clock.
I shall be waiting for you at the Grosvenor's gate.
Brevard

She folded the note, then set it back down on the tray.

Lance had said nothing to her last night about wanting to ride today. Perhaps he was feeling impulsive this morning. She certainly hoped nothing was awry. Of course, if something were wrong, he would have come here to the townhouse. Odd that he wanted to meet her at the park.

She caught her maid's attention. "Lord Brevard has written inviting me to ride with him this morning. Please be so good as to set out my riding habit, Lucy."

Her maid dipped a curtsey and moved toward the wardrobe while Eliza sat down to eat a hurried meal.

An hour later, with just enough time to spare, Eliza made her way downstairs. Earlier, she had sent word to have Cassiopeia saddled. The horse and her groom were waiting as ordered when Robert let her out the front door.

"Have a good ride, miss," the footman called.

Perched on her mount, she gave him a jaunty wave. "Thank you, I shall."

With a gentle flick of the reins, she rode away.

Kit strode up the steps to Raeburn House, glad to finally be free of the coach.

He wanted a warm bath, a change of clothes and a hearty meal, in that exact order. While he was bathing, he decided, he would have one of the servants liberate a fine bottle of Burgundy from the cellar to enjoy with his meal.

The notion of the small indulgence lifted his spirits a touch.

"Welcome home, my lord," the footman greeted, holding open the front door. "Did you have a pleasant time at the races? Lay money on any winners?"

Kit removed his hat and gloves and passed them to the other man, together with a smile. "One or two, Robert. I didn't disgrace myself by losing a fortune to the bet-makers, at any rate. I actually came away flush by a few extra pounds."

The footman grinned. "Well done, my lord."

Kit glanced around the large entry area. "Is the family about?"

"The duke is in his office and her Grace is meeting with Mrs. Litton about the menus, I believe."

"And Miss Hammond?" Kit knew he shouldn't ask, but found himself prompted as if by the devil.

"Gone out, my lord. She left not long ago to ride with Viscount Brevard."

Relief dueled with disappointment, his jaw tightening at mention of Brevard. Nodding his thanks to the servant, he turned to climb the stairs to his rooms.

Kit hadn't gone two feet when the sound of a new arrival scratched at the door.

The caller was Brevard.

"Good morning," the viscount greeted as he strolled inside. Removing his beaver top hat, he handed the headgear and his cane over to the servant.

Kit offered a cursory welcome. Firming his resolve, he readied himself to come face-to-face with Eliza for the first time since their volatile encounter in the upstairs corridor. After the things he'd said to her, she might not even return his hello.

Yet as the moments slid past, Eliza did not appear.

"Where is Miss Hammond, Brevard?" Kit asked. "Surely you didn't let her ride around to the stables on her own."

A line of puzzlement creased Brevard's forehead. "I don't know what you mean. I assume she is here in the house."

"She's not with you?"

"No. Why would she be?"

Alarm coiled like a serpent inside Kit's gut. "Because the two of you went out riding this morning."

"We did not go riding. I only just arrived."

"Pardon me, my lord Brevard," Robert interrupted, "but I saw Miss Hammond ride out with a groom. She told me herself that she would be joining you in the park."

Concern darkened the viscount's gaze. "I made no such arrangements with the lady. Why would she think such a thing?"

March entered the hall and was quickly apprised of the situation. "Let me send for her maid. Perhaps the girl can shed some light on the matter."

Kit nodded in agreement. "Meanwhile I'll saddle my horse," Kit said. "One of us should go out and find her."

Brevard retrieved his hat. "I shall join you."

Before either man had a chance to act, a hurried clamor of horses' hooves rang out in the street. Beyond the open door, they watched Eliza's groom ride up, leading Cassiopeia behind him. The horse's saddle lay empty.

Kit hurried down the steps, Brevard on his heels.

The groom slid off his mount, blood glistening in a violent smear across his temple, more matted in his hair.

Kit caught him before he fell to his knees. "Joshua, what happened?

"My lord, I got here as soon as I could," Joshua panted.

"Got here from where? The park?"

The groom nodded, wincing in obvious pain. "Bloke came at me, took me unawares and clubbed me good over the head. My lord, I'm sorry. They took her. They took Miss Eliza, and there was naught I could do."

Panic struck Kit like a hard, crippling punch. "Who took her? Who took Eliza?"

"Don't know for sure, my lord. Another fellow had a big black coach up ahead. Must've been waiting fer us when we got to the park."

"What did he look like, this man?" Brevard demanded in a calm, yet implacable voice.

"Tall and thin, dark hair, mean eyes. He were dressed like a gentleman, all in black. I remember that. Miss Eliza called him her cousin."

"*Pettigrew!*" Kit met Brevard's steely gaze with a matching look of his own.

Brevard nodded in agreement. "But why would he do such a thing?"

Fury roared through Kit's veins, knowing precisely why. "He must mean to force her into a marriage. He wants her money."

"But what chance has he at succeeding? Surely he is aware we'll give chase."

"It won't matter if he marries her before we find them."

Distress and anger swept through Kit, emotions directed as much at himself as they were at Pettigrew. He'd told Eliza he would keep her safe, and now the villain had her. Kit had let down his guard and failed her. He would not fail her again.

Handing Joshua over to the care of one of the footmen so they could tend the man's wounds, Kit turned back to Brevard. "Once Pettigrew and Eliza are wed and she is compromised there'll be nothing any of us can do. He'll have what he wants, control of her fortune. We haven't a moment to lose. We have to stop the blackguard."

"I suppose he's taken her to Gretna," Brevard said.

"It would seem the most likely place, although he

might have thought of something else. I've heard tales of couples fleeing south to Guernsey in order to throw off their pursuers."

The viscount shook his head. "I'm not so sure. Guernsey seems a long shot. What if you're wrong?"

Yes, Kit mused, *what if he was wrong and completely misjudged the situation? If he made a vital error, Eliza could be lost forever.*

"Exactly the reason we must cast as wide a net as possible and cover the greatest amount of territory. We'll enlist Adrian and Darragh's help in the search. With the four of us giving chase, we're certain to run Pettigrew to ground."

And God help the little weasel when they did, he thought.

Yet what if it was already too late and Pettigrew had forced Eliza to marry him by the time they caught up? If that was the case, Kit vowed, he would see matters put right. After all, a woman could be as easily widowed as wed. Of course, the coward would likely have violated her by then.

Bitter gall rose into Kit's throat, the idea of Eliza injured and terrified making him literally ill. But as much as he would rage over and lament her abuse, to him she would be no different. He would love her no less.

Love her?

His muscles quivered as the words reverberated through his mind, a wave of profound emotion threatening to bring him to his knees.

Heavens above, he *did* love her. Adored her, in point of fact.

He nearly laughed, feeling half-crazed. What a blind, stupid fool he'd been all these many months, incapable of recognizing the truth of his own emotions. But suddenly he understood, aware that his heart had not been his own for a very long time, perhaps from that first innocent pull of desire.

No wonder he'd been so miserable these past weeks, his senses comprehending what his intellect could not.

And now Eliza was missing.

He must find her, *would* find her, and once she was back home in his arms again, he would set about claiming her for his own.

Seconds later, he stiffened, noticing Brevard. How easily he had forgotten about the other man, forgotten too that Eliza had already pledged her troth to the viscount. But engagements could be broken. Kit would simply have to convince Eliza that she belonged with him, not Brevard.

Now was not the occasion, however, to be dwelling upon such topics. Time enough later, once Eliza was safe and sound.

"Prepare yourself to ride, Brevard," Kit ordered, striding in the direction of his brother's study so he could apprise Adrian of the situation. "We leave within the hour."

Eliza's head ached as if an entire band of monkeys were jumping up and down on it and screeching out their primate lungs. She bounced against the seat as the coach hit a deep rut, only then becoming gradually aware of her surroundings.

She lay prone, one cheek pressed into faded cloth upholstery that held a musty odor, as if the coach had not been used in some while. The wheels creaked, the vehicle swaying on sets of poorly fitted springs.

Count on her cousin, she thought, to be a pinchpenny even when it came to procuring a vehicle he planned to use for a kidnapping. It might have been amusing had the circumstances not been so grim, and had she not been the one currently being kidnapped.

She kept her eyes closed and willed her headache away. Her stomach roiled, nauseous from whatever vapor he had used to subdue her. Sealing her lips closed, she prayed she wouldn't embarrass herself by vomiting. Although it would serve Philip right if she was sick all over his shoes. Casting up her accounts would almost be worth it just to see him fuss and jump around in disgust.

But if she did vomit, whether accidentally or on purpose, he would make her pay later on; she knew him well enough to be certain of that. Keeping her eyes closed, she tried to curl more tightly into herself and discovered, to her horror, that her hands and feet were bound.

"I know you're awake," Pettigrew said from where he sat on the seat across from her. "So you might as well quit pretending."

She shivered but did not reply.

"Go back to being the silent little mouse, if that is what you want," he disparaged. "It will make no difference to me. You and I will be wed either way. Besides, I think I liked you better when you knew enough to keep your mouth shut. Mother had a way with those slaps of hers, didn't she?"

Her eyes popped open at that, revulsion loosening her tongue. "I will *never* marry you."

"Oh, you'll marry me and don't think you won't. I already have a minister lined up who doesn't care much about consenting brides so long as he's well paid for his trouble. So you see, your willingness is not of concern."

She swallowed against her terror. "Where are you taking me?"

"What does that matter? You'll go *where* I say and do *what* I say until you have served your purpose."

"And what purpose is that?" she dared to question. "If it's my fortune you want, I'll . . . I'll give it to you. Just draw up the papers and—"

He turned his malevolent gaze upon her. "If only it could be that simple, but it isn't. Your fiancé, for one, might have some objection to your giving away your wealth, not to mention those interfering friends of yours. Don't think I've forgotten how the high-and-mighty Lord Christopher treated me that night at the theater. He and the others would see to it that any legal agreements made between us were voided as soon as you were set free."

He caught hold of the coach strap as they hit another rut. "Of course, all this trouble could have been avoided if you had simply agreed to marry me when I asked. I would have treated you with some respect then, found you a nice little house where you could quietly live out your days."

"While you went off to spend my money."

Color rushed into his cheeks, mottling his pallid complexion. He jabbed a finger toward his chest. "*My* money, you mean. I was the heir, that was *my* inheritance you took. It would all have come to me if that stupid old crone hadn't cut me off. If I'd known she had so much money hidden away, I would have done more to ensure she didn't change the will."

"Why *did* Aunt cut you off?" Eliza asked.

He smiled, the expression holding no warmth. For a moment, he paused, clearly considering whether or not to answer her.

Finally, he gave a shrug. "A minor indiscretion while I served as vicar. Seems my benefactor took exception to some yeoman's lies about my having carnal knowledge of his daughter. They claimed I took advantage of her, when she was nothing but a common little trollop. How was I to know she was only thirteen?"

Eliza bit her lip to hold back a gasp.

"They said there was another girl but she was a whore, gave it away to anyone who would pay her price. In spite of my protests, they forced me to resign my living. When Mother heard, she cut me off." He grumbled under his breath, "Old witch.

"Anyway," her cousin went on, "once I am safely in possession of *my* fortune, then I'll consider what to do about you. After all, it isn't as if I am really interested in having you for my wife, Cousin." He leered. "Though we will have to consummate our wedding in order to satisfy all the legalities of our union."

She quailed inside but did her best not to let it show. "They'll come for me, you know," she said.

His face hardened. "Let them come. By the time they do, it will be far, far too late."

Eliza closed her eyes and prayed he was wrong.

Kit drew up his mount, slowing the lathered animal to a walk. He'd ridden the beast, and others like it, hard throughout the course of the day, pushing for as much time and speed as he could safely manage.

Back in London before he'd set out, he and the other men had met. After a quick debate, the decision was made that Adrian and Brevard would ride north to Gretna Green. Darragh would ride to Dover and make inquiries to see if Pettigrew and Eliza planned to cross into France through Calais. And Kit would head to Southampton, then make the crossing to the island of Guernsey if he discovered evidence that the pair had passed in that direction.

Anyone else would have gone to Gretna Green, and

sent Brevard chasing south to the shore instead. But Kit's gut instincts had called for him to take the less likely course, and he always followed his gut.

To his relief, his intuition once again had proven correct.

At the last coaching inn, while waiting for a fresh horse to be readied, he had questioned the stable hands. When one youth began to describe a slender, brunette lady accompanied by a tall, black-haired scarecrow of a fellow, Kit knew he'd hit the mark. The stable boy recalled them most particularly because the gentleman had given him such a miserly tip for his service. The boy also recounted how the man had yelled at the young lady when she had balked at stepping back inside the coach as they were preparing to depart.

Heartened by the fact that he was definitely on the correct trail, Kit composed hurried messages for Darragh, Adrian and Brevard, and sent them off with runners. He also wrote a note to be express-delivered to Violet, whom he knew must be worrying herself ill back in London.

Now on the road again, he raced fast, knowing he was no more than an hour behind Eliza and Pettigrew. If he caught them before they set sail, he could put a quick end to Pettigrew's vile plans. But even if he missed them, he would find Eliza. He would never stop searching, not until he held her safe inside his arms.

Chapter Twenty-two

The sea crossing was rough and miserable and, unlike in the coach, Eliza had not been able to keep from being violently ill. Despite the agony of her queasy, churning stomach, a part of her had been glad of her suffering since her illness kept Pettigrew at bay.

Had she not been sick, she feared he might have decided to force himself upon her to consummate their "union," as he called it. The idea of him touching her in such a manner only increased her nauseated state. Given that, she didn't begrudge the long, cold hours spent inside the tiny cabin belowdecks, her head bent over a wooden bucket. In her estimation, her miserable state had been worth every last wretched heave.

Morning sun was just lightening the sky when their ship docked and Pettigrew came for her. Disgust wrinkled his face as he sniffed the squalid atmosphere, his eyes raking over what she knew must be her wan complexion and disheveled appearance. If she looked as dreadful as she felt, she must truly be a sight.

He led her to an inn, where he procured a bedchamber for himself and his "wife."

A maid brought her hot water, towels and a comb for her hair. Eliza had no idea what excuse Pettigrew had used to explain her lack of luggage and other traveling amenities. A meal arrived not long after, and was set upon a small, drop-leaf table near the fireplace.

"Clean yourself up," Pettigrew ordered once the maid had gone. "I am going to find the minister and make sure everything is in order for the ceremony. Be ready by the time I return."

"And how long will that be?" she said with more spirit than she felt.

"Midday most like, so I suggest you get some rest while I am out." A crude, ugly light shone in his gaze. "You'll be needing your strength for later."

She shuddered as he let himself out the door, the key scraping audibly in the lock. If she'd had any doubt, his last words assured her that he meant to force himself on her tonight. He would have to take her against her will, she promised, since she would never let him touch her any other way.

Ignoring the fatigue that dragged upon her like chains, she went to the door and rattled the knob, confirming that it was indeed well barred. Then she crossed to the window.

Peering out, her heart sank as precipitously as the sharp drop beneath, the land sloping off toward a rough, rocky shoreline that led straight to the sea.

Cousin Philip had chosen her prison well. She wondered how long he had been planning this. Some while, she decided, since he already had the minister under his control.

She considered banging on the door and yelling but didn't know if he had hired a guard—one of the men from the ship, perhaps—who was willing to see she did not gain help from any of the inn staff.

Dejected and weary, she crossed to the washstand and rinsed her face and hands. The maid had also left a toothbrush and tooth powder, which she used to scrub her teeth. Mildly refreshed, she moved to the table, dropped onto the single, hard wooden chair and studied the tray of food. She knew her efforts were not aided by starvation and so forced herself to eat a few bites of bread, and drink some hot tea.

The last of her nausea eased, hunger surprisingly replacing the ache in her stomach. Picking up a knife, she reached out to cut a tiny wedge of cheese, then paused, her interest caught by the implement. In speculation, she turned the knife over in her hand, then gazed again at the window.

No, she thought, shaking her head at the wild idea that popped into her mind. Trying such a thing would be sheer folly. But what other options did she have? Kit and the others would be searching for her, she knew, but they might not reach her in time. Either she should act now or wait meek as a lamb for Cousin Philip to return.

Knowing she had not so much as a second to waste, she hurried to her feet.

"I'll have that key now." Kit fixed the innkeeper with an implacable stare as he pushed a pair of coins across the wooden bar top between them.

"You're her brother, you say?" The man eyed the coins assessingly.

"That's right." Kit added another coin to the pile, then one more when the first few failed to elicit results.

The innkeeper's large fist came out and scooped up the money. Unhooking a key from a nail beneath the bar, he passed it to Kit. "Wouldn't want to keep a man from his family, now would I?"

Without acknowledging the man's lascivious wink,

Kit folded the metal key into his palm and strode toward the stairs.

"First door at the top of the steps," the older man called after him.

Kit knew Eliza was alone and presumably locked inside, the innkeeper having previously volunteered the information that her *husband* had taken her up to their room, then had come back down and gone out.

Kit didn't believe it. Surely they couldn't already be wed, unless the ship's captain had performed the ceremony on the voyage over. But if the man had, Kit thought, silently reaffirming his vow, Eliza would not remain a bride for long.

Up the stairs he went into a narrow, dimly lighted hallway. Crossing to the first door, he fit the key into the lock and gave it a turn. The door swung open on silent hinges.

He expected to see Eliza. Instead the room appeared empty, the window sash full open, cheap gingham curtains billowing inward on a stiff, salt-scented breeze. Shadows crowded the room, the morning sunshine grayed by a band of dark, lumbering clouds that were rolling in from the sea.

He scowled, his gaze flying to the bed, which had been stripped free of its linens. Walking forward, he moved to investigate. To his left, the floorboards creaked ever so lightly, and the fine hairs on the back of his neck stood straight up.

Acting on pure instinct, he shifted on the balls of his feet and flung up an arm. He took a glancing blow to his shoulder from the china washbasin that had been intended to crack open his skull.

Whirling around, he prepared himself for a fight. A pair of soft, fear-glazed gray eyes collided with his own.

Suddenly the blue and white basin clattered to the floor as Eliza tossed the crockery aside and hurled herself into his arms. "Kit, my God, you're here! I thought you were Philip. I thought he'd come back for me."

Kit clutched her tight and squeezed his eyes shut. Cradling her to him, he savored the sensation of her lithe body pressed against his own. Without thinking, he crushed his lips to hers and breathed in her warm, vital scent, overwhelmed to be holding her once again in his arms. Deepening their kiss, he gave himself over to the moment, blood thundering in his head, pounding through his veins with a mixture of complete relief and immense joy.

Eliza responded, returning his kisses with an eagerness that rocked him to his core. Gentling his touch, he let both of them savor the connection, rejoice in the unbridled exhilaration of being together once again.

At length, he forced himself to draw away, resting his forehead against her own. "Are you all right?" he whispered, his voice a low, thick rumble.

She leaned back enough to gaze up at him. "Yes. At least I am now."

He kissed her again, a soft, gentle joining of lips. "I thought I'd lost you. My heart nearly stopped when we realized he'd taken you."

She trembled. "I knew you'd come after me, but I didn't think any of you would realize his destination, not right away. I assumed you would all be headed to Scotland by now."

"Brevard and Adrian are traveling there now. I'm sure they're still en route. All of us, including Darragh, set out as soon as we realized you'd been abducted."

"Thank heavens for your quick thinking." She cast a

rueful glance toward the floor. "Sorry about attacking you with the washbowl. I'm glad now that I missed."

He grinned. "I'm glad that you missed too. You'd have left a wicked knot on my noggin, not to mention given me a raging headache."

"When I heard footsteps in the hall, I assumed he had returned early, come back before I had a chance to escape."

"And how were you going to do that if not with the basin?" He gazed around the room, only then noticing a strip of cloth—seven feet long at least—lying on the floor at the base of the window. "Are those bedsheets? Or should I say, *were* those bedsheets?"

She nodded. "I cut them into strips and braided them together in hopes of using it as a rope. I didn't think I had enough length and was about to start on the curtains when you arrived."

"A rope for what?" He released her and crossed to the open window, his stomach lurching as he saw the drop down to the cliff below. "Lord have mercy, Eliza, you weren't going to try climbing out the window, were you? It would have been nothing short of suicide. You'd never have made it down in one piece."

She crossed her arms. "I had to do something. I could not sit by and let him force me into marriage."

"So you aren't married, then?"

She shook her head. "No, not yet. That's where he went, to consult with the minister. He may return anytime. We really shouldn't linger."

"She is right, you know," declared a grim male voice from the hallway. "You ought not to have stayed."

Pettigrew stepped into the room and slammed the door closed behind him. In his hand, he held a pistol.

Eliza sucked in an audible breath.

Kit reached out, caught her hand and tugged her behind him.

Pettigrew smirked. "Hiding her will do you no good. I am the one who has the advantage here."

"I assure you, Pettigrew," Kit drawled, "you have no advantage, nor will you ever have."

Fury flashed in Pettigrew's gaze, his nose jutting out like a great vulture's beak. "Unlike the last time, you're in no position to offer insults, so I would advise you to curb your tongue. And I'm sick of your interference, Winter. How did you find us here?"

"Simple deductive reasoning. There are only so many places you could have fled with Eliza. I sent a man to every one."

Pettigrew's hatred shone brighter.

As though he wasn't in the least concerned, Kit placed a hand on his hip. "If I were you, I would run while I had the chance."

Pettigrew's lips parted, incredulous amusement showing on his face. "*I* should run? *I?* You are the one who is a fool, Lord Christopher. A self-indulged, careless second son, who hasn't the wherewithal to succeed at anything that is of the slightest worth in this world."

"Maybe so, but at least I've never crawled so low I've had to resort to kidnapping an innocent woman for her money."

The other man's eyes burned hot as coals. "*My* money," Pettigrew spat, gesturing toward himself with his gun. "She's got *my* money and I want it back!"

Kit sprang, using the instant of distraction to grab for the weapon. He nearly managed to wrench the gun free of the other man's hand, but Pettigrew countered just in time and held firm, his grip like a vice. They wrestled, grappling between themselves. Muscles straining, Kit fought for possession of the pistol, ignoring any inkling of worry about the gun going off before he could pry it free.

The bastard is strong, Kit thought, far stronger than he would ever have imagined.

Still, Pettigrew was no match for him, Kit using brute force to gradually twist the scoundrel's hand and arm up over his head. Tightening his grip, Kit forced Pettigrew's wrist back, pressuring it into an unnatural angle that threatened to tear muscle and snap bone.

Arms straining, Pettigrew's face contorted with frustration and pain, then he gave a shout and let the gun clatter to the floor. He bit out a vicious curse as Kit kicked the weapon behind him.

"Eliza, get the gun," Kit ordered.

She didn't hesitate, racing forward to retrieve the weapon from the floor. Visibly shaking, she picked it up and held it out in front of her, aiming the firearm directly at her cousin.

Unable to restrain his anger, Kit smashed his fist into the other man's jaw. Pettigrew cried out as he stumbled back, whimpering in his misery.

"I should horsewhip you for what you've done," Kit told him, "and afterward set the magistrates on you. The charge of kidnapping alone could send you to prison for a long, long time. But doing so would inevitably bring Eliza's name into the matter, and she has already been harmed enough. I'll not see her reputation smeared by the likes of you. So as much as it galls me, I'm going to let you go, but only if you swear never to set foot in England again, so long as you live."

"And if I refuse?" Pettigrew challenged, cradling his injured wrist to his chest.

Kit narrowed his eyes as he shot the other man a dan-

gerous stare. "Then you had best be prepared to watch
your back, because I promise you this, if you ever come
near Eliza again, I will kill you. It's as simple as that.
Leave, Pettigrew. My suggestion is France, since it's a
quick crossing from here. Or go to America. They say it
is indeed the land of opportunity."

Pettigrew stood his ground for another long moment,
his jaw thrust forward at a pugnacious tilt. Then abruptly,
his shoulders sagged. He cast one final venomous, black-
eyed glare at Eliza before spinning on his heels and slink-
ing from the room.

Kit didn't allow himself to relax until the door closed
behind Pettigrew. Crossing, he turned the key in the
lock and flipped the night latch to guard against any
further intrusions. Hurrying back to Eliza's side, he
eased the pistol from her tremulous grip and set the
weapon aside, careful to make certain the trigger was
not cocked.

Drawing her comfortingly into his arms, he held her
tight and let her burrow close. "It's over, my little wren.
I have you now and nothing and no one will harm you
again."

Her melting gray gaze lifted to his, and in the space of
a single heartbeat, they were kissing.

Fervent and needy, he took her mouth with a kind
of savage desperation, releasing all the pent-up fear and
anguish and apprehension that had besieged him over
the last twenty-four hours. Closing his eyes, he lost himself to the dulcet sweetness of her touch, exalting in the
disparate sensations of blessed relief and smoldering
passion, the inner fire that always burned for her leaping
to life in his blood and vitals.

Stroking his hands over her back, he caressed her
hips, then glided up again to trace the tensile length of

her spine. Sliding low, then lower still, he curved his palms over the rounded softness of her bottom, cupping her, gently kneading her flesh, before lifting her toes off the floor to fit her tight against his frame. Devouring her mouth, he reveled in the mewing sounds of pleasure he coaxed from her throat, the marvelous, sensuous weight of her slight figure cradled inside his powerful grasp.

Eliza clung, wrapping her arms around Kit's neck as she poured herself into his ardent embrace. His hair held the scent of the sea, or maybe it was the storm-tossed breeze whipping into the room through the open window, the wind bold and robust, but no competition for the mastery of Kit's touch.

Widening her mouth, as he'd once taught her to do, she invited him to take more. To dive deeper. To plunge them both into a world of hunger and possession, where they could revel in dark, wet delights and silken pleasures. Shuddering, she sighed in hazy bliss, his kisses the nearest thing to perfection she knew she would ever find on this earth.

A harsh gust of wind puffed into the room, sending her curls dancing around her face, yanking at her skirts like the hands of an impatient tot. Shivering, she held Kit tighter and kissed him until she wondered if she might explode, bright and dazzling as a Roman candle in a fireworks show.

A loud clap of thunder boomed outside, hard enough to rattle the walls of the inn. An instant later, sheets of rain broke loose, slicing a diagonal path to the ground below. Carried aloft by the unrelenting wind, icy droplets of rain sprayed inward, splattering her skin and Kit's, and dampening their clothes.

Gasping, the two of them broke apart, shaken by the frigid damp. Blinking in confusion, they watched water sluice into the room, pouring across the floor like a falls. Lightning flashed and cut a jagged arc in the sky, turned inky black despite the morning hour. Unleashing its full fury, the rain pounded harder.

Springing into action, Kit set her on her feet and rushed to the window. Fighting the wind, he closed the panes and shut the downpour outside. As if in complaint, the tempest beat a relentless tattoo that pattered and pummeled against the glass.

He turned, rainwater glistening in his hair, on his skin. Crossing to her, he bent and scooped her off her feet, then carried her to the bed.

"No sheets," he murmured, nuzzling her neck as he lay her down, "but I suppose we can make do. Let me get the quilt. I'll be back in a moment."

But a moment was long enough for her conscience to kick in and give her a sudden, painful jab.

Mercy, what am I doing? She was about to sleep with Kit. Again. A kidnapping, a rescue, a consoling hug, and she'd practically thrown herself at him, ready to surrender, body and soul. But despite his gallantry in saving her, nothing between them had changed.

Shivering now with cold, her mind began to clear as though emerging from an intoxicated stupor.

He returned with the coverlet and spread it over her. "This should keep off the chill."

"Kit, we can't do this," she stated, struggling to sit upright against the lumpy mattress that seemed determined to draw her downward.

Setting a light hand against her shoulder, he tumbled her backward, then followed her down. "Can't we?"

"No. In case you've forgotten, I am engaged."

A heavy scowl settled over his brows. "You don't have to be."

Surprise rippled through her. "What?"

"Don't marry him." Leaning over her, he gazed into her eyes, his own glittering like fragments of green and gold glass. "Marry me instead."

Confusion knotted beneath her breast. "We've been through this before. You don't want to marry me."

"Don't I?" A soft breath soughed from his chest as he glided his lips across her cheek.

She shook her head. "You only want my body."

He nipped her earlobe, then feathered a series of kisses along the column of her throat. "Is that right?"

"It's obligation talking," she rushed on, "because you desire me. Because we are here together alone, and if we do this I will be quite thoroughly compromised yet again."

Lifting the quilt, he slid under it. "I should say you will be, since I plan to ravish you until we both collapse from fatigue. But this," he paused, pressing the unmistakable length of his iron-hard erection against her hip, "has nothing to do with obligation."

"Lust, then." She struggled to move away.

Catching hold, he gently pressed her back onto the mattress, capturing her wrists to pin her hands next to her head. In the dim stormy light, she met his gaze. "Please, Kit. Please let me go."

Slowly, he shook his head. "I can't. Believe me, I've tried, but it quite simply cannot be done. And though I unquestionably ache with lust for you, my emotions run far, far deeper than that." His expression serious, he brushed a kiss across her mouth. "I love you, Eliza."

At first she didn't think she had heard him. "What?"

"I love you. I should have told you sooner, but I was too much of a fool to even realize it myself. When you were taken . . . well, I knew my life wouldn't be worth living anymore, not without you in it."

The air rushed from her lungs, leaving her head spinning as though she had taken a bad fall. He couldn't be saying these things, she marveled. She must in truth have hit her head and was hallucinating. All of this, perhaps even the kidnapping, nothing more than a fantastic dream.

The tantalizing stroke of his thumbs against the inside of her palms brought her back, let her know that everything she felt was indeed reality. His touch set her body aquiver, her nerves ablaze.

"Say something, sweetheart," he urged. "Tell me if you think you could feel the same. If you could stand to marry me and share my life and bear my children. I know you want babies. I assure you, it will be my very great pleasure to get you with child, and keep you that way, as many times as you wish. All you need do is say yes. Please, Eliza, please say yes and let me spend my days making you happy."

Her lips trembled, a torrent of emotions building up inside her. Like a spring dam overflooding its gates, she burst into tears. Turning her head, she began to sob.

Kit stared, devastation filling him as he watched her cry. Releasing her wrists, he hovered for an uncertain moment, stroking her hair away from her wet cheeks as tenderly as he would a child's.

Yet as much as it pained him, he had to ask, his voice ragged when he finally managed to choke out the words. "Do you love him, then? Brevard? Is it him you truly wish to wed?"

Weeping, she shook her head. "N-no."

"No?" Perplexed, he rubbed a hand along her arm. "Then why? What is it, sweetheart? What's wrong? If you don't want to marry me, I'll wait. I know you may not love me now, but—"

A muffled laugh hiccuped through her tears as she reached up and looped her arms around his neck, urging him to silence. "Shh, you d-don't understand."

"Don't understand what?"

"That I love you. So much, too much. I've loved you for years, so long I'd given up hope of you ever feeling the same about me."

"You have? Then why did you refuse me before when I asked you to marry me?"

She sniffed and curled closer. "I thought you were only being honorable. I suppose most women would have accepted, but I couldn't trap you—or myself, for that matter. We both deserved more than being shackled inside a loveless marriage. I couldn't bring myself to settle for less than the full measure of your love."

"Nor should you have. God, what an idiot I was to talk of duty and honor when I should have been telling you how much you mean to me." Bending downward, he pressed his lips against hers in a slow, gentle merging that left both of them trembling. "Forgive me for being such a slow-top. I don't know why it took me so long to see the truth, to recognize the treasure I had, waiting right there in front of me all this time."

Her lips curved in a radiant smile. "You see me now, that is all that matters. There is nothing to forgive."

Joy burst like a radiant sun inside his chest. "Say yes, then. Tell me you will be my wife. Tell me you'll be mine."

Her eyes turned dreamy. "I am yours, Kit. For now and always. Of course I'll be your wife."

Crushing her lips beneath his own, he sealed their promises, using his touch to forge vows and bonds in the oldest, most intimate way a man could with the woman he loves.

Neither one of them was breathing steadily by the

time he raised his head from their tempestuous kiss. His body rampant with need, he yanked off his coat and tossed it to the floor.

After doing the same with his waistcoat, he reached for the fastenings on her dress. "Let's get you out of these damp clothes. I wouldn't want you to take a chill."

Her hands moved to his shoulders, fingers shifting impatiently. "Yes, we both should be careful."

She lay quiescent as he stripped her to her thin, linen shift. Leaning down to plunder her mouth, he swallowed the humming sounds of pleasure she made, fondling her as he untied the ribbon on her undergarment to free her breasts.

Outside, rain drummed on the roof, the wind howling and whining around them like a banshee. But Kit heard nothing beyond a dim hiss, a whisper, drowned out by the pounding of his own heart. The pounding increased to an almost deafening roar when Eliza's small hand slid beneath his shirt and traced the hard plain of his chest.

Shuddering beneath the power of her still innocent touch, he let her caress him, trail the edges of her small, inquisitive fingers over his skin. As though dipped in fire, she set him ablaze, heating him from the inside out. He groaned aloud when her fingers circled one flat male nipple, then the other, flicking each with the tip of one nail before gliding lower. Slipping just beneath the top edge of his trousers, she stroked his belly, the light sensation enough to push him right to the edge.

"I never did get to see you," she murmured, unknowingly coquettish.

Brain buzzing, he had to focus on her words. "What?"

"When we made love the first time, I never really got to see you."

His brow arched upward. "Did you not?"

"No."

A slow, crooked grin tilted his lips. "Well then, shall we rectify that omission?"

She nodded, the eager look in her eyes confirming her answer.

Leaning up, he peeled his shirt over his head, his arousal thickening in response to her gasp of appreciation. He stiffened even more when he shucked off his trousers and bared himself fully to her gaze.

"Oh, my," she exclaimed, staring straight at the part of him he could no longer even attempt to control.

"Too much?" he asked, reaching for the quilt.

She stopped him. "No, don't." Her cheeks pinked at her boldness, her eyes skittering away. "May I touch?"

His erection twitched as if she had already wrapped him in her little fist. He nearly groaned, forcing himself to relax. "Be my guest."

Instead of beginning with the part of him that was obviously begging for her touch, she laid a palm against his upper thigh. His muscles jerked and tensed, her hands delicate and cool as they traced his heated flesh, flesh that burned hotter with her every caress.

Eliza swallowed and put aside her qualms, refusing to let herself feel shy or hesitant. Kit had taught her to be confident. He'd helped to make her the woman she now was.

Independent, assured and no longer afraid—not even of herself.

Feeling bold, she stroked his skin. From thigh to foot, belly to arms, she traveled a wondrous path, learning his shape and texture, fascinated by the fundamental differences between his masculine physique and her own.

Hard where she was soft. Large where she was slight.

Strong where she was frail. Yet she didn't feel frail, realizing the power she held over him, his body literally trembling beneath her questing hands by the time she eventually paused.

He groaned aloud when she curled her hand around the most obviously male part of him, awed by the sensation of holding him so intimately. Arching into her grasp, he urged her to touch him as she'd never thought to do.

And she again became the attentive student, letting him instruct her in all the ways he yearned to be pleasured.

After long minutes, he clasped her wrists and drew her hands away. "Enough, you siren, before you make me lose what little control I have left."

Rolling her onto her back, he stripped off her garment, baring her naked body to his fiery gaze, his eyelids heavy with undisguised hunger. "My turn now."

Before she could take a full breath, he claimed her with his touch. Senses whirling, desire spiked hot and wet between her thighs as he caressed her. She didn't know how, but with a few deliciously magical strokes, he brought her to peak, her sighs ringing loudly on the stormy air.

Then with a dazzling flick of his fingers, he did it again.

But he wasn't through. "One more time, Eliza. You're so pretty when you come. Come for me again."

"I can't," she panted.

"You can," he promised.

Then he was driving her up again. Impossible as it seemed, he soon had her melting, making her arch hard against his fingers as the most devastatingly intense pleasure lashed her from within and without.

Helpless, she twisted beneath him as he built her

hunger higher, made the quivering ache rise and go deeper, so deep she feared for a moment it might claw her apart.

Then the rapture caught her, her wail of completion drowned out by a crash of thunder, as if the heavens were urging her on. Thick and golden, an exhilarating joy spread through her like hot, viscous honey.

Stunned, her arms fell limp at her sides.

But Kit was far from finished.

Feasting upon her, he took her mouth in a series of long, deep, drugging kisses that made her blood sizzle and her brain grow muzzy. Then he began to kiss her breasts, drawing upon her, caressing her in a way that, to her awe, brought her need roaring back to life.

She was ready for him by the time he parted her legs, her body welcoming his, gladly accepting his impressive penetration.

There was no pain, she discovered, only pleasure as he plunged deep. Intense, unrelenting pleasure that wrung little gasping cries of delight from her throat, sounds she could no more stop than she could stop her own lungs from breathing.

Establishing a primal rhythm that vibrated through her, he thrust and thrust hard, over and over again. Doing her best to match his pace, she held on as she climbed toward her peak. Yielding her body utterly to him, she let him guide her, knowing he would lead her where they both most longed to go.

Another clap of thunder splintered the air, the storm rattling the windows as her climax hit, shaking her like a rag doll. She screamed against the intensity of her release, nearly overwhelmed by the profound depth of the sensations. Carried aloft, she sobbed out her ecstasy.

Kit stroked inside her a few more, almost brutal

times, then stiffened. "God, I love you, Eliza," he called out as he claimed his own, plainly devastating, satisfaction.

"I love you too," she murmured, holding him as he quaked. Stroking her hand over his hair, she cradled him close, smiling as he nuzzled his face against her neck.

Savoring their connection, they both drifted to sleep.

Chapter Twenty-three

Eliza and Kit arrived in London two afternoons later.

Seconds after the coach Kit had hired for the journey rolled to a stop, Raeburn House's front door flew wide.

Violet raced down the steps. "You are home!"

Kit barely had time to lift Eliza free of the vehicle before Violet crushed her in a fierce embrace. Happily Eliza returned her friend's hug.

"Are you well?" Violet demanded, worry crashing like a rough sea in her blue-green eyes.

"Quite well," Eliza reassured.

"He didn't harm you?" She clucked, outraged as a mother hen whose chick had been endangered by a fox.

"No, though he would have if Kit had not found me when he did."

"Well, thank the stars for Kit." Violet showered her brother-in-law with a jubilant smile. "He is a prince."

Eliza met Kit's gleaming hazel gaze with a special one of her own. "Yes, he is."

Too excited to notice the import of the intimate exchange, Violet continued. "Darragh is here. He received Kit's note from the road, and returned only a few hours ago. Jeannette and the girls are waiting inside as well. And we're expecting Adrian and Lord Brevard to make it home by this evening. Once everyone has arrived, we shall have a special meal in celebration of your safe homecoming. And as an additional thank-you to Kit, I shall have François bake an extra tray of honeyed Bath buns, just for him."

"Bath buns for me!" Kit's handsome features creased with clear appreciation. "I see I shall have to rescue Eliza more often."

He waggled his brows, causing them all to laugh.

"Well, come inside where you can tell me everything," Violet said, slipping her arm around Eliza's waist. "And once you are finished, we shall never again mention that man's name. I always did think Philip Pettigrew was a thoroughly loathsome toad."

"You'll get no argument from me." Eliza hooked her arm around Violet's waist in return and let her friend ferry her inside.

In her bedchamber, Eliza bathed and washed her hair, then changed into one of her own freshly laundered gowns. All the while, she regaled Violet with the details of her harrowing adventure, careful to omit mention of the most important part of the tale, the glorious turn of events between her and Kit.

As much as she was dying to confide in Violet, Eliza decided she owed Lance the dignity of telling him first. Once she had broken off her engagement to him, she would share her ecstatic news with her friend. She couldn't wait to see Violet's reaction, since she knew Violet would be so surprised.

A few hours later, she sat on the saffron-and-white-striped sofa in the family drawing room, sipping a predinner sherry. The others were gathered with her, including Darragh and Jeannette's entire brood, all of them awaiting the anticipated arrival of Adrian and Brevard.

Not long after, soft footfalls tread across the Turkey

carpet runners in the hall, Adrian and Lance striding unannounced into the room.

Abruptly nervous, Eliza set her drink aside and climbed to her feet. Guilt assailed her when she saw the viscount's travel-stained condition. His jaw was unshaven, eyes red-rimmed with clear exhaustion. Without pause, he crossed instantly to her and pulled her into his arms.

Before she could say a single word, his lips were upon hers and he was kissing her passionately, uncaring of their audience.

"Darling," he said, "I am so grateful you are safe. I was frantic until I had Winter's note, and all the way home, well, Raeburn and I didn't know if he'd found you or not. I am so relieved you are here. I assume you are well?"

"Yes, I'm fine."

Eliza plunged into the same series of reassurances and explanations she had already given everyone else. Cradled inside Lance's grasp, she delicately tried to extricate herself without making an obvious issue of it.

But Lance wasn't letting go.

Aware of the glower of jealousy and displeasure that must be riding Kit's face, she kept herself from glancing in his direction.

"Lance," she said in a low voice, "we need to talk."

Gently, she tried again to remove herself from his embrace, but he failed to take the hint.

He smiled down at her. "We will talk later, dearest. First, just let me hold you, let me feel that you are all right."

Fighting the urge to squirm, she forced herself to stand acquiescent for another long pair of moments. "See?" she murmured with false brightness. "I am quite well. Now, let me go, Lance. We are in company."

He dismissed her request. "Everyone here is family. No one can object if we share an embrace. We are an engaged couple, after all. Allowances are always made for engaged couples."

She could think of at least one person who must be dying to object. Once again, she did not glance his way. "Yes, but—"

"But what?" A slight line creased Brevard's patrician forehead. "What is it, Eliza. Something *is* wrong, isn't it?"

On an inward sigh, she met his gaze. "Let us go into the other room, where we can be private."

The lines on his forehead deepened to a heavy frown. "Why do we need privacy? What is it you must tell me so urgently?"

A silence descended over the room, everyone else—save one—clearly wanting to know the answer as well. A leaden lump of panic settled in her throat, her heart suddenly beating as frantically as the wings of a small, caged bird. Needing reassurance, her gaze finally darted up and across to Kit, seeking his strength and guidance. His eyes locked with hers, conveying a silent message of resilient calm.

The brief contact was obviously enough to alert Brevard, whose muscles stiffened. The viscount flicked a long, inquiring glance between her and Kit. Slowly, his arms slid away, finally setting her free.

"Just what exactly is going on here?" Brevard asked.

"Come out into the hall. Please, Lance," she beseeched, a bitter shower of guilt raining upon her.

Kit strode forward. After a brief moment of hesitation, he laid what could only be seen as a proprietary hand on her shoulder. "I think it's a little too late for secrecy. I believe he already knows the truth."

Brevard stared for another long moment before his eyes narrowed upon Kit, turning vicious. "Why, you contemptible blackguard! You've compromised her, haven't you?"

Gasps echoed around the room.

Eliza extended a hand. "Lance, it isn't what you think."

"It's exactly what he thinks, sweetheart," Kit declared in a soft, pragmatic tone.

"*I'll kill you!*"

In a blink, Brevard's fist shot out and connected squarely with Kit's chin.

Kit's head snapped back, more gasps filling the room, along with a few wincing *oohs*.

Eliza cried out and reached for Kit.

Shaking his head to clear out the stars, Kit stood his ground. Slowly, he reached up to rub a hand over his abused jaw. "I suppose I deserved that punch," he told the viscount, "but if you want to try for another, we'll have to take this to an alternate location."

Eliza laid a restraining hand on his arm. "You will do nothing of the kind. I will not have you fighting, either of you. And certainly not over me."

"Sorry, Brevard. Eliza and I didn't want to tell you this way, not so openly and with so little finesse." Kit paused, then looped an arm around Eliza's waist. "But the lady and I are in love. Whatever may have happened between us over the past few days was born of that love. And just so there are no misunderstandings, Eliza has agreed to be my wife."

Brevard's skin paled, his gaze shooting to her. "Is this true, what he says? Have you promised to marry him?"

Remorse stung her as she read the abject pain in the viscount's eyes, along with a measure of his rising anger. "Yes."

"Is it because the two of you were alone? Because you feel you must wed him?"

Part of her wished she could salve his pride, wished she could soften his hurt and let him believe a lie. But such dishonesty seemed wrong, seemed unworthy of them all.

Slowly she shook her head. "No. I love him. Oh, Lance, I am so dreadfully sorry."

"He's the one, isn't he?" Brevard sent a curt nod toward Kit.

She nodded.

"I thought you said it was over."

"I thought it was. Please, you must believe me, I never intended to hurt you."

His shoulders lowered in sudden resignation. "No, I suppose you did not."

Not knowing what else to do, she twisted off her engagement ring and held it out to him. "Lance, I . . . forgive me."

His anguished blue eyes met hers for a long moment before he took the ring. "Be happy, Eliza."

Gripping the stone tightly inside his palm, Brevard turned and strode from the room.

Trembling, Eliza let Kit draw her close. Dusting a kiss over her cheek, he stroked a palm in soothing arcs across her back. They remained silent, both sad and awash in regrets.

"It had to be done," he murmured against her ear.

"I know, but did you see his face? He was so hurt."

"Yes, but he'll heal in time."

"I suppose. I feel so very dreadful. He didn't deserve this."

"No, but there was no alternative."

She sighed. "I only hope he finds someone else someday. Someone who will love him with all her heart."

"I hope so too." Dismissing the avid interest of their audience, Kit bent and kissed her. "I love you."

Her arms crept around his waist and squeezed. "I love you too, so very much."

Leaning back, she studied the bruise beginning to color his jaw. "Oh, darling, just look at your poor face. You're going to need an herb poultice and a fresh piece of steak for that wound."

"And here I was looking forward to eating dinner, not wearing it on my face." He laughed, then groaned, grimacing against the pain.

"So, do I presume there is a wedding in the offing?" Adrian interrupted, crossing the room toward them.

Eliza huddled against Kit as he turned them to face his brother. "There certainly is, as soon as the ceremony can be arranged. Eliza has made me the happiest of men by agreeing to be my bride."

When Adrian fixed a stern gaze upon Kit, Eliza stiffened and raised her chin.

"She has done you a great honor, agreeing to put up with you and your antics," Adrian said. "A gift I trust you will not soon forget."

"Never," Kit promised.

A wide grin stretched across Adrian's mouth, his gaze shifting to her. "Welcome to the family, Eliza. I can't think of another girl I would rather have as my sister."

She beamed and stepped forward for a familial buss on the cheek. "And thank you for searching for me."

"You are entirely welcome."

Having restrained herself long enough, Violet rushed forward, squealing out her delight. The two women hugged, jumping up and down like giddy schoolgirls.

"Are you angry?" Eliza asked.

Violet raised a golden brow. "About what?"

"My not telling you. Were you shockingly surprised?"

"A little shocked but not all that surprised. I've always known you carried a secret tendre for Kit."

"You did?"

"Of course. I'm not blind."

"Neither am I," Jeannette piped.

Eliza's lips parted, a frisson of astonishment tingling through her as she stared at Jeannette. "What?"

"Well, your adoration was plain to see, if one only cared to look," Jeannette said. "I am just glad Christopher finally decided to come to his senses. I was worried he was actually going to let you marry Lord Brevard."

"Good heavens," Eliza exclaimed. "Did you all know?"

Darragh and Adrian had the grace to glance at their shoes, while Darragh's four siblings observed the proceedings with great interest and rounded eyes.

"Seems we've both been deluded, sweetheart." Kit hugged her to him again. "But it doesn't matter. We've found each other now and we'll never be apart again."

"No. Never, ever again, my love," she murmured, smiling as she gazed into his eyes.

Jeannette cleared her throat. "Well, now that we're all in agreement that the two of you belong together, we must discuss this wedding. It simply will not do for you to rush to the altar."

"I planned to procure a special license," Kit stated.

Jeannette made a noise of dismissal. "Eliza must have a church ceremony and a beautiful gown, nothing less will do. I have already been in talks with Madame Thibodaux about her dress, so that is already under way. The banns must be read, which means you will need to decide whether you wish to be married here in Town or at Winterlea. Personally, I think the country would be far nicer now that the Season is nearly finished."

Kit scowled.

Eliza sighed.

Violet grinned and leaned near. "You might as well give in. You know how she loves to plan festive events."

Eliza exchanged a look with Kit.

Moments later, they began to laugh.

Epilogue

"Oooh, that was lovely." Eliza fought to catch her breath as she fell back against the sheets next to Kit.

He angled his head toward her, his own lungs pumping for air. "Lovely? It was better than lovely. It was fantastic."

A happy smile teased across her lips. "You're right. It was fantastic. Stupendous, actually."

"Magnificent, especially there at the last."

She laughed and rolled over to lean against his chest. "Yes, that last was quite delicious. You nearly made me faint."

His large palm came down across her bare buttocks in a playful swat. "Perhaps next time, I shall."

If he gave as splendid a performance as the one just past, she decided, he had an awfully good chance of achieving his aim. She shivered with anticipation.

"I'm glad we decided to spend our honeymoon here in Scotland." She gazed at the gleaming gold band and the accompanying emerald that graced her ring finger, a fresh thrill running through her to know she and Kit were actually married.

"Hmm, I thought you'd love this house. It's quiet and secluded, with only a pair of servants to cook and clean. If we want, we don't have to leave this room except for food."

"Well, we didn't leave yesterday. I don't think I've ever eaten dinner *in bed* before."

"But you liked it, I could tell. Most particularly dessert."

Her cheeks heated, recalling the dollops of beaten cream he'd coaxed her to let him eat off her naked breasts and belly and thighs. She had to admit, she'd ended up liking it very much. Very much indeed.

He gave her a devilish grin. "Besides, we needed to make up for lost time."

"Are you still lamenting our decision to wait until our wedding night to make love again?"

"*Your* decision. I would have been perfectly happy to sneak down the hall to your bedroom every night. I've never taken so many cold baths in my life as I did over the past three months."

"It was hard for me too, but I thought it would be better if our first child was actually conceived *after* we took our vows. Besides, I had that specially designed wedding gown to consider. What if it had no longer fit?"

"It would have fit, a couple months gone or not. But this will save us the trouble of making up claims of an early birth." He brushed a curl off her forehead. "And though it pains me to confess, the results were well worth the wait, both in bed and out. You were beautiful. The most perfect bride I have ever seen."

"The power of our love made me that way. In those moments when I stood next to you at the altar, I felt truly beautiful."

He cupped his hands against her cheeks and urged her to meet his gaze. "Because you *are* truly beautiful. I don't know how I could ever have thought you anything else, since every time I see you, you quite simply take my breath."

"Oh, Kit."

His lips met hers—slow and dreamy. She kissed him back, melting like steamed chocolate into his embrace. Eyes closed, she trailed her hand along the smooth skin and firm muscles of his body, pausing in her exploration when she encountered a firmness of another sort. "I see you've recovered your strength."

He chuckled. "How could I not with that wandering hand of yours. But don't stop now. Please, keep wandering."

She laughed and did exactly as she was instructed.

When they surfaced a long, long while later, Eliza cuddled in repletion against him, her head pillowed comfortably on the breadth of his naked shoulder. Despite a slight nip in the early autumn air, they'd kicked all the covers to the foot of the bed.

One thing she knew for sure, she would never be cold at night again. The man was like a furnace.

"Eliza?" He played his fingers over her arm.

"Hmm?"

"There's something about which I've been meaning to talk to you. Remember your suggestions?"

"What suggestions?"

"About my future, our future now. I've been thinking about what you said. Actually I've done a bit more than think, I've been talking to a few people."

Her interest piqued, she opened her eyes. "Really? Which people?"

"A couple of lords and a government minister attached to the foreign service. I understand there's an interesting assignment available, a liaison of sorts. If I put in the word, the position could be mine."

She sat up. "Really? What would you be doing?"

"Assisting with the postwar rebuilding efforts, coordinating between the British and the French."

"Oh, it sounds exciting, if you think you'd like it."

"I think I would, at least enough to give it a try. But it means we would have to move to France, perhaps for several years. I know it's asking a lot of you, giving up your home and your friends. I know how close you and Violet are."

Catching her lip between her teeth, she gave the matter a moment of thought. But only a moment. "Of course we shall go." Leaning down, she kissed him. "Without question, I shall miss Violet and Adrian and the children, but I want to do what's best for us. Anyway, France isn't so far, they can come visit."

Kit smiled, eyes lighting at the idea. "You're right. With the war done, it's not such a great journey these days. They can be across the Channel in a thrice."

"And surely you will get an occasional leave, so we can come home to England."

"Yes, I am sure I shall. A couple months a year, I believe."

"If you want the assignment, then all you need do is say yes."

"All right, then, yes! I shall write to Lord Exmeyer to accept directly when we return home."

They cheered each other with an exuberant kiss.

"Paris," she mused. "I've never been to Paris. Oh, just think of all the books. Why, there are texts there that have been inaccessible to the rest of the world since before the Revolution. It's simply thrilling. Violet will be quite jealous."

"Jealous, is it?" he teased. "I see I shall have to work hard to get you with child."

"I can still study and have babies, you know." She paused. "Unless you dislike the notion of having a scholarly wife."

With a gentle hand, he tumbled her across him. "Of course I do not dislike the idea, not since scholarly pursuits make you happy. Just be available for the occasional dinner party."

Delight spread through her like rays of morning sun. "I shall accompany you to all the dinner parties of your choosing." She kissed him. "You are my heart."

He kissed her back. "And you are my soul. Which means, I guess, that neither of us can do without the other."

"Quite right."

He claimed her mouth again, to her immense enjoyment.

"Speaking of books," he said at length. "I brought one along I thought we might enjoy."

"Oh, what is that?"

Climbing out of bed, he strolled across the room and reached inside a travel valise. Her eyes widened when she saw what he held, recognizing the familiar green binding. He waggled the volume between his fingers. "I suppose you might call it an old friend. In a way, this helped bring us together."

Albanino's Postures.

"But I put that back in the drawing room escritoire," she sputtered.

"Not this copy. I went to Jeannette's bookseller and had him locate one just for us. The other volume must still be where you left it, unless Violet decided to retrieve it for her and Adrian's use, after all."

"Mercy me." A rush of color stained her cheeks.

He winked and handed her the book. "Consider this a little wedding present. Not that we actually need the help, but I thought it might be fun."

"Fun, hmm?" Unable to resist, she opened the book and began to leaf through. She paused at a particularly contorted position. "Do you really think *that* looks fun?"

He peered over her shoulder. "It might, if I were an acrobat. Pick another, then."

She thumbed through the pages, then thumbed back. "Well, I have to admit number nine looks intriguing."

He studied the drawing and grinned. "Is that your choice?"

"It is." She nodded, abruptly shy.

Setting the book onto the nightstand, he opened his arms. "Then come get me, my love."

On a laugh, she dived toward him, and together they gave number nine a very fine try.